THE
AMANT
CHRONICLES

❖

JENNIFER'S LEGACY

Volume I of IV

M. J. BRUNNABEND

Published by "Fairy Godmother" Debbie Horovitch of Social Sparkle & Shine

This is a work of fiction. Although the author may have been inspired by real-life facts, the names, characters, places, events and incidents are fictitious. Any resemblance to real, living or dead people, or real events would be purely coincidental.

Cover Image by Rebecca Whitman:
Cover Design & Interior Formatting: Rodolfo Samson

Social Sparkle & Shine is a publisher of legends and tales, renowned for putting accomplished authors in the limelight, with editions of professionally produced books, also recognized for its thought leadership on media channels (strategic advertising), as well as for its consulting services "Fairy Godmother" in order to create for its authors the impact and the repercussions of their works as they imagined them. For a free evaluation of your publishing and bestseller potential, email Debbie Horovitch at debbie.horovitch@gmail.com.
Visit our website www.DebbieHorovitch.com

Library and Archives Cataloging in Publication Data:
ISBN-13: 978-1-77316-028-3
ISBN-13: 978-1-77316-029-0 (ebk.)

Published in Canada
SECOND EDITION

Acknowledgments

IT'S NOT EASY TO THINK of all of the folks who helped out along the way. The time taken to finally craft this story from bizarre thoughts while driving to work one day to this edited four-volume novel series took more than just a little time. So if you're not listed, it's not that your efforts weren't appreciated; it's more a case of me being overloaded and forgetful. My sincere thanks to all who contributed along the way. But specifically, I'd like to call out the following:

To Rebecca Collins—The very talented artist who painted the front and back cover for this novel. I am impressed by all of your art but also especially by what you've done here. Your craft is well honed and such a delight to behold. I look forward to working with you again soon. Thank you!

To Patrick Simmons—You did some great work on the character drawings. Thanks so much for putting my vision of the main characters to paper.

To Geoff Flederbach—Many thanks for the words of encouragement. Without them, the haters might have won out. But instead the creativity was fostered and grew. Thanks buddy, you helped me with the initial editing and gave me the courage I needed. I owe you the first round at the next big UFC fight!

To Miss Karen—Always ready to listen to ramblings of my bizarre imagination, you've been a constant source of support in every aspect of my life. Even though you do fall asleep while I narrate my stories to you.

To Mom—Of course, without you, I wouldn't be. You're my number-one fan, although I think there might be some favoritism there. Ha!

To Miss Fresca, my loving little birdie: You were my energy when I took breaks from writing, and of course you made it monumentally harder by trotting across my hands and keyboard while I tried to type.

To you, the reader—Thank you for picking up a copy. You could have bought that really large sticky bun and that double mocha latte, but instead you used the money for this book. Awesome!

I do hope that you enjoy my efforts on this story. So much thought, time, and editing went into this first volume, and the story only builds up from here. With your support, I'll be able to continue this adventure. So get comfy and enjoy the ride. Oh, one more thing: A beloved relative left me a very huge sum of money that I would like to share with you as a part of this story. The location of the money can be found if you look * at the /> pages & whervx I have fds wth.. sdfl _# $ % (Transmission lost).

- **Stay in touch with me at <u>www.mjbrun.com</u>**

Chapter 1

"TRANSPORT PASS PLEASE," STATED THE attendant mechanically as he tapped the keyboard and stared at his monitor. I reached into my purse and placed it on the counter. His tired eyes peered up at me, and he shuddered, staring at my larger alien eyes while his color paled and his mouth slowly drew open. The moment turned into two as his hand slowly, blindly slid across the counter and fumbled into my ticket.

"Oh, are you one of those crossbreeds?" he whispered drily in response.

"Excuse me?" I snapped. "It's Qyron-human!"

I felt the hair on my neck bristle. Only the ignorant used the term "crossbreed" to label us.

His hand quivered as he gave me a nervous smile and then fumbled on his keyboard. The feeble smirk he presented reminded me of a plastic grin that a woman gives her annoying, ugly mother-in-law at Christmas time. I stared at his bad comb-over, which left obvious gaps on his scalp, making it look more like satellite terrain than a greasy head of hair. Thick-rimmed glassed hung clumsily on his thin nose while he clicked away at his console.

I turned away in disgust and peered down the passageway, noting that the renovations of the old airport were finally completed.

"Uh, as a translator, you have a first-class suite available to you on the transport. Is, uh, there anything else I can do for you, Miss Ducet?"

I turned my glance back to him as he shifted his stance nervously and extended the boarding pass. I leaned back across the counter and snatched the pass from his wiry fingers.

"How soon does the transport leave for Beta Lyrae?"

He peered back to his monitor and adjusted his glasses. "You have an hour and twenty minutes, and you're at gate two." He gave out a dry cough and then looked across to me again. "I was screened for translator," he blurted out.

"Really?" I scoffed. "Sorry that it didn't work out for you." I exhaled loudly.

I quickly spun around, reached down and grabbed my leather bag, and then turned and stormed down the walkway.

I'm so tired of these interactions, between the uncomfortable stares and everyone wanting this job. No one realizes just how demanding this is. They see only the money to be made and not the lifelong commitment, protracted travel times, and extended working hours.

I glanced at a painting on the wall of a moonscape from colony Theta Nine. I've actually stood on Theta Nine and can say that being there in person is so much more breathtaking; something this painting could never hope to relate.

The soft feel of the bright, new, rubberized carpet under my heels cushioned me as I strode down the passageway. Lush plants and flowers guarded the hallway as their fragrance delighted in tickling my nose. Clear, curved skylights allowed the sunlight free reign to pour down, fully illuminating the passageway and adding a true warmth to the walk. A smooth jazz tune echoed through the hall as my scowl faded into a gentle smile.

The airports of old had finally been remodeled as today's transport stations. At first there was resistance, as many groups moaned over the loss in historic value. But once the more popular airports, such as LAX and Narita, were lavishly remodeled, few could argue against it. Drab waiting areas and sterile walkways now exploded in rich color with local flair. All of the latest in amenities were available to travelers, including up-to-date linked planetary Wi-Fi. In addition, the huge tracts of land needed for the runways were torn up and repurposed for housing and office buildings.

As I strolled to the opening of gates 1 and 2, the smooth sound of jazz was slowly overtaken by the background clamor of thousands of conversations. I peered at the bank of seats on the first level.

Ugh, the great unwashed masses.

As I surveyed the room, looking for an empty seat, a rubber kickball rolled across the passageway and bounded into my leg. A small child of maybe six, laughing and shrieking with joy, ran after it. As he caught sight of me, his patter screeched to a halt. His wide, happy eyes and huge, laughing smile froze into a look of shock while his arms remained outstretched for the ball.

"Here you are," I said with a smile as I tapped the ball with my foot.

It slowly rolled back to him and gently bounced off his leg. His expression remained unchanged as the ball slowly rolled back toward me.

"Get your ball!" I huffed. "You little mongrel," I finished in an angry whisper.

A woman twice the width as she was tall stood up and waddled her way over to him. Wearing the same offensive stare, she latched onto his arm and tugged him, pulling him off balance.

"Come nah, Tannah!" she yelped in a southern drawl while keeping solid eye contact on me.

"Really? I'm not a monster!" I hissed as I took a step toward them.

She immediately jerked him to her side as he let out a scream. Several other passengers stopped talking and directed their attention to us. I shook my head in disgust then turned and continued my search for an empty seat.

A single voice suddenly rang out over the din.

"Amant!"

I quickly turned to the right and spotted a man dressed in a dark suit, waving in the distance.

Who is that?

I slowly walked toward the figure and squinted as the distance closed. As I approached, I felt a surge of adrenaline and exclaimed in shock, *"Johnny?"*

I instantly felt flush, and my heart stopped for a moment. John quickly dashed the last few steps and hugged me tightly. Still in shock, I let out a squeak.

"Wow, I can't believe it; it's you, Amant! I'm speechless. My gosh, where have you been?" John rattled off, his eyes wide as he wore a huge grin.

My breath was still hostage; my heart fluttered. I could only smile as we stared at each other for a moment. Johnny was so stunning in his dark gray suit. His jet-black hair was nicely slicked back; this was funny because, as a kid, he never combed it. I always liked his eyes—so thoughtful and caring. As I stared into them, they seemed to be an even darker brown than I remembered. He had actually grown too; he now stood several inches taller than me.

John's expression was bright and jubilant as he exclaimed, "What happened? Why did you leave so suddenly all those years ago?"

John's questions came at a bullet's speed. I continued to stare in shock, my mouth open while I shook my head.

"Oh, I'm sorry; um, let's sit down!" Johnny said as he hurriedly grabbed my hand.

I could feel his soft touch as he escorted me back to his seat. He moved his jacket from the adjacent chair and pointed to the plush leather seat as I sat down, my eyes still locked on him.

"Wow, I can't believe it. You look incredible, Johnny—so ... so grown!" I exclaimed as my senses finally returned.

John blushed as I said it. I then noticed his ears turn red. I couldn't hold back the smile.

"Nice red ears, mouse!"

John burst into laughter.

"You will *never* let me live that down!" He moved his hands to cover his small, rosy red ears. "It's been a long time—at least ten years. Wow, how have you been?" John said, shaking his head. "I have so many questions. I just can't believe that I bumped into *you! Here!* After ten years!"

John paused a moment. His eyes, which were darting back and forth, now focused firmly on my face.

"My God, you ... you look i-incredibly ..." He smiled. "You are so beautiful, Amant!" he whispered.

His hand slid over mine. His fingers gently caressed while his eyes sparkled. Now it was my turn to blush. My face even started to hurt from smiling—something that I realized was foreign to me.

"So how are your mom and your dad? I haven't talked with them in a while. Oh, and your job?" John asked with an ear-to-ear grin. His hand squeezed mine in excitement.

"Well," I took in a deep breath, still reeling. "I've been quite busy translating," I panted. "So much travel and always on the go, plus all my studies to get my degrees," I squeezed his hand back, nervous and trembling. "The schedule has been torture, really!" I gave out a nervous laugh and then a dry cough. "So much so that I haven't been back to Earth in quite some time. My, um, dad? Uh, yes, he's doing fine."

I paused a moment, breathing heavily as his words finally registered.

"Wow, ten years, Johnny?"

John gave me a stunned look; it must have been in response to my expression. If you had asked me five minutes earlier how long had it been since I left the neighborhood, I would have said "maybe five years" with utter confidence. John nodded, pushing me to continue.

"Wow, um, where to start? Well, I've been to eight other colonies and all over planet Earth. I've met with every political leader, industry mogul ..." I paused again and shook my head. "It's really been nonstop with work. Plus I went from finishing my high school diploma to a dual master's degree. I ... I haven't vacationed in years!"

My voice trailed off as the realization struck with me like a stiff wind. The time really had flown by, and I hadn't done a thing for myself in far too long.

John peered down at my hand.

"So, not married, I see," his sparkling eyes drew back up to meet mine. I blushed again and gently nodded.

"Wow, traveling all the time? I can only imagine the sights you've seen," John said with a smile. "This is my first trip ever off Earth. Oh, I did see a special on Theta Nine the other day; it looked stunning. Have you been there?"

"Are you kidding me, Johnny? Of course!" I shot back with a giggle. "It's the jewel of all the colonies!" I slapped his hand playfully, and he smiled.

"Oh, Johnny. I can't begin to describe the absolute majesty of the sight from the moon. The binary stars electrify the oxygen and hydrogen gas, and it just spirals and swirls as it's being absorbed into the massive gas giant Theta. It's like an aurora everywhere in the sky, but it's most brilliant at nighttime. And I was even lucky enough to see a spiral of nitrogen—the colors ... just breathtaking!"

"Wow, so it's all that it's cracked up to be," John responded. He shifted in his seat and then cleared his throat. "Why haven't you been back to the neighborhood? Why didn't"—he paused and swallowed hard—"Why didn't you ever call me!" The cheer and excitement he had oozed a moment before were completely gone. His eyes tightly focused on mine as his smile stiffened flat. The words hung in the air as the mood crashed down.

"Please, with what time?" I nervously laughed aloud. I could feel a slight tremble in my hands.

"My … my life has just been so crazily busy with one conference after another, nonstop transports while brokering deals, and studying for my degrees. It's actually been quite ridiculous." I shuffled my hands and shifted in my seat.

"I have five homes on five planets, and I can't tell you the last time I spent two weeks straight in any of them. I'm too busy, you know, um."

I noticed a man pass by me with a tattered shirt and dirty pants, glaring at me as he walked by.

"Oh, really? Okay." John's voice drew down; it lacked the rich enthusiasm of earlier. "Well, quite a bit has changed since you've been gone. The Wilsons sold their place and retired."

My gaze stayed on the man as he sat down an aisle away.

"The new owners finally changed the color of the house," John stated, his left brow raised.

"Wait, what? The Wilsons?"

I couldn't for the life of me remember which family they were on the block.

"Seriously? You don't remember the Wilsons and their electric-pink house? It's no longer pink!" John's eyes opened wide with anticipation.

"Oh my," I laughed, "those were the Wilsons? Ha! Yes, I remember thinking that I loved that house when I was five, but by age ten I wanted to sneak over at night and paint it any other color!"

We both burst out laughing. John then started talking about other neighbors while I panned the first area of gate 1 and noticed something rather odd. Many of the passengers were dressed quite poorly. I glanced at a few dozen of the people across from us; they were wearing nothing more than dirty T-shirts and jeans. Worse than the sight, though, was the odor. An older man of maybe sixty strolled by, and I was awash in a hideous stench that was wholly unbearable. I could have slept in a garbage bin and smelled a world better than he. I then panned down one tier, to the second level. It seated about a thousand, and it too was packed. I couldn't spot a clean shirt or washed face in the entire group; perish the thought of finding any man clean shaven or in a suit like Johnny.

"… so then he burped! Can you believe it?" John exclaimed. I immediately jolted back to the conversation. John sat with his eyes wide and mouth open, waiting for me to respond.

"Oh, I apologize, Johnny; I wasn't paying attention."

John frowned, and the excitement drained from his face. I leaned in toward him.

"Did you notice the condition of these people?" I whispered. "It seems that everyone just walked out of a dust storm or something."

John pivoted in his chair. He gazed around the area and then turned his view back toward me.

"Yes, they do seem a bit worse for wear. Why, what's the concern?" His eyebrow rose, and he squinted at me.

"Well, not a concern as much as an observation, John. I mean, they're disgusting and unkempt."

"I'm not sure I'd use the word 'disgusting' to describe them. It looks like a few of them could use a shower, but—"

"A few!" I couldn't believe he wasn't alarmed by this. "John, some of them stink like they haven't bathed in over a week. It's utterly uncultured!"

John turned his head slightly as he looked at me. A moment passed, and a smile then returned to his lips.

"Well, yeah, I did get a whiff of that one guy who walked by us— quite powerful." He laughed. "I thought the leaves on the plants would have fallen off."

I burst out laughing; the comment just tickled me. John joined me, and we both laughed aloud for a minute.

"Well," John said as he wiped his eyes, "I think they're all on the transport to Gamma Five. It's a new colony, so maybe they're all workers or something."

I was still laughing and finally stopped.

"John, seriously, it's 2280, and even the lowliest of workers make

7

a hundred grand and can afford a nice house, clean clothing, and a shower."

"I don't know; maybe it's their religion," John riffed sarcastically. "They pray to dirt and this is a holy day?"

I completely lost it.

I laughed so loudly that several people stopped talking and stared angrily at us. I can't remember a time before when I laughed so hard. Wait; yes I can. It was when I was with Johnny. He always had the ability to make me laugh, many times, until my stomach hurt.

How could I have forgotten that?

"Oh, Johnny, you have to stop it!" I slapped his hand playfully. My face ached from smiling.

An overhead announcement called for the boarding of the transport to Gamma Five at gate 1. We were still giggling when many of the people around us stood up and began to collect their things.

John then took to his feet.

"Where are you going, Johnny?"

"This is my transport; I'm going to Gamma Five for a new job."

"Oh please, stop; no more jokes," I laughed. "My side's going to split."

I continued to giggle as John picked up his bag.

"No, I'm serious, Amant. I'm starting a new job on Gamma Five. I'm going to work in new product development. I start a week after we land there."

I stood up, alarmed. It suddenly seemed surreal, as though I had found my long-lost brother and now he was stepping back into oblivion.

"No, wait! You—you can't go now, Johnny!"

I felt a sharp twinge in my throat, and my heart beat faster. My face felt flush, and I had a hard time breathing. John set his bag on the seat and reached in as I grabbed his arm. He paused and stared into my eyes. Time seemed to stop; nay, it seemed to warp back ten years, to when we were younger. All of the noise of the other passengers washed away. I stood there grasping the hand of a fifteen-year-old boy, his dark brown eyes probing mine. My body tingled.

"Amant?" John said, shattering my trance. "Before I go, can you tell me why you left so abruptly ten years ago?"

My heart ached at his question. I felt paralyzed, his words were like a dagger plunging into my chest. My eyes opened wide, and I sucked air into my mouth. I heard a slow but audible "uh" escape my lips as I finally exhaled. John's eyes remained locked on mine.

"Oh. Johnny, I, um," I stumbled.

"Boarding on gate 1 for Gamma Five!" The announcement droned overhead.

John sighed and nodded. The edge of his mouth drew down, and he blinked slowly.

"Here, this is my business card, and here's my signal code. Call me when you get a chance; I'd love to catch back up with you," John whispered as he stared into my eyes.

He leaned in and gave me the warmest hug I can remember. My knees buckled, electricity coursed through my body, and my breath drew short as he gently rubbed my back. A tender trace of his cologne wafted up. It was intoxicating. He pulled back and looked down at me. I felt woozy.

"It was truly mind-blowing seeing you again, Amant," he paused. "After so many years."

John took a half step away.

"I wish we had more time to catch up, but …"

He looked down for a moment, gazing at his shoes.

"Please, keep in touch!"

His eyes commanded my attention. They pleaded with me. I stood like a statue.

John quickly moved in close and kissed my cheek. I felt a tingle that shot through me, and I shuddered. John then picked up his bag and turned, walking toward the loading doors.

I suddenly realized that my lips were pursed and I was still leaning backward. I must have looked like a silly little ten-year-old schoolgirl who had just gotten her first kiss, frozen in the moment.

"Uh, bye Johnny. Thanks!" was all that I could muster. Inside I was screaming and kicking myself. I translate for a living between the Qyron and the leaders of industry, countries, and worlds. I am never at a loss for words, yet here I stood, dumbfounded and nearly speechless.

John peered back one last time and nodded at me as he stepped through the entry doors.

Amant Ducet

Chapter 2

I EASED BACK DOWN INTO my seat. I felt sick and broken; I couldn't concentrate. As my mind raced, I peered over at a group of people across the aisle. They were staring intently at me as they gathered their things. A few of them whispered and shook their heads. I leaned down and grabbed my leather case and pulled out my laptop. I tapped a few keys and quickly opened an application—the stellar map. After locating Earth and Beta Lyrae, I then searched for Gamma Five. I couldn't find it.

How is that possible?

I then performed a full-level search and finally located it. The Gamma system was part of the same cluster of stars directly between Earth and Beta Lyrae. I jumped out of my seat, as if launched from a coiled spring, and ran over to the attendant counter. As I reached the ticket counter for gate one, the associate looked up at me.

"What da *yew* want?"

I gave the attendant a sharp glance as I frantically pulled out my ticket. He was a stout man with thick, hairy arms. Yellow teeth drew the eyes in and away from the mangy assortment of hair he called a mustache. A brown chunk of some food item clung precariously to the side of his mouth. As I peered up, I noted the thick brown curly hair that swirled around his hat. It was a tattered baseball cap from some old movie called *Rocky*. He stood behind the counter, chewing loudly on gum, and produced a sour look. I quickly pushed the ticket out in front of him.

"I need to change my trip from Beta Lyrae to Gamma Five."

The attendant snatched the pass from my hand with a jerk and a look of displeasure. He exhaled loudly and then looked at the pass and shuddered.

"Oh, you're a trans-lay-tore. *Pssh!*" He rolled his eyes and gave me a salty look. "Yew get paid millions uh dollars and suck up the rich life. Yeah, I seen ya on the teevee a lot." He sighed and rolled his eyes as he waved the ticket at me.

I continued to stare at him and drew my hands to my hips. He chortled and then looked up from his monitor.

"You *shure* ya want ta go tuh Gamma Fyive?"

The smacking of his gum punctuated every other word.

"Did I stutter? Are you hearing impaired! *Yes, damn it!* Put me on that transport!"

I could feel the fire inside me building. Time was quickly rushing away, along with Johnny. I wanted nothing more than to jump over that counter and slap the ugly clean from his soul. His rudeness was equaled only by the nauseating stench of his body odor. I quickly glanced back over my shoulder. The huge throng of people at the boarding doors was now a thinning trickle of passengers, and John wasn't among them. He began to chew the gum in his mouth louder and slower; then he peered up at me.

"This is a basic transport; there ain't no first class fer *yew*, Missy."

He said the last part with a slight lilt in his voice and a queer little smile. I could barely contain myself; the anger now roiled inside me. I had no time to waste, and he was dragging his feet just to provoke my annoyance.

"Last call for boarding on the shuttle to Gamma Five," squawked an announcement overhead.

That was it; I reached across the counter and grabbed the troll's hand. I clenched it hard. At first, he didn't resist and continued to give me a sick little smile. But then I squeezed harder—much harder. His eyes opened wide, and the gum fell out of his mouth.

"Ow, by dammit!" he screamed.

He tried to snatch his hand from my grasp, but I pulled him hard toward me. His stomach slammed into the counter. A glass bottle jangled and fell over while several pens danced about on the countertop.

"You'll dispense with the foul attitude," I seethed, "and *get me on this transport before I crush your fat little hand!*"

"Ow, let go!" he pleaded. "I can't dew that if ya break mah hand!" he cried out.

I released my grip, and he pulled his hand close. He had just begun to massage it when I flinched forward again. He jumped back. His cheeks flushed, and his bottom lip quivered.

"*Now!*" I screamed.

My patience was razor thin. I wanted to be on this transport in the worst way, and this disgusting creature's poor attitude was not going to cause me to miss it. He lurched at the terminal and furiously began to type. His bottom lip trembled, and his hand shook, but he continued to clack away on the keyboard.

"Aw, what's dis shit?" he bellowed.

I shifted my view and leaned over the counter to spy the screen. The display continued to pop up a bright red bar that flashed "DENIED" when he tried to move me over to the Gamma Five transport. He then backed out and looked at the manifest. It listed 4,720 people and the total capacity of the shuttle was 5,000. He glanced at me quickly with a hurt look and glassy eyes.

"I been doin this fer years, and this ain't never happen'd," he whimpered.

His eyes were large, and his earlier defiant look was replaced with a woefully sorry pout.

"If you're stalling on purpose, so help me!" My voice steamed with anger as I clenched my fists.

"Naw! I'm not!" He shot back with a pained look. "I never had dis issue before; lemme see if I can change dis," he yelled back nervously.

His fingers trembled as he punched a few more keys. I looked over my shoulder again to see the last few passengers walk through the boarding gate.

Finally a boarding pass issued from the printer. He grabbed the ticket and gave me a solemn look. I peered down at it. It was a general boarding pass with no identification.

"No first class! Can't you bump someone?"

I had never traveled in anything but first class and didn't want to start now.

"I done tol' ya, there ain't no first class wit' dis shuttle," he sniveled while massaging his sore red hand. "Yew got da same room as ever'body else."

He took a step backward, maybe in fear that I would launch my-self across the counter and slap him unconscious. I wanted to. Oh, I *so* wanted to. I took a step forward and leaned over the counter.

"I appreciate you working through this issue, but I must say that I am sorely troubled by your lack of respect and discourteous behavior. If I had the luxury of time, I would discuss this gross shortcoming with your supervisor. And be clear on this," I hissed. "It would lead to your dismissal."

I turned and dashed over to my seat and hurriedly grabbed my bags. I noticed several people staring at the two of us in shock as I ran by them. I arrived at the door to the shuttle as they prepared to close it. A boarding agent glanced at me and smiled as the door slammed closed behind me. I gave out a large exhale and thanked the female attendant. She scanned my ticket, and an audible tone sounded from her handheld device. She looked up at me confusedly as she scanned it a second time and another tone sounded.

"I'm sorry; not sure why this won't work." She then clicked a few buttons and handed my ticket back.

"I just overrode the error. But that's weird," she mumbled to herself.

I gazed at my ticket; I was in room L-109.

As I made my way to my room, I felt the shuttle begin to pull upward. In seconds we were moving up quickly and the announcement was made that we had left the Earth's atmosphere. I felt a twinge of dizziness, but it quickly abated as the artificial gravity came online.

As I walked to my room, I was immediately stricken with the obvious difference in this shuttle: the pale gray passageways were completely void of character. No pictures hung on the walls. No flowers or green plants stood along the passageway. The standard rubberized carpet was missing; I heard only the tinny clacking of my heels on the deck. Even the lighting in the passageway was substandard and yellowish. It seemed that every other light was out, and only the dull hum of the transport filled the air—an air which, I might add, smelled more of mildew and sweat than a warm spring day.

I finally reached my room and opened the door. A horrible, tangy odor rushed at me—a blend of stinky feet and onions would have been my guess. I paused at the terminal and tapped my cell phone to upload my preferences. It took my musical tastes, movie selections, and even my favorite drinks, which would be automatically shuttled to my mini fridge. Jazz music began to play, and the lights softly illuminated. That's when the full view of the room overwhelmed me. A small brown couch with faded cloth covering, accented with various stains, sat in the center of the room with two chairs and a monitor that appeared to have been cleaned with a Brillo pad. The carpet looked as though it was decades old, with a few tears and a plethora of blemishes. In front of the couch sat a tired and worn coffee table. Several gouges in the wood and various water stains adorned its top. I just stared in disbelief.

I walked over to the table and picked up the remote. I turned on the monitor and was amazed that the picture was rather clear despite the various scratches on its surface.

On the opposing side of the room, I noted two cupboards with one door slightly askew and a sink that framed the tiny kitchenette. It was apparent that cleanliness was next to nothing in this room. Various food stains were everywhere, and as I took a step, something sticky tried to keep my foot planted on the floor. I quickly strolled into the bedroom to see a queen-size bed with two dressers. Not to be outdone by the ambiance of the kitchen or living room, the bed sported several gross blemishes that I wasn't brave enough to guess the origins of, and the thin carpet squished under my feet. A fake plant sat atop the one dresser, covered in a thick layer of dust, and a faded print, torn in the center, hung on the wall. To the right was a small bathroom; I wasn't feeling the confidence at this point to venture in.

"Ugh, this is so disgusting and primitive," I exhaled aloud.

A tone sounded.

"Come in," I yelled in disgust.

The front door opened, and an attendant rolled in a cart holding my three large pieces of luggage. He started to shove them off of the cart. The first one toppled over and slammed into the wall, followed quickly by the second one.

"Excuse me! *Can you treat them with a little respect?*"

The attendant stopped and gave me a blank stare. "Uh, sorry." He grabbed the last piece and placed it on the floor.

As he turned to leave, I walked over and asked him, "Can you tell me why this room is such a filthy, stinking mess?"

The attendant only returned a dead stare. I immediately sensed that his amount of enthusiasm rivaled that of the hairy troll I had dealt with moments before at the ticket counter. He then peered around the room and finished his gaze back to me, all with his mouth slightly ajar.

"Uh, I mean, I just started, but I can look into it and, like, let you know," he said with a meek tone and one eye half closed.

I had to stifle a laugh. I was almost expecting a whole crew to jump out from behind the door and yell 'surprise'. Every transport I had traveled on was impeccably clean and furnished with the very best furniture and decorating flair. This room was more akin to an animal pen than a room fit for humans—especially in odor. I shook my head in revulsion at the slack-jawed attendant as he turned and quickly pushed the cart out the door and into the passageway.

I tromped over to the terminal, batting away the sticky strands of hair from my eyes.

"Computer, are there any other rooms available for transfer?"

A standard computer voice responded, "All room assignments are final. If you have any issues, you may call for a steward or maintenance technician."

"You have got to be kidding me!" I yelled.

"Please restate your question," the computer replied.

I exhaled as I closed my eyes and shook my head. I couldn't believe that this was the room that I had been given and was stuck with! The thoughts of the other passengers then popped into my head. For them, this would be home. Filthy, disgusting, and stench ridden—they would be delighted, I'm sure.

"Computer, location of the nearest laundry facility," I huffed.

An overhead map illuminated on the terminal. The laundry was a few doors down from my room.

I spent the next several hours washing my bed linens and blanket while I scrubbed the kitchen and bathroom. I also placed a repair order for carpet cleaning and was given a response that it could be three days until that could be completed. I guessed I would need to keep my shoes on until then.

Hot, sweaty, and tired, I asked the terminal one last question: "Location of John Crowley?"

The terminal responded, "John Crowley is in room Alpha 42." A passageway map illuminated on the monitor, showing the route. As I stood there contemplating and sweating, a sudden growl broke the silence; my stomach was tired of being ignored and not to be denied.

I walked over to the bathroom. As the lights illuminated, I looked into the mirror. My painstakingly detailed hair, which I had coiled into a bun, now fell about. Strands of hair clung to my sweaty face. The gray business suit I wore was splashed with the foul food and funk of the room as I had cleaned. My crushed suede gray shoes were sticky with filth. I felt torn between the urge to scream in anger and the building demand to cry. As I turned to open the shower door, my hand bumped the counter and I broke a nail.

"Damn it!" I yelled out.

The proverbial camel's back broke, and I started to cry. The anger and emotion issued forth as I quickly undressed. I sniveled as I stepped into the shower.

The hot water felt so good. The warm pulses massaged me. I closed my eyes for a solid ten minutes. It was the first right thing in my room, and it not only washed away the sweat and grime but also carried some of my angst with it.

After the shower, I dressed in some clean clothes and made my way toward the dining hall. I walked by several passengers who thought nothing of gawking at me while I passed by. I was too tired and hungry at this point to care.

When I reached the cafeteria, I grabbed a tray and started to gaze at the food. Two men in front of me were staring and whispering to each other. The first man, with a small, stocky frame; greasy hair; and a bushy beard, grunted and finally mumbled aloud over his shoulder.

"What's *that* doing here?"

I quickly shifted my scrutiny to him and placed both hands on my hips.

"Is there something you want to say to me?" I uttered loudly enough for most people in the dining hall to overhear.

Several other passengers stopped eating and turned their glances in our direction. The loud conversations that had been deafening the room now ceased, and an eerie calm settled over us. The two men gave shocked looks. The fat man's buddy then whispered aloud.

"It can talk!"

Beyond those words, neither of them moved an inch.

"Oh, so now you're all quiet!" I yelled back at him.

I was in no mood. I had spent the last three hours cleaning copious amounts of unknown filth from a transport room that was no larger than many of the closets in my house. I was tired, and I was hungry. My dealings with the gate 1 ticket troll and the luggage attendant had left my patience on a razor-thin line that this bigot was trampling on.

The first man finally turned around to face me. I took my hands off my hips and clenched my fists. I felt a surge of adrenaline as I awaited a response. The second man grabbed the arm of the first and started to pull him away. While I felt that a fight may have been a fitting release for all of my anger and tension, I was glad that it failed to materialize. I was reaching a point of exhaustion. I just wanted to eat my food and enjoy a solid bit of sleep. The two men turned and pushed their trays along.

I turned back, grabbed my tray, and continued on with my food selection. I passed over the seafood, steaks, and pasta. After grabbing a salad, two hot roast beef sandwiches, a bowl of soup, green beans, corn, a side of garlic mashed potatoes, and three brownies, I sat down at a corner table. A few of the other passengers gave me curious looks while I dined, but no one uttered a word, and I was fine with that.

When I finished eating—the roast beef was delicious—I decided to take a walk around the transport. I found the gym on Echo Deck. I almost screamed out loud. The gym was a fraction of the size of those that all other shuttles enjoyed. It lacked a swimming pool and racquet-ball courts. Even the equipment was in less-than-stellar shape. The area reeked of month-old sweat, and many of the machines were not wiped down. There was no cooler of flavored waters or fresh towels; nor was there an overhead stream of music. As I looked across the gym, several men stopped and stared. I suddenly felt like a piece of meat on display for a pack of hungry wolves. One man stood up from a weight bench, his buddies slapping his back as he began his strut toward me. I turned and strolled out of the gym, as the odor was beginning to make me queasy.

"Hey, hold on please!" called out a voice from behind. I stopped and slowly turned, now standing outside the gym in a more suitable space. He trotted over to me—a large man, over six feet tall with a dark complexion. He had a very impressive physique, with bulging, veiny arms; a nicely chiseled broad chest with rock-hard abs; thick, muscular legs; and a sheen of sweat. I peered back up to notice that he caught me looking him over.

"If you like what you see, feel free to touch," he said coolly.

I rolled my eyes and frowned.

"What can I do for you?" I sighed loudly, with tired annoyance in my voice.

He gave me a slight smile and looked me up and down while nodding.

"I just wanted to make sure that you weren't scared away," he said in a smooth, deep-toned voice. "I saw you looking into the gym, and I know how some of those guys can seem a little intimidating. I would be more than happy to show you around, and if you like, you can work out with me."

I had to bite my lip. I wanted to laugh out loud, because his come-on seemed a bit tired. But another part of me found his muscular body enticing, and his voice and demeanor exuded a bit of confidence, which I found sexy.

"Maybe another time. I just ate, and I feel tired."

"That's fine too. How about I tuck you in?"

I giggled. He had caught me off guard with that one.

"There, I like that smile," he said as he took a step forward. "Your smaller Qyron mouth is so sexy."

He grabbed my hand in his and looked into my eyes.

"I have never seen anyone as gorgeous as you. If you don't mind me asking, do I detect a little African along with the Qyron in you?"

I'm not sure if it was the exhaustion or the full belly, but I suddenly felt a little warm.

"Uh, why yes, actually." The words were barely louder than a whisper. "I'm Qyron, German, and African."

"Wow, that's quite a fascinating mix; I'm mostly African," he said as he slowly walked around me.

Part of me wanted to slap him for being a pig by checking me out so blatantly, but I had to admit I was starting to feel it.

"So I missed your name, sweet miss; I'm Brad," he said as he sauntered back into view.

"Amant, my name is Amant," I said softly.

He tenderly grabbed my right hand, brought it up, and kissed it.

"Amant, what a beautiful name, befitting a Nubian queen. It suits you well." His eyes were probing me, and a slight smile crossed his lips. "So, Amant, why don't we ..." He grabbed both my hands and began to pull me close.

I immediately pulled back.

"No, I'm sorry," I blurted out as I withdrew my hands. "I'm tired, really. It's ... it's been a very long day for me."

I felt my rate of breathing increase, and Brad gave me a look of surprise.

"I'm sorry; I ... I should go now," I stuttered as I took a step back.

Brad reached out, trying to grab my hand again. I turned and took hold of his hand firmly.

"Brad, I appreciate the attention; really, I do. But I'm exhausted, and I'm going back to my room alone. I'm sure that I'll see you around."

I released my grip and turned around. I noticed that all of the gym rats were hanging at the entrance of the gym, staring on.

"I certainly look forward to it. It was a pleasure meeting you, Amant," Brad called out as I walked away.

It took me a few minutes to digest the whole interaction in my mind. I know I was blushing, and I'm not easily moved by men, but Brad seemed to cut right through my defenses. He did have a drop-dead sexy body and a suaveness about him. Talking to him, though, I suddenly felt—well, I felt scared, and I felt the need to retreat for some reason. I took my time thinking about it while I slowly ambled my way to Alpha Deck, but my thoughts continued to circle back to John.

I finally came upon room 42—John's room. I took a moment to compose myself and then pressed the door sensor. "Enter" sounded over the speaker, and the door opened. As I stepped into the room, John was leaning over from the couch to see who was at his door.

"Amant!" he exclaimed as he jumped up from his seat. "Wow! What are you doing here?"

He stepped in close and gave me a hug.

After a long, soothing moment, he tried to pull away, but I clutched him tight.

"I missed you, Johnny," I whispered. "More than I realized."

He allowed me to hug him firmly for a whole minute. I felt his hands as they gently caressed my back. His warm breath on my neck tickled and gave me goose bumps. The light scent of his cologne and his strong embrace felt so welcoming.

John finally pulled back.

"So you're going to Gamma Five now?"

I looked up at him and smiled.

"Well, no; actually, I'm heading to Beta Lyrae, but after we chatted, I checked and found that Gamma Five is about midway between. So for now, here I am, Johnny!"

I gave him a big smile and hugged him again. When I let go, John slowly walked into his kitchenette and grabbed a drink. I gave a cursory look around his room. This apartment, while having the same layout and furniture, was in much better condition. First of all, it didn't reek of burnt onions and butt. The air was rather pleasant with a light undertone of flowers. His carpet and furniture were stain-free, and the lighting was bright and inviting.

"You want one?" he asked softly, holding up a bottle of flavored water. I nodded, and he grabbed two.

"Oh, peach water, my favorite," I said as I opened the bottle.

I was still surveying his room. He had the same pictures on the wall; one was of a comet streaking across a planet with a moon in the background. He also had several pieces of luggage still sitting against the wall.

"I know," he said with a smile. "I remember everything about you, Amant." John winked at me as he sat down on the couch. "Including what you love to drink."

John slowly sipped his drink.

"Is there something you're looking for?" he said as he followed my eyes.

"Huh? Oh, no, sorry," I giggled. "It's just that the quality of your room is leagues above mine."

"I would think that they're all the same. Why not put in for a room transfer?"

"I did; it denied me."

John jumped up and walked over to his terminal. He clicked a few buttons and inquired about a room transfer.

"You have one hundred eighty-six rooms to choose from," the computer voice stated. A map showed on the monitor, detailing the adjacent open rooms in green.

"What the …!" I exclaimed as I shuffled over to look at the screen.

"If you need help, I can—"

"I'm good, Johnny; I can manage on my own, thank you!" I snapped.

John turned with a raised eyebrow. He then slowly walked back to the couch and sat down. I eventually followed him and took the seat next to him.

"I'm sorry, Johnny; I didn't mean to yell at you," I said with a sigh.

I put my hand on his. A smile replaced his shocked look, and he gently patted my hand.

"You look tired," he said calmly, "and I know when you get tired, you get crabby." His words were delivered with a loving smile, which melted my scowl. I smiled back.

"Yes." I nodded. "I'm overdue to get some sleep. It's been more than forty hours."

John stood up. He outstretched his hands, and I put mine in his. He gently raised me up from the couch.

"You get your sleep, then let me know when you're awake and we'll do some breakfast. Sound good?"

I paused and looked longingly at Johnny. His dark brown eyes were actually smiling at me, comforting me. I could feel the warmth and love from my old friend. This was *my* Johnny, my childhood pal. I leaned in and gave him a hug.

"Thanks, Johnny. Good idea."

He grabbed my hand and slowly walked me to his door. His touch was soft but firm. When I reached the door, I gave him a smile and a nod. I stepped out into the passageway, and I could feel him watching me as I walked. I stopped halfway down the hall and turned around. I gave him a wave. He waved back, smiling, and returned to his room.

When I finally reached my door, I felt exhausted. I had no energy, so I stripped out of my clothing as I walked through the living room and collapsed into bed. "Lights off," I said as I pulled the freshly washed covers over me. A light tone sounded, and the lights turned off. "Smooth jazz, volume of 1." A very soft jazz tune began playing. I didn't make it thirty seconds before I drifted off.

A tone rang out, and I stirred awake. It took me a moment to realize where I was as I came out of a deep sleep. I leaned over and checked my watch. Twelve and a half hours had passed. Another tone sounded.

"Enter!" I exclaimed before adding, "Lights on."

The lights illuminated, and I heard the door open.

"Amant, are you awake?" John asked as he stepped into the room.

I quickly wiped the sleep from my eyes and hopped out of bed. After pulling on a pair of clean pants, I grabbed a shirt. My head was spinning as I ramped up from the deep sleep, but I felt energized hearing his voice.

"Yeah, I'm here, Johnny," I yelled back as I buttoned up my shirt and stepped into some shoes.

I quickly walked out of the bedroom, feeling a little woozy, and noticed John staring at me.

"What?" I exclaimed as I tousled my hair.

"I'm sorry," John said as he smiled and averted his eyes. "It's just that you're …"

I slowly walked over to him, still shaking off the feeling of sleep.

"I'm what?" I said with a smile.

"You're so beautiful," he mumbled bashfully.

"What?" I repeated loudly as I stepped within a foot of him.

He was so adorable when he blushed. Those little ears glowed red, and he still had the cutest little-boy smile—the same smile he had when we were six. John continued blushing and fumbled his fingers together.

"What did you say?" I said softly but with authority.

John looked down and into my eyes.

"I'm just so captivated by you." John's voice wavered as he continued. "I mean, you were so pretty when we were young, but now you've blossomed into such an incredibly gorgeous woman."

I could feel my face go flush as I smiled back. I felt so warm hearing Johnny compliment me. I knew I was attractive; so many men looked and stared, but so few had the courage to date a Qyron-Human.

"Thank you, Johnny; your ears are glowing, Rudolph." I giggled and pushed his shoulder, making him roll backward.

"Bully! Do you want to get some breakfast?" John asked playfully.

I strolled over to the couch and sat down. John took a moment to check out my room.

"I see what you mean now. Phew!" he said as he pinched his nose and waved his hand. "No offense, but this room smells like a trash dump."

"Yeah, right?" I said, feeling validated that it wasn't just me being picky.

"I'm sure you're just bugging out," John said with a chuckle as he slapped my arm.

"Yes! I spent three hours cleaning up this disgusting dump and doing laundry."

John walked over to my terminal and clicked a few buttons. A large red "denied" block came up on the screen, along with an audible honk in response to his room transfer inquiry. John laughed aloud.

"It looks like you've made some enemies," he laughed as he turned from the terminal. "I see nothing has changed with you in that respect."

John walked back into the living room and sat down on the couch beside me. An image of the hairy troll at the ticket counter flashed in my head. I felt a tinge of anger, knowing he must be the one to blame for this.

"So let's talk breakfast there, little lady." John's face was bright and happy.

"I'm not really hungry. I got a good night's rest, but I feel like I want to jump into work right now."

"Work? What do you need to do?" John asked.

"I have to chair a forum on Beta Lyrae for the job of translator. To prepare for it, I am going to do some Psy-logging."

John leaned back and gave me a confused look. "What's Psy-logging?"

I shifted myself, raised my legs onto the couch into a triangle, and faced John.

"It's a fully immersive mental blog. It's like being that person. You see what the other person sees, feel what the other person feels. It's like a movie, but you get to live the life of that person through all of his or her senses. I'm going to research the past several generations of translators so I can have firsthand knowledge when I lead this forum."

"Wow, so you get to relive past people's lives. That's really neat!" John stood up. "Do you mind if I grab a drink?"

I gave him a nod. He walked into my kitchenette.

"So why do you need to chair this conference? I thought being a translator only meant getting a brain scan, and if you have the unique brain pattern, you have the job?"

He opened the refrigerated food conveyor and grabbed a flavored water.

"Yes, that's true," I said to him, shaking my head as he motioned to ask if I wanted one. "But the position of translator is so understaffed; Beta Lyrae has only one for the entire planet."

John sat back down beside me and took a sip of the water.

"No one likes the talk boxes that the Qyron wanted to use, so we're left with the only option being human translators. But the population of Beta Lyrae is unsure and fearful of the process, so this forum should answer all questions and clear up any misconceptions. I'll be giving a few speeches about the job duties, its history, and its scope."

John took another sip of his water. "History? How long has it been?"

"It's been about two hundred fifty years. Actually, I'm the ninth generation of the very first translator, Jennifer. And, well, I'm ashamed to say that I don't really know a whole lot about her or my lineage."

John's mouth dropped open.

"Jennifer? Wow, I had no idea you were related to Jennifer. I remember reading about her in history class!" John sat up straight, eyes wide.

"Yes, I have only faint memories of what my mother relayed to me, so I'll be spending a lot of time with my Psy-logs of her."

I reached over and grabbed the bottle from John. I took a long drink. I didn't realize how thirsty I was from all that sleeping.

"I'd like to get started today—maybe join you later for dinner?" I handed the bottle back to John. He looked at the mouth of the bottle and then motioned with his arm as if he were wiping the bottle.

"Girls have cooties," John said with a smirk as I giggled. "Yeah, that would be great. How long will you be doing this psy-thingy?"

I unfolded my legs and stood up.

"Um, give me a solid eight hours and I'll be ravenous and ready for a break by then."

"Ravenous. Yeah, I remember your monster Qyron appetite. Okay, it's a date then," John said with a smile. "But make sure you dress better for dinner; I have a reputation to uphold."

We both laughed.

I reached my hands out, he grabbed hold, and I pulled him up from the couch. John shot me a little smile. He slung his hands through mine and gave me a big hug. I felt myself blush after the hug and walked him to the door.

"See you at dinnertime, Johnny," I said softly.

I opened the door, and John walked to the opening. He turned to face me.

"Nice touch with the music, by the way," he whispered with a wink. He then smiled and walked out of my room and down the hallway.

"Music off," I said, shaking my head as I strolled back to the living room and sat on the couch.

I opened my leather bag. I pulled a small case out of the bag and placed it on the table. Opening the case revealed a thin black headpiece with four white plastic tabs on each corner. I grabbed the small, pea-sized memory orb marked "Jennifer Winston" and slid it into the memory slot. It clicked into place, and a little door closed tightly over it. I placed the headset on my head. There was a bright white light, some hissing noise, and then darkness.

John Crowley

Chapter 3

+ + + + + +

June 20, 2021

THE SOUND OF FEET SHUFFLING. A tingling sensation. Jennifer opened her eyes. Her head felt funny, and she tried to move. Jennifer jerked her arms against something, and her shoulders only twitched. She realized she was lying flat, naked, and in a stark white room with bright lights shining down upon her. She tried to move again, but her arms and legs were tightly restrained. She gazed around, realizing nothing in this room looked familiar. Her heart beat faster as she tried in vain to move her head, but it too was being held firmly in place.

"What the?" she huffed aloud.

She pulled on her arms again, but this time she felt the thick straps holding them back. Her heart now quickened, and her mind raced.

How did I get here, and where the hell is here? I don't remember.

"Hello!" She called out. She could move her fingers but felt nothing to grab. Her breathing quickened, and she could feel the blood coursing through her veins. She frantically tried kicking, but this too was no use.

"Hello? Help me! *Help!*" she yelled out, but only silence greeted her.

Her heart pounded faster, and fear had her eyes tearing up. She suddenly felt sick to her stomach. Jennifer closed her eyes and tried to concentrate.

What is the last thing I can remember?

She heard her heart banging loudly in her ears, and her whole body trembled.

What did I do before now?

Jennifer began to cry as her mind raced. Her chest heaved as she bawled.

"Hello? *Help me!*" she sobbed loudly.

She could only wiggle in place. Her breathing was faster than it had ever been. She felt light-headed. The feeling of nausea rose to a peak when Jennifer hyperventilated and finally passed out.

***

"Jennifer, thanks so much for coming!" Tasha leaned over and hugged me tight.

"I wouldn't miss this; you know I love you like a sister!"

"Yeah, it's too bad Tom couldn't be here; he missed out on a great party," Tasha said with a touch of sarcasm.

I hate it when she attacks Tom.

I felt my heart beating faster, and a warmth engulfed my face as it flushed.

"Well, he said he wasn't feeling well, and I—"

"Oh, come on! He never 'feels well' when you ask him for anything!" Tasha fired back. "He never supports you in any way, Jennifer, and every time I see you with him, he's rude and mean to you! Wake up, girl!"

A tight sensation clutched my chest.

"He's really nice to me. You ... you just don't know him well enough," I sputtered back.

"Sure, he's nice to you when he wants sex, right? And he's happy when he wants you to cook him dinner, yes? He's really sweet to you when he asks you for money?"

Tasha fired the words hard and fast. Her green eyes squinted at me.

I leaned my head back to check the clock on the wall. 9:40 p.m. The tightness in my chest increased, and I felt a bit of tingling in my eyes. I sensed them starting to well up.

"That's what I thought. Damn it, girl, you're too nice, and he's just a leech. You've dated through high school, and all he's done is use you. Woman up and dump him!" Tasha steamed. She shook her head, and her bright red hair fluttered in the air.

"Well, he loves me, and I ..." a tear gently rolled down my cheek. I removed my glasses and wiped my tear-streaked cheek with my arm.

"Ugh! Jen, you are far too sweet for this jerk."

Tasha's tone changed.

"I'm sorry; I don't mean to bring you down." She grabbed my hand. "I've known you my whole life, and I just hate seeing this guy use you like this." Tasha's eyes were wide, and her stare was sincere. She pulled me close and then gave me a hug.

"Thanks, Tash, I know you care." The tightness in my chest started easing up, and I wiped my eye again. "So I'll see you tomorrow at lunch?"

"I'm sorry, girlfriend," she said as she stared at me and hugged me again.

"It's okay," I whispered. I then gave her the best smile I could muster behind my tears.

"Yup, tomorrow we get our nails done first; then it's time to pick out a bridesmaid dress for you." Tasha beamed.

We hugged once more, and then I waved and walked to my car. After turning the key, soft music came on, and I glanced at the clock. 9:45 p.m.

Ugh, Tom's going to be angry that I'm not home already.

I slapped it into drive and pulled out of the driveway and started down the road. After ten minutes, I got onto Horsethief Road.

Another fifteen minutes and I'll be home.

"*Ka-thunk*" rang over the music, and the car began to sputter.

"Oh shit, not again!"

I banged my fist on the dashboard. A bright light suddenly shone on the car from above. I pivoted my view from the front of the windshield to the driver's-side window.

Is that a helicopter?

The car finally stalled, and I fought to steady it over to the side of the road. The bright light now hovered directly over the car. The intensity of the light then increased to a blinding brightness, and then ...

***

Jennifer jerked back to consciousness. It took her a minute, but she finally realized she was back in the white room. A sound from behind startled Jennifer and wrenched her from her thoughts.

"Hello?" she yelled out. From the corner of her eye, she could make out a figure. Her glasses weren't on her face. Jennifer blinked a few times and now was able to see a short humanoid—gray in color, with no hair—turn and walked toward her.

What the hell is that?

Jennifer blinked a few more times to remove the tears and squinted hard. She saw the figure more clearly: Its eyes were large, dark, and angled, and it had a very small nose and mouth.

Oh my God! What is that?

She tried to scream, but nothing came out; she was frozen in terror.

***

There was a bright light and a hissing noise, and I then pulled the headset off my head. My heart raced, and I was sweating. I can usually control myself in a Psy-log, but Jennifer's emotions were so high that they overwhelmed me. I was covered in sweat, and I thought my heart was going to leap from my chest. I walked into my kitchenette and grabbed a flavored water. Several deep sips and a stroll to the bedroom felt good. After changing my shirt, I sat back down on the couch. My heart finally returned to a calm rhythm. I focused myself, took a few calming breaths, and then grabbed the headset and put it back on. There was a bright light and a hissing noise, and then …

***

Jennifer's heart pounded like a jackhammer, and tears streamed from her eyes. The alien creature extended a hand, its long fingers and small palm now held up in the "stop" gesture.

I've been abducted! I've been taken by aliens!

Jennifer's heart pounded so loudly in her chest that she heard it banging in her ears. Her whole body was drenched in sweat, and a bitter taste filled her mouth. She continued to heave wildly against the restraining straps. The alien again pushed its hand out as if to say "stop."

Oh my God. I'm going to pass out again.

She could barely get enough breath. Her chest heaved wildly up and down. She swallowed roughly; it felt like grinding sandpaper. Jennifer closed her eyes and tried to slow her panicked breathing. She didn't hear any sounds and opened her eyes again. The creature held its place a few feet away. Her head spinning, still wrenched against the restraints, she could feel exhaustion setting in.

31

"What?" The word creaked out of her dry mouth.

She swallowed again; this time a little wetness soothed her dry throat.

"What are you?" Jennifer heard her words croak out.

The alien waved both hands downward, as if to say "calm down."

Jennifer blinked a few more times, cleared more tears, and was now able to see clearly again. The alien creature's large black eyes studied her, but it moved no closer. She could see the tiny nostrils of the alien's nose move in and out as it breathed. Its head was large in proportion to its body. She scanned its head but couldn't see a single hair—not even eyebrows. As Jennifer continued to stare at the alien, she could feel her breathing slow. The alien just continued to move its hands in a downward motion, and Jennifer slowly gained more control over herself. It then raised up two fingers and made a V shape.

"Peace?" she asked. "Oh, you come in peace?"

She continued to slow her breathing and exhaled deeply. The alien nodded at her and then turned and left the room.

Jennifer continued to work on calming herself. She felt several beads of sweat rolling off of her naked body. She thought that the slick sheen of sweat might make it possible to slide out of the restraints, but it was no use. She was held firmly in place.

A second alien then entered the room. This alien wore a white smock like that of a doctor. It was taller than the first creature, and a little more tan than gray. Its features actually looked more human to her.

It stepped slowly alongside Jennifer. She looked at its eyes; they were angled but smaller than the first alien's. This alien had some hair, too. The creature slowly nodded its head. Hundreds of images and memories instantly flooded into Jennifer's mind.

"*Ahh!*" she screamed out, in shock over the intrusion into her mind.

It was as if someone had opened several books and movie clips into her head and hundreds of images and conversations had poured in. She sorted through the images: a spaceship with several aliens, some of the Earth. Now she saw images of her car from above, and then a few of her frozen in her car. Jennifer watched as they took her and the car into the spaceship. They removed Jennifer from the vehicle, removed her glasses, and tore off her clothing. Now there was imagery of Jennifer in a room, several shiny instruments on trays, and bright lights. The room—it was this room!

"Did you do surgery on me?" She yelled up at the alien.

The alien nodded slowly, and another flood of images rolled into Jennifer's mind: Her scalp was being pulled back, a bright laser cut through her skull, and they removed the bone. A small grape-sized object, as shiny as silver, was placed in her brain. Thin, spiderlike tentacles wiggled and extended from the shimmering round object and into the gray matter of her brain.

"What did you *do!*"

Tears again welled up in her eyes, and Jennifer pulled hard against the restraints.

"Why?"

Her body was now heaving hard against the restraints, and her breathing was frantic.

The alien continued to push its hands down as if to say, "Calm down." It squinted its eyes, and then a few more images entered her mind. First there came some memories of a waterfall and then a warm sunny beach. She actually felt the sun on her skin. The smell of the ocean and a sensation of a warm breeze rolled across her body, and she gave a shiver. Another memory came; this time she was holding a newborn puppy. It was so soft, so cute. The puppy whimpered in her hands. She could even smell it. Jennifer smiled, and her breathing slowed.

The memory slowly faded away. Jennifer was now calm, and the alien stared at her. A few more images of the surgery entered her mind: the object was now fully implanted in her brain, as the spiderlike tentacles were firmly attached to several areas of her gray matter. They put the piece of skull back, and a bright blue laser sealed it tight. The scalp was then pulled back into place, and a thin green laser was meticulously drawn between the folds of scalp.

"This thing—it's allowing me to see these images?" Jennifer nervously asked.

The alien nodded. It gently took hold of a strap and removed it. Jennifer's left arm was free. It moved across her, grabbed the other strap, and released it. She looked at her arms; both bore thick black-and-blue bruises in ring shapes where she had pulled and fought against the manacles. The locks on her legs were removed, and then the table slowly moved and lifted her up toward a standing position.

The alien gently extended its hand. Jennifer cautiously grabbed it and stepped off the table from a nearly vertical position. She looked down and saw deep red welts across her legs; they were similar to the ones on her arms but not as pronounced. The creature slowly walked her toward another table, where it grabbed a cloth item. It reached its hand toward Jennifer. The alien's fingers were long and thin. It handed her a smock similar to the one it was wearing. As she placed the robe over her sweat-covered body, the fabric pulled on the wetness. In seconds her sweat was gone and a warm sensation replaced her cold shivers.

The alien then reached over and grabbed her glasses. She took them from it and placed them on her face.

"My name is Jennifer," she said, and instantly several images flooded in.

Jennifer saw this alien being born. It was a crossbreed of a human male and an alien female. The mother smiled at the newborn and thought "Xho"—the creature's name.

Jennifer felt along the surgery site on her head. It was tender, but she couldn't feel any scars or stitches, her fingers were clean of any blood, and there were no bandages on her head. She then stared at Xho, seeing clearly now with her glasses.

Xho stood five and a half feet tall. She looked into his eyes. They weren't as dark as the other alien's, and his mouth and nose were larger.

"So you are a mix of human and ...?" She then saw a few images of their home planet and a name—Qyron.

They spent the next few minutes walking through the spaceship. Every passageway looked like the next. They were all light gray, smooth, and sterile. No pictures or windows marked any hallway. It felt cold and bland. Jennifer was shown the propulsion area of the ship. Several large containers with bizarre markings stood floor to ceiling. The room echoed with a loud humming sound. The walls were lined with various panels covered with flashing lights and alien symbols.

She was then shown the control room. Jennifer viewed the outside through a video screen. She saw various stars and other objects but could not see Earth. Other aliens sat around control panels, tapping on images and nodding at each other. After a few moments, they left the control room and walked along the hallways.

Jennifer communicated with Xho and began to feel more comfortable with the flow of images and thoughts. She was given a room on the ship and joined several other aliens, Qyron, for a meal. The food looked so different; the colors and textures bizarre. But when she tasted each item, it was an enjoyable experience. She discovered new fruits and vegetables that were amazing. One fruit actually tasted like a soft orange Creamsicle. Jennifer was amazed; it was like being a baby again, where everything was fresh and unique.

She noted too that the other Qyron all looked alike. They had no differences in features to distinguish one from another. Every one of them was about four feet tall. All were naked and pale gray in color yet very warm to the touch. Their genitals were quite small, and Jennifer tried not to stare. Only Xho had a slight tan tone to his skin and towered over them at five foot six.

Jennifer was aware of the passage of time as she continued to learn from Xho. She was given a vast array of imagery and dialogue on their history, science, philosophy, and culture. She viewed numerous planets, moons, and stars. Their existence had lasted a far longer span of time than that of the human race. It made Jennifer feel so much like a child that their civilization was far more advanced in technology and principles. She also learned that the Qyron communicated with Xho, who then communicated to her. Their direct communication was far more intense and would be too much for Jennifer to comprehend.

Jennifer was then informed of their offer for the people of Earth. Xho finally relayed to her that it was time. As they stood in the control room, she saw that the ship was nestled in a sea of other large objects. It seemed that they had been hiding in the asteroid belt, away from the prying eyes of satellites and telescopes. The ship quickly moved into orbit around Earth. It was so beautiful seeing the world from here. The blue was so brilliant, and the clouds, with their bright white swirls, gave it the appearance of a marble. Jennifer felt a surge of pride and majesty as she stared down upon her planet.

They waited until nightfall in Montana, and then the ship descended quickly. After the craft landed on the outskirts of town, Jennifer sat down in her car.

"I'll see you soon!" she said to Xho.

He nodded, and she drove the car down the ramp and away from the spaceship.

29 June 2021

The clock in the car showed 3:20 a.m., but she had no idea what day it was. The bright light subsided, and Jennifer watched the spaceship zip up and out of sight within a few seconds. She was alone, for the first time in a while, on the road. A huge yawn overcame her. She took a deep breath. The air smelled different but familiar. Jennifer suddenly realized that the thin smock she was wearing did little against the cold morning air on her legs. The gravity was also not the same; she felt much heavier, and her head felt funny. She rolled down the window and took another deep breath. Jennifer plugged her cell phone in, since it had run out of juice a long time ago. She yawned again and then stomped on the gas and drove the quiet twenty minutes home.

As she pulled into her driveway, she peeked at her phone. She had been away for nine days and had over two dozen messages. She stepped out of the car, her eyes bleary with exhaustion, and noticed a large sticker on the front door with police tape across the entrance.

The home was an old single-story farmhouse. It had a weathered stone stucco exterior, and the original windows rattled with every gust of wind. A small front porch with rickety loose steps and more coats of paint than Jennifer's years of age framed the front of the home. The grass in the small yard was thriving and long, having not been mowed for over two weeks.

She looked back at the house. No lights were on, and it was dead quiet. She gave out another huge yawn and stumbled up the steps, kicking up dust with every stride. Jennifer tore through the police tape and put the key in the lock. She pushed open the door with a slow, loud creak.

"Hello?" She yelled into the darkness.

Only silence. She snapped on the light and peered across the living room. She saw that many things had been moved around since she left.

All of the mail was scattered about on the desk in the living room. She peered to the right and noticed that every cabinet and drawer in the kitchen was open. A sudden waft of rotting garbage overwhelmed her. The pungent and rancid odor was beyond horrible; she dry-heaved and almost threw up as she ran into the kitchen.

No surprise, though. Obviously Tom didn't bother to empty it after I left.

Jennifer grabbed the trash bag and tossed it outside. The drawstrings held it closed, and it quickly rolled to a stop in the tall grass.

"Tom! Tom, are you here?"

She slowly walked into the bedroom, finding an empty bed. The rest of the bedroom looked like the other two rooms. Every drawer had been opened, and all of the clothing was strewn about in the drawers. A sock hung precariously over the edge of one drawer, clinging to the handle. The closet door was open too. The overwhelming feelings of exhaustion finally overcame her. She could barely keep her eyes open. She took two steps, tossed her glasses on the nightstand, and collapsed onto the bed. Jennifer pulled the covers over her and quickly slipped into a deep sleep.

"A change, a change, will do you good!" blared out of the clock radio.

Instinctively, she rolled over and slapped the alarm clock. 11:45 a.m. It was time to get ready to go to work. She lay in bed, still shaking off the sleep. It took a few moments, and then the past week's events suddenly came rushing back to her. She bolted up in bed and reached for the cell phone.

She called her mother, and the answering machine picked up.

"Hey, Mama, I'm back. I have to go to Washington, DC. I'll tell you about it later. I love you, Mama!"

She quickly dialed another number.

"*Jennifer?*" came the frantic yell over the phone.

"Tasha, I'm home and I'm all right. What's been going on?"

"Damn, girl, I have the same question for you! Where the hell have you been?"

"It's really complicated, but it will all make sense soon."

"What does that mean? Where are you?" Tasha screamed

"I'm home. I got back early this morning."

"I'm coming over!" Tasha yelled before hanging up.

Jennifer still felt tired, but she knew there was too much to do and she had to get moving. She slowly rose to her feet, feeling dirty and gritty, and started walking toward the bathroom. There she peeled off the Qyron robe. It floated gently to the ground. After starting the shower, she looked in the mirror. Her head looked normal—no scars and no way to tell where the surgery had been performed on her. She stepped into the shower and turned up the heat. The hot water sprayed over her; it felt so good. The Qyron used a water-based gel to clean with, so she hadn't had a real shower in over nine days. Worse yet was the fact that she hadn't shampooed her hair that whole time. Since the Qyron don't have hair, there was no provision for shampoo.

Jennifer just stood against the wall and let the hot water beat down. Like a parched, dry desert welcoming that first rain, she reveled in the rhythmic beat of the water and massage of heat. Eventually she grabbed the shampoo bottle and lathered her oil-soaked hair. After washing it twice, she soaped up her whole body. She took her time rinsing off; it felt so good she nearly fell asleep—and she likely would have if it hadn't been for the loud bang of the front door slamming shut.

A second later, Tasha came bursting through the bathroom door.

"Jennifer?" She ripped open the shower curtain and then lurched and hugged Jennifer. The hot water sprayed all over her back and dripped onto the floor.

"Are you nuts?" Jennifer yelled, pushing her back. She pulled the shower curtain across her.

"Oh my God, I thought you were dead! Where the hell were you?" Tasha's eyes were bleary with tears.

Jennifer leaned over and shut off the water. Tasha handed her a towel.

"Come on! What happened, damn it? Where were you?"

As Jennifer toweled the water off her face, she gave Tasha a smile.

"I missed you too, girl."

"Come on! Where the hell have you been? *Tell me!*"

Tasha was jittering with excitement.

"What is this?" Tasha screamed as she grabbed Jennifer's wrist

The bruising from the restraints had not fully healed. There were still purple rings around both wrists and her ankles.

"Did Tom do this?" Tasha's angry voice echoed through the bathroom.

"No. You have to promise that you won't call me crazy."

"Shit, girl, I already know you're crazy!" Tasha nervously laughed.

Jennifer ran the towel over her chest and then started on her legs.

"Tasha, I was abducted by aliens."

"What? Oh, come on!" Tasha took a step back and folded her arms.

"I'm serious. I was abducted by aliens. Look, I'm not about to spend a lot of time explaining all of this, because I know it sounds redneck crazy. But I was taken by aliens over the last week. I have to get to Washington, DC. Please tell everyone I'm sorry for making them worry. I'll call my mom as I drive."

"Call? Oh no! You need to see her, Jennifer; your mom is a freakin' mess," Tasha stated as she walked over to Jennifer.

Jennifer stopped for a moment and stared into her eyes. She finally gave Tasha a nod, as she realized Tasha was right. As Jennifer was an only child, her mother constantly worried about every little thing in Jennifer's life.

"Holy shit, wait. You were really abducted by aliens?" Tasha's voice got quieter. "So, like, did they probe you and—"

"Knock it off. No, they didn't probe me, you sicko. Get your mind out of the gutter!"

They both laughed as Jennifer walked out of the bathroom and into the bedroom. The sight of her bedroom in disarray angered her.

"Tasha, what happened in here?"

"Well, when you didn't show up, I came looking for you. You didn't answer your phone, and no one knew where you were. So after three days, the police searched everything. Tom was questioned a few times. Wow, was he pissed. He thought you ran off with someone else, and everyone in town thought he killed you!"

"No, I was stuck on a spaceship far away."

"You're serious, aren't you?" Tasha flashed her a devilish smile.

"I'm dead serious, girl. This is big, Tash—real big. They want to make contact with us."

A large growl interrupted the conversation. They both peered down at Jennifer's stomach.

"Sorry; I'm starving," Jennifer said as she blushed.

"Then let's get some food; it is lunchtime, you know!"

Tasha threw Jennifer a pair of panties that she scooped up from the floor as Jennifer grabbed a shirt. Five minutes later, they were driving down the road.

They pulled into the Busy Bee Café. It was their favorite place to eat and always stocked delicious pies. When they entered the café, several people recognized Jennifer. They stopped eating and ran over to her. She told everyone it was just a crazy mix-up and that she had just been visiting family and her cell phone had died.

As the two of them sat down at a booth in the corner, Jennifer quietly related her story of her time on the ship to Tasha.

When the food finally came, Jennifer wasted no time. She quickly wolfed down a cheeseburger, fries, and a nice slice of pie. The Qyron food was delicious, but she sorely missed her food from home and hadn't had a meal in almost twenty-four hours.

"Wow, I've never seen you so hungry," Tasha said while she worked on her Philly cheese steak.

Jennifer started to get restless, so they had the rest of her food wrapped up. On the way out, Jennifer bumped into Tyler, one of Tom's buddies. He wanted to play fifty questions, but she just yelled "I'm back!" and ran to Tasha's car.

"Look, Tasha; I have to get on the road to DC. But I don't think I have enough money. Can you lend me some?"

Tasha pulled out of the café lot and onto the road, shooting a quick glance of bewilderment at Jennifer.

"You serious?" Tasha shot back. "You picked a really stupid time to ask for money. I'm tapped out from planning this wedding!"

Jennifer winced, and her eyes dropped.

"But I think Craig can spare some. How much?"

Jennifer's face lit up. "I'm not sure. I mean, I know I'll need to stay in a few hotels, and I'm thinking maybe a week."

"That sucks that you're spending your own money," Tasha said, grimacing at Jennifer.

"Well, I have five hundred, but I think a grand is what I'm gonna need. Can you spare five hundred?"

Tasha nodded and smiled.

"Anything for you girlfriend, as long as you can pay it back within two weeks. Craig won't miss it till then." Tasha giggled.

Jennifer grabbed Tasha's hand. "Thanks, Tash, I owe you!"

They pulled into Jennifer's driveway, and Jennifer opened her car door while Tasha turned off the ignition.

"Hey, don't you have to go back to work?"

"Nah, I yelled to my boss that I'm taking a half day as I ran out of the office. I have all day," Tasha said as she shut her car door.

"So what are you planning, Jennifer?"

"Well"—Jennifer opened the front door of the house—"I'm gonna finish packing, stop by my mom's house, then race to DC. Once I get the message to our government, then I have to contact the Qyron before Monday. Otherwise, they are going to land at the White House."

They stepped into the house. Jennifer walked into the bedroom and grabbed her suitcase. She spent the next fifteen minutes trying to find outfits that looked professional enough for talking with politicians.

"What about this top with those cream slacks?" Tasha asked, holding up a tan blouse.

Jennifer looked over at the top. "Well, I think if I—"

They both heard the unmistakable sound of the front door being opened.

"Jennifer? You here?" bellowed Tom's voice.

Jennifer's face went pale, and her heart sank.

"Oh shit!" Tasha murmured. She dropped the blouse on the bed and ran out of the bedroom. Jennifer dropped the slacks and moved around the bed, chasing Tasha.

"Jennifer!" Tom yelled.

"Yeah, she's here," Tasha spat back, "and she doesn't have time for *you!*"

Jennifer finally cleared the bedroom in time to see Tom and Tasha standing nose to nose. Tom's long brown hair curled around the outside of his ball cap. A smear of mud on his cheek matched several clumps of dark brown on his tattered T-shirt. He was pointing a dirty finger at Tasha's face. At five foot seven, he stood a few inches taller than Tasha.

"I didn't come to see you, bitch!" Tom now turned his eyes toward Jennifer.

41

"Bitch?" Tasha reached out and grabbed Tom's arm as he tried to push by her.

"Who are you calling a bitch, you redneck motherf—"

"Cut it out! Both of you!" Jennifer screamed.

Tom took a step forward; mud clomped out from under his boots. His job at the quarry always meant that his boots carried a pound of mud in them—mud that was always left for Jennifer to clean off of her floors.

"Where the hell have you been!" Tom roared. "The whole damn town thinks I killed you an' been hatin' on me!"

Tasha moved to Jennifer's side, her arms outstretched and fists clenched.

"I'm sorry, Tom. I was—"

"Do you have any idea what I've been through?" Tom yelled. A small, frothy bit of spittle flew out and landed on Jennifer's face. "The cops were interrogatin' me for hours over the past week. People I don't even know are flippin' me off everywhere I go!"

"Sounds like they know you well enough!" Tasha quipped.

Jennifer couldn't help smiling at that.

"Oh, you think that shit's funny!" Tom roared at Tasha. He shook Jennifer, and her glasses dislodged and fell to the floor. "You fucking disappear, and I get hated for it?" he screamed as he looked back to Jennifer.

Jennifer bent down to retrieve her glasses. Tom lashed out with his right hand and punched her face. A second punch landed on her left eye. She fell to her right and knocked over a lamp.

Tasha exploded.

She dived across, throwing a hard right that connected on Tom's jaw. He never saw it coming and sprawled sideways. Tasha's momentum carried her across Tom, and his head smashed against the side of the kitchen cabinet as they rolled to the ground. Jennifer jumped to her feet but wobbled as her head spun. As she turned, she saw Tasha throw a few more punches at Tom. Jennifer darted over and grabbed Tasha's shoulders and pulled her off of Tom.

"*You worthless loser!*" Tasha screamed. "*I'm tired of you beating on Jennifer!*"

Tom grabbed the edge of the counter and raised himself up. Blood flowed from a split lower lip. As he tried to steady himself, his knees buckled. A large knot appeared on his forehead where his head had struck the cabinet.

"You bitches," he sputtered, "are crazy!" Blood sprayed at the two of them from his fat bleeding lip. He staggered across the kitchen floor toward the door.

Jennifer reached a hand out. "Tom, please, I—"

He slapped her hand away. "Don't touch me! I'm done with you!" He continued staggering toward the front door.

"You're done with her?" Tasha raged. "She's done with you! Yelling and beating her, you fuckin' coward!"

Tom finally reached the doorway and spun around.

"I oughta kick your ass, you red-headed bitch!"

"You as much as touch me and Craig will stomp your guts into a grease spot!" Tasha yelled.

Tom turned and staggered down the steps. Jennifer ran to the door as Tasha blocked her path.

"Tom, I'm sorry; please!" Jennifer screamed over Tasha's shoulder.

Tom continued staggering slowly toward his truck, wiping the blood from his mouth and looking over his shoulder at them. Tasha pulled Jennifer back from the open doorway.

"Are you mental? Let 'im go!"

She slammed the door behind them. All of the emotions finally overcame Jennifer, and she began to cry, crumpling to the floor. Tasha had turned and looked out the window, watching Tom get into his truck. She spun around when she heard Jennifer crying.

"Aw, come on, girl." She knelt down beside her and grabbed Jennifer's shoulders. "You know he's no good for you."

She held her tight as Jennifer cried.

"I, I, I know," Jennifer struggled to say through the tears.

Tasha gave her a smile and then hugged her. They sat on the floor for a solid five minutes while Jennifer cried herself out. Tasha finally pulled back and looked into Jennifer's bleary red eyes.

"Get to DC and do what ya gotta do. Get Tom out of your head. Heck, find a *real* man while you're there!" She pulled back and gave Jennifer a big smile.

"Some big, well-to-do kinda guy. Rich and powerful!" Tasha boasted as she wiped Jennifer's cheek.

They both giggled. Jennifer touched her sore eye and winced. Tasha stood up and walked over to the freezer and opened the door.

"Awesome!" she screamed, and she pulled out a quart of chocolate ice cream.

"Yeah, we'll celebrate with some nice double chocolate!"

Jennifer picked up her glasses. They were bent from someone stepping on them. She sat down at the kitchen table, still sniffling, while straightening up the frames. She picked up a napkin and blew her nose while Tasha grabbed two small bowls. Tasha then took a few ice cubes, placed them in a dish towel, and handed them to Jennifer. Jennifer placed the ice on her sore cheek and eye. They sat at the table for the next ten minutes, spooning ice cream and making fun of men.

"How long will you be gone?" Tasha asked as she licked her spoon.

"Um, I don't know. I hope to be back in a week."

Jennifer removed the ice from her face. Tasha gave her a shocked look.

"Oh damn, girl, you're gonna have one heck of a shiner," Tasha said as she looked hard at Jennifer's left eye. "Well, you have 'til next Saturday to heal up and look pretty. I've got a wedding, and you're my bridesmaid, girl!" Jennifer smiled at Tasha and then stood up.

"I need to get going; I have a long trip ahead of me!" Jennifer dropped the ice in the sink and paused a moment. "Hey, why don't you come with me? It would be an awesome road trip."

Tasha flashed her a huge smile, and her eyes lit up. She was about to say something when her face changed.

"Aw, ya know, that would be great," Tasha paused for only a moment, but there was already a "but" in the air. "But I have my wedding, girl. It already sucks that you can't be here to help me with the last-minute things."

They both nodded, knowing that each had her priorities.

Jennifer went back into the bedroom and finished packing. After wiping the bits of Tom's blood off her face and checking the redness of her cheek and eye, she grabbed a few things and opened the front door.

"I sure wish you could come with me; I'm so scared about all of this."

"I know, and I'd love to come with you Jen, but,"

"Yeah, I know," Jennifer relented. "I feel guilty not staying here and helping you."

They walked to Jennifer's car. After they had tossed the luggage in the trunk, they hugged and said their good-byes.

Jennifer drove to the ATM with Tasha following in her car. Tasha withdrew the five hundred and gave it to Jennifer. After another set of hugs, Jennifer drove the next few blocks to her mother's house. She was busy outside, gardening.

When she saw Jennifer pull up, she dropped her mini rake and ran over to her car with tears in her eyes. She yelled at Jennifer, kissed her, hugged her, and then yelled at her some more. Jennifer crafted a story that she had gone to a series of job interviews out of town and her phone had died. She knew it would have taken hours to convince her mother of the real truth, and she just had too many hours of driving in front of her. The easiest part was telling her mother how she got the swollen eye—no phony story needed for that.

Jennifer felt bad about lying to her mother but knew that soon the real truth would come out and she wouldn't have to deal with everyone thinking that she was some stupid, crazy blonde. She shared a glass of lemonade with her and then finally hit the road. It was past four when Jennifer finally got out on the highway.

She only made it as far as Glendive, Montana, before her eyes got heavy. She stayed in a cheap little motel off the interstate. By 8:00 a.m., she was back on the road. Jennifer called and chatted with Tasha for a solid hour. They laughed about the day before, and Tasha told her that Tom chased her down at Craig's house and cried to her that he was sorry. Jennifer felt a little bad for Tom, but she was glad to be away from him. She told Tasha that she was sporting a badly bruised eye.

During the drive, Jennifer thought long and hard about the time she and Tom had spent together over the past four years. He really was mean to her most of the time; it was clear to her now. He yelled a lot, and he slapped her from time to time, causing several fat lips and two black eyes; this was her third. The long drive allowed her to play back so much, and it all seemed clear to her now. She had to put Tom out of her life.

Jennifer tried to drive eighteen hours, but after almost fourteen, she was exhausted. The signs on the interstate said Madison, Wisconsin. She pulled into a Motel 8. The room smelled like week-old food, but she didn't care. It was cheap, and she was dog tired.

Thursday morning she grabbed a quick breakfast and hit the road. As she was searching for a radio station, her phone went off.

"Hello?"

"Hey baby, where have you been? I camped out at your house all yesterday," Tom said softly.

Her heart sank.

"Hello?"

"Yeah, Tom, I'm here," Jennifer sighed. "I'm on my way to Washington, DC."

"What? DC? Why?"

"It's for a job; it's a long story, Tom."

"Is that where you were the past week?"

Tom's voice was soft and pathetic, like that of a broken man. His tone was so calm and quiet. He normally just yelled or demanded things when he spoke, but this was completely different.

"Yes, and my phone wasn't working, so I couldn't call you," Jennifer replied.

A moment of silence passed between them.

"Oh, okay. I'm sorry, Jennifer. I know that I've—"

"Tom, listen; I'm sick of apologizing to you for everything. I feel like I've been your property: doing what you want, saying what you want to hear, being the person that you demand. Everything finally came clear to me over the past week. I need to get away. I'm done, Tom."

"No, look. Come back. We can take a nice, hot bath together," Tom gushed. "I got that bubble bath that ya like. Then we can—"

"No, Tom." Jennifer took a deep breath. "I'm not coming back to you." Her chest felt tight, and she was holding back her tears. "You'll be fine in a few days, and you can move on with your life," she said as her voice wavered.

"No, baby, I miss you too much. I'm sorry I—"

"No, Tom. Good-bye!" She clicked the disconnect button and let out a huge sigh.

Tasha was right; she had been such a fool for far too long. Jennifer had a good final cry, counted the mile markers, listened to her music, and finally felt free. The rest of the day's drive went by with a calmness she had not felt in years.

After an exhaustingly long drive, Jennifer finally pulled into the Hilton Garden Inn in Washington, DC. She checked into her room at 11:00 p.m. and then collapsed into bed.

"Mmm." She gently opened her eyes. The clock showed 6:48 a.m. "Damn it!" Jennifer hopped out of bed and took a quick shower. By eight fifteen, she was walking up to the White House.

Qyron Alien

Chapter 4

JENNIFER KNEW SHE HAD TO speak with the president to tell him of the plans of the Qyron and make sure the first contact went well. But during the whole drive, she never really gave a thought as to just how she would do it. She suddenly felt overwhelmed and stupid, like a stereotypical dumb blonde. She stood in front of the White House at 1600 Pennsylvania Avenue.

It was a nice, warm summer day. The breeze gently blew by her while she stared in awe. She couldn't believe that she was here, looking at *the* White House. It was just as she had seen it in movies. A shiver went up Jennifer's spine. She suddenly felt nervous, scared, and alone. She walked up to the main gate and was told by a guard that all tours and inquiries must go through the South Gate.

Jennifer turned and walked down the street and around the corner, and she finally reached the south gate. Tour busses were driving in, and a sea of tourists flocked the area, taking pictures and chatting. Another breeze blew by her, wafting a slight fragrance of cut grass. As she approached the guard house, she saw a tall, rotund black man in a white police uniform behind a counter. He appeared to be in his fifties, with baggy eyes and a receding hairline. He was slouched behind a tall desk, and his name tag said "Marvin." She sauntered up to him with a smile.

"ID, please," stated Marvin.

She handed over her driver's license. He paged through a list on a monitor, and his brow furrowed.

"I don't see you on the approved list for a tour, Miss Winston." He looked over his monitor at her and stared for a moment at her black eye.

"Um, I know; I'm here to see the president." She flashed him a nervous smile.

Marvin exhaled loudly and shook his head. "Miss …" He peered down at her license again. "Miss Winston, you have to possess the correct background clearance and approval before being allowed to enter the White House or meet with anyone." He handed her back the ID and gave her a disproving look.

"I know I'm not doing this right, but I must speak with the president, please!"

"Ma'am, I can't allow you past this point." He reached behind the counter and handed her a thick pamphlet.

"You have to follow these instructions." Marvin outlined the steps with his thick finger. "In about three weeks, you'll be able to take a tour of the White House or speak with a staff agent." Jennifer glanced down at the papers and frowned; she could feel her heart pounding.

"I don't have the time for all of this; you don't understand!" Jennifer pleaded with urgency in her voice.

"No, you don't understand, miss." Marvin now stood up straight. "You have to follow proper protocol. Next!"

Marvin looked beyond her, and a large woman with a short, greasy-haired man stepped alongside Jennifer. They handed their IDs to Marvin. Jennifer stayed frozen in her spot, mouth open as her eyes darted back and forth. Her heart was now pattering in her chest, and she was breathing fast. Marvin looked at his monitor, nodded at the couple, and then handed them back their IDs.

Jennifer exhaled loudly. "Okay, is there anyone I can speak with about a very serious matter, please?" Jennifer's heart pounded in her chest, and she gave Marvin a pathetic look as her bottom lip quivered.

Marvin stared at her for a long moment—what felt like an hour to Jennifer. He turned and grabbed a phone and then waited.

"Yes, are there any staffers available to speak with someone here at the south gate?" He said with a huff. "Okay, thank you." He ended the call and then turned and stared at her. "Have a seat over there, and someone will be with you shortly." He pointed to a chair in the corner.

"Thank you so much, Marvin; you have no idea how truly important this is." She nervously extended her hand.

"I'm sorry, Miss Winston; I can't shake your hand. Protocol." Marvin turned back and continued to screen more tourists.

After five minutes, a man in a suit entered the gate. He stood six feet tall with dark brown hair that was all slicked back. He had a square jaw and a small, pointed nose. He reminded Jennifer of a secret agent—so prim and perfect but with a bit of a male swagger. His suit fit him like a glove. Even his shoes sparkled. Jennifer smiled.

He looked over at Marvin. "Hey, Marvin, where's my target?" Marvin pointed over to Jennifer while she stood up from the chair. She walked over to him, hand extended.

"Hi, I'm Jennifer Winston." He shook her hand. His palm felt strong but cool to the touch. His eyes pierced into her, studying her intently.

"How can I help you, Miss Winston?" he said with cold precision, his eyes studying her battered eye.

"I'm sorry—your name?" she replied with a smile.

"Taylor. My name is Taylor. Now how may I help you, please?" His demeanor did not waver; it was all business with no humor or happiness in his voice. A few other tourists looked on and listened in.

"Is there someplace private that we can speak?"

"No, miss, this will have to do," Taylor stated a little louder. He cleared his throat, glanced down at his watch, and then looked directly at her. His gaze again focused on her left eye. Jennifer felt nervous, and she could sense that she was starting to tremble.

"Okay, I need to speak with the president about a race of aliens I have encountered who—"

Taylor exhaled and finally cracked a smile while a few tourists laughed behind her. He looked over his shoulder at Marvin.

"I thought I could get through the week without one of these."

Marvin looked over his monitor, shrugged, and smiled at Taylor.

"No, wait; I'm not." She could feel her heart beating faster, and now her chest started to tighten up.

Taylor placed his hand behind her back and started to lead her in the direction of the exit door.

"Why don't you just go back to your trailer and—"

"That's rude," Jennifer said with a hiss, and she slapped his hand away from her.

"Look, miss, I don't have time for this, and I really—"

"No, you look, Taylor!" she said with a start. "I have the most important information that you'll ever hear in your life, and—"

Taylor turned to walk back to the secured doorway. She lunged out and grabbed his arm.

"Look; I know I sound like a nut job!" she yelled.

Her heart was now beating faster, and her voice quavered. Marvin took a step forward, but Taylor waved him off.

"Please! Please, I know you probably hear this kind of crap a lot; I'm sorry. But just think for one minute. Taylor, would you like to be the person responsible for pushing me away and having a UFO land on the front lawn of the White House in three days?"

Taylor now lost his smile and opened his mouth to respond.

"Please, just take this; it will prove me right!" Jennifer took a deep breath. She reached into her purse and pulled out a shiny object.

Taylor looked at the item. It was a metallic cloth, with a variety of numbers scribbled on it. The shine of the cloth was so bright it twinkled in the light. He peered back at her with a confused look on his face as she placed it in his hand.

"These are the coordinates of the waiting ship that is in orbit above us. Just have any telescope or satellite view that area, and you will see the ship. Please!"

Taylor peered down at the object in his hand again. He rubbed it between his fingers and then crumpled it into a ball. When he opened his palm, the object unfolded flat again with no wrinkles at all.

"What is this?"

"It's what they use as paper. I think it's an alloy of aluminum and carbon created under a helium process. They told me about it, but it's complicated to explain, and well, I forgot."

Taylor looked at her and cracked a smile. Jennifer felt herself trembling, and her heart played that familiar jackhammer song in her ears.

"Okay, um ... okay, try to rip it," she said to him, her hands trembling as she pointed her finger at the shiny paper.

Taylor grabbed the item and tried to tear it. Marvin watched with interest and a growing smile of disbelief. Taylor shifted his grasp on the item and pulled harder. After grunting, he finally gave up and looked seriously at Jennifer.

"This thing is lighter than paper, and yet—"

"Yeah, I know," she said with a little relief. "Now can you please verify the information on that so we can get to what I need to tell the president?"

His gaze went from the metallic paper to slowly meet hers. Jennifer stared confidently into his dark brown eyes. She gently grabbed his hands.

"Please?"

Jennifer could feel her own hands trembling, but she gave Taylor a serious look. Taylor peered at Marvin and then back to her. He nodded.

"Okay, I have to go to lunch and after—"

"Look, you really don't have the time to waste. Please get this done now. *Please!*"

Jennifer felt hot all over but a bit more confident. Taylor blinked and slowly nodded again. She reached into her pocket and pulled out a second item. This was just a normal piece of paper with the hotel letterhead and her cell phone number scribbled on it.

"I will be going back to my room at the Hilton. Call me when you've verified the UFO in orbit."

She turned and walked to the door. As she opened it, she turned around and gave one final look at Taylor.

"Please hurry!"

Taylor gave her a final nod and then turned around and walked back through the secured door toward the White House. Jennifer felt that if she hadn't gotten outside in the fresh air, she would have gotten sick all over the floor. The breeze helped to cool the sweat on her forehead, and her stomach started to calm down as her heartbeat finally slowed. She sighed aloud as a huge weight was lifted off of her. But she felt the harder part was yet to come.

That whole process wiped her out. She couldn't recall when she had been so nervous—well, with the exception of the abduction. As soon as she got back to her room, and lay down on the bed, she fell into a deep sleep.

A gentle song played. Jennifer suddenly jolted awake, realizing it was her cell phone. The clock showed 10:43 a.m.

"Hello?"

"Hello, Miss Winston. It's Taylor."

"Jennifer. Please, call me Jennifer." She was a little dizzy from jolting awake. The room seemed to waver a bit.

"Okay, Jennifer, we would like to meet with you immediately. Could you please come back to the White House?"

"I'll be there in ten minutes." She slowly slung her feet off the bed, yawned, and headed out the door.

As Jennifer walked up to the south gate, she noticed four men in suits shuffling about in front of the building. When she got to within ten feet of them, she peered behind her and saw three other men in suits closing quickly. As she reached the gate, she looked at one agent.

"Hi, I'm Jennifer." No sooner were the words out of her mouth than the seven men surrounded her.

"Come with us," the one agent commanded. Two sets of hands grabbed each arm, lifted her, and quickly escorted her directly through the door. Marvin held the door open for the secured door and gave Jennifer a curious look. They marched quickly through the second guard area and into the basement of the White House. After passing by several rooms, they entered through a doorway into a dimly lit room. Twelve other men stood alongside a table, and a large, burly woman approached her.

"I need to frisk you," she stated gruffly in a Russian accent. Jennifer raised her arms, and the woman started slapping and groping her.

"Ow! Ease up there, Large Marge!" Jennifer protested. She heard a few muffled giggles, but the woman continued to quickly grab, slap, and probe Jennifer's body. When she finished, she gave a nod to a man in a light tan suit. Jennifer quickly looked around the room again. While doing so, she felt a set of hands push her firmly down into a chair.

"Where is Taylor?" Jennifer shouted out, her voice already tense and nervous.

At five foot nothing, Jennifer sized up everyone in the room; no man in here was under six feet tall. A Hispanic man in a gray suit leaned across the table.

"We will be asking the questions here," he said with a deep and gravelly voice.

She closed her eyes for a moment and took a deep breath. When she opened them, Jennifer locked her gaze on the man in the gray suit.

"Look; I-I'm not going to be bullied by you. I have—"

A second man, this one in a silky black suit, stepped forward. "Miss Winston, I apologize. My name is Dan Williams."

He extended his hand from across the table. Dan was a large man, both in height and in girth. His hand was thick, like one of Fred Flintstone's, and his knuckles were hairy. Jennifer looked him in the eyes, seeing only a stone-cold poker face. Jennifer kept her arms folded and lips pursed, and she continued to stare coldly back at him. Dan withdrew his hand and sat back in his chair.

"Everyone here is quite curious to know what you have to tell us about that object in orbit."

After another deep breath, Jennifer relaxed in her chair.

"Then find Taylor, and I'll tell you."

Dan paused, gave her a serious look for a moment, raised his right eyebrow, and then nodded at one of the men. Ten seconds later, Taylor was ushered into the room.

"This is how you treat me?" Jennifer shouted at Taylor as she jumped up and slapped his arm. She immediately felt two large hands grab her shoulders and slam her firmly back in her seat.

"Ow! Damn it!" She screamed, causing several men in the room to jump.

Dan rose from his seat and gave the man behind Jennifer a stern look.

"We're sorry."

Jennifer shifted her look to Taylor as he sat down next to her.

"What *is* all of this, Taylor?"

Taylor's expression was different than before. His eyes quickly darted about, he looked pale, and his lips were white and dry.

"I'm sorry, Jennifer; I'm just a staffer. I did what you asked, and now—well, this is all out of my hands." His voice was higher and was devoid of the commanding and sure tone it had possessed earlier. She could see that he was breathing heavily and was nearly as nervous as she was.

"Okay, let's get down to brass tacks," Dan blurted out. "Jennifer, we need to know what this object is and what you know about its intent."

Dan slowly leaned forward in his chair. Jennifer continued to give Taylor an angry look as she slowly turned to face Dan. Dan's expression had also changed. His stoic poker face was now slightly softer, his eyebrows raised.

"It's a scout ship from the Qyron. They are a peaceful race of beings who are traders and explorers just like us. They—"

"If they're like us, then why—"

"Dan, did your mama raise you to be so rude?" Jennifer's voice echoed in the room.

Three men chuckled from across the darkness. Dan's expression turned from one of seriousness to a look of surprise as he leaned back in his chair.

"You ask me to tell you about the object and its people, and then you interrupt me. Where I was raised, Dan, we call that rude."

Several other men in the room cracked smiles. Dan looked over to his left, and the man straightened up. He leaned forward in his seat and exhaled.

"You are correct, Miss Winston; that is rude, and I apologize. Please, continue."

"Thank you. Now, as I was saying, the Qyron are a peaceful race who wish to make contact, trade with us, and help us to colonize other planets. They have been a civilized race for nearly a million years, and their technology is far more advanced than ours."

Jennifer took a deep breath. She sensed that the tension in the room had broken from its earlier height. She also felt her trembling subside and heartbeat slow.

"How did they come to know you?"

"Well, they abducted me over a week ago. Then implanted something in my head that allows me to hear their thoughts. They don't talk like we do; it's all thoughts. They've tried this on thousands of other people over the last few hundred years, but it never worked—until now."

The mood in the room shifted. A few men shuffled about and murmured. Jennifer tried to see who was talking, but it was too dark. She finally caught sight of one man whispering. He immediately stopped.

Dan peered at Jennifer's left eye.

"Did they do that to you?"

"What? Oh, no!" Jennifer snapped. "My stupid boyfriend did that."
Dan nodded.

"Why can't these—Qyron, is it?" Dan asked, and Jennifer nodded back. "Why can't they speak?"

"Well, they evolved, um, telepathy hundreds of thousands of years ago, so their vocal cords died off a long time ago. Now they only communicate through thought."

"Miss Winston?"

"Jennifer, please."

"Jennifer," Dan continued, "so they have you under some form of mind control?"

Jennifer stifled a giggle and then slowly leaned forward. Dan responded in kind, leaning in closer to her.

"No, Dan; the Qyron are not *Independence Day* aliens. They aren't looking to conquer us, and they don't want to butcher every human. It's not mind control. They implanted a tiny device that allows their thoughts and images into my head. To be honest, they've explained it to me twice, and I still don't really understand how it works much."

"Can you communicate with them now?"

"No. I have to be within a few feet of one of them to link with their thoughts. But I do have a transmitter that can reach them on the ship. Look; this is not what I asked for. I need to speak with the president." Her words were louder, surer. "They're waiting for a response from me; otherwise, they will be landing their ship on the front lawn on Monday."

Dan leaned back in his chair for a moment. He looked up at the ceiling, and his thick hand stroked through his thin hair. He then sat up and looked Jennifer squarely in the eyes.

"Jennifer, we need to make certain that you don't pose any threat to the president or our way of life."

"Then it all starts with a little bit of trust, doesn't it, Dan?" Jennifer stared back at him, unwavering. There was another round of murmurs. Jennifer slowly rose to her feet. She leaned over the table at Dan.

"I came here as a messenger to bring about a whole new way of life for Americans. There will be more jobs than we have people to do them."

Jennifer now turned her gaze to the right side of the table.

"We will have more food and technology than we've ever had before, and they have cures for just about every ailment we suffer from." Jennifer shifted her gaze to the other side of the room. "Our president can be the leader who creates this new friendship, this new way of life, for everyone around the world." Jennifer noticed wide eyes among the crowd. "Look; I came here with nothing but good faith and trust." She turned to face Taylor; his mouth was open, and he was following her every word. "I met Taylor earlier, and I gave him my trust. He believed in me over all of the crackpots who come to the White House every day, and look where we are now. Please, what we have in front of us is so much bigger than you could imagine. But if you wait, if we all don't get this right, there will be mass panic and hysteria when the Qyron land."

Jennifer now leaned back on the table, turning her view to Dan.

"Look at how you've handled this so far. I'm in a darkened room, molested by some large Russian woman, surrounded by a dozen men, and feeling completely intimidated. I'm so scared that I'm trembling."

She raised her quivering hand out.

"Please, let me speak with the president."

Dan stood up from the table. He nodded as he maintained eye contact with Jennifer.

"Trust, eh?"

Dan then spoke a few words into his right sleeve. The door opened, and Taylor and Jennifer were asked to follow.

Jennifer Winston

Chapter 5

THEY WERE QUICKLY ESCORTED INTO another room. This time the room was very well lit, with far fewer menacing figures standing about. There were a few pictures on the wall—one of the White House lawn, and another of the Pentagon from above. A few plants in the corners gave the room a warmer feeling. Taylor and Jennifer were given a seat at one end of a very large table. Four other men walked into the room. Behind them was the president.

Dan turned toward the president. "Mr. President—Jennifer Winston."

Jennifer sat in shock. The immediacy of the moment struck her like a bus. Here she was, in the White House, and the president of the United States, Kennedy Myers, stood before her. She peered up at him, marveling at how tall he was.

The president extended his hand.

She continued to stare in awe. Of all things, his nose caught her attention. It was stern and perfectly shaped—the kind of nose you would see on Washington or Lincoln.

"Miss Winston?" the president whispered, hand still extended. She saw that a slight sheen illuminated the tip of it.

"Jennifer?" the president said.

"What? Oh, I'm sorry, Mr. Sir—I mean President."

She quickly shook his hand.

"Good day, Miss Winston. Jennifer?"

"Yes, Mr. President, Jennifer is fine, thank you," she said nervously. A rush of adrenaline surged through her.

Holy shit, this is the president!

Her whole body tingled with excitement. Jennifer could barely sit still as the rest of the men sat around the table.

"Jennifer, I have a member of the Joint Chiefs of Staff here today, as well as my top advisors. So let's get to it, shall we?"

Jennifer looked at one man who was in a military uniform with several colorful ribbons on it. Jennifer swallowed and nodded. She took a deep breath.

"I … I wanted to relay to you that the Qyron want to meet with you and form a group. I mean, an alliance."

Her voice was still shaky, but she started to feel the adrenaline rush subside.

"Right now I would like to assess their military capability," the president uttered. "I need to have a complete attack and defense plan in place so that we can be fully pre—"

"Mr. President," Jennifer blurted out. She leaned forward and put her hands on the table. "Please, we can react in fear and take a defensive military stand, or you can lead with trust and confidence. The Qyron don't have offensive weapons. Their ship in orbit is only a scout ship."

"How would you know what weapons they have?" The man in the military uniform added.

Jennifer quickly peered at him and then turned back to face the president.

"When I linked with Xho, my liaison after my surgery, I was able to read many of his thoughts and memories."

Jennifer peered around the table while she continued.

"I spent nine days learning all about them and being taught many things. I could see most of his life experiences, as well as the past hundred thousand years of their history. It was like a movie on fast forward. The way they communicate is so much quicker and more detailed than how we talk. In a few days, they can relate years of information. But nowhere in any of that did I see a single image of any wars, weapons, or violence."

The president snapped a quick look toward the man in uniform and then locked eyes with Jennifer.

"Is it possible that this creature can shield parts of his memory from your perception?" The president asked as he shifted in his chair.

"What? No. I mean, not that I'm aware of. But please—I never felt any negative emotions in any of their culture."

"Miss Winston," the man in the military uniform said, "enemies will rarely show up as adversarial at first meeting."

Jennifer balled one hand into a fist. She shook her head, gave out a sigh and took a deep breath.

After a second deep breath, she said, "Look, the Qyron are willing to share much of their technology with us. They have a form of propulsion that will replace our filthy car engines. They have cures for most of our diseases and can help us clean up the pollution in our environment. They have more jobs available than people on this planet. What more do they need to do to prove that they're friendly?"

A few hushed statements sounded around the table.

"I see," Kennedy began. "So how do the ... Qyron ... see this proceeding?"

"The Qyron know that our planet is broken up by languages, values, and fear. So they would be willing to wait for the world leaders to meet and adapt to the idea of change. They also know that every leader must prepare his or her people for this transition. But right now, they are waiting for me to respond to them with a time, a date, and a location."

The president nodded, leaned back in his chair, and stroked his chin for a moment. Jennifer held her breath. She could feel her hand tremble slightly.

"You have a detailed knowledge of these plans?" he calmly inquired.

"Yes sir," Jennifer said confidently.

Although she felt a glimmer of hope, she still felt nervous and unsure. Her stomach was tight, and now she was trembling all over.

"Jackson," the president barked, "let's set up an emergency meeting called for all nations. See if we can do this at the UN by Monday."

A man at the end of the table stood up, nodded, and exited the room.

"John, I want all of the financial, economic, domestic, and foreign advisors for a Saturday conference—9:00 a.m."

"Uh, Kennedy, that may be difficult, considering that we have—"

"John," the president said sternly, "I'm not asking!"

"Yes sir." John rose from the table and turned to leave.

The president pivoted and faced Taylor.

"So now we have to frame your position in all of this. Taylor, you seem to have a growing rapport with Jennifer, and I'm impressed with your work so far. I'd like to promote you to chief domestic liaison. We'll bump your rating and give you a full staff. Is that acceptable to you?"

Taylor, who sat entranced while listening to the conversation unfold, sprouted from his passive daze.

"Sir, uh ... yes, that would fine. Thank you."

Taylor peered over at Jennifer, grinning. She again shot him an icy glare.

"As for you, Jennifer"—the president looked at her as she rose up from her chair—"as I understand it, you're the only person who can communicate with the Qyron?"

It suddenly hit Jennifer. It would have felt no different if Kennedy Myers had punched her square in the face. She felt a spurt of adrenaline and gave an immediate look of shock.

"What's wrong?" the president uttered as he leaned forward. Other men around the table stood up.

Jennifer locked eyes with the president and felt her bottom lip begin to quiver. She sat back down, hard, in her chair.

"I, uh ... I just realized that I don't have a choice."

Jennifer's face paled. Her eyes stared through the president, off into the distance. Kennedy returned a confused look to her.

"I was thinking that I would just have to come here and get the process started, and then I could go back to Roundup, Montana."

The president let out a chuckle.

"No miss. I'm sorry, but it seems like you've just earned yourself a longstanding position."

Jennifer suddenly felt short of breath, and her head started to spin. She slowly stood up from the table. Taylor stood up as well, a confused look on his face. Jennifer could feel her eyes begin to well up. Kennedy shot Taylor a sharp look and then motioned for him to help her. Taylor turned toward her, as she could no longer hold back. Jennifer burst out crying and fell into his arms as he leaned in to clutch her.

All of the fear, tension, and exhaustion had finally combined at that moment. Jennifer could barely hold herself up, she was crying so hard. Taylor stood with a confused look while the president told an aide to get some refreshments. Another man grabbed a box of tissues and quickly slid it across the table to her.

She felt the strong arms of Taylor hold her while she shuddered and cried. After a few minutes of full-on bawling, she began to pull herself together. She grabbed a few tissues, wiped her eyes, and blew her nose.

"I'm sorry," Jennifer blubbered. "I just … I don't know if I can do this."

Her crying began again as Taylor held her.

The president rose from his chair and adjusted his suit jacket. *"Are you kidding me!"* he exploded.

The loud tone shocked everyone in the room. Jennifer recoiled from Taylor's embrace, and the chatter in the room ceased as everyone froze. All eyes were now firmly on the commander-in-chief, the room now in dead silence.

"Jennifer, you drove all the way across this country, barged into the White House, bullied your way beyond my staff, and orchestrated this meeting. You are most *certainly* ready for this task."

He stated the words as he walked around the table and firmly grabbed her hand. Taylor backed away. Jennifer gave a quick snivel and looked up to his face. A tear streamed down her cheek.

"I understand your fears," he said softly. "Leading is never easy, and blazing a trail with no guidance is fraught with unknowns."

The president looked down at her and smiled. Jennifer now experienced firsthand why he had won his election in a landslide. He was a strong, decisive, and quite handsome man. The president was a model of confidence even in the face of uncertainty. He always stood tall, spoke clearly, and understood the situation in a moment. Many people drew a likeness between him and John Kennedy—but not just in name recognition. Both had boyish good looks, light brown hair, and eyes that twinkled when they smiled. However, this president was not just large in stature—the tallest president yet at six foot five—but was also large in action. His decisive nature grabbed everyone's attention. He had immediately quelled the drug-sales-funded uprising in Columbia two years ago. When Hurricane David wiped out the Carolinas, he had evacuations planned and executed before the storm hit. Now here he was, standing in front of Jennifer like a father with a crying child.

"But we are all in this together," he said, "And we'll help each other through this. Now it's your turn to trust." The president smiled. "Trust *me!*"

Jennifer smiled, and the president pulled her up and gave her a nice, warm hug. Jennifer hadn't felt this secure since she was nine and crashed her bike on the pavement. Her father gave her the same warm, secure hug.

After a long moment, she pulled back and looked up at him with a wide smile.

"Thank you, sir."

"It's my job," he said with a smile, "but I relish the challenge, because honestly"—he leaned down close—"there's never a dull moment in this position."

Jennifer giggled as he grabbed a tissue and wiped her cheek.

"Thank you, Mr. President."

"Please, call me Kennedy."

Jennifer nodded.

"This is just so much, all at once. I'm only twenty-two," she sniffed. "The only job I ever had is at McDonald's. But here I am, in the middle of this whole, crazy thing. I'm so scared."

The president gave her a reassuring nod and smiled.

"We are all scared, Jennifer," he said thoughtfully. "But fear is a great motivator. It keeps us alert and forces us to find solutions quickly. You've done well. You met with the aliens—Qyron, sorry. You've learned their culture and now have communicated this to us. Be proud of that; draw strength from your success."

He pulled out another tissue and wiped her face, giving a subtle smile.

"If you don't mind me asking, how did you get that?" He pointed to her left eye.

"Oh," Jennifer said with a frown, "My *ex*-boyfriend," she said as she looked down at the floor. Another tear streaked down her cheek.

"I promise that will never happen again," Kennedy said solemnly as he looked down on her with a mix of anger and pity.

A moment passed, and the president surveyed the room. All of the men were still frozen in position, mouths open, staring at the unfolding drama.

"Well, let's get to it!" Kennedy yelled.

The men instantly began to scatter like cockroaches in a room with the light switched on. Jennifer let out a laugh as the men scurried.

The president turned to face Taylor.

"I want you to stay with her; help her with anything she needs. You will be my direct contact with her through this process. Make sure you select your staff and Jennifer's this weekend, and be ready by Monday."

Taylor nodded in compliance.

"Make that by tomorrow," Kennedy added. "Time is too short!"

The president pivoted to face Jennifer again.

"I will have you moved to a secure location. We can't risk anything happening to you. I'll have security placed with you, and we'll get you a staff."

A man in a blue suit stepped up.

"Sir, we have all of her items now in a suite downtown."

He handed her a key card.

The president nodded, and the man walked away.

"I also have a doctor waiting to give you a complete physical. We need to make sure you're healthy, with no side effects or issues from your time with the Qyron. Jennifer, everything from this point forward is top secret. We need to ensure that there are no leaks and no unnecessary panic before we go public. Whom have you told your story to?"

She took a moment, looked down, and shifted her stance.

"Well, I told my best friend back home, Tasha. Actually, it's Natasha—Natasha Mills. I explained a good bit of my story to her. I'm not sure if she completely believed me, though."

The president turned to face another man and gave him a nod.

"I'm going to put someone with her to make sure that she fully understands the gravity of the situation."

"Okay, she lives in—"

"We know," the president finished. "We know all about you, Jennifer."

Jennifer recoiled.

"How the hell?" She took a look around the room. "Oh, of course, you're the government."

The president grabbed her hand as she sat back down. He knelt down next to her.

"As soon as we verified the spaceship was in orbit, we performed a complete background check on you. We had to know; we had to be prepared."

Jennifer gave him a smile.

"Yeah, I understand," she said with a sheepish grin.

"For now you'll be staying at a secure location downtown. We will have a staffer assigned to you—an admin assistant of sorts. This person will handle all travel plans and assist with setting up meetings and scheduling. Taylor will fill you in on the rest of the details."

Taylor nodded.

"If you need any other staff, let us know," the president added.

A woman entered the room pushing a cart filled with donuts, drinks, and fruit. Jennifer looked at the cart and sighed.

"What's wrong?" Taylor asked.

"I'm hungry for lunch." She peered over at the clock on the wall and saw that it was 12:03 p.m.

"Then lunch it is," Taylor said as he extended his hand.

Jennifer gave a look to the president, and he nodded back. She reached out and grabbed Taylor's hand.

"Wait a moment. Tank!" the president called over at a large black man in a pin-striped black suit standing in the corner.

"Yes sir?" He quickly walked over to the president.

"I want you to cover Jennifer. I'll have Atkins finalize the rest of the details on her assignment later."

"Yes sir," Tank replied.

"You see this?" The president pointed to the sore black eye that marred Jennifer's face. Tank nodded. "Nothing more happens to her—understand?"

Tank stared directly into the presidents' eyes. "My life before hers, sir. You have my word," Tank shot out without hesitation.

The president turned to face Jennifer.

"Jennifer, this is Terry Brown; he prefers to be called Tank."

Jennifer slowly panned up the hulking figure that was Tank. He stood six and a half feet tall, and she hazarded a guess that he must have weighed close to three hundred pounds. His large, thick frame easily surpassed that of the president or anyone else she had ever met. He almost reminded her of a cartoon character. His arms were as thick as her legs. The suit he wore was so wide in the chest that she thought it would hold two men. His face was very serious, and his eyes were machinelike as they scanned her while she looked up at him.

He had short stubble for hair, with long sideburns that connected to a pencil-thin beard along his thick, square jawline. He reminded Jennifer of those football players who seem to have a head on top of shoulders with no neck. He extended his hand, and she slowly presented hers. His large palm dwarfed hers as he gently shook it.

"I, uh, I really don't need this," she said as she continued to stare up at Tank.

"You don't have a choice; it's not your call," Kennedy responded. "I have to ensure your safety, as you're too valuable to lose, so from this point forward you will have full Secret Service coverage. Tank is one of our very best; he will be in charge of your protection." He looked at Tank. "I feel confident that you'll be safe with him in charge."

"Safe against *what?*" she said abruptly as she shot the president an alarmed look.

"All threats," Kennedy began as he took a step closer to Jennifer. "Jennifer, once this story breaks globally, there will be no end to the number of scared people out there, and scared people can do some strange, dangerous things. You're going to be at the epicenter of this change, so it's my responsibility to keep you safe."

He motioned to Tank. "Take her to the doctor, and then go get some lunch!"

The three of them ambled toward the door. Jennifer grabbed a doughnut and looked back and caught a glance of the president. He was immediately surrounded by men as he talked and pointed with his hands. It was like watching a coach barking out orders to his team.

"Where do you want to eat?" Taylor asked as they walked down the hall. She turned and shot a stiff look at Taylor.

"This is your town; you pick the place," she barked with a dead tone.

Taylor stopped walking, grabbed her shoulder, and spun her around to a stop. Tank halted two steps behind.

"Where's the attitude coming from?" Taylor asked, his eyes wide and a touch of anger in his voice.

Jennifer quickly averted her eyes from him and peered over to Tank. "I don't like the way you set me up," she pouted.

"Set you up? Are you kidding me? You dropped a mind-numbing thing like a UFO hovering above the planet. What did you expect—a tea party? This whole thing was completely out of my hands as soon as they verified the craft with the coordinates you gave me. Top military advisers were instantly alerted, and the president was immediately notified. You should be happy they didn't storm your hotel room and drag you out of there!"

Taylor shook his head, turned in disgust, and continued walking down the hallway.

Tank stepped up behind Jennifer as she watched Taylor, and he leaned over. "He's right," he whispered. "This thing had the whole White House on lockdown. I've never seen such buzz around here."

She gave Tank a nod and then turned and trotted to catch up to Taylor. As Taylor turned a corner and reached the exit, she grabbed his arm.

"Look; I'm sorry. I overreacted. I just didn't expect … well, I guess I didn't know what to expect."

She looked up at him with sullen eyes.

Taylor gave her a quick glance and then exhaled, "That's fine; now let's get you to the doctor and then find something to eat."

When they arrived at the café, Jennifer was still complaining about the visit to the hospital.

"They didn't have to jab me with so many needles. I felt like a pin cushion," she moaned.

"You got the very best care as quickly as possible by a top team of doctors," Taylor huffed. "You wouldn't have been able to afford that kind of care otherwise, so quit your whining!"

He shook his head as he stepped by her and up to the counter to order his food. Tank held the door open as Jennifer and a second agent followed him in. Jennifer stood with her mouth open in affront until Tank ushered her toward the counter.

After they ordered their food, Tank and Jennifer joined Taylor at a table alongside the far wall. The other agent was chatting with Taylor when Jennifer sat down.

"You know," Jennifer said sharply while locking eyes with Taylor, "You sure are a—"

"So tell me about yourself," Tank burst in loudly.

Jennifer whipped her head around and peered at Tank.

"Where are you from?" he prodded Jennifer.

Jennifer smiled.

"Well," she grabbed the glass of water at the table and took a sip. "I was born and raised in Roundup, Montana. I graduated high school a few years ago. I never went anywhere or did anything, really. This is the first time I've been outside of Montana, now that I think about it."

Taylor slowly shook his head with a terse little smile on his lips.

"Did you have a job?" Tank continued.

"Yeah, at McDonald's. I started working there when I was seventeen as a cashier, then fry girl, and finally got promoted to shift supervisor. Not much else to tell, really."

Tank smiled. "That sounds like a nice, quiet life actually. I was born in Harlem, dropped out of school in the seventh grade, and learned to fight on the streets. I then decided to take karate and tae kwan do and do it right. After getting two black belts and getting my GED, I joined the navy and became a SEAL. I then got a job with the Secret Service. I've been in the White House for the past seven years."

"Wow, that's amazing," Jennifer said as she stared at Tank. She couldn't help but gawk at his large frame. She even noticed that the buttons on his suit strained under the pressure.

"Well, I was born and raised here in DC," Taylor said with an arrogant air. "My father was a congressman, and I always wanted to follow in his footsteps—surpass him, actually." He chuckled. "So my plans after this assignment are to push for a House of Representatives seat, and then maybe a governorship, and after that, who knows—maybe shoot for the big chair."

Tank gave Jennifer a crooked little smile and she let out a giggle.

Taylor shot her a quick look. "What's so funny?"

"Nothing," she said over another giggle.

Taylor sneered at her. "At least I'm not some hick from Oregon."

The laugh died in her throat, and she felt a touch of heat as she gave him a hurt look. Jennifer could swear she had heard Tom's voice through Taylor's.

"I'm from Montana, not Oregon, stupid!" Jennifer shot back.

Tank squinted at Taylor and leaned over. "That's harsh; say you're sorry to the lady!"

The tone from Tank was deep and heavy. Taylor peered over to him for a moment and then turned his gaze back to her.

"I'm sorry; that was cruel of me," Taylor mumbled. She gave him a nod as the waitress approached with their appetizers.

They enjoyed feasting on chicken wings, which helped to break the tension, and the rest of the food quickly arrived to the table.

"So will you be moving full time to DC?" Tank asked as he bit into his sandwich.

Jennifer was enjoying a hearty broccoli cheese soup with a grilled cheese sandwich.

"I'm not sure. I guess for now I'm staying here on the president's tab. I'll have to see how all this plays out." She sipped another spoonful.

Taylor was busy with his hamburger and let out a sneer.

Jennifer pivoted to face him. "What now?" she sighed.

Taylor swallowed and then turned to her.

"You know, I just have issue with …" He peered over and caught a stern look from Tank.

"What?"

Jennifer looked hard at Taylor. He had a smug look on his face and a touch of mustard on his chin. The more she looked at him, the more his face and tone reminded her of Tom.

"Finish your thought," she said as his smug smile grew.

"It's just that you're rubbing elbows with the president and you didn't even earn it." He swallowed and continued. "It's like watching a cross between *Legally Blonde* and *Mr. Smith Goes to Washington*. I had to go to school for years. I've been doing this job for a while, and you just strolled right into it."

Jennifer sucked air through her teeth in disgust. Her immediate animosity toward Taylor quickly turned to humor, though. He really was Tom: small, arrogant, and mean. A part of her wanted to yell out at him, but when she looked harder at Taylor in that moment, all that she could see was a jealous child. She gave Tank a quick look and then smiled and turned to Taylor.

"Yes, I did kind of fall into this thing, didn't I, Taylor? I didn't grow up with a silver spoon up my ass like you did. My daddy wasn't no congressman; he worked in a mine shaft and died when I nine. So I grew up poor and didn't get an education like you were given. No, instead I was abducted and brutalized by aliens against my will."

Jennifer suddenly realized that she was talking loudly, so she quickly hushed her volume. Tank and Taylor leaned in to hear her clearly.

"I had surgery; my skull was opened up like a can of soup, and a device wiggled its way in and attached itself to my brain."

Both Tank's and Taylor's eyes opened wide.

"I was then awakened on a table, naked and terrified at meeting a whole new race of beings. But now I'm the only person who can communicate with this race of beings who are about to make all of our lives so much better. Oh, and let's not forget *you*, Taylor, just got given a promotion with a full staff. So please tell me who didn't earn what now?"

Tank exploded in laughter, leaning back in his chair. His deep, loud, gut-busting laughter brought the entire café to silence. Jennifer joined him with a hearty laugh herself.

Tank finally stopped laughing, and Jennifer turned back to face Taylor.

"I know things are crazy right now, and I'm sure they will get a thousand times worse in the next few weeks," she said as she took a drink. "I guess we have to just take things as they come."

Taylor gave her a solemn stare for a moment and then smiled.

"You know, you're right, and I'm sorry. It's just that things aren't going at all as I had planned," Taylor said sheepishly.

"Hey, that's life; you just have to roll with it," Tank quipped.

"So what did you do to deserve that?" Tank pointed to the side of Jennifer's face and her black eye. Jennifer quickly lifted her hand in embarrassment to shield it. Her eyes and smile dropped.

"I laughed at my boyfriend."

Taylor turned his gaze away and shook his head. Tank pursed his lips and sighed. He reached across the table and patted her hand. She gave him an acknowledging nod.

Taylor looked back at Jennifer. He stared at her bright blonde hair.

"What?" Jennifer asked softly.

"I was just looking for the scars," he said as he surveyed her head. "Did the surgery hurt?"

She took another spoonful of soup.

"I was actually unconscious for the whole process. It was only after that I was able to see it all through Xho's eyes."

Taylor sharpened his look. "Xho? Who's Xho?"

"Oh yeah, sorry. Xho is a half-human half-Qyron. He interprets everything from the Qyron to me."

Jennifer sat back in her chair and laughed aloud. Taylor and Tank both leaned in again, waiting for the punch line.

"He's doing your job on the Qyron side," Jennifer laughed.

Taylor shook his head and continued working on his burger.

They finished their lunch and headed back to the White House.

There was a bright light and some hissing, and I pulled the headgear off of my head. It took me a few seconds to readjust.

President Kennedy Myers

Chapter 6

I PLACED THE HEADSET BACK into the case and looked at my watch. I had been in the Psy-log for seven hours, and my stomach rumbled loudly. I got to my feet and started to walk toward the bathroom.

"Computer, messages." The computer responded by playing the one message on the monitor.

"Hey, Amant, it's been seven hours, and I'm ready to eat." The message had been recorded twenty minutes ago.

"Computer, record message," I said as I stripped out of my clothing. A tone sounded. "John, I'm done with my Psy-log and I'm going to get a shower." I walked into the bathroom and turned on the shower. "I'll meet up with you in the dining hall in twenty minutes. End message." A tone sounded. "Computer, deliver message to John Crowley."

I took a shower and then got ready.

As I walked down the passageway toward the dining hall, I reflected on the journey of my great-grandmother Jennifer. I marveled at the courage she'd had over two hundred years ago. As I turned a corner, I heard a familiar voice.

"Yes, I'd definitely be interested," echoed John's voice down the passageway.

I spotted him talking with another man, and John caught my approach.

"Oh, this is the lovely lady I was telling you about," John said with a smile as he extended his hand to me.

I grabbed Johnny's hand and said hello to the man. He was smiling as I looked at him. He had a full head of curly red hair and bushy eyebrows to match. His smile evaporated as we were introduced.

"Amant, this is Jeremy. He owns a construction company and is moving to Gamma Five."

I shook Jeremy's hand, and he blatantly avoided eye contact.

"Hi, Amant," said Jeremy. "Okay, I should be on my way. So much to do." He turned quickly.

"Excellent, I'll keep in touch," John called out as Jeremy walked away.

I had to take a second to compose myself; it would do no good to get upset now. I gave John a smile.

"So are you ready to eat?"

"I could eat the ass end of a bus I'm so hungry," John replied as he walked me into the dining hall.

After we selected our food, I got two fluffy omelets with spinach and onions, hash browns, several pieces of sausage, a bowl of oatmeal, a large stack of pancakes, and a cup of yogurt. We sat down at a quiet table in the far corner.

"You sure you have enough there?" John asked with a smile. "So how was your work?"

"Yes, I have plenty there, funny man; we Qyron have huge appetites," I replied with a smile. "Oh, wow, it was so fascinating, Johnny. Jennifer was so interesting I could hardly tear myself away."

"Was? Oh right, sorry. I wish I could join you on this Psy-log thingy. So I guess you'll just have to fill me in as you go," John said with a smile. "I'm equally excited about talking with Jeremy. He's looking for a manager for his company."

I already had a juicy bite of the omelet in my mouth; it was so delicious. I frowned and shook my head on hearing John's last statement.

John caught my response. "What?"

"Well"—I swallowed—"I'm sorry that I queered your deal."

"What do you mean?" John's eyebrow rose.

"Didn't you catch Jeremy's face as he saw me? Did you see how quickly he exited after I joined you both? Come on, John!"

John sat silent for a second, his spaghetti dangling on the tip of his fork. John slowly put his fork down.

"I can't believe that ... as beautiful as you are?"

I shook my head. I could feel my stomach tighten up.

"Jeremy said he was busy and—"

"John, how did the conversation go before I arrived? What were you two talking about?" I stopped eating and focused on John.

"Well, we were talking about the open position, and we were going to talk more in depth about it." John's voice trailed off.

I nodded. "But suddenly he's too busy and has to leave the very moment I arrive?"

"That doesn't make sense, though. You're so attractive and—"

"John, please, you have to stop. I'm half Qyron and half human. There are still a lot of people out there who can't see past the human side. Why do you think I don't have a man in my life? Every time I find a nice guy who finds me attractive, it ends when he introduces me to his family or friends. I've seen it too many times. Now it's happened to you." I exhaled loudly and dropped my fork on the plate.

"No, I wouldn't let something like this stop us if we were a couple."

John reached over the table and grabbed my hand.

"Sweet of you to say that John," I said as I pulled my hand away. "But wait a while and you'll see. Racism has a funny way of messing everything up."

"I would love the chance," John volleyed back. "Are you too soured to give me, to give *us*, that chance?"

"John, you just don't know."

"And apparently I never will—is that right?" John's voice got louder. "So you're just going to quit with me like you did ten years ago? You're going to be a coward and run away?"

The anger and disappointment streamed off of his words. It was as if he plunged a knife straight into my heart. I gasped and dropped my napkin. I could feel my bottom lip begin to quiver.

"Oh, John." I was short of breath, and I felt my eyes begin to well up. "I'm ... I'm done."

I quickly rose from the table. John dropped his fork and jumped up. "No, John, *no!*"

John froze in his place while I quickly walked away. As soon as I left the dining hall, I broke into a run down the passageway. I arrived at my room, and as soon as the door closed behind me, I burst into tears.

A tone sounded. "Incoming message."

"Ignore!" I screamed through the tears. I quickly tore off my clothes and stormed into the bathroom. I started another hot shower and jumped in. For the next fifteen minutes, I cried as the hot water beat down.

After I finished my long shower, I wrapped myself up in a thick terry cloth bathrobe and plopped down on the couch. I grabbed a pillow, hugged it close, and curled up on the couch. I saw that there were three messages waiting for me. I just lay on the couch for another few minutes, and then I took a deep breath and sat up. I felt the strong urge to escape. I pulled the case from the coffee table and grabbed the headset. I placed it on my head, experienced a soft hiss and white light, and then …

Jennifer spent the next few hours in the White House dealing with administrative issues. She answered questions for a background check, received an ID badge and security clearance, and interviewed candidates for her administrative assistant position. Taylor walked her into a room with three people.

"Jennifer, this is Jodi, Thomas, and Rachel."

She greeted all three, and then Taylor pulled her aside.

"You may interview to select your admin assistant." Taylor leaned in close. "You have interviewed before?"

"Of course. I was a supervisor at McDonald's. Duh!" Jennifer huffed as she turned to face the three candidates.

Taylor snickered. She peered back to catch him looking at her with a smile. Part of her wanted to laugh too, as this position was going to be far more serious than a job for some high school kid flipping a burger. But the other part of her wanted to be serious and professional to show Taylor she wasn't some stupid, redneck blonde.

She spent a solid hour performing individual interviews, and it didn't take long for Jennifer to notice a take charge person in the group. She still wanted to think a few things over, so she dismissed the candidates.

"I want to thank everyone for applying; I will be contacting my selection later today."

Jennifer took the next few minutes to check over the written answers to the questions Taylor had given them. One in particular stood out: "You're in an important meeting, and your boss is absent. A negative comment is made about your boss. How do you react?"

Rachel's answer read, "While I know my boss can stand on her own feet and defend her honor, I would still take it upon myself to challenge this person to see what his or her reasoning was for disrespecting my boss."

Jennifer grabbed her phone and made the call.

"Hello, this is Rachel."

"Hi, Rachel. It's Jennifer. Please turn around and come back."

"Really? Oh my gosh, thank you so much!" Rachel exclaimed with excitement.

Jennifer walked to the south gate to meet her. As Jennifer approached the gate, she spotted Rachel walking up the sidewalk, grinning from ear to ear. Rachel was a year older than Jennifer, but her résumé had her working with a congressman and, previous to that, the president's election team. Jennifer watched as her wavy auburn hair flitted in the air. She looked so professional in her navy-blue business suit, and Jennifer marveled at her shoes. As she approached, Jennifer saw Rachel smile at Marvin. She had a large, beautiful smile. Marvin handed her a visitor pass and stared at her butt as she walked by. Jennifer shook her head but couldn't fault Marvin, as her body was quite shapely, with not an ounce of fat on it.

"Hi, Jennifer. Thank you so much for the chance," Rachel exclaimed as she gave Jennifer a hug. "You won't be disappointed. I've worked in the political field for the last five years, and I'm so hungry for a new challenge."

Jennifer smiled back. "Well, this will certainly be political all right, and like nothing you've ever done before. I just hope you can handle diversity."

Rachel looked over her shoulder and spotted Tank standing by.

"What's with him?"

"Oh, I'm sorry. Rachel, this is Terrance. You can call him Tank. He is here for my security."

Rachel and Tank shook hands. Rachel gave Jennifer a questioning look.

"So why do you need a bodyguard?"

"He's Secret Service, and it was the president's idea," Jennifer mumbled as they turned and walked back into the White House. Rachel continued to shoot her a dumbfounded look.

"Nice answer, by the way," Jennifer said as they walked down the hall. "I like that you have such loyalty to your boss."

Rachel nodded. "Well, it may sound cliché, but I see myself as a team player, and if anyone attacks my coach, I take it personally."

Jennifer smiled at Rachel and then continued.

"Okay, so what I'm going to need from you in this position is complete scheduling to include world leaders, diplomats, corporate heads, and, well, the others. I'm also going to—"

"Excuse me?" Rachel's expression shifted to a more confused look with a crooked smile. "What is 'the others'?"

"We'll get to those details later."

Jennifer noticed Taylor approaching them.

"Mr. Atkins, head of security, needs to speak with you, Jennifer."

They walked to the end of the hallway with Taylor and then went into a conference room. Taylor introduced her to Mr. Atkins.

"Jennifer, this will be your full-time security detail." Mr. Atkins pointed to the eight men standing behind him. "You will have two agents with you at all times. We will take care of their scheduling. All we need from you is a week's notice of your plans and destinations. Is this your assistant?" He pointed to Rachel.

"Oh, yes, I'm sorry." She quickly introduced Rachel to Mr. Atkins.

"We also have all of your belongings in your new residence. Whenever you're ready, our team is prepared to escort you."

Jennifer stopped for a moment.

"My stuff was in two suitcases. Did your men go through them?"

"It's standard protocol to ensure there are no weapons, tracking devices, or listening devices."

"So you found my transmitter?"

"Your what?" Mr. Atkins said with a blank stare.

He was a short man with a thin nose. His thinning hair made him appear birdlike and frail.

"A small black box—feels lighter than air."

Mr. Atkins continued to stare at Jennifer for a moment.

"Yes ma'am," he finally answered reluctantly.

"I'll need that back."

"When we're done with it, you'll get it back," Mr. Atkins said assertively.

"Mr. Atkins, that's the transmitter that I need to make contact with the scout ship. I've seen enough movies to know that you're probably already in DEFCON 1 mode, so you've taken my transmitter and are trying to figure out what it does."

Mr. Atkins continued to give Jennifer an authoritative blank stare.

"Two things. First, it's technology you won't be able to understand, and it will be pointless in a few weeks anyway, as much of their technology will be shared with us. Second, and most important, if you break that box and I can't contact the scout ship, then *you* can answer to the president and the rest of the world as to how this entire situation is now out of our control."

Mr. Atkins took a deep breath, and his expression changed to one of concern. His eyebrows rose, and then his pursed lips shifted to a frown.

"I'll get that box for you."

"Thank you," Jennifer said, barely able to contain herself.

She had no idea where her courage came from. She gave a look at Rachel, who had a stunned expression on her face. Jennifer then peered over to Tank, who sported a huge grin.

"What?" she whispered to Tank.

He stepped forward and walked her to the corner of the room. He peered over her shoulder and then leaned over and whispered in her ear.

"I've been working here for seven years now, and I've never seen anyone handle Mr. Atkins like that. For a small-town girl, you sure have big-time attitude."

Jennifer let out a little giggle and slapped Tank's arm. "I surprised myself too!"

It suddenly felt like being in church and having been told a joke. Both of them turned bright red and tried to hold back their laughter. When Jennifer finally composed herself, she turned back toward Tank.

"This is the first time in my life that I've been a part of anything important; I just wanna get it right."

Tank shook his head and smiled. "You're doing just fine; let's go," he said.

He and another agent escorted Rachel and Jennifer to a waiting car.

They slid into the backseat while Tank got into the passenger seat. The whole car lurched as he did so. Mr. Atkins ran over to the car. He handed the small black box to Jennifer through the open car window.

"Thank you," Jennifer said to him with a smile.

Mr. Atkins turned and walked away. As they pulled out, Rachel turned to her.

"Okay, what is this position about?"

Jennifer paused as she gave Rachel a stern look.

"I guess I can tell you. You're going to hear it all tomorrow morning at the next meeting. For now, though, this is top secret, so it stays with you. Okay?"

Rachel nodded slowly, her mouth slightly open and her eyes fixed on Jennifer's.

"I have made contact with a friendly race of aliens. I will be handling all aspects of communication between them and us."

Rachel's mouth dropped open and the agent driving the car gasped.

"No way!" Rachel said with her eyes wide.

Jennifer gave her a minute to process it as they turned down a street and then into an underground garage.

Tank pivoted around in his seat. "You won't have any concern about safety. The government owns the entire city block, and it's constantly monitored."

As they exited the car, Jennifer peered over at Rachel. She still had a look of shock on her face, her eyes wide and her mouth still agape. Jennifer reached over and grabbed her arm. After she pulled her out of the car, they walked into the waiting elevator. The other agent pressed 2 as the doors closed. After reaching the second floor, they escorted the ladies to room 3.

Jennifer stepped through the doorway and walked inside. A brightly lit apartment greeted her as she took the first few steps. The walls were painted in light cream with tan accents. A few large paintings adorned the walls, and thick plush carpet softened every step. Jennifer was stunned as she continued to look around. She gazed at the shiny hardwood floors in the kitchen. Maple cabinets and stainless steel appliances were connected with a dark green marble countertop. Across from the kitchen was the living room. Beautiful plush couches surrounded a large

TV on the wall. A small desk on the far side of the room overlooked a picture window. Jennifer couldn't help but gawk, as this apartment was a world of difference from the ratty carpet, broken cabinets, and cracked walls of her rented home. Jennifer stared at the leather couch, figuring it was more expensive than her monthly rent.

"You have two bedrooms, each with its own bathroom," Tank said to her. "You have windows, but they're four-inch-thick bulletproof glass, so you won't be able to get fresh air that way."

He walked over to a panel on the wall and tapped on the touchscreen.

"If you want air conditioning …" He peered over and saw that Jennifer was still marveling at the apartment. He walked over to her, gently grabbed her hand, and walked her over to the touch panel. "If you want heat, you press here. If you want air conditioning, click here. And if you want fresh air, you select this."

Jennifer gave him a blushing smile as she tuned in to his instructions. He walked her through the entire screen, but she was catching only parts of his speech as she continued to steal glances at the apartment.

"Wow," she muttered as she slowly walked back through the apartment. "I've never seen such a beautiful place."

"I'm glad you like it," Tank said with a large grin as he walked behind Jennifer.

"If you need us at any time, you just hit this button," the other agent added.

Jennifer's head was on a swivel as she continued to look around.

"Miss?"

Jennifer shook off the trance and turned to face him. "I'm sorry."

"That's fine," he said with a smile. "Again, if you need us for anything, you can hit this button. In addition, you have a remote button in both bedrooms and at the door." He pointed to the doorway.

Tank stepped forward. "We work in shifts and will stay in an apartment on the bottom floor, so we're always close."

Jennifer gave them both a nod. "Thank you, guys; this is … wow, it's incredible."

The two of them exited, and she closed the door behind them. Jennifer turned and walked back toward Rachel, who was still standing in the living room. "Can you believe this?" she gushed.

"Huh? Yeah, nice place," Rachel said flatly. "So you met up with aliens. What are they like?"

Jennifer spent the next few minutes discussing the Qyron and some of her time with Xho. Then they spent the next two hours setting up a plan of action for the meeting tomorrow. Jennifer felt good getting back into typing and spreadsheets instead of hamburgers and fries. She finally felt needed, wanted, and useful.

When the time approached 5:00 p.m., they decided that they had reached a solid point and then chatted a few minutes about their lives.

"So he was being such a jerk, I dumped him," Rachel said.

They both laughed.

"Me too! I finally reached my limit with my old boyfriend this past week. He was such a tool!" They both broke out laughing again.

"Is, uh, that where you got …" Rachel said as she motioned to Jennifer's eye. Jennifer nodded. "I'm sorry," Rachel mumbled softly. "Okay, well I need to get going. I'll see you tomorrow at 8:00 a.m.," she said as she walked toward the door. "Oh, since parking is easier, mind if I come by and drive in with you?"

"Sure, that's fine. I guess I'll see you at seven forty-five then."

Rachel left, and Jennifer closed the door. Jennifer took a slow stroll through the apartment and gazed at her new accommodations. She walked into her bedroom and admired the queen-size bed. She ran her hand along the plush comforter. A few steps and she was in her bathroom. She unpacked her toiletry bag and then decided to lie down on the bed. As soon as she got comfortable, she heard her cell phone ring. She jumped up from the bed and ran to the counter in the kitchen.

"Hey, Mama. Yeah I'm here in DC."

Jennifer strolled back into the bedroom.

"Oh, Mama, you should see the apartment that they put me up in. It's so incredible. The kitchen is beautiful, and it has the best furniture I've ever seen." She leaned back on the bed and stretched out.

"No, I'm not going to get back with Tom." Jennifer sat up, an angry look on her face. "No, Mama, I'm tired of his games, and I'm tired of him hitting me."

Jennifer slid to the edge of the bed.

"Look, I have to get up early, Mama, so I have to go. Love you too."

Jennifer ended the call and walked out to the kitchen. She grabbed the black transmitter box from the counter. The box was similar in size to a large ring box. Jennifer held it up to her head and closed her eyes. She focused solidly through the day's meetings. A few seconds later, a stream of thoughts flowed into her mind.

We will be landing at 9:00 a.m. local time on the south lawn of the White House in Washington, DC, on Friday. We will have Xho for your link. Our leader will be available to meet with your leaders.

Jennifer then received a large block of information. It was almost painful because of the amount of information that streamed in, so she sat down at the kitchen table and tried to process all of the data. Jennifer then jumped up, ran to the living room, grabbed the laptop, and furiously typed the information into the outlines she and Rachel had worked on earlier. When she finally finished over an hour and a half later, she was exhausted. She thought of the times in school when she'd had final exams, and recalled how tired her head felt from so much thinking—and this was worse.

As she went into the bathroom to wash up and brush her teeth, a wave of fear and doubt overcame her. Tomorrow she would be in front of the top political people in America. Her thoughts then floated to Monday, when she would stand at the United Nations in front of every diplomat from around the world. Then images of next Friday, the day of the first meeting with the Qyron, floated through her mind. She stared into the mirror, looking at this twenty-two-year-old blonde who two weeks ago had been a manager at a fast food joint. She replayed the secretary of defense yelling at her, questioning her background and skills. Jennifer began trembling all over and felt her chest heaving as her heartbeat and breathing increased. The tension and fear became palpable. Her arms and legs shook, and she began to sob. She dropped her toothbrush and tried to steady herself over the sink. Her legs gave way, and she slid down to the floor. For a solid ten minutes she cried, gripped by fear, lying on the bathroom floor.

Jennifer had finally stood up to grab a tissue when the house phone rang. She picked up the receiver from the bedroom nightstand.

"M'low," she slurred out through the tears, panting and whimpering

"Jennifer? Are you okay?" Tank's voice blared out.

Jennifer crumpled to the floor again and began bawling.

"Meh flaawb" was all she could get out over the sobbing.

Fifteen seconds later, the lock on the door was activated and Tank and another agent pushed through quickly. Jennifer was sobbing on the carpet as Tank ran over to her, gun drawn.

"Clear!" the other agent called out from the guest bedroom. Tank leaned over and scooped Jennifer up. His large arms lowered her gently onto the bed.

"Are you okay, Jennifer?" He looked into her eyes.

She nodded slowly.

"I'm sorry," she cried. "It's just that my mom is pushing me to come home. My old boyfriend is being a jerk. I'm so scared about tomorrow. I have no idea what I'm doing, and I've never felt so much pressure."

The other agent joined them in the bedroom. Tank sat down on the bed next to her.

"Look, I know that you're shouldering a lot right now," Tank said as he stared into Jennifer's eyes. "You just have to take it a step at a time," he softly reassured her. "Know that you have a whole team here to help you. Taylor will assist with everything on the government side, Rachel is here to help you with administrative work, and our team is always ready with the heavy lifting. And my team won't let anything happen to you—you got my word!"

He gave Jennifer a smile as his large brown eyes reassured her. She smiled back through the tears. The other agent handed her a tissue, and she wiped her eyes and blew her nose.

"I'm sorry for being such a baby."

"Don't even start that!" Tank said in a low tone. "Look; I've felt like you have in many situations; it's normal. You just have to assess the situation and use all of the tools at your disposal. For me it's other agents, guns, and my martial arts training. For you it's having Rachel do your admin work; it's Taylor being the go-between with the president or his cabinet members." He softly patted Jennifer's head and gave her another smile. "And what happens with us here stays with us. So let it all out, and then let's go out and grab some dinner. That was the reason I called. Are you hungry?"

She slowly nodded as she sniffled.

"Then clean yourself up and let's go; I can't have you starving under my watch."

He helped Jennifer to her feet. She walked into the bathroom, splashed some water on her face, put on a little makeup, and they were out the door.

"I feel like a mess," she huffed as they walked out of the elevator.

"You look fine," Tank reassured her as they strolled to the car.

There was a bright light and some hissing, and I pulled the headgear off. It took a moment for me to adjust to the present reality.

Terrance "Tank" Brown

Chapter 7

MY STOMACH RUMBLED LOUDLY, UNHAPPY with the few bites I had eaten earlier today. I checked my watch and saw that I had been in the Psy-log for five hours. A quick glance at the monitor showed that I now had five unheard messages. Four of the messages were from John; the last was from the flight administrator. I opened the note from the administrator. It explained the unique aspect of my general ticket and then asked for the full details of my identification and the reason for the trip. I saved the message. *I'll get to that later, after I've eaten.* I deleted the other messages from John and then grabbed my gym bag from the bedroom and moved to leave.

When I opened my door, a bouquet of roses stood guard in the hallway. I bent over and picked up the two dozen blooms. I sauntered back into my room and set the flowers on the coffee table. I pulled the card from the top and read it.

> These are just 24 ways to say I'm sorry. I have at least a dozen more if you would give me the chance.

I smiled and put the card in my pocket. I hoped those roses would not only make the place a little more colorful but fight the horrible odor too. I left the room and walked to the gym. My stomach was screaming for food, but I had to burn off some anger and needed more time to think.

After donning a jogging suit, I ran on the track for three miles. During my run, I remembered the times in the neighborhood with John: sitting with homework together, fighting over a candy bar, laughing over a comedy program. A flood of memories came rushing back to me.

When I stopped my run, I walked into the equipment section. I lifted weights on a few machines and then stepped over to a heavy bag.

"Well hello, Amant," a voice said behind me.

I pivoted around to see Brad in a pair of shorts and a ratty T-shirt. His arms were thick, and his abs showed through the tears in his shirt. He also had a few days' worth of scruff on his face; it gave him a rugged, sexy look.

"Glad to see you in the gym. So what are you working on, because you look perfect to me," Brad said as he stepped into my personal space.

I smiled; his come-on was cheesy but cute. I was still breathing heavily from my weight lifting.

"I'm just working out some stress. And before you say it, no I don't need to work out *that* kind of stress."

Brad grinned back at me. "Am I that obvious?"

"As subtle as an air horn in church," I replied.

Brad laughed aloud. "Wow, I must be slipping then, because I used to be smooth."

I turned and began to punch the heavy bag.

He slowly walked around me, looking at me as I continued to punch the bag. I caught him staring at my chest as I threw a punch. I stopped abruptly.

"Ya know, it makes me feel more than a little awkward, you staring at my breasts while I work out!" I panted angrily.

Brad slowly stepped forward.

"It's not that I'm ogling your breasts, although they are spectacular. It's your form when you punch; it could use some refining."

"I've had my share of mixed martial arts training," I huffed.

"Yes, I see that," he said softly as he continued to move alongside me, "but you could benefit from some additional training."

He peered again as I punched the bag.

"When you punch"—he stepped close behind me—"you have to move your hips."

He firmly placed his hands on my hips. I let out a little gasp.

"Relax," he said softly.

He gently pressed on my hips, turning me.

"When you punch, you want the power and force to be generated from your hips. You want to use that momentum."

He continued to push back and forth. Brad also swung his hips, showing me. He then released his grasp on me and punched the bag hard. I watched his form as he punched the bag again and again. I continued to swing my hips in time with his. I then launched a hard punch. It connected with so much force that the bag let out a large thud that echoed through the gym. Brad's eyes opened wide, and he nodded. I punched a few more times, hitting the bag harder. It felt good to punch with so much more force; I was really burning up my earlier aggression. My breathing was faster now as I continued to jab.

"Very good," Brad said as he walked around me.

I threw a few more punches and then stopped. I was panting and sweating, but it felt good.

"You're a quick study; I'm very impressed," Brad said with a smile.

I went to throw another punch but felt a bolt of pain shoot up my back.

"Ow! Damn it!" I leaned over, clutching my right side with my right arm. Brad stepped around to the back of me.

"Easy," he said as he gently put his right hand on my lower back.

"Ow, yeah, right there," I said, wheezing and grimacing in pain.

"Yeah, no kidding. You've got one hell of a knot."

He began to massage that spot with his palm. It hurt as he pressed on it, but the pressure he applied started to feel good. He swirled his right hand in a circular motion. Slowly, the pain began to decrease, but I could feel the round knot of muscle as he massaged it. I then felt his left hand grab my left shoulder. He gently eased me to a standing position as he continued to massage my lower back.

"Ooh, yeah, that's it," I said softly.

The pain was beginning to dissipate. He continued pressing and massaging; it felt so good. His left hand then slid across my upper chest, and he grabbed onto my right shoulder. He drew his right hand up and down my spine, pushing and kneading as he went along. The massaging and pulling slowly forced my back into an arched position.

"Ooh," I said.

It tingled, and I moaned again. As my back arched, it loosened up the muscles and the tension dropped.

"I'm glad that feels better," he said softly.

I felt his breath on my ear. A shiver ran up my spine, and I quivered.

"You should do some yoga; it will loosen you up and prevent this from happening again."

His voice was low, and his warm breath was in my ear again. I giggled a little and shivered.

"Sorry," he said in a low whisper, "would you like me to stop?"

"Oh no, please don't," I moaned back to him.

It felt so good as his hand massaged my muscles and his stretching loosened up my spine. He then released the grip on my shoulder with his left hand. He dragged it slowly across the front of my breasts.

I gasped and tried to turn. He hooked his right arm around my lower back and spun me around. It was one fluid motion, akin to a dance move, as he twirled me around and pulled me tight. We were now face-to-face. He leaned in and placed a soft kiss on my lips. I gasped again, in shock.

He tried to put his tongue in my mouth. I pulled back quickly.

"No, wait. Stop!"

I pushed hard. Brad had me tight, so it took a second effort. I finally pushed out of his grasp.

"I'm sorry; no, I can't!"

Brad gave me a stunned look and reached out.

"No, please. I … I just can't." I backed away.

"Amant, I'm sorry," he said as he extended his hand.

I shook my head and continued to backpedal. Part of me wanted him—wanted to be taken by him. But a bigger part of me saw John. It was so confusing. I turned and ran for the doorway.

"Amant, wait; don't go!" Brad yelled out as I ran down the hallway.

I didn't stop until I reached the end of the deck. I was sweaty, tired, confused, and incredibly hungry. My stomach was now roaring, and hunger pains were shooting through me. I just wanted to walk; I needed to calm down and sort things out. I entered a lift and hit the button for F Deck. The screen responded with a red "denied." I angrily hit the button a second time, and again I heard an alarm tone, with the red letters flashing "denied."

Why would an entire deck be off limits? That doesn't make any sense.

I then pressed *E*, and the doors closed. I wiped the sweat from my face, and as I reached Echo Deck, I stepped off and began to walk. I passed a small entertainment area. Kids were laughing and playing Ping-Pong; a few others were shooting pool. I then caught a whiff of food. My stomach broke into a chorus of "feed me," so I began walking in the direction of the wafting odor.

A short walk and a turn of the corner and I was staring at the Echo Deck dining hall. I grabbed a tray and began to survey the variety of foods. My mouth watered at the sight of the lasagna. I grabbed four pieces of it along with some corn, cauliflower, and a brownie. I shivered as the sweat slowly cooled my body. A tall glass of lemonade completed my tray. I ate quickly, as my stomach was well past hungry. I wasn't even ladylike. I ate like a starving wolf and didn't care who saw me. I also drank down the entire glass of lemonade in one moment. After a second glass of lemonade, I slowly enjoyed my brownie. I peered up from my tray to see a family looking at me in disgust.

"Sorry, I'm so hungry," I said sheepishly.

If my mother had been there, she would have scolded me for being so crude. She always disliked that trait in me. I used to be crude, boorish, and crass just to upset her. I guess I got that from my father, as he enjoyed pushing my mothers' staunch barriers. I found it sporting, at times, to push her limits too.

I finally finished my meal and quickly walked back down the passageway. I stopped at a general terminal.

"Message to John Crowley," I said. A notice flashed back immediately. "John Crowley is asleep".

I walked away from the terminal and onto the lift. I pressed the *L* and within seconds was on Lima Deck. A few seconds later I was at my doorway. As I opened the door, I heard noises. The hairs on my neck stood up as I cautiously walked into my room. Two attendants were busy shampooing my carpets. I exhaled loudly and relaxed.

One attendant was actually cleaning my couch. I cringed when I saw a very dark brown fluid being suctioned from the cushions. The one doing the carpet stopped when he saw me.

"Oh, I'm sorry, Qyron, I was told to—"

"You're fine," I said with a smile. "Please don't stop on my account."

"Oh wow, you can speak!" he said with excitement.

"Yes," I said while I suppressed a laugh. "I'm only half Qyron."

"Okay, um, we'll be done soon. We already completed your bedroom."

I nodded and looked over at the coffee table. My headset was not there. I quickly peered over at the kitchenette counter and saw it sitting there. The second attendant caught my gaze.

"Sorry, I moved it there. Um, what is that? I put it on, and it made my head hot."

I gave him a startled look. "It's my Psy-log headset. It shouldn't be used by normal humans. Actually, you should have a scan performed to ensure you didn't do yourself any harm."

He gave me a wave of his hand. "Nah, I feel fine now."

He then turned around and continued to clean the upholstery. The first attendant also returned to his carpet cleaning. I walked over and grabbed my headset. I then did a double-take and took two bottles of flavored water. My workout had really dehydrated me. I walked back to my bedroom, grabbed some clean clothes, and went into the bathroom.

The steamy hot shower made me feel a world better. My stomach was digesting nicely, and now the only noises it made were gurgles of happiness. I toweled off and got into some clean sweatpants and a T-shirt. When I opened the bathroom door, I noticed the attendants were gone. Best of all, the room smelled clean and fresh. The roses were also back on the coffee table, along with my headset case.

I went into the bedroom and lay down on the bed.

"Computer message."

My words were followed by a tone.

"John, I got your roses. I deleted the other messages before listening to them; for that I am sorry. I would like to talk with you. I'm going to do some more Psy-logging—maybe eight hours' worth. I'm going to go to sleep shortly after that. I hope to catch you somewhere in between. Computer, send message to John Crowley."

Another tone sounded.

I decided to meditate. I wanted to clear my head, as the time with Brad and my thoughts for John had me in a twist. When I finished my session, I felt calm but was still ambivalent about John and Brad. I reached over and grabbed my headset. I placed it on my head.

There was a white light and some hissing.

Chapter 8

"THAT WASH A REALLY NICE dinner and a fun time; shanks, Tank!" slurred Jennifer as she giggled.

Tank smiled. "Glad you had a good time. Will you be ready in the morning? You had a lot to drink."

"I'll be … I'll be fine, but chu be reaby though," Jennifer laughed back, wavering a bit as she walked.

"I'll be off," Tank replied, "but there will be two new agents with you."

"Oh, okay. Enchoy your time off."

Jennifer turned and opened her apartment door. As she stumbled into the living room, she recalled her evening. She had had a wonderful dinner with Tank and Marcus, the other agent. Afterward, they sang some Karaoke while having a few drinks. Jennifer had enjoyed trying a few different martinis. The evening had ended when she stumbled off the stage. Tank said that she "had had enough."

She staggered directly into the bedroom and fell onto the bed, clothes on.

"That's right, 40 percent off!" blared the radio.

Jennifer opened one eye and hit the snooze button on the alarm clock. Ten minutes later, the alarm went off again.

She finally crawled out of bed. She plodded into the bathroom, peeling off her clothing as she went, and opened the medicine cabinet.

Awesome, it's stocked with aspirin, she thought.

Jennifer quickly downed two and hopped into the shower.

Forty-five minutes later found her in the car with two new agents and Rachel strolling across the parking area. She opened the door.

"Good morning!" she said with a cheery Saturday voice.

"Ugh" was all Jennifer could muster as Rachel slid in next to her.

"Uh oh, what's wrong?"

The car moved forward and Jennifer leaned her head back and closed her eyes.

"A little too much chocolate martini. No, a lot too much," Jennifer mumbled.

She reached into her pocket and handed Rachel a USB drive.

"I worked on some additions to the plans last night. Please photocopy them and be ready to hand them out as soon as the meeting starts."

Rachel then said a few things, none of which Jennifer heard, as they finally pulled into the White House. Fortunately for her, the aspirin was starting to take effect as they walked from the car. Taylor was standing outside, waiting for them with a smile.

"I heard you had a good time last night," he said in a cheery tone.

"Did you plan that?" Jennifer grumbled as she gave him a sour look.

"I may have had a hand in it," Taylor said with a smirk. "I mean, you were quite stressed, so I thought a nice evening out would do you some good. From the looks of it, though, it ran over you."

Jennifer shot him a smile and stifled a giggle.

"Yes, it backed right over me. Maybe next time you can ditch the wife and join us?"

"Sorry, no wife," Taylor said smugly as they walked into the building.

"Boyfriend?" Jennifer replied with a devilish grin.

He only flashed her a grimace while Rachel let out a laugh.

"Okay, let's get down to business. The president has every cabinet member and at least one staffer at the ready. No one is in a good mood, so you had better be on your game," Taylor warned. Jennifer moaned in response.

They finally reached the large meeting room. No fewer than thirty people were in attendance.

The president greeted Jennifer outside as Rachel ran to a copier.

"I would have liked to have seen your work last night."

"I'm sorry, sir," she said sheepishly.

"It's difficult for me to get on board if I don't have the data first, so I'm hoping you have some convincing information at the ready."

"I do, sir, and it won't happen again."

Kennedy nodded and then leaned in closer.

"I know you're new at this, but there cannot be a next time." The president's face was dead serious. "This is the single most important event in human history, so we must be prepared. I need to get in front of this."

Jennifer bobbed her head. He paused for a moment and then gave Jennifer a pat on the back.

"Let's nail this," he said confidently, and they stepped into the room.

All of the light chatter ceased, and the president began by introducing Jennifer to his cabinet. Rachel finally returned to the room as he finished the introductions.

Jennifer leaned over to the president. "Please excuse me for just a moment."

She pulled Rachel aside and told her to grab some more aspirin and be ready with a recorder.

When Jennifer turned back around, all eyes were on her and the room ached with silence. Jennifer took a deep breath.

"I want to thank everyone for meeting on short notice. I'm sure your first question is "Who the hell is she?"

A collective nod was given, and a few chuckles floated around the room.

"My name is Jennifer Winston, and I'm about to become the second most important person you'll ever meet."

She gave the president a smile as she handed out the stapled booklets to every cabinet member.

"Over a week ago, I was abducted by an alien race, the Qyron."

Several faces suddenly changed in the room; there were looks of shock and a few disbelieving smiles and nods.

"I was given the ability to communicate telepathically with them. I learned all about their history and culture. The Qyron have been a civilized race for nearly a million years. Their technology is far better than ours, and they are looking to form a partnership with our planet."

She finished handing out all of the packets, her hands cold and clammy.

"My assistant and I have outlined all of the proposed changes to our way of life. Every cabinet member here has a very large to-do list that needs to be looked over and prepared for before we officially meet them. Please check that you have the right copy." She glanced over at Rachel, feeling dizzy and weak. "This coming Friday, they are scheduled to land a scout ship on the White House lawn and make the first official contact with the human race."

A growing swell of chatter now filled the room. Everyone began tearing through the pages with startled, confused looks. The president was also busy flipping through his sixty-page review document.

"Excuse me!" Jennifer yelled. Her head thumped, and her stomach tightened. All eyes suddenly returned to her, and much of the banter stopped.

"We have very limited time to get our plans together. Monday we will be hosting a UN meeting, and we need to have our plans underway."

The secretary of defense stood up.

"Thank you for this, little lady, but aren't we putting the cart before the horse?"

Jennifer snapped her attention to him. He was a tall but stocky man. A thick, bushy mustache matched the sandy brown gray-peppered hair that was receding on his head. His big puffy cheeks with a shade of red would have given him a Santa Claus look if it hadn't been for his dark gray suit and gruff demeanor.

"How in the hell do we know these aliens are friendly? How can we be sure that—"

"If you continue to read my document, it will explain much of this, sir." She let out a small, quiet burp. "But let me sum it up for you: Within a day, the Qyron are prepared to set up stations in every city hospital in America, as well as one hundred thousand more across the world. They will be able to quickly diagnose every person and provide rapid solutions to nearly every medical problem we have. Just one hospital will be able to cure approximately twenty-five hundred people a day of such serious diseases as cancer, AIDS, and Ebola, as well as arthritis, birth defects, and bad breath. They realize that we will be incredibly fearful of them, so they want to establish goodwill immediately."

Every eye in the room was plastered on Jennifer; the only motion in the room was coming from her stomach.

"They will also be bringing enough food to feed every person on this planet, so starvation will be eliminated within the week. Transportation, housing, and tools will be provided for us to fill hundreds of millions of jobs."

The secretary of state, Tom Franklin, rose up.

"Oh, come on; we're supposed to believe that this loving, philanthropic race of beings will swoop down on unicorns and immediately solve all of our problems? What's in it for them?" An immediate buzz of agreement flooded the room.

Jennifer exhaled. She could feel the tension rise, and her stomach continued to tighten and churn.

Tom Franklin, unlike some of the other cabinet members, had a long-standing bulletproof reputation in politics. His clean-cut appearance, from his crew cut and precisely tailored suit to his squeaky clean lifestyle with a loving wife and three kids, framed his thirty years in politics. Tom was a by-the-book Boy Scout that many admired and few distrusted. Jennifer knew very little about politics, but she knew that this was a man of power and respect, from what she had heard in the news.

"Okay, let's play a little game," Jennifer responded as her chest tightened. She took a calming breath to steady herself. "I call it 'suppose.' You ready?"

Tom gave her a stern look and slowly nodded.

"Let's suppose you're one of a million humans who are on this planet called Earth. Now let's suppose that Earth is, say, fifty percent larger than the current pile of dirt we're living on. Let's say that this new Earth is just overflowing with natural resources—more than the million people can ever hope to use. Now suppose that in our solar system there are three other habitable planets—two slightly bigger than ours and all three also rich in resources."

She noted that a few people leaned back in their chairs, sporting more relaxed expressions.

"Now let's suppose that the mindset of your race is to have small but loving families that are dedicated to work and purpose. So you go to work every day, and you make"—she paused for a moment to quiet another burp—"cars for a living. Since the population doesn't grow very much, you make cars for ten years, until everyone has a car. As your race is purpose motivated, you continue to go to work and make cars. After stockpiling millions of extra cars, you decide to start building houses. You then build enough extra houses that you can stockpile another couple million homes."

Everyone was intently listening to her every word; only a few were glancing at the handouts.

"Now let's suppose that your lifespan has expanded to, say, five hundred years. Over your lifetime in your job, you stockpile millions of cars, millions of houses, millions of everything. So when your grandkids now hit their stride in the workforce, there isn't really a fulfilling purpose left for them. But now, suddenly, you discover a much more primitive race."

Jennifer swiped her forehead with her hand; it was lightly sweaty.

"'Wow,' you say to yourself. Now you suddenly have a great new purpose. You can educate this new species, share in your bountiful resources, and finally have greater meaning in your life."

Jennifer took a second to compose herself. Her stomach was feeling increasingly uneasy, and her head was thumping to a louder beat. The stress had her stomach in knots. She looked over at the president, who was wearing a slight smile and nodded to her. She turned back to the group, took a big gulp of air, and continued.

"The problem with our race is that we have too many people and too few resources. So greed has made us evil, angry, and untrusting. The Qyron don't know deceit, theft, anger, or greed. They understand the principles but have no experience with them in practice, as they've been peaceful and content for nearly a million years. They don't even understand the term 'murder.'"

The secretary of the interior chimed in. "So your plan is to just trust them immediately and have them integrate with our race?"

Jennifer shot the president a nervous look.

"Well, the ultimate decision is the president's," she said nervously, "but from my point of view, why not?"

"Excuse me—your point of view?"

The secretary of defense butted in. "Who *are* you? What is your title? What experience have *you* had with diplomacy? Hell, girl, you barely look old enough to drive!"

The room now erupted in a sea of dissent.

The president stepped forward. "Silence! I trust Jennifer and what she's shared with us." The quick uprising in tension immediately ceased. "This is a critical issue that needs calmness and reasoning. Our race is about to transition to a completely new way of life. We can't be blinded by our fears. From what I've read here, we have a solid outline to forge ahead with this new partnership."

"With all due respect, sir, what do we know about these Qyron?" Tom asked. "Has anyone else met with them?"

The president stood a little taller. "No. Jennifer is the only person to have spent time with them."

"Mr. President, can we really trust … well, a girl, with our—"

"A girl!" Jennifer burst out. She felt a spat of rage inside her as her stomach tightened and her head throbbed.

The president put his hand up. "Enough of this! We have a scant few options," he began. "The first is that we tell the Qyron we're not interested and we continue on with our lives as before. I'm not even considering this."

A few members looked back and forth at each other.

"The second option is to do nothing and meet with them this Friday and take matters as they come. I don't particularly like that option, as it makes us look soft and weak."

A few heads nodded in agreement.

"The final option is that we prepare for these changes, gaining an edge over the rest of the world, and emerge as the global leader in a completely new world."

"If I could add a few thoughts?" Jennifer said to the now quieted crowd.

The president nodded and turned sideways.

"In my report, I do mention the fact that the Qyron would like our planet to move toward a single language, currency, and political system to make all transactions easier. So if we establish a strong transition early, then they will most likely push for English, the dollar, and democracy as the planet's standard. Otherwise"—she paused to wipe more sweat from her forehead—"we all may need to learn Chinese or Russian."

She saw a few raised eyebrows around the table.

"So as I see it," the president continued, "we have only one choice, and that's to move forward now. I'm open to options if anyone has a better plan."

The room shifted to several hushed tones and side conversations. Jennifer looked to the president.

"I'll be right back."

She ran out of the room and down the hallway to the nearest bathroom. Her stomach had finally reached its limit. She pushed through the door and reached the toilet in time to empty the contents of her stomach. When she finished, she walked to the sink to rinse off her sweat and freshen up. Rachel stepped in close.

"Too much partying?" she said with a smirk.

Jennifer wiped her face dry with a paper towel.

"I wish. It's actually nerves."

"Really?" Rachel said loudly enough to echo through the bathroom. "Wow," she said in a more hushed tone, "you could have fooled me. You were a rock in there, girl."

Jennifer gave her a smile. Rachel pulled out some mints from her pocket. Jennifer gratefully smiled and took two mints, chewing them immediately. They quickly returned to the conference room.

The president turned to Jennifer. "Are you okay? You looked a little green."

"Yes sir, I'm fine; thank you."

"I've skimmed over this report; it's quite thorough. We all need to digest this and design detailed plans to implement by Monday."

"I thought I could give each secretary about half an hour to discuss and answer questions," Jennifer added.

The president gave her a solid stare and then nodded and smiled.

The rest of the morning and early afternoon plodded by. Each secretary had more questions than Jennifer had anticipated. Jennifer frequently had to place her transmitter to her head and ask questions to Xho. Moments later, she would receive a flood of answers. What Jennifer couldn't process, she quickly dictated to Rachel. A brief catered lunch broke up the morning from the afternoon, and by the time four thirty approached, Jennifer was mentally exhausted.

Taylor leaned over to her. "You look like you're done."

Jennifer had just finished discussing the plans with the secretary of energy. Within a year, all fossil fuel power plants would be offline, replaced by Chaqxa, or what we call dark energy, generators. In addition, an army of solar panels would be placed in orbit around Earth, providing more than enough power for everyone.

The secretary of energy was extremely concerned, though, over the impact caused by the loss of jobs. Jennifer reassured him that having completely clean renewable energy was the only way to go and that there would be many other jobs and opportunities available.

"Yes, I am so tired my brain hurts."

Jennifer couldn't even fake a smile. Taylor put up a finger, telling her to hold on, and walked over to the president. They chatted for a moment, and then Taylor walked back over to her.

"I told him that you're done for today, and he agreed. He asked if we could have some time tomorrow. I bargained with him; I think you'll like what I got for you."

Jennifer gave Taylor a blank stare. She could tell he wanted her to play a guessing game, but she wasn't in any mood. Her head was still thumping an angry tune, and her nerves were thin from the stress.

"Taylor, please."

"I'm sorry," he relented with a grimace. "We will reconvene tomorrow at 8:00 a.m. and be finished by lunchtime."

Jennifer stared at him with a tired look and frowned.

"Then I'll take you shopping with a fifty-thousand-dollar credit card. We've noticed that your wardrobe is, well, lacking in professionalism and style, and we need you to look your very best at the UN and to the public moving forward."

Jennifer was stunned. She had heard his reference to the fifty grand, but between being tired and the shock, it took her a few moments to process his statement.

"Um, what? Really!"

Taylor's face reminded her of the Grinch. His crooked little mouth slowly grew to a huge, curling grin.

"Wow, that is … that's so nice of you; thank you," Jennifer sputtered.

She felt a jolt of energy and couldn't contain her smile. Taylor seemed very genuine, and that struck her as a refreshing change. Jennifer answered a few more questions from the room and then said her good-byes to the group. Rachel and Jennifer were quickly escorted back to her apartment.

As soon as they entered her room, Jennifer went right for the couch. Rachel stopped in the kitchen.

"Mind if I get a refreshment?" she said as she strolled to the refrigerator.

"I don't have anything in the—"

Rachel opened the refrigerator; it displayed fully stocked shelves.

"Wow, I wish your anything was my anything," Rachel quipped as she pulled out a bottle of wine.

Jennifer jumped up from the couch, peering at the bottle of vino Rachel held above her head.

"I didn't know," she said as she walked into the kitchen, mouth open.

Jennifer opened a few cabinets to reveal cereal, soup, and all sorts of boxed and canned goods. She reached up and grabbed a box of crackers.

"Oh, there's some cheese in the fridge that would go great with that," Rachel added as she grabbed two glasses.

Two minutes later, they were on the couch, eating cheese and crackers with some grapes and washing it all down with some white zinfandel.

"So I caught Taylor looking you over earlier," Rachel said with a smile.

"Ugh, he's been such a jerk since I met him, and he was so mean to me the other day!"

"What's his problem? He was short to me as well!"

Rachel grabbed the bottle and poured some more wine. Jennifer just shook her head.

"He was born into money and privilege," Jennifer sighed.

"That would explain it," Rachel laughed. "Not me, I have school loans!"

They both laughed.

"But today he ..." Jennifer began; she then stopped and grabbed some more crackers.

For the next few minutes, they chatted about their lives. Rachel had just started dating a nice guy who worked construction in the area. She was hoping to get her master's in business and move into management. Jennifer told her about her life in Montana.

"Wow, so you've had a pretty sheltered life," Rachel quipped.

"Yeah, it's quiet. And, well, I always wondered what a fast-paced lifestyle would be like."

They both exclaimed, "Be careful what you wish for!" and broke out laughing.

"Okay, let's get to some business so we can finally quit for the day."

Jennifer reached over and grabbed her Qyron transmitter from the counter.

"Prepare your recorder," she told Rachel.

Jennifer put the transmitter to her head and began to reflect on the last dozen questions posed near the end of the meeting. She received numerous responses and then relayed them to Rachel. After a half hour of back-and-forth communications, she finished and put the transmitter down on the coffee table.

Rachel gave her an inquisitive look. "So what's that like?"

"It's so weird; you think of what you want to say, and then a second later you get this massive dump of information into your head."

Rachel continued her quizzical look.

"Imagine you read a chapter in a book, with pictures and even video. Now imagine all of that information suddenly being in your head at once. That's what it's like."

"Wow, that sounds a little scary, but neat," Rachel droned as she studied the transmitter.

"It took a lot of getting used to, but I'm getting better at understanding and organizing it every day."

Jennifer now felt quite tired and dizzy, thanks to the wine. She glanced at the time; it was almost 7:00 p.m.

"Okay, I think I'm done for the night."

Rachel stood up. "Yeah, I'm a bit drunk and tired myself." She gathered her purse and laptop and then walked toward the door.

"Okay, so tomorrow at 8:00 a.m. again?" she said with tired eyes as she yawned.

"Yeah, sorry, but I'll make it worth your while afterward," Jennifer replied with a smile.

"As tired as I am"—Rachel opened the door and took a step out—"it will have to be a Hawaiian vacation or something."

She giggled and walked down the hall.

Jennifer closed the door and cleaned up the kitchen. She then made a few edits in her files and grabbed a hot shower. Her day ended by crawling into bed, feeling dead to the world. As she was about to drift off, her cell phone rang. It was Tasha.

"Hello?"

"Hey, Jennifer. So why didn't you call me and tell me about these agents?"

"Oh, Tash, I'm sorry. It's been crazy, stupid, busy around here. I worked all day today and have a half day-" Jennifer yawned. "Sorry. A half day of work tomorrow too."

"So, like, these two guys in suits show up at my door. They tell me that they're with the government, and then they tell me that everything you discussed with me is top secret."

"Yeah, it's hush for now girl, but by next week."

"Really, Jennifer, I don't even remember half of it. I've been so busy with all of the final details of the wedding."

"Mmm, I can imagine," Jennifer exhaled. Her head felt as if it were floating. "Sorry I'm not there to help, Tash."

"Oh, no problem. Funny thing—the agents that came to tell me to keep quiet are here all week. Since they tag along, I put them to work. They've been setting up chairs and helping me with picking stuff up."

They both laughed.

"So now that you're some important muckety-muck with the government, I guess I'll have to schedule time with your secretary?"

"Her name is Rachel," Jennifer added softly as she yawned again.

"No shit? You got a secretary? I was only kidding!"

"She's an admin assistant or whatever. She's really nice; I think you'd like her."

"I miss you, Jennifer."

"Yeah, I miss you too, Tash."

"Jennifer, will you be able to make it to my wedding on Saturday?"

"Tasha, I'm going to try; really I am. I'll see what I can do." Jennifer gave out another huge yawn. "Oh, I'm sorry."

"Tired? It's only six forty-five."

"Not here; it's eight forty-five, and I'm bushed."

"Well, get some rest, girl. Oh, and Tom is being a big jerk. He came by again, and this time he was a little angry. He misses you, and now he's getting all uppity. Alex had to get up in his face."

"Alex?"

"Oh, that's the one agent; he's actually really cute. If I didn't have Craig … Well, okay, girl, get your sleep. Let me know if you can make the wedding, *please!*"

"I will, Tasha. Love you."

"Love you too, Jennifer."

Jennifer ended the call and turned off the lights.

Chapter 9

THE NEXT MORNING CAME QUICKLY, but Jennifer took a hot shower and was ready on time. The meeting went by without too much fanfare. Jennifer distributed her answers from the Qyron the night before, and they recorded several hundred more questions.

Jennifer was finishing a discussion with the secretary of health and human services on the hospital planning. She motioned to Rachel.

"Okay, Rachel, I need you to get the rest of the questions. Is there anything else?"

"Nothing yet," the secretary replied.

Jennifer stood up from the table and walked over to Taylor.

"Okay, I think that's everybody for today. I also wanted to let you know that I've set up a system with every cabinet member to provide me with questions as they pop up. I'll translate and then have Rachel provide reports with answers within a half hour."

Taylor gave her a look of approval. "That's an excellent idea. Good job."

Jennifer had been stealing glances at Taylor over the past two days. He was very busy with setting up side meetings with the cabinet staffers and informing other members of Congress. At many times, she noticed him reach a near climax of wanting to scream while several staffers shouted demands at him, but he always took a deep breath, smiled, and continued on. She was also told he had spent the past night here till 2:00 a.m., took a four-hour nap on a couch in the other room, and returned to his duties. Taylor then pulled her aside.

"The president would also like to have a direct pipeline of all information—but more of a summary. He will also need you close on Monday at the UN. Oh, and one more thing: we will be pulling out in a caravan at 4:00 a.m. to reach New York City tomorrow. Don't be late."

Jennifer nodded but gazed over his shoulder.

"What's wrong?" Taylor asked.

"Huh? Oh, well, um, it's my best friend, Tasha," Jennifer said softly.

Taylor stared at her, waiting for the rest. Two other staffers approached him, but he waved them away.

"She has a wedding; it's on the tenth."

"Of July?" he asked incredulously.

"Yeah, and I'm the bridesmaid," Jennifer said, cringing, waiting for the inevitable response.

"Are you out of your mind? That's day one after first contact!" Taylor exclaimed loudly enough for others to overhear. Several heads turned, including that of the president. Jennifer stared at Taylor with an angry look.

"You wanna type that up into a memo for those that didn't hear that?" she shot back.

Taylor frowned and shook his head. "Look; I'm sorry, Jennifer!" he panted. He ran his hand through his already disheveled and greasy hair, a look of pain on his face. "Seriously, I don't see how that will be possible. Montana, right?"

Jennifer slowly nodded.

"For the love of ..." Taylor sighed, and he turned away, shaking his head. He put his hand to his forehead and brushed his hair back again, thinking. He took a few steps away from Jennifer and then paced back to her. "Look; I doubt you can make it. I mean, the whole world is going to be on the tenth level of crazy!"

"Believe me; I understand that," Jennifer pleaded back. "I didn't plan all this. Well, I mean, I kinda did, but I just want to know if it will be possible for me to make it?" Jennifer's eyes were large and imploring. Taylor opened his mouth to respond, gazing down at her. He then paused.

"No promises, but I'll look into it," he sighed.

"Thank you." Jennifer leaned in and gave Taylor a hug.

When she pulled back, Taylor's eyes were wide. She then looked to her right and saw several people staring.

It was 1:30 p.m. when Jennifer and Rachel left the White House. They were then escorted through a bevy of downtown shops as she picked up several professional business outfits and shoes. It was convenient that she had three agents with her, as they did most of the heavy lifting of boxes and bags back to the car. Around 4:00 p.m., one of the agents actually drove back to the apartment to unload the car, as there was no more room. He returned with a larger black SUV. By 7:00 p.m., they were back at the apartment.

"Oh my God, that was so much fun!" Jennifer cried out as she plopped down on the couch.

Rachel stood in the kitchen, grabbing some snacks. She sat down next to Jennifer and gave her a look.

"I gotta say, that was the most surreal shopping I've ever done. You were like *Pretty Woman* out there today. I just can't believe they gave you fifty grand to spend!"

Rachel grabbed a handful of chips and began to munch on them.

Jennifer looked over at her and smiled.

"Hey, you got a few grand in outfits too."

"I know," Rachel shrieked. "I can't thank you enough." She beamed. "That was really sweet of you, Jennifer."

One of the agents opened her door, his hands full of boxes. The other agent was behind him with his arms full of bags. They walked in, and Jennifer directed them into the second bedroom to set the clothing down. As they walked out of the bedroom, Jennifer stood up with her hands on her hips.

"Wait, you're not going to put it all away and color coordinate it?"

She held a solid look of anger on her face for nearly five seconds. When one agent started to turn to walk back into the bedroom, Jennifer finally broke out laughing. She sauntered over to the couch, still giggling. She thanked them both and walked them to the door.

"Thanks, guys!" she stated, still giggling as she closed the door.

Rachel was already in the second bedroom, sorting out the clothing.

"Hey, the least I can do is help you put it away," Rachel said as she started to open the bags.

The two of them spent the next hour and a half putting the clothes away. When they finished, Jennifer sat down on the bed. "Oh jeez, I have to get up at 3:00 a.m. to be ready to go by three forty-five."

Rachel moaned. "I am so not going to get enough sleep."

Jennifer thought for a moment and then smiled.

"Why not stay here tonight?"

Rachel gave her a pensive look, and then her face brightened.

"I do have an overnight bag in my trunk."

"Seriously?" Jennifer's eyes opened wide.

"Yeah, I always want to be ready for anything, and, well, this qualifies."

"Sleepover! Go get it, and I'll whip up some food and then we can crash," Jennifer said as she left the bedroom and headed to the kitchen.

Jennifer cooked up a quick dinner of steak sandwiches and green beans. The two chatted for a little bit after they ate, and they then drifted off to sleep.

As expected, 3:00 a.m. came very quickly. Jennifer was still sleeping when Rachel finished her shower and dressed. A speed shower and no makeup had Jennifer on schedule. She figured she could apply a little bit of her makeup on the way. Tank drove them to the White House, and they rode with the president in his limousine to the airport.

Jennifer gawked as she walked aboard Air Force One. It was another thing that she had only seen on TV and movies.

The hour long flight was a quiet one, as everyone slept while the president read over various factual materials on the Qyron.

The motorcade from the airport to the United Nations building was another first for Jennifer. She sat glued to the window as they drove through New York City. She had only seen it on TV, and she pointed and stared as they passed familiar landmarks. As they approached the United Nations, she gawked at the Freedom Towers from afar.

"Sorry we can't sightsee today," the president mused.

"That's okay; I'm sure I'll get the time to take in the sights someday," Jennifer said as she snapped a few pictures.

"Oh, and that's a very professional outfit you have on today," the president complimented.

Jennifer blushed. "Thank you so much for your help with my wardrobe."

"Thank *you* for preparing me for this day," the president added.

The next two hours were spent in a private conference room at the U.N. Kennedy Myers performed a question-and-answer session. Jennifer had Rachel catalog more questions, and Jennifer briefed the president on more of the history and culture of the Qyron.

When their private meeting ended, Jennifer walked in line behind the president. Many of the world's leaders were in attendance. A few noted holdouts were China, Russia, and North Korea. The president stepped through several meet and greets before officially beginning the meeting.

As everyone was seated and the conversations died down, the president surveyed the dignitaries in attendance, took a deep breath, and opened with his speech.

"There are times in human history when discovery and ingenuity cause significant change in our way of life. Mastering fire, inventing the wheel, designing the microchip, and landing on the moon were all momentous strides for humanity. But I present to the assembled leaders of the world here today the single most critical watershed event in global history." He paused for effect while panning the world leaders. "We have made contact with another species from a distant planet."

The entire forum erupted in gasps and outbursts. The president allowed a full minute for everyone to process his statement through translation and return to calm.

He then detailed the current plans for the Qyron in making first contact. The president described how they would transition immediately by providing healthcare to everyone as well as food to all third-world countries. He explained their strategy to open up billions of jobs, including asteroid mining, environmental cleanup on Earth, and new planet colonization and exploration. Taylor's team distributed a massive publication in various languages for all of the leaders and diplomats in attendance. The document included the Qyron history, physiology, and society.

The secretary of state then took over and detailed the massive logistical operation with every country for receiving food and medical assistance from the Qyron. Lastly, a framework was outlined on how local government's military would offer the Qyron a complete security detail.

Taylor wrapped up the session by explaining how all questions would be routed through his department and answered by Jennifer. Many of the diplomats and leaders were still reeling at the completion of the eight-hour session.

When it was over, the president gathered everyone together.

"You've all done well in preparing for today. We obviously have a big head start over all countries in preparation for Friday's first contact. At tomorrow's meeting, I would like a detailed report to see where we are in preparation." He turned to face Taylor. "It's obvious now that we need to enlarge your staff, as the rest of the world will be funneling questions through you."

Taylor nodded. The president pivoted and then turned back again to face him.

"As a matter of fact, once we're past Friday, I will make an executive order creating a new cabinet post. You will be promoted as the secretary of Qyron affairs."

Taylor's eyes lit up, and everyone took turns in congratulating him. As the group made their way back to the caravan to return to Washington, DC, Taylor pulled Jennifer aside.

"Jennifer, I can't thank you enough." Taylor's smile was Christmas-morning huge. He grabbed her hand and looked her in the eyes. "This is more than I could have hoped, and I have you to thank." He squeezed her hand. Jennifer smiled back.

"That's okay; I mean, you deserve it, Taylor."

Taylor leaned in and gave Jennifer a hug. When he pulled back, Jennifer's mouth dropped open.

"Oh, I'm sorry," Taylor said as he took a step back. "I'm just over-come with—"

"No, it's fine; you just surprised me," Jennifer said, stunned.

"Let's go!" shouted the secretary of state, now waiting to pull out.

Jennifer trotted to her limousine. Rachel was standing at the car door, holding it open for her.

"What was *that?*" she whispered as Jennifer hunched down to get into the back of the limo.

Jennifer smiled as Rachel sat down beside her.

"It's the 'new' Taylor, I guess," she whispered back.

The trip home was even busier. The president and Tom Franklin were setting up meetings and video conferences between nations. Thirty minutes into the trip, they received confirmation that many of the world's leaders were onboard with welcoming the Qyron into their countries. As a discussion ended, Jennifer turned to the president.

"Sir, I think it would be a good idea for everyone to be off from work to hear this news. I mean, I know if I were to hear something like this, I wouldn't be able to function at work for the rest of the day. And, well, if people were at work and happened to panic, that would make things worse."

The secretary of state raised an eyebrow and then nodded.

"She's right," he said.

The rest of the staff in Air Force One looked around and nodded in agreement. The president smiled and then turned to Jennifer.

"So I guess that means I have to declare Friday a national holiday. What do I call it—Jennifer Day?"

Everyone in the vacinity smiled. Jennifer looked over to the president.

"Well, as cool as it would be to have a country of schoolkids praising me for a day off, I suggest you call it Qyron Day. But of course you'll have to wait till after Friday to make that have meaning to everyone."

The rest of the flight back was frantic with coordinating meetings and updating schedules. Rachel and Jennifer worked on more questions together. They finally arrived back at the White House by 9:00 p.m. Jennifer turned to Rachel as they were about to part ways for the evening.

"How about we start at 9:00 a.m.; I could use the rest."

"Deal!" Rachel said with a tired smile.

The following few days were a blur of meetings and staging for Friday. By Thursday morning, the military was ready for mobilization in every major city. All state employment agencies were prepared to add massive amounts of job entries for the US government. Hospitals had identified rooms to provide for this "special government program." CEOs of major industries were contacted to be ready for a special government conference on the following Saturday. Every cabinet member was successful in preparation, with the exception of one—the secretary of transportation, Butler Andrews.

Jennifer saw him as the stereotypical nerd. He was pudgy with a pencil-thin neck, round face, and short, shaved head. He wore glasses and always spoke with an air of superiority. But his looks weren't the biggest issue. Butler was becoming increasingly combative in the daily meetings. He argued with every request and delighted in always having devil's advocate questions in response to every statement. Even the president grew more irritated with him at every gathering.

Kennedy began the meeting on Thursday morning with a quick status update and then turned it over to hear progress reports. Every secretary took twenty minutes to step through an appraisal. It was impressive to hear how many aspects had been made ready in so short a time. The biggest issue present, though, was the fact that the media was abuzz with wild speculation as news of Saturday's corporate meetings, the domestic military deployment, and some of the preparations filtered down to the public, yet no one had a reason for these occurrences. The president decided to make a public address. He would announce that Friday would be a national holiday and ask all television channels to cover this special global Friday address at 1:00 p.m. EST.

As the president asked for Butler's update, he turned with a scowl.

"I don't have a progress report," he exclaimed, rubbing his hands together.

The room suddenly fell to a hushed tone. The president, now focused squarely on Butler, turned his head slightly and waited.

"You know, this is completely ridiculous," Butler began. "We're all busting our asses working eighteen hours a day because some stupid blonde is telling us to!"

A collective gasp sounded in the room while the president's brow rose. Taylor, who was sitting next to Jennifer, jumped up from his seat.

"Look; you're—" Taylor began, but the president stepped forward with his hand extended. All eyes now focused on the commander-in-chief.

"I highly suggest we take this conversation private, Butler."

"I'm not afraid to air my concern to everyone in this room!" Butler raged, his face red. "I can't believe that we're all taking orders from some country blonde fresh out of high school. We haven't verified anything she's said, and now the entire world is focused in and asking questions." Butler took a step away from his seat. "What if, God forbid, all of this is a setup for global domination?" His voice heightened. "I mean, at the very least, what if this all doesn't work out?"

Butler nervously panned the room. His face twitched. The president took a few steps around the table and now stood two paces from Butler.

"You!" He turned to face the president. "You're in your first term, and if this thing blows up, it won't just take you down; you and everyone in here will be finished!"

The president remained emotionless, his face a picture of calm.

"I can't believe I'm standing in a room where everyone is afraid to question you about what's going on. I almost feel like she's in charge here!" Butler pointed to Jennifer with a trembling hand.

Jennifer sat speechless, mouth open and eyes wide.

"I've heard enough, Butler. It's obvious you're allowing your fear and emotions to overwhelm you," the president stated in a calm tone. "Instead of lashing out at Jennifer and me, why not take stock of the facts? She provided precise coordinates in space for their scout ship. We verified that. She has extensive knowledge of them, and they're offering us a better way of life. As leader of this country, I'm bound by my office to provide the very best for all Americans. If that means placing faith in something, then so be it. This country was based on faith in God." He paused a moment and then continued. "The process I'm coordinating now will ensure that the United States is poised to accept this change quicker than any other country, which will allow us to be the hub of all change."

"But how do you *really* know if they're seriously altruistic? How do we know that we're not being set up for slaughter?"

Butler was now visibly shaking, and beads of sweat began to form on his forehead.

The president pivoted to face the group.

"Does anyone else here seriously doubt my guidance with this issue?" He panned the room. "Please people, moving forward, I can't have any further dissension in the ranks. I give you my solemn word that there will be no reprisals. I need to know—now."

He slowly looked over the group. Jennifer stood up.

"Sir, I am telling you the God's honest truth, so help me."

Taylor stood up next to her.

"I'm with you sir, one hundred percent."

Jennifer turned her head. Taylor gave her a confident look and a smile.

Two more cabinet members stood up. Then, one by one, others raised up around the conference table. Eventually everyone was standing, silently pledging faith with the president and his plans.

"Then it's settled," the president said as he nodded and turned back to face Butler Andrews again. "We all agree that this is the best path for success."

"This is insane!" Butler screamed. "You people are all sheep being led to slaughter! How can you trust aliens you've never met?" His eyes were wide and he panted wildly.

The president took one step forward and placed a hand on his shoulder. "Why don't you take some time off and—"

"Why don't you get screwed!" Butler yelled, his voice cracking with emotion as he slapped the president's hand away. Three agents quickly stepped forward and grabbed Butler. the president dropped his gaze to the floor, shaking his head.

"I can't believe you people!" Butler shrieked, tears streaming down his face.

Two agents restrained him and dragged him out of the room. The third agent stepped alongside the president.

"He's finished. Take him to a psych ward for observation. Process him out, but make sure he cools off and isn't released until 5:00 p.m. Friday."

"Understood, sir," the agent replied.

He turned and left the room.

The president allowed a moment for everyone to calm down and then spoke again.

"I want to thank everyone for standing firm and believing. Butler, while flying apart at the hinges, did have a point in that if things don't go smoothly, then we'll have to answer for it." Kennedy Myers paused for the briefest of moments. "No, I will answer for it," he stated with an unwavering tone. "But I firmly believe Jennifer and I trust in the experience, dedication, and planning of everyone in this room."

Several people nodded back to him, and the meeting continued.

Jennifer then walked over to the president.

"One last thing, sir," she said with a little smile. "Do we have a gift to present to them tomorrow?"

The president's face went blank. He quickly looked over his right shoulder and called a staffer.

"We need to have a grand gift to present tomorrow by 1:00 p.m.; get it done!"

The staffer's stunned look lasted a mere second, and then he nodded and trotted away.

Jennifer smiled and turned. "Men!" she uttered. The president just laughed and nodded as Jennifer walked away.

"Never a dull moment," he quipped.

An hour later, after all of the last-minute preparations, discussions, and meetings, the president left to deliver his speech to America.

The president announced to the people that vast unprecedented changes were coming for not just Americans but to everyone the world over. He stated that the event would occur at 1:00 p.m. on Friday and that it would answer the many questions that have been theorized and debated on every newscast. Further, he declared that Friday will be a national holiday and urged every person to remain home for this monumental announcement. The end of his speech created an explosion of questions from news agencies and a flood of speculation on social media. After the presidential address, the cabinet was dismissed for the day, although few people left.

Jennifer finally decided to wrap up her day a few hours later. She gave Rachel a final set of notes to distribute. A few secretaries gave her another handful of last minute questions. Taylor then ambled over to her.

"Hold on," she said to Taylor. She placed her transmitter to her head. A minute later she dictated a few points to Rachel.

"So tomorrow's the big day. Nervous?" she asked Taylor.

"Yes," Taylor said. "There are so many unknowns. I won't lie; I'm more than a bit nervous."

"Well, I think we're ready for whatever happens." Jennifer said as she smiled at Taylor. "Oh, and thanks for sticking up for me earlier, Butler had me nervous."

She grabbed his hand and gave it a gentle squeeze.

"Ah, well, he's always been a jerk," Taylor said as he gave Jennifer a smile. "His specialty has been to backstab everyone in an attempt to further his own gains. I think the president just wanted a reason to discharge him."

"Well, Butler sure gift wrapped that one, eh?" she giggled.

Taylor turned for a moment and then paused. Jennifer looked at him and realized how much he had done in the past week. Taylor had assembled a crack staff that had prioritized all cabinet members' plans and issues. He maintained a solid pipeline for questions and answers and kept the president fully informed. She also noticed that his childlike outbursts that had irritated earlier were no longer. He was even being thoughtful and kind. But there seemed to be something more. Taylor opened his mouth to say something.

"Yes?" Jennifer prodded.

"Do you, uh, do you think the Qyron ..." Taylor stammered with a pained look on his face. He stopped and shook his head.

"Think they what?" Jennifer asked, her curiosity piqued.

"No, nothing. Okay, I have a ton of work to get to. I'll see you tomorrow."

He gave Jennifer a quick handshake and trotted off with his staff. Rachel walked over to join Jennifer.

"Okay, I have a pile of inquiries from just about everyone. It may take you an hour to sort through these. I wonder why everyone waited to the last minute," Rachel grumbled with a sigh. "I'll bet the Qyron are getting tired of hearing from you."

Rachel smiled, expecting Jennifer to respond. But Jennifer was still gazing at Taylor's exit.

"What? Sorry," Jennifer said as she focused on Rachel.

"What's wrong?"

"Nothing. Well, just Taylor," Jennifer said distantly as she continued to stare at him.

"Is he being a jerk again?" Rachel's brow was raised, and she was grinning.

"No, actually he's starting to be nice; that's what's confusing me."

Jennifer shook her head and then grabbed the list of questions. She then turned her gaze back to Rachel.

"Okay, look. I will get you answers to all of these questions, but since we've been running nonstop for a week, I'll let you go home now. Spend some time with your boyfriend."

"My who?" Rachel said with a smile.

"Exactly! Go home, shower, get into a nice, slinky outfit, and remind him that you're all woman!"

They both giggled. Two male staffers and the secretary of defense overheard the comment and smiled along with them. Jennifer and Rachel blushed and left the room; then they laughed even harder.

Chapter 10

WHEN JENNIFER MADE HER WAY through the White House, Tank joined her.

"Howdy stranger," Jennifer said as Tank walked alongside.

"Hello, Jennifer. I regret to inform you that you're stuck with me for three whole days," Tank stated with a grin.

Jennifer put her arm over her forehead in mock drama. The two laughed as they made their way to the truck. After a quick drive from the White House to the apartment, Jennifer walked with Tank to the elevator. The other agent stayed behind to fill out paperwork in the truck and waved them on.

"So what do you have planned this evening?" Tank asked while pressing the elevator button.

"Nothing, really; this is like the first quiet time I've had without a bazillion things to do. What are you doing this evening?"

The door opened, and they stepped in. Tank shrugged and hit the button for the second floor.

"How about I make some dinner and we watch a movie?" Jennifer posed, smiling up at him.

Tank peered down at Jennifer and thought for a moment.

"I'm not supposed to associate with my charge."

"Your what? What the hell is a charge? Is that code for a blonde?"

Tank burst out laughing. The elevators doors opened on floor 2. Jennifer took a step out and then reached in and grabbed Tank's hand. Tank leaned forward and took a hesitant step.

"You're not afraid of a five-foot, one-hundred-ten-pound blonde girl, are you?" Jennifer batted her eyelashes.

Tank took another step and cleared the elevator.

"Well, yes, yes I am."

Jennifer laughed. She walked down the hallway, opened her door, and stepped into the apartment. She set down her laptop, paperwork, and transmitter. Tank slowly walked in behind her and closed the door. Jennifer sauntered into the kitchen, gave out a sigh, and then started to look through the freezer.

"So what do you feel like?" she asked with her head in the freezer. She stood up on her tip toes, peering at the frozen foods.

Tank peered over at her. He stared at her shapely body just as Jennifer poked her head back out of the freezer.

"You checking out my butt?" she snapped, smiling.

Tank blushed.

"No, I was ... uh, I was thinking."

"Thinking about my butt?" Jennifer giggled. She paused for another moment, staring at Tank. "Lighten up; relax!" She laughed a bit and then turned around and opened up the refrigerator. After a moment, she pulled out a block of meat.

"I was thawing this out; I'm thinking spaghetti and meatballs?"

Her voice was cheery, and her eyes sparkled. Tank nodded. He picked up her transmitter and slowly rolled it over in his hands. Jennifer was busy grabbing the spaghetti from the cupboard. She started opening up the meat and pulled some spices from a cupboard.

"So how does this work?" Tank asked, pivoting the small box in his hand.

"I'm not sure how the internal junk works. I just put it to my head, think all of the questions I have, and even step through memories of conversations. A moment later, I get a stream of information into my head from Xho."

"That's amazing," Tank gushed, setting it back down on the counter.

"Yeah, and we'll have that technology soon. So I'm sure our cell phones and computers will get much smaller and more powerful."

Tank nodded back at her. He continued to stare at the transmitter.

"So why don't you give a look on the TV. See if you can find us a good movie," Jennifer said as she started to season and roll the meatballs.

Tank walked into the living room. He turned on the TV and started to look at the guide.

"What kind of movies do you like?" Tank asked.

"Anything but scary movies. But it's your choice, so pick wisely there, agent man."

Tank let out a laugh.

"No pressure!" he said as he continued chuckling. "Here's something," he called out.

"What?" Jennifer replied as she turned her head to catch his gaze.

"*Independence Day* is on."

"Uh, yeah, no, we're not watching that," she cautioned, dropping two more meatballs into a bowl.

"How about *War of the Worlds*?" Tank yelled out toward the kitchen, smiling as Jennifer caught his expression.

"Cut it out!" She said softly with a touch of seriousness in her voice.

Tank continued to look through the guide. Jennifer grabbed some frozen veggies from the freezer. She continued to work on the food while Tank surfed.

Jennifer finally finished with the food preparations. The spaghetti was in a pot of boiling water. The corn and green beans were heating up. The meatballs and sauce were bubbling away. Jennifer walked into the living room as Tank gazed over at her.

"Okay, there are two movies starting in five minutes, both are chick flicks."

Jennifer gave him a smile as she slowed her walk toward him.

"Chick flicks huh?" she replied with an air of sarcasm.

Jennifer paused for a moment with her hand on her hip. Tank peered back at the TV. She smiled and then started to slink seductively at him. He caught her approach and stiffened. When she reached the couch, she bent over, put a hand on his thigh, and planted a knee between his legs. She placed her other hand on his chest, doing a crawl up to his face. She got nearly nose-to-nose with him and then exhaled slowly.

"What makes you think I want to see a chick flick, there, tough guy?" she moaned in a low, sultry voice.

Tank was frozen. He let out more of a slow grunt than a word.

"Uuughhh."

Jennifer pulled back and started laughing. She rolled backward and fell onto the carpet, now in a full giggle. Tank exhaled and shook his head. Jennifer finally finished laughing and propped up on her knees.

"You enjoy tormenting me, don't you?" Tank sighed.

"You blush so much you turn jet black!" Jennifer quipped while standing up. "Heck yeah, I think it's funny how such a big man gets all nervous."

"Uh huh," Tank said as Jennifer looked at the guide.

"So what two movies?"

"*Field of Dreams* and *The American President*," Tank replied.

Jennifer stiffened up.

"Wow, you have good taste in movies; they're both awesome classics. I misjudged you, Terrance."

Tank gave her a mildly agitated look.

Jennifer smiled. "What, you don't like a little girl calling you Terrance?" she asked, smiling. "I like that name; it's softer and sweeter than Tank."

He continued to stare at her.

"Relax; I won't call you Terrance when the rest of your crew is around. Deal?"

He exhaled and finally nodded.

Jennifer walked back into the kitchen. She stopped and spun around.

"Wow, I'm sorry; do you have a wife or a girlfriend?"

Tank's view quickly shifted from the TV back to her.

"What?"

Jennifer started to walk slowly back toward Tank.

"I was just playing with you, and I realized how uncomfortable that would be if you had a wife or girlfriend."

"No, I don't." Tank said.

"Whew. Good. Now I can go back to being annoying and teasing you," she said with a laugh.

She walked back into the kitchen and grabbed some plates. As Jennifer started to plate out the food, she yelled back into the living room.

"Why not?"

Tank looked up. A minute had passed since the last conversation, so he had to pause and reflect for a moment.

"Just don't have the time. That and assignments like this, where I have to stay overnight here, make it a little harder. If I'm in a relationship, then I want to be *in* a relationship and around her as much as I can."

Jennifer continued to put more food on the plates.

"Yeah, that's very thoughtful of you to say Terrance. I've never had a relationship where the man actually looked out for *me*."

Tank stood up from the couch. "What about you? Are you still dating your boyfriend in Montana?"

Jennifer shook her head. "No, I broke up with him when I decided to come out here."

"That's understandable," Tank said as he walked into the kitchen.

He peered at her eye. The dark black and blue around her left eye was now clear. What little color remained was hidden behind her makeup.

"Do you miss him?" he added.

Jennifer paused, serving spoon in hand. She looked down for a moment and then up to Tank.

"In some ways, yes, I do. But"—she stopped for a moment and looked away—"I'm tired of him using me and hitting me," she finished softly.

A sizzling noise came from behind them. Jennifer quickly turned around. She had forgotten to turn off the burner for the sauce, and it was bubbling wildly. She turned off the stove and put a lid on the pot.

She gave him a weak smile.

"Let me know if you want any more," she said softly.

Tank grabbed both plates and walked into the living room. She picked up the two glasses of juice.

"You do like grape juice?"

Tank nodded to her as she walked into the living room. He sat down and grabbed the TV remote.

"*The American President* it is," he said as he pushed the button.

They sat and ate their dinner while watching the movie.

"Hey, there you are!" Jennifer said when the president made a comment to a Secret Service agent named Coop. Tank smiled.

"So, would that make you Sydney Ellen Wade?" Tank replied with a smile.

Jennifer turned slowly to face him. "Nah, I'm younger and cuter!"

126

"Yeah, well, I'm bigger and blacker than Coop!"

The two burst out laughing.

When the movie was over, Tank slowly got up from the couch. Jennifer had been leaning against him while they were watching the movie. He gently peeled her away as he stood up. The warm feeling he had on his arm quickly cooled as he stood up.

"That was a lot of fun," he said with a slight smile. He grabbed the plates and turned toward the kitchen as Jennifer slowly stood up from the couch.

"Yeah, it was," she said as she stretched. "Let me help you."

"Nah!" he called back over his shoulder loudly. "You cooked a wonderful meal, so let me clean up."

Jennifer smiled and stopped at the entry to the kitchen. She stood and watched as Tank rinsed the plates and placed them in the dishwasher. He then took the extra spaghetti and sauce and put them into a Tupperware container.

"You make such a cute kitchen helper," Jennifer said softly.

Tank just peered back at her and winked. She returned to the living room and sat back on the couch. He finished cleaning up the kitchen and then walked back into the living room. He put his shoes back on and turned to her.

"Thanks again, Jennifer; this was really nice," he said.

Jennifer walked him to the door. She turned the knob and slowly pulled it open.

"Yeah, this was fun," she cooed softly. "We should do this again soon."

She smiled and grabbed his hand. He gave her hand a gentle squeeze and then pulled away and walked out the door. She watched him as he strolled to the elevator and then slowly closed her door. She leaned against the door and smiled. Her cell phone rang and jolted her from her thoughts. Jennifer ran over to the coffee table and grabbed it.

"Hello?"

"Jennifer, what's going on?" Tasha said.

"What do you mean?"

"I heard the president's speech. Wow, a holiday and everything.

So is this all going to be done in time? Will you be at the wedding on Saturday by noon?"

"I'm not sure, Tasha, I'm going to try."

"Try? Did you get a plane ticket yet? You can't drive that in a few hours!"

Tasha's voice was loud and made her sound very nervous.

"I asked when I can leave; I'll see about a plane ticket then. I can put it on a credit card. I just don't know if or when I can leave."

Tasha sniffled and then cleared her throat.

"Okay, well please call me tomorrow and let me know. I really want you to be here, Jennifer. It won't be the same without you!"

"I know, and I'm trying," Jennifer volleyed back.

"I'm sorry, Jennifer; I don't mean to be such a pushy bitch. I just miss you and want you to be here for my wedding!"

"I know, Tasha. Believe me; I *want* to be there."

They both paused for a moment, and then Tasha chimed in.

"So how is everything else going?"

"Well, I may have met someone!" Jennifer said as her voice turned from solemn to giddy.

"Really? Tell me about him!!"

"Well, he's huge—like six foot six—and built like a tank." Jennifer then giggled.

"What's so funny?"

"Well, that's kind of his name. It's actually Terrance, but he goes by Tank. Anyway, he's really nice and sweet. I really like him."

"What's he do?" Tasha asked. Jennifer paused a moment.

"Well, he's kind of my bodyguard."

"Oh, no way!" Tasha screamed. "You're banging your bodyguard. Wait, you have a bodyguard? Damn it, girl, you can't keep this kind of juicy stuff from me!" Tasha yelled through her laughter.

"Well, we haven't done anything yet. I mean, he's nice, and I like him, but we haven't even kissed or anything."

"Bodyguard?"

"Well, he's Secret Service actually."

"Oh, no way! Come on!"

"Yeah, he is. I'll tell you all about it later. It's kinda gettin' late, and

I have some more work to do. Tomorrow is going to be so crazy. I'll call you as soon as things calm down, okay?"

"Why don't you just tell me everything at the wedding?"

"Okay, deal. All right, I gotta go, Tash; love you!"

"Love you too, girl; see you Saturday."

They ended the call, and Jennifer set her phone down, grabbed her transmitter and Rachel's notes, and got back to work.

By 10:30 p.m., Jennifer was dead on her feet. She set down her laptop and crawled to bed.

There was a bright light and some hissing, and I removed my headgear. I sat back and reflected for a moment.

So that's where my African blood came from.

I stood up and stretched. I felt a little sore from the workout. I noticed a computer message. "Computer, play message," I said as I walked toward the kitchenette.

"Hi, Amant, I am so sorry about earlier," John's voice stated. "Please call me when you're free."

I grabbed a water and slowly drank it down. I felt hungry. I walked to my terminal.

"Location of John Crowley." The monitor showed him in his room. "Call John Crowley." A tone sounded.

"Hello?"

"John, it's Amant. Are you hungry?"

"Yeah, but I'm more sexy—dripping with it, actually. Sorry, it's this Adonis body of mine; it's my curse, but I'm struggling through life with it!"

I laughed. What a character.

"Thanks, Johnny, I needed that. How about we meet for lunch?"

"Excellent idea. Where?"

"I'll come to your deck; see you in a few minutes."

A tone sounded. I quickly changed from sweat pants and a T-shirt to some comfortable slacks and a really nice blouse. I was out the door in a minute.

I met John at the lift. The doors opened, and he was there, waiting with a smile and a hug. He leaned in and gave me a soft, warm embrace.

"I'm sorry I upset you earlier," he whispered.

I could smell a waft of light cologne. It was very understated—so Johnny.

"I'm sorry too, Johnny. I really haven't been myself lately. I don't know why."

John gave me a thoughtful look and nodded. He grabbed my hand, and we walked to the dining hall. Although it was lunchtime for me, I felt like waffles—craved them, actually. I loaded up with six waffles and two omelets. A large bowl of fresh fruit cocktail, some toast, two cups of yogurt, and a tall glass of orange and cranberry juice finished my tray. John sat down in the far corner of the room. There weren't many people in the hall, and we were as distant as we could be from anyone else. I was fine with that; I enjoyed the privacy. When I sat down at the table, John gave a stare at my tray.

"I guess this blogging thing gives you an appetite," he said with a grin. John then yawned.

"Sorry, am I boring you?" I said loudly, as if I were angered.

"Not just that; I can barely tolerate you, between the smell and your attitude," John said.

We both laughed and then dug into our food. The waffles were delicious; I savored the fruit-blended syrup. I was never one for the maple kind. John yawned again as we were finishing our meal.

"Is it bedtime for baby?" I said with a smirk.

"Yeah, definitely getting late. I was busy viewing some programs, so I didn't get dinner. I was planning on just going to bed when you messaged me."

"Ah, you funny sixteen-hour creatures," I said.

John smiled and then reached over and grabbed my hand. "I wish I could go for forty hours awake like you."

I smiled, but I felt tense and nervous.

"John—wait, do you mind that I call you Johnny?"

He smiled and then peered down for a moment. His eyes then locked again with me.

"If it were anyone else, I would. But I so truly miss hearing you call me that." He smiled and stared into my eyes. "So please, by all means, call me Johnny."

His fingers caressed my hand. I looked down at my hands and then into his eyes. I wanted to tell him so many things. I felt like a volcano waiting to explode, but I wasn't sure where to begin.

"Yes?" John said. He gave me an inquisitive look. "You have a really pensive stare; I can tell there's something on your mind."

I smiled. I could never keep anything from him; nor he from me.

"It's you, Johnny. You bring back so much, and I'm so confused right now."

John sat up straight. He pulled his hand away and stopped eating. He wiped his mouth with his napkin and then leaned in to me.

"Funny you say that. You bring back so much, but I couldn't be clearer."

"What's that mean?" I leaned closer, truly confused.

John smiled and grabbed my hand again.

"When you left me abruptly ten years ago, it was like half of me was instantly ripped away. You were gone on the morning of your sixteenth birthday, and it just destroyed me. I had planned a nice birthday celebration for you. I had a whole list of games and things to do. I was devastated."

John maintained a smile, but I could hear his words had pain behind them.

"Your father wouldn't tell me anything, and, well, your mom doesn't speak. I begged your dad for an hour. All that he said to me was that you were happy. But I was miserable and incredibly selfish. So I became angry and bitter. I couldn't make any sense of it, and I lashed out at everyone and everything."

John took a sip of his drink. I was frozen, listening to him.

"I didn't do well in school after that, and I only spiraled down from there. In my eight years of working since then, I went through no fewer than five jobs. I couldn't keep any good friends, and I was always getting reprimanded at work—and then fired. I was a big, hot mess." John took another drink. "Two years ago, I finally hit my rock bottom. I was standing in line at a grocery store, and a guy in front of me was just going off on this woman. They started arguing, and then yelling. I watched in delight, as I used to find things like that entertaining. In a span of two minutes, I watched and listened as the two argued. Then the man escalated it. He unleashed everything he had, and it was brutal. I saw this woman—his wife, I assumed from the ring on her finger—transform in front of me. As he pulled out every deep, dark secret of their relationship and spit it back at her in a venomous, angry tirade, I saw the love she had for him just die right in front of me. It was vulgar, disgusting, and gut-wrenching."

I was on every word. John took another sip.

"She just collapsed mentally. She began sobbing so loudly; then she screamed holy murder when he tried to touch her. The entire store came to a halt, yet no one knew what to do or say. It became a horrid spectacle. The wife looked up at him and said through a stream of tears, 'My God, I love you; why do you hurt me like this?' I actually started to cry, there in the line. I felt in that moment that all the anger, confusion, and bitterness I had bubbled up to the surface. I saw in me that man. I hated you, Amant, with a passion. And I let it completely consume me. I was that ugly man, and I saw it crystal clear, as if I were looking into a mirror."

John took another bite of his food and then a drink from his glass. I blindly shoved another forkful of food into my mouth. He leaned forward again.

"I then told myself that I would no longer keep secrets from myself and I would no longer allow anger and bitterness to control me. The next day, I enrolled at the university. I took classes in psychology. I needed to know what made me think and act the way I did. I also went to the library and checked out several books. It was the start of the new me. I read a few books on meditation and expanded from there. I changed my whole routine. I began working out my body, mind, and soul. I hit the gym three times a day and even changed my diet. I got so into health that I took a mixed martial arts class. I dropped the mean and nasty friends that I had. I was thirsty for more, like a man crossing a desert."

John grabbed another fork of food and chewed it slowly.

"Wow, Johnny, that's incredible. I'm so proud of you," I said in awe. John gave me a smile as he swallowed.

"I finished my psychology degree and then decided to leave my last job. I needed to take the last step in my transformation. I had to get away from the current job because I had made too many mistakes and yearned for a fresh start. So it led me to Gamma Five, where there are a host of new companies and positions." He gave me a thoughtful stare. His eyes twinkled, and he squeezed my hand. "So you can imagine my utter surprise when I saw you in the transport terminal. It was like I was taking my final exam. Everything suddenly came full circle; here was the catalyst that started me on the path, and now there before me stood my last great test—you, Amant."

"How did you do?" I heard myself say in a whisper.

"Amant, all the anger, bitterness, and hate were gone. I was left only with the fond memories of you and the love in my heart. It seems my biggest challenge was just holding back all my feelings for you. But the new me doesn't fear your response. I don't need you to complete me, but I am excited about exploring a possible relationship between us."

I was in shock. John's stark honesty had me speechless. My mind raced but was clogged with thoughts. More images of our youth flashed back. I had thoughts about how we would proceed, with me traveling all the time. There was so much all at once; I didn't know where to start.

"I'm speechless, John" finally rolled from my tongue.

He smiled and sat back. "That's fine," he said. "I know I've thrown a lot at you; all my cards are on the table, as they say. Take your time, Amant. But do you mind if I comment on my thoughts about you?"

A sudden shock went through me. I pulled my hand away from John. I was actually afraid to hear it. But I felt my head nod. My eyes were wide, and my mouth was open; I was unable to do much else.

"I see and feel a lot of conflict in you. I have started to see sparks of the old Amant I knew—the carefree, fun-loving, and happy girl that I fell in love with in our youth. But now I see a gorgeous and vibrant but very cautious and restrained woman in front of me. I can actually sense pain in you. I see it in your face, in your expressions. I hear it in your words. What I said to you before about you being a coward and not trying with us—the old you would have fought back immediately. That's what I was waiting for, but instead, it hurt you."

John squeezed my hand. "I'm truly sorry that I uttered those words. I'm apologize that I upset you, Amant."

I shook my head and pulled my hand back.

"No, that's okay, John."

"No, it's not. I'm a man, and men don't go around hurting women. What I said was cruel and hurtful, and I'm truly sorry for saying it. But I think it does touch upon something that we need to discuss, Amant."

He reached across the table and grabbed my hand again. He gave me a surprised look.

"Your hand is cold," he stated matter-of-factly. I pulled my hand back quickly and clasped both hands together. John recoiled.

"I think I'm done eating, John." I stood up from the table.

John rose and walked around the table.

"Amant, please, take the time to think about everything I've said. I do want to talk; maybe I can help you with some of the things that are troubling you?"

He looked into my eyes. I felt scared, nervous, and now short of breath. I opened my mouth to speak and nodded, but nothing came out.

"Please take all the time you need, and let me know when you feel comfortable to chat."

He gave me a smile and a brief hug, and he then turned and walked away.

I stood frozen for a moment, not sure what to do. My mind was a racetrack full of cars that were moving at top speed. Some cars were going in the wrong direction. It was chaos; it was maddening. I finally snapped out of it and slowly walked back to my room.

I meditated for a half hour. It didn't help. I was still confused, tense, and anxious. I did have renewed feelings for Johnny, and I wanted to explore a relationship, but I felt anxiety, fear, and something else. I jumped up from my couch. I realized I was tired of me. My thoughts began to bother and haunt me, I needed to escape. I went back into the bedroom, grabbed my headset, and put it on. There was a bright light and that familiar hissing noise.

Chapter 11

July 9, 2021

JENNIFER'S ALARM CLOCK WENT OFF. She rolled over and stared at it for a moment. 6:03 a.m. Her mind started slowly. *It's Friday*. She sat up in bed, threw the covers off, and jumped out and hit the floor. In minutes she was in the shower and racing. In less than twenty minutes, she was strolling toward the door, where she hit the call button.

"Yes?" came Tank's low voice over the intercom.

"Are you ready to go?" Jennifer asked.

"Ready when you are" was his response.

Jennifer giggled into the open microphone.

"I'll be down in two minutes."

She grabbed her purse, leather briefcase, and transmitter.

When the elevator door opened on the first floor, Tank gave a startled look.

"Wow, you look incredible," he said as he and another agent stepped into the elevator.

"Thank you," Jennifer replied as she looked up at him.

He smiled back and then faced forward in a professional manner. She gazed quickly to her side at the other agent. He had a slight smile on his face. When the doors opened, the first agent walked out and Jennifer grabbed Tank's arm. She pulled him downward and whispered in his ear.

"What's he smiling about?"

The first agent, now several steps ahead, looked back and paused.

"Start the car," Tank called out.

He turned and faced Jennifer.

"I'm not sure; maybe he's just happy that you look so nice."

"I can tell you're lying," Jennifer said with a dry look on her face. "You're a bad liar."

She turned and started walking toward the car. She peered back at him a few feet from the car and smiled. When she got in, she called Rachel.

"Hey, I'm heading in now."

"Okay. I'm already here. I've been here for an hour now. Taylor called me—said he had a lot of issues to discuss. It seems several other leaders have additional questions and concerns."

"Well, they'll have to wait," Jennifer said as the car pulled out of the garage. "At this point, it's all preparations for the meeting at 1:00 p.m."

Jennifer ended the call, and the car soon pulled into the White House parking area. Jennifer opened the car door and stepped out on the passenger side with Tank. As they walked into the White House, Jennifer bumped Tank's arm and smiled.

"You look so dapper," she whispered to him.

They finally reached the main staging room. It was abuzz with conversations, staffers running about, and phones ringing. Taylor was pointing and yelling at someone in the corner. She spotted Rachel across the table, sorting out papers and looking at a monitor. A staffer tapped Jennifer on her shoulder.

"The president wants to speak with you in the Oval Office."

Jennifer nodded and walked over to Rachel. She handed her the additional work from the previous night.

"Here, take care of this."

Jennifer leaned in closer.

"And since when do you come to work on Taylor's call?"

Rachel shot Jennifer a puzzled, shocked look. Her eyes darted over to Taylor.

"You're *my* assistant. If anyone contacts you, I need to be informed; is that clear?"

Rachel nodded again and stole another glance over to Taylor. Jennifer turned quickly and walked over to Taylor at the rear of the room.

"It doesn't matter what he said," Taylor said defensively to the secretary of commerce.

He was extremely tense. His skin was already slick with oil, and his collar was loose, with his tie pulled to the side. His sleeves were rolled up, and two people already flanked him with papers in their hands and tentative looks on their faces. Jennifer was prepared to pull him aside but thought better of it as she assessed his already stressed demeanor. She turned and gave the staffer a nod. They both walked quickly to the Oval Office.

When she entered the room, the president was at his desk, edged on both sides by staffers with tablets. The president was also in high-speed mode. He answered a question from the person on his left and then quickly looked right and answered a question. Jennifer sat down and waited. After ten minutes of questions and orders, Kennedy looked up and pointed to Jennifer. She jumped up from the chair and approached his desk.

"Okay, I need you to preview the government website on the Qyron. I also need you to, uh, here." He pushed forth a stack of paperwork. "Please look it all over; verify that it's all correct." He took a deep breath. "Sorry I had you wait, but Taylor looked as if his head was going to pop off, so I thought I would discuss these things with you directly."

Jennifer gave the president a smile.

"No problem, sir; I'll check all of this over and let your staff know if it needs edits. And yeah, Taylor is going to need new batteries by lunch."

The president smiled and then returned to his fast pace of preparations. Jennifer made her way back to the staging room. She spent the next hour fact-checking and reviewing the government's new website on the Qyron.

It provided a wealth of information on the Qyron as a race. It detailed many facets of their physiology: four feet tall, strength of two to three adult human males, telepathic means of communication, forty waking hours and twelve for sleep. It even mentioned that their bones were comprised of iron and calcium which greatly increased their weight. The website listed various facts on their three home planets and two colonized moons. It explained their current system of living and their principles as a people. Their very small government was also discussed in detail on the web page, which was fully integrated through advanced computers to receive all of the population's input on issues and resolutions.

Lastly, it listed the overwhelming stockpile of finished goods and natural resources they possessed.

Jennifer noted a few small discrepancies, and she added in a variety of other facts. She continued to check through the progress of the other cabinet members. It seemed just about everyone was ready for this meeting, save for the secretary of transportation. Butler was relieved of that post, and the deputy secretary was currently in the role. Their main objective was to ensure we were prepared to receive millions of new propulsion engines and then discuss the transition with the automakers on Saturday. Jennifer had planned to meet with the acting secretary of transportation, but everyone was currently at a feverish pace to be ready by 1:00 p.m.

When noon arrived, the tension was palpable. Several carts were wheeled in with snacks and drinks. Kennedy Myers then walked into the room and raised his hand. It took several seconds for the attendees to finally come to a halt and direct their attention to him. The president grabbed a drink from the cart, slowly popped the top, and took a leisurely sip. He let out an "ahh," and the crowd nervously laughed.

"That's what I want everyone to do now. I know that we've all been running around like mad trying to prepare for this day. I applaud everyone here; you've all done a remarkable job in blazing a trail through unknowns and getting America ready for the single most important time in our history."

The room broke out in a round of applause. Several people grabbed snacks and beverages from the carts.

"What I want everyone to do now is relax. We have just about an hour before the scout ship lands. My speech before the ship lands will take about ten minutes. Our military is completely deployed in all major cities and many smaller towns, as are all police and firefighters. Most companies have complied with my request as a national holiday and have kept their doors closed. Many of the interstates are clear of traffic."

The president took another sip from the can.

"What I demand of everyone now is to just relax. We are the leaders. I need everyone who will be with me"—he surveyed the room and nodded at all of his cabinet members—"to not just *be* calm but also *look* calm. We need to remember that America will be initially alarmed and afraid. They will look to us for confidence and strength. Let's be sure that we give them precisely *that*."

Everyone then took the next half hour to get a little something to eat and calmly get a few more things done.

The president motioned to Jennifer and the rest of the cabinet staff. She joined him as they walked the hallways of the White House.

"I have to admit," he said as they strolled toward the awaiting media at the South Lawn, "I had my doubts, but I feel confident that everything will go well. Thank you for being strong and seeing this through."

Jennifer looked up at him.

"Me? Strong?" Jennifer giggled. "Thanks for believing in me and taking me seriously, sir."

"Any last-minute advice?"

Jennifer stopped walking. Her face changed to a look of shame. The other cabinet members stopped in their tracks.

"Well, I have one thing." She gave him a wince. "Think happy thoughts, because their leader will be able to read your mind." The slight smile on the president's face dried up. "I didn't mention it before because I thought it might hinder you in your preparation."

The president stood motionless for a moment. He then turned to her.

"It would have been nice to have known that sooner, but honestly, I don't see how that would have changed anything too much. How much can they read?"

"Well, as you speak they can read your related thoughts. But since you have no malice in your plans, it shouldn't be an issue."

"True." The president then began to walk forward. "Once this meeting is over, I have a present for you."

Jennifer trotted to catch up to him.

"What? I only caught a part of that, sir."

"When the meeting is over, I have a surprise for you," the president repeated with a smile.

"And that's it; you're just going to leave it like that? Torture me, eh?"

The president nodded and arrived at the South Lawn. The rest of the cabinet members slowly exited the White House and joined him. Taylor stepped alongside Jennifer.

It was an incredible sight to behold: The stage was a huge

platform—large enough to hold the entire cabinet staff and then some. To the left and forward of the staging area, red ropes isolated a large section of grass. That was where the ship would land in the next fifteen minutes. The front of the stage was crowded with hundreds of reporters and camera crews. Along the far outside of the entire White House lawn, soldiers stood arm-to-arm. There were also several types of military vehicles, completing a solid wall of men and machines around the entire White House and its grounds.

Jennifer just stood in awe at the magnitude of the scene. She finally looked to her right, at Taylor.

"Ready for this?" she said to him.

Taylor looked like a wreck. He was nervous and pale, and his breathing was rapid. She grabbed his hand; it was clammy. Taylor looked as if he were about to pass out. Jennifer felt alarmed.

"Damn, are you okay?"

Taylor turned and looked at Jennifer. "I should will then, yes," he blurted out in a nonsensical haze. He stared straight ahead.

Jennifer thought he looked more zombie than human.

"Listen; this is going to go just fine," she whispered to him. "They are going to land; their leader, Thoona, will greet the president; and it will be a very brief exchange. No reason to panic."

She patted his hand, but he didn't seem to respond. The president began to speak with the press. He introduced his cabinet members one by one. As he peered back and saw Taylor, he raised a brow. Taylor continued to stare on in the distance—bleak, white, and clammy. When he finished with his cabinet introductions, Kennedy Myers then began his official speech. Jennifer quickly turned to Taylor and gave him a soft, wet kiss on the lips. He shuddered and stared at her, blushing.

"There, that's better," she whispered.

"My fellow Americans, today, July 9, 2021, is a monumental day that will be recorded in history as the day that we, the people of Earth, made contact with beings from another planet."

He paused for a moment while the press corps gave out gasps. Many of the people peered around in shock and then looked back to the president.

"These beings, the Qyron, are a friendly advanced race that are eager to share their knowledge, skills, goods, and services with us. They will help us bring a swift end to many of the blights on our planet: starvation, disease, unemployment, pollution, and, of course, an isolated galactic existence. My administration have been preparing for this change."

The president paused again to survey the stunned crowd.

"Effective later today, they will set up diagnostic and curative stations in many of the hospitals here in the United States. They have the ability to cure nearly every ailment and affliction known to mankind. Several supply vessels will land in Africa, Asia, and South America to distribute much-needed food and hydroponic technologies."

As the president continued his speech, Jennifer looked over at Taylor. Much of his color was restored, and he was actually looking closer to normal. She leaned in and whispered, "You look better."

He turned and gave her a smile. She then panned the cabinet members, who were smiling and standing tall.

"… and we have prepared detailed outlines of all aspects of change. The site www.Qyron.gov will cover every facet of this change. I will not be taking questions at this time."

The president turned around and motioned to Jennifer.

"Now let me introduce Jennifer Winston. She has been given the ability to communicate with the Qyron telepathically, and she will have them land here on the South Lawn."

Jennifer stepped next to the president. She smiled at the cameras for a moment and then placed the transmitter to her head. She then turned to the president and spoke into the microphone.

"Ten seconds, Mr. President."

Everyone looked up, and all cameras immediately panned the sky. A small, shimmering blue spot appeared and rapidly grew larger. It descended very quickly, coming into view for all to see. The ship was oval in form, like a slightly flattened egg, but with an extended lower section. It almost gave the impression of an egg that was pregnant. The craft was large and shiny in the summer sunlight. It was chrome in appearance but gave off a glow of a brilliant light blue. With the glow came a low bass hum that grew lower in tone as the craft continued to approach the ground. The crowd gave out a collective "Ooh!" and the oblong vessel then slowed and hovered a hundred feet above the ground. It was large in size—about the diameter of three city busses.

It then lowered the final distance and touched down on the grass. The outcropped lower section had several protracting arms that acted as the landing struts. The low hum and blue glow then ceased, followed by a brief hissing noise. The side of the craft then opened up.

Several people in the crowd were talking in hushed tones, and everyone's eyes were wide, while only a handful of people were heard screaming. Three Qyron then exited the craft. The first to step forward was Xho. He was wearing a shining gold robe that glittered as he walked toward Jennifer and the president. A second Qyron dressed in a dark brown robe then stepped forward. Closely following was Thoona, with a shiny iridescent robe and points of light across his chest. Thoona was much taller than the standard Qyron. He stood nearly six feet tall and had a slight, green hue from the normal grey Qyron skin tone.

Xho stopped in front of Jennifer. She raised her hand up at an angle as Xho raised his. They touched hands, forming an inverted V. She turned to face the president.

"Mr. President, may I introduce Thoona, leader of Qyron."

She then turned to Thoona.

"Thoona, I introduce to you Kennedy Myers, president of the United States."

The president stepped forward and extended his hand. Thoona extended his. The three long fingers and thumb slowly grasped on to the president's hand, and they gently shook. Thoona then raised his arm up at an angle. Kennedy followed his lead, and they touched. The secretary of state stepped forward, holding a large, shining golden item. The president turned and gently grabbed it. He took a step forward and presented it to Thoona.

"Thoona, I present to you a golden statue of the bald eagle, our national symbol, which signifies liberty and freedom. In one talon are thirteen arrows, which represent the power of our united people. In the other talon is an olive branch, which signifies peace."

Thoona took the golden eagle statue and gave the president a nod.

Jennifer then spoke up. "It is with great honor that Thoona accepts this generous gift from your people of the United States."

The Qyron in the dark brown robe then reached into his robe and pulled out a small crystal orb. He handed it to Thoona. Thoona then quickly clasped both hands, creating a slapping sound. A bright light instantly blazed forth. The orb glowed brightly, in bluish swirls, and a collective gasp was heard from the assembled crowd.

Jennifer turned to the president.

"Mr. President, Thoona of Qyron offers you the Orb of Chade. It signifies a lasting peace and friendship. It shall shine brightly for one thousand orbits of your planet. Oops—I mean a thousand years."

Jennifer blushed, and a few outbursts of laughter came from the crowd. The president extended his hands and held the orb. Its brilliance was stunning, and it gave off a warm sensation.

The president stared into the orb for a few moments. "I thank you, Thoona, and your people, for this breathtaking Orb of Chade. We welcome the start of a long-lasting friendship and alliance with your people."

The air sat silent for a moment. Jennifer began to clap, and then the crowd joined in and clapped for a full minute. Jennifer walked over to the president and whispered in his ear while the crowd was clapping. He nodded to her and then took to the lectern again. The crowd immediately grew silent.

"I would also like to inform the world that this friendship and alliance is extended to all people of Earth. A conference was held with nearly every nation earlier this week. All nations will be following our lead in establishing the same government and Internet resources globally. I now offer an invitation to Thoona and your crew to dine with me and my staff."

Jennifer paused briefly. "It would be our honor to join you."

The president, his cabinet members, Jennifer, and the Qyron then entered the White House. Tom Franklin, secretary of state, remained outside to answer the flood of questions from the media. The assembled leaders then sat down to a grand buffet. The Qyron were thoroughly impressed with the many varieties of food. Although they stood a mere four feet tall, their appetites far exceeded our own.

After nearly an hour of dining and light banter, Jennifer turned to the president.

"Thoona would like to know if it is acceptable to begin landing supply ships with food. Thoona feels it is not polite for us to feast while others on this planet hunger for sustenance."

The president stood up from the table.

"I give you my deepest apology. Yes, please do so. It is extremely rude and selfish of me to dine with so much excess before those in need."

Thoona also stood up from the table, walked over to the president, and extended his hand again.

"Three thousand ships are now landing across Africa and Asia. Mr. President, you are truly a wise and compassionate leader," Jennifer said as she nodded to Thoona. "At this time, we will now take our leave. Mr. President, thank you for your gracious hospitality. I look forward to hosting you on Qyron. I will leave Xho with Jennifer to assist in coordinating this transition."

Thoona then shook the president's hand, and they walked back to the South Lawn. The secretary of state was still busy answering questions when they exited.

The president took the lectern.

"We now have thousands of ships landing and distributing food across Africa and Asia. Later today more ships will land and begin to set up facilities in hospitals across the globe. At this time, they will see only those who are critically ill. Thoona will now return to Qyron, but we will continue to move forward in establishing trade and services."

Thoona and the dark-brown-robed Qyron then walked back to their ship. The door closed, the blue glow reemerged, and seconds later the ship elevated and then zipped up and out of sight.

The president and his cabinet members then walked back inside the White House.

"Status report!" he said as he paced back to the west wing. A staffer ran alongside.

"There are only isolated reports of violence. It seems that everyone is currently stunned but calm. The ships have begun to land in every major city. They are being escorted to the hospitals by police and the military."

The president stopped and turned quickly to face the staffer.

"No, I want my marines guarding the Qyron. We need to be prepared for anything, so get them on it now!"

The staffer returned a shocked look but nodded and ran back down the hall. Jennifer, Taylor, and Xho walked along with the president. Jennifer peered at Taylor; his color had returned, and he no longer appeared ready to pass out. However, he did have an uncomfortable stare locked on Xho as they walked. They finally entered the Oval Office, and the president sat down.

"Okay, I'm very impressed so far with our progress," he said as he leaned back in his chair. Taylor continued to stare at Xho. Tank stood guard at the door. The president then looked to Jennifer.

"So, Sho is it?"

"No sir, it's pronounced 'Zo'," Jennifer replied

"My apology, Xho. So you'll be assisting with the entire process?"

"Well," Jennifer replied, "he's actually going to be my permanent liaison for all communications through the Qyron."

The president nodded and then peered at Taylor, who had a zombie-like gawk focused on Xho.

"Taylor!" he shouted.

Taylor's fixed gaze on Xho was broken as he snapped his view to the president.

"Knock it off; you're being rude!" Jennifer laughed, and Xho turned to look at Taylor.

Taylor froze in his place. Jennifer walked between the two.

"Relax, Taylor; Xho won't bite," Jennifer said. Xho smiled. "So now imagine being naked on a surgical bed and having the Qyron walk into the room while you're strapped down, Taylor. That's part of what I went through. I think you would have died."

The president was unable to stifle a laugh. Jennifer followed.

"Taylor, this is Xho. Xho, this is Taylor."

Xho extended his hand, which unlike those of the other Qyron had five fingers. Taylor's face was bleak white again, and he appeared to be frozen in place. Jennifer slapped him on his back.

"Don't be rude!" she scolded.

Taylor blinked and then slowly extended his hand, and they shook.

"There, now that didn't hurt, did it?" Jennifer said, and again the president laughed. He then stood up from his chair, came around his desk, and shook Xho's hand.

"It is a pleasure to meet you, Xho." Xho nodded. "If you don't mind me asking, you seem different from Thoona and the other Qyron."

"Yes, Xho is a mix of human and Qyron," Jennifer began.

The president gave her a thoughtful look.

"You have to understand that many of the alien abduction stories were actually true. And they did experiment with breeding. It's good that they did; otherwise, we would not be able to communicate. A full-breed Qyron is far too telepathically powerful for me or any human to understand. I can only communicate through Xho."

"Ah, so that's why Xho will be your permanent liaison," the president exclaimed. "Then it's prudent to give him a full security detail."

He peered over at Tank, and Tank nodded back. Kennedy then turned to Jennifer.

"Well, how about you let Xho get on with his weekend and you make preparations for a wedding."

Jennifer's eyes grew large. The president looked over at Taylor, who was still trying to regain color in his face.

"Taylor told me that you need to get back to your best friend's wedding tomorrow. So, as a present for your outstanding work, I would like to give you a free ride."

Taylor looked at Jennifer and smiled, still pale and a little off balance. She turned and gave him a big smile back.

"So what I have for you is extra special."

"I get a ride on Air Force One?" Jennifer asked.

The president chuckled. "No, I can't swing that," he said, smiling. "I called over to Andrews Air Force Base and found two junior pilots who need flight time. They will escort you and Tank in F-18's to Billings, Montana. From there you'll be escorted to your friend's wedding in Roundup."

Jennifer stood stunned; she was nearly in tears. With eyes wide and mouth open, she lunged at Taylor and gave him a big hug. In his present state, it nearly toppled him. The president laughed, and even Xho smiled. She then turned and gave the president a big hug.

"Oh thank you, thank you so much! You don't know how much this means to me!"

The president smiled and then added, "No, you don't know how much everything you've done means to me—and will soon mean to the American people."

Jennifer smiled and turned her head.

"I was thinking," Jennifer began. "How about when I get back on Saturday, we set up to have the vice president healed by the Qyron?"

The president flinched.

"He is still in isolation for the Ebola virus, yes?"

"Yes he is, quarantined for the next month," the president said as he walked back around his desk.

"What better way to promote the Qyron than to show them curing the vice president, who's sick with Ebola."

Kennedy sat back in his chair.

"That's an excellent idea. I think it's also prudent to show them curing people in the hospitals as well. How soon will that be set up?" He looked at Xho. Xho nodded, and then Jennifer turned.

"He says they should be ready within thirty minutes of getting a room at the hospital. They only need a minimum of space and very little setup time. By the end of today, they should have at least a few thousand people cured nationwide."

"Excellent!" The president leaned back in his chair with a smile. "I love this job—never a dull moment." He grinned.

"We have everything ready, sir," Tank chimed in.

"Okay, well, Jennifer you have a great time at your friend's wedding. Tank, make sure Jennifer is kept safe. Xho, what are your plans?"

Xho nodded to Jennifer.

"Xho has a place on the command ship; he'll return when we're ready to work," Jennifer replied.

Jennifer, Xho, and Tank turned to leave. Jennifer stopped and grabbed Taylor's arm.

"I guess I will call you on Sunday, then, so we can get caught up?"

"Yes, that will be fine," Taylor said, still staring at Xho.

His color had again returned, but he kept an eye on Xho as they walked. Jennifer smiled and shook her head. They passed by the main meeting room. Jennifer flagged down Rachel, who quickly trotted over to her.

"I'm so sorry about this morning," Rachel began. "Taylor called me and—"

"Oh, never mind about that. We're fine. Listen; I'm going to be leaving for my friend's wedding. I won't be back till Sunday. Please keep tabs on Taylor on Saturday, and I'll give you a call when I get back."

"Sounds good. Enjoy the wedding!" Rachel gave Jennifer a smile.

"How much longer are you staying tonight?" Jennifer asked.

"I'm finishing up now actually, so I'll relax 'til I hear from you."

Jennifer nodded and then continued with Xho and Tank down the hallway.

Xho took a small transport ship back to the command ship while Tank and Jennifer walked to their truck. The streets were fairly clear, so it took less than a minute for them to reach the apartments. As they were walking toward the elevator at the apartment, Jennifer looked over to Tank.

"So how will this work? What time are we leaving?" Jennifer asked.

"Well, it all depends on you. When is the wedding?"

"It starts at noon, so we should be there well before."

Tank looked down at a set of papers.

"We can leave here at 4:00 a.m., be in the air before five, and be landing by eight. It's then an hour drive, so you'll be there by about 9:00 a.m.," Tank explained as they walked into the open elevator. They talked a little more, and when the door opened on the second floor, Jennifer grabbed Tank's hand.

"I need to discuss something else with you," she said. Tank gave a nod to the other agent, and they walked down the hallway toward her apartment. Jennifer opened her apartment door and then stepped inside.

"You need to step in so I can close the door, Terrance."

She reached out, grabbed his hand, and pulled him inside. She then closed the door and turned back around. Tank had an inquisitive look on his face. She took a step, threw her arms around his neck, propped up on her tiptoes, and planted a wet kiss on his lips. When she rested back on her heels, Tank's eyes were wide, and his mouth stayed open slightly. She smiled and then jumped back up on her toes. She gave him another long, sultry kiss.

"Wow, that was much better," Jennifer said as she looked back up at

Tank. Tank seemed nervous; he gave her a pensive look. "What? What's wrong? Don't you like me? Don't you find me attractive?

"I do; you're very attractive, but—"

Jennifer then jumped back up. She gave him another long kiss. She put her arms around his neck and continued to kiss him. When she finished, she leaned back slightly and exhaled slowly in his face.

"That was hot!" she moaned. Tank slowly brought his hands up and grabbed her wrists. He gently pulled them away from his neck and down to her sides.

"Oh yeah," she said seductively.

"No, Jennifer, I can't," Tank said softly. "My job is very explicit about not getting involved with the people I'm charged to protect. I'm sorry. I find you quite attractive, and I'd like to have a relationship with you, but my job—"

"Job schmob!" Jennifer stated defiantly. "I really like you, Terrance; you're strong, quiet, understated, and sexy as hell!" She took another step forward. Tank stood straight and backed up.

"Please, I really wish I could. But I take my job very seriously, Jennifer. I value honor and duty, so I can't disregard them and forsake my job."

Jennifer stared at him for a moment. "Not even for a hot, sexy, young blonde?"

"Especially not for a funny, beautiful, creative, and strong young woman such as yourself," Tank said solemnly. He turned and opened the door. "I'm sorry," he said as he stepped out and closed it behind him.

Jennifer stood stunned for a moment. She felt hurt and wanted to be angry but couldn't. Tank wasn't just right; he was a pillar of virtue. But that just made Jennifer want him all the more. She wanted to continue thinking about it but realized that she had a little more work to do and needed to be up by 3:00 a.m.

She opened up her laptop and dived into the last bit of work that she had from Rachel. The TV was on in the background, so she was able to listen while she worked. As she typed on her laptop, the pundits spoke about the positives and pitfalls of this new alliance. They flashed a few images from around the country of people rioting and trying to loot, but the police and the military were in force to suppress it quickly. Finally she saw a story on a few people who were healed by the Qyron at the hospital. It seemed that many of the Qyron had visited the ICUs and healed those in the greatest of need first. Lines were already beginning to form outside of hospitals, like those that form for black Friday sales. Jennifer smiled and then turned off the TV and got ready for bed. She decided to make a few phone calls, the first to her mother.

"Oh my gosh, baby, I saw you with the president. How did all of this happen? Why didn't you tell me?"

"Mama, slow down. I will tell you about everything tomorrow. I'll be at Tasha's wedding."

"Oh, that's wonderful, sweetie."

"Okay, Mama, I have to go. I love you!"

"I love you too, baby."

Jennifer then made a second call.

"Jennifer?"

"Hey, Tasha, did you see me on TV?"

"I sure did; you're famous, girl!"

They both laughed.

"Huh, I never thought about that. I'm just glad we're past this first day. I was a little nervous."

"Yeah. So are you going to be at my wedding tomorrow?"

"Yes!"

Jennifer had to pull the phone away from her ear, as the screaming was so loud.

"*Yeaaaaah*! That's awesome. Do I need to have someone get you at the airport?"

"No, I have my own ride. Just make sure you have my dress ready, girl!"

"It's here and ready for you. Oh, this is so awesome!"

"Okay, Tasha, I have to go. I need to get to bed now, because my flight is really early."

"Okay, see you tomorrow! Love you, Jen!"

"Love you too, Tasha."

Jennifer ended the call and then nestled under the covers. The day's events and all of the related stress were so draining that Jennifer was asleep in minutes.

Chapter 12

As expected, 3:30 a.m. arrived very quickly. Jennifer gently crawled out of bed and grabbed a shower. By four fifteen, she hit the intercom button.

"Yes?" said the voice on the other end.

"Tank?" Jennifer asked.

"No, this is Mike. Tank is almost ready."

"Okay, I'll be down in five minutes," Jennifer said.

She grabbed her overnight bag and her camera. When Jennifer's elevator stopped on the first floor, Tank stood waiting as the doors opened.

"Good morning," Tank mumbled.

He was tired—too tired to hide it or care. His eyes looked heavy, and he walked slowly. Mike also joined them on the elevator. It was a quiet walk to the black SUV. Jennifer got into the backseat and slid down. She rested her head and, before she knew it, was fast asleep.

Tank's voice shattered her slumber. "Let's go; we're here."

"Wha?" Jennifer mumbled.

"We're here at Andrews Air Force Base. Let's go, sleepyhead."

Tank reached his hand in the backseat. Jennifer grabbed hold, and Tank slowly eased her out of the truck. She leaned into him, and he bent slightly and grabbed her overnight bag from the backseat. Jennifer slowly stood up and looked around. They were standing on an airstrip next to a enormous hangar. Two large men dressed in flight suits and helmets stood waiting. The cool early morning air gave her a shiver.

"Hey, you're that woman," the one pilot exclaimed. He reached out and shook Jennifer's hand. "You were with the aliens?"

Jennifer nodded. "Yeah, sort of."

"Okay, let's get rolling," Tank blurted out.

The pilots nodded and then walked back around the hanger. Two F-18s stood ready. The first pilot reached over to a cart and pulled up a suit.

"This is the smallest we have." He handed it over to Jennifer.

She stepped into the suit. It hung a little on her. He then gave her a helmet. She felt a little silly but gave the pilot a smile.

Tank was busy trying to fit into his suit. The other pilot let out a chuckle.

"We have both extremes—five foot nothing and, what, six six?" he said with a smile.

Tank nodded as he cinched himself into his suit.

"Yeah, six foot six," he mumbled as he grunted while pulling the suit on.

When they were finally suited up, the pilots gave them a quick overview of their cockpit.

"So, if we should have an issue and need to ditch," he said as he pointed, "pull that bar, and it will eject you out."

Jennifer's eyes went wide.

"Oh, that's crazy; we're not going to crash, are we?"

"Not on my watch, ma'am!" the pilot stated as he helped her into her seat. The overnight bag was placed in her lap.

After a few preflight checks, the pilot throttled up the engines and they began rolling down the runway.

"We have clearance; you okay back there?" radioed the voice into Jennifer's helmet.

"Yes!" was her nervous reply.

They accelerated down the runway in mere seconds, as Jennifer was thrust back in her seat. When the jet finally lifted off the ground, the pilot pulled the stick back and they climbed quickly, nearly straight up. Jennifer grunted and let out a squeaking noise as the force slammed her into her seat.

"Are you okay?" crackled the pilot in her ear.

"Oh my God, this is insane!" she yelled. The pilot leveled the jet a bit but continued to climb.

"Sorry, ma'am, but we need to get some altitude above the commercial jets."

After a few minutes, she heard him radio to the other pilot; then he called to her.

"Okay, we're cruising at about five hundred knots. We'll be here for about four hours, so feel free to kick back and snooze if you're tired."

"Wait, four hours? I'm going to be late!" Jennifer exclaimed.

"We'll be on the ground in Billings at 8:00 a.m., ma'am. We're crossing two time zones."

"Oh," Jennifer mumbled. "Okay then!"

Jennifer was anything but tired at this point. Her stomach felt as if it were being pushed back into her spine, and any grogginess had been replaced with adrenaline.

"Um, can you roll the plane so I can see the ground?" she asked.

"Roger that," he replied, and the jet quickly swung left, twisting them into a horizontal spin. The night sky was a clear dark purple, but as the jet spun, the light orange horizon and then speckles of light from the ground came into view. Her overnight bag tumbled around the cockpit as they spun.

"Woohoo!" Jennifer screamed. "This is fucking awesome! Oh, sorry!"

The pilot laughed, "That's okay, ma'am; we all feel that way. I've got one of the best jobs around."

He then leveled the jet, and they continued on. Jennifer eventually drifted off to sleep, as viewing the sky became boring in short order. The next time she heard a voice, it was the pilot radioing to the tower in Billings, Montana.

"Roger that, cleared to land," he replied to the tower. "You with me, Tiger Seven?"

"On your six there, Tiger Five," radioed the other pilot.

"Is Tank still alive back there?" Jennifer chimed in.

An audible grunt came across the radio, and Jennifer giggled. In ten minutes, they were touching down on the runway. It was now sunny and bright as the sun was cresting above the horizon. Jennifer stretched as she stepped out of the cockpit. She glanced over at the other jet. Tank was slowly exiting. When Jennifer finally stepped on the runway, she walked over to Tank as he climbed down from his seat.

"So how was your flight?" she asked.

Tank removed his helmet and gave her a frown. "Very cramped."

Tank was stretching out his legs and flexing his knees. He winced a few times as he moved.

Tank's pilot chimed in from behind him. "Sorry, sir; we don't make 'em for larger people."

A black SUV quickly pulled alongside them. The door opened, and Tank gave a nod to the agent, Alex. He then opened the door and looked across to Jennifer. Jennifer turned to her pilot.

"Thanks so much; I had a really good flight." She shook his hand.

"Yes ma'am, I heard ya snoring back there for most of it." He gave her a wink.

Jennifer smiled back as she walked toward the waiting SUV.

"We will be back later this evening," Tank said to the first pilot.

Jennifer was sliding by Tank and stepping into the back of the truck. She gave Tank a smile.

"Party pooper. I was hoping to dance well into the night."

She giggled and took a seat in the back. Tank closed the door and got into the front passenger seat.

"So you were cramped in your cockpit?" Jennifer asked.

"Like a sardine in a can," Tank mumbled back.

On the drive to Roundup, Jennifer gave Tasha a call.

"Hey, I'm in Montana and on my way to you now, girl!"

"Awesome! You might as well come right to the church. I have your dress here, and I'll be getting ready soon."

"Okay, we'll be there in about an hour," Jennifer said as she ended the call.

The drive went by quickly, and heeding Jennifer's directions, they pulled up at the church.

"Please don't go running off; we need to stay close to you, Jennifer," Tank cautioned.

Jen nodded and then walked into the church with Tank and the other agent. Tasha was getting ready in a back room in the church. She was sitting in a makeup chair while another woman was busy applying foundation on Tasha.

"Oh, you'll never get all the ugly off of her!" Jennifer said. Tasha spun around in the chair.

"Jen!"

Jennifer ran over and gave Tasha a hug.

"I can't believe it; it's finally here!"

"I know!" Tasha exclaimed. "Craig is so nervous!"

They both laughed.

"Hey, Alex!" Tasha said.

Jennifer turned around. Tank and Alex stood in the doorway.

"Alex has been a big help getting my yard ready for the reception. I'm sorry to see him go."

She gave him a wave. He smiled back at Tasha.

"I told Alex that if Craig gets cold feet and doesn't show up, I'm going to marry him."

The girls laughed while Alex smiled.

The makeup woman continued on with Tasha. Jennifer slinked her into the bridesmaid dress. It was a stunning light yellow with plenty of flowing lace. As she looked into the mirror, she wondered if she would ever wear white herself.

She smiled and walked out into the church. It slowly began to fill up as noon approached.

"Jennifer!" came a yell from the room.

She walked back into the prep room.

"Why don't you get a little makeup done? I've paid for the service; you might as well use it," Tasha said as she began to dress into her wedding gown.

Jennifer sat down at the makeup chair. As the woman began to apply some foundation, she whispered, "I saw you yesterday; you're the one who can talk with the aliens?"

"Yeah, that's me," Jennifer whispered back.

"Can they cure my sister? She has diabetes." The woman continued to brush on makeup.

"Yes, I believe they can. Check out the website to see which hospitals they're at."

"Thank you. This would mean so much to me. My sister has suffered for so long now."

Jennifer finished in the makeup chair and then joined Tasha. They talked for a few minutes about Jennifer's time in Washington and her flight out here.

"Damn, girl, I can't believe you. You get abducted, and now you're rubbing elbows with the president and have your own staff, a set of bodyguards, and a free apartment. You always were lucky!" Tasha said.

"Hey, you're marrying a great man. He's good-looking, has a solid job, and loves you to pieces. That's lucky too, ya know!"

Tasha slid in close and whispered into Jennifer's ear, "That big black guy—is that who you're dating?"

Jennifer frowned and looked back at Tasha. "No, he can't because of his job."

Tasha shot another look at him as he stood by the door. "Damn, girl, you should at least ride him once!"

Jen slapped her arm, and the two broke out laughing.

A few minutes later, the wedding began. It was a truly wonderful event. Tasha was stunning in her long, white wedding gown. Craig was nervous but dashing in his tuxedo. The two stood and exchanged vows with gentle music playing in the background while Jennifer cried. The wedding procession, three limousines and a black government SUV, drove through town and stopped at a quiet park. The bride and groom had several pictures taken and then arrived at Tasha's house for the reception.

Her backyard was elaborately decorated. Two large circus-type tents were erected with enough seating for seventy-five guests. A large dance floor sat in front of the band, and the entire yard overlooked a quiet pond. Bunting was strewn from the street to the first tent and throughout the yard. The day could not have been more perfect. The sun was high in the sky, providing the perfect eighty-degree day with only a lone cloud gently wafting across the bright blue background.

The day drifted by, much like that cloud. Food was served, everyone danced, and Jennifer enjoyed the celebration of Tasha and Craig. As the sun began to creep close to the horizon, Jennifer caught up with Tasha, who was dancing with Craig.

"Hey, Tasha, this was absolutely wonderful; I'm so happy for you both." She gave Tasha a hug. "I hope you'll forgive me, but I didn't have time to get a card."

Jennifer reached into her purse and pulled out the Visa card she used to shop for clothing. She handed it to Tasha.

"Here, this has a little over four grand on it. How's that for a wedding gift and interest on your loan?"

Tasha's eyes opened wide. "Wow! Thanks, Jen, that's great!"

She gave Jennifer a hug. Tasha then peered over Jennifer's shoulder. Both Alex and Tank were standing at the edge of the dance floor. Tasha pulled back from the hug.

"I guess you have to get going, huh?"

Jennifer grimaced and looked down. "Yeah, sorry girl, but we have a flight to catch back to DC."

Tasha smiled at her. "Listen to you, all important now. I'm so proud of you, Jen!" She leaned in and hugged Jennifer again. "You keep making me proud, girl."

"I will. This was a great wedding, Tash. Love you!"

Jennifer was then escorted up the hill and back toward their SUV. As Jennifer reached the top of the hill, she saw Tom angrily walking toward her. He dropped a beer bottle and staggered forward. Jennifer stopped in her tracks.

"Oh no, that's Tom!" she screamed nervously.

Alex reached a hand out and grabbed Jennifer. He quickly pulled her behind him. Tank took a step forward.

"I got this," he said as he unsnapped the gun from his holster.

Tom continued storming forward, now three steps away. Tank pulled his pistol out from his suit jacket. The .45-caliber gun was pointed down at the ground.

"Don't take another step toward Jennifer or I'll be forced to drop you! This is your *only* warning!" Tank shouted. The band played on at the party down below. The crest of the hill hid the scene from the wedding party.

Tom stopped abruptly. "Aw, what, you gonna shoot me, you fuckin' monkey?" Tom slurred to Tank as he stood tall.

"I'll get her to the truck!" Alex shouted out, his pistol also drawn as he kept one hand firmly on Jennifer and scanned the area around them.

"I'll shoot you if you force me to!" Tank yelled back at Tom. Tom took a side step toward the SUV. Tank raised up his weapon.

"Not another step!" Tank yelled out. Tom stopped; he locked eyes with Tank.

"You don't unnerstand," Tom stammered. "I love her. I jus' need ta talk with her."

"Sober up and call her later!" Tank said.

He heard the doors to the SUV open. A second later, the truck fired up. Tank slowly eased his gun back into the holster, keeping a lock on Tom.

Tom then took a step toward Tank. Tank raised his hands.

The SUV roared in behind Tank, and Tom lurched forward. Tank threw a hard right hand, connecting solidly with Tom's jaw. He sprawled backward and onto the road. Tank opened the rear door, jumped in, and slammed the door behind him. Alex hit the accelerator, and Tank leaned over, smothering Jennifer.

"Stay down," Tank yelled as the SUV sped away. Tom rolled on the pavement as the truck roared down the road.

"Clear!" Alex yelled.

Tank slowly sat up. He grabbed Jennifer's arm and pulled her upright.

"Are you okay?" he asked.

Her eyes wide and mouth open, she stared at Tank for a moment. He studied her with a piercing scan. *"Are you—"*

"Yes!" Jennifer spat, "I'm fine, and it was only Tom. You could see he was drunk!"

"I could see that he was unstable, and I know he has a history of violence," Tank responded without hesitation. "Our job is to protect you, Jennifer, and a drunk person is unpredictable. You told me that he used to hit you?"

Jennifer slowly nodded.

"Can you say that he would never use a knife or a gun on you, especially when he's drunk and upset?"

Jennifer just sat and stared at Tank for a long moment. She then turned her head away and watched the road zip by as they drove back to the Billings Airport.

After a half hour, Tank pulled out his gun and inspected it. Jennifer turned her gaze back to him.

"Wow, that's a really big gun," she said softly, eyeing it intently.

"It fits my hand well, I like how it feels, and it has the stopping power in a time of crisis," Tank responded coolly. Jennifer looked at him for another moment. He was as cold as steel—no trembling, no sweating. She reached her hand out and tapped his shoulder.

"Thanks for protecting me," she said gently. Tank turned his gaze back to her.

"It was our pleasure," Tank said.

The rest of the drive went quietly. When they arrived at the airport, they drove back to the hangar and waited for the two pilots. Tank shook Alex's hand and then donned his flight suit. Jennifer got out of her dress in the SUV and put on her flight suit. The two pilots finally walked over to the hanger.

"We ready for some fast flying?" the first pilot said with a grin.

Jennifer was closing the door on the SUV. She walked over to the waiting group.

"I am, but you'll need a can opener for the Hulk." She pointed at Tank and giggled.

Alex gave him a laugh as he slapped Tank's back. Tank just grumbled and put his helmet on.

They seated themselves back in their aircraft and were off the ground in fifteen minutes. The flights went by quickly as dusk turned quickly to night. Jennifer again drifted off to sleep. The descent into Andrews Air Force Base woke her up. Twenty minutes later, they were on the ground and exiting the jets. Jennifer was happy to reach solid ground. She was exhausted, even with the three-and-a-half-hour nap during the flight. As the pilot helped her step down to the ground, he grabbed her arm.

"Ma'am, I want to thank you. My grandmother was in a hospital bed, dying of leukemia. My mother called me earlier and said that she was given some kind of shot today by your aliens. She's now responding and is being told that she'll make a full recovery in about a month. I can't thank you enough."

Jennifer smiled. The pilot was nearly in tears.

"You can pay me back by telling everyone how the Qyron helped your Grandma," Jennifer said. She grabbed his hand and then gave him a hug.

"You bet, ma'am," he said.

They walked over to the other jet in time to see Tank slowly step down to the ground. He was mumbling and stretching out his legs again. He caught Jennifer's smile as he turned.

"You find that you need another quick flight somewhere, you can count me out!" he said, shaking his head.

Jennifer gave him a serious look. "Do you need me to carry you?"

Tank mumbled, shook his head, and then walked to the waiting vehicle.

Jennifer arrived in her apartment just after 1:00 a.m. the next morning. She clicked on the news while she lay in bed.

The top story was the quick recovery of the vice president from his Ebola virus. There were other stories about healings by the Qyron of bedridden, near-death patients. But those stories were set next to several protests and marches. People all over the world were voicing their fears over the intrusion of the Qyron. Jennifer eventually drifted off to sleep.

Chapter 13

THERE WAS A BRIGHT LIGHT and a hissing noise. I pulled the headset from my head.

Hmm, so it looks like Tank isn't my link with African blood.

After another moment, my current reality came back to me. I did feel better after viewing Jennifer's life, but I knew I had to address my own—and now.

I was getting tired and would need some rest soon, but I wanted to talk with John before I went to sleep.

"Computer, location of John Crowley?"

"John Crowley is in Lima Entertainment Hall," responded the computer.

I grabbed a snack and some water and then trotted out the door. In two minutes, I was outside of the entertainment hall on Lima Deck. It had several computer and virtual games, as well as pool and Ping-Pong tables. The sounds of zapping and laughing echoed throughout the large room. I walked in and finally spotted John in the corner. He was playing air hockey with another man. The man was short with blond hair and a big smile. I slowly approached from behind John. I looked at the scoreboard; they were tied 9–9. Both men were yelling and wildly flailing their hands, slapping the puck back and forth. As I got to within a step of John, he slapped the puck at an angle and it zipped by the other man for a goal. The machine gave out a huge cheer with flashing lights and a horn while John yelled out.

"Yeeeaahhh!" He jumped up and cheered again.

"Nice game, Johnny!" He startled and pivoted around.

"Hey, Amant! Yeah, that was a really good game!" He leaned in and gave me a hug. The other man caught my eyes, and his smile flattened. John broke from the hug and turned to face him.

"Hey, that was really fun, Chet. How about we play another?"

Chet's eyes left John quickly, and he briefly looked me up and down and then slowly shook his head.

"Nah, that's all right. I should get going."

"What? I thought we were going to shoot some pool?"

"Yeah, I wanted to, but I need to leave. I'll catch you around."

Chet turned and walked away. John's face had a look of surprise on it, and his mouth hung open slightly.

"I'm sorry, Johnny; should I go?"

John turned his focus back to me.

"What? Go? Hell no, you just got here!" John's eyes panned my face quickly. "What's wrong?"

I exhaled and just shook my head.

"Nothing, Johnny." I turned to walk away. John reached out and grabbed my hand.

"Hey, come on, now. You came to find me; don't walk away," John pleaded as he squeezed my hand.

I was just tired of this reaction. People would see me and either frown and turn away or gawk. It was draining and depressing. I just wanted to go back to my room and sleep. John took a step in pace with me as I walked out of the room.

"Amant, come on; talk to me." John now pulled my hand, turning me around to face him.

"I'm just tired, Johnny."

"No, you're not running away again," John said.

He then walked alongside me, pulling me with him. We were at his room in no time, and John opened the door and stopped. He threw his arm forward, gesturing for me to enter. With arms crossed, I sighed and walked inside.

After taking two steps inside, I saw another dozen roses and a box of chocolates on his coffee table. I stopped and turned to face him. John's glance quickly spied the roses and chocolates as well.

"Damn, those were supposed to be a surprise!" he uttered.

I gently touched his face with my hands and drew his attention to me.

"Success," I said as I took a step and gave him a hug. It felt so good. His hand rubbed the middle of my back while his other hand caressed my side. The fragrance of the roses tickled my nose. They were delightful. "Mmm," I said as I hugged him back. I could feel his strong arms now grab tight and squeeze. My heart beat faster as his hands continued to caress my back. His left hand slid up, and he began stroking my long brown hair while his right hand circled my lower back. I felt every part of him pressing against me.

I moved my head back and locked my eyes with his. The dark brown eyes twinkled, and his hand slowly pushed my head forward. His lips gently touched mine. I let out a light moan, and he kissed me again. The kisses were smooth and slow. I savored every one. As I pulled back, I looked deeply into his eyes.

"Johnny, I'm scared."

He kept his gaze on mine and slowly processed my words. I waited for him to respond. He finally took a step back. He moved his hands from around my back and clasped both my hands in his. Johnny walked me over to the couch. A gentle push from him and I was lowered down onto the couch. He followed me and sat alongside, never losing his lock on my eyes.

"Scared of me—how is that possible?" he said in a slow, deep voice.

"Well, I—" I began. I felt nervous and scared, as if I were being interrogated. My heart continued to beat faster, and my breathing sped up. John leaned in. He kissed me gently and slowly. It was as if the only way to calm me was to provide this gentle kiss. And he did.

He slowly pulled back to his seat on the couch. My eyes were still closed. As I opened them, his loving gaze waited.

"Please, go on, Amant."

I swallowed and then took a deep breath.

"Johnny, this thing we have—"

"Thing?" he said louder than his last words. I gave him a smile and paused.

"This new relationship. It scares me, Johnny." John now straightened his smile and turned his head slightly. He nodded for me to continue. "I so want to be with you. I remember how we were, growing up, and I see so much more now, but …" I stopped. I was almost afraid to continue. I wanted John—his love, his touch—but I wasn't sure if I wanted to lose this newly awakened relationship.

"Please, Amant, continue," John urged.

"I'm afraid our relationship won't last, Johnny."

"Why is that?" he said with a professional calm.

"I see how people treat you when I'm around. I see and hear how they treat me. People aren't ready for a half-Qyron, half-human hybrid."

"You're not the first one, ya know," John interjected.

Damn him. Of course I'm not the first. He's not getting it.

"Yeah, John, I know! But people still aren't ready to accept it."

I felt myself tense up. I don't know how he couldn't see this.

"So you're leaving to go and live on Qyron?"

"What? No! Wait; don't twist my words, John!"

I felt my heart beating faster and my face growing flush.

"I just don't think we'll last, John." I shook my head.

"Because of how everyone else feels?" John said as he raised his right eyebrow.

"Yes, and then I'll lose you."

John nodded. I think he was finally getting it.

"So this is a new thing then? You just became a half-human, half-Qyron in the past year?"

"What? Don't be ridiculous! What are you talking about, John?"

"Amant, I don't know why you seem to want to block out our past."

"I'm not, John!"

The volume and tone of my voice shocked even me as the sound echoed off of the wall. John shuddered, gave me a startled look, and then slowly blinked and continued.

"Amant, I don't know why you seem to want to forget the past. I can recall as far back as four years old. You lived two doors down from me; we met and became instant friends. We played in your backyard as well as mine. We shared the swing sets and—"

"I remember it, John; I'm not stupid!" I screamed.

John's mouth dropped open, his eyes opened wide, and he sat back and folded his arms.

"I'm sorry for yelling, Johnny," I said as I reached out and grabbed his hands. John took another deep breath.

"Amant, do you remember the other neighborhood kids? The names they'd call you and then me? You remember the fights we were in—how we were always outnumbered? Can you recall all of the taunts in school?"

I felt angry, but I closed my eyes and nodded. Suddenly a wave of memories of our childhood engulfed me. I saw the other kids' faces; I heard their words and taunts.

"And who was beside you with every bloody lip and every skinned knee, every single day?"

I opened my eyes. John's expression was pleading. I could see the hurt in his face. More memories washed into my mind. I saw the kids cornering us, yelling and screaming at us, pushing me down and John trying to stop them. I felt tears well up in my eyes, and my throat tightened.

"Why do you think I'm going to abandon you after standing by your side for so many years? I love you for you *in spite* of you!" I leaned in quickly and hugged him. I couldn't stop the flow of tears. He held me tight, again caressing my back while I began to cry.

"I know people can be mean and nasty when they're scared. I'm okay with that; I have *always* been okay with that." His words were soft, and his hug was even softer. "You can't change the world overnight, Amant, but you can try to change it a little every day."

I just cried and continued to hug him. I did remember those days now, after having pushed them so far down in my mind. The kids would yell "sugar glider" and outline their eyes with their fingers. They would outrun us and corner us when we tried to walk home from school. As a child, my strength was greater than theirs, but there were always six or seven of them and just me and Johnny.

That's when the rest came back to me—when it all came through so clearly. Johnny *was* always there, taking a beating right next to me. But never once did he hold that against me. Never did he blame me for his fat lip, black eye, or bruised knee. He never said a word. And even after we would get bloody and muddy, John was there to walk me home. He would tell me that I wasn't ugly and that I wasn't stupid, all the while bleeding and limping alongside me.

"Oh Johnny, I'm so sorry!" I blubbered. I cried for the next ten minutes. I suddenly realized that Johnny always took the more severe beatings. It was he that shouldered the brunt of the taunting; it was Johnny who threw the first punch when I cried. It was the kids who would beat him harder for being a traitor. Yes. It all came back now. While the kids would yell "sugar glider" at me, they would hurl "traitor" and "alien-lover" at him.

John just continued to hug and caress me back as I cried. I felt so horrible, so ignorant—so selfish. I pulled back and looked at him. I suddenly saw the small scars on his face: a pencil-thin scar on his lip where he was punched the one morning on the playground; the small, round scar on his cheekbone where a boy threw a stone at him; and the little break in the hairs of his eyebrow where a boy kicked him in the head. I raised my finger and gently traced the scars on his face. They were faded and as white as his normal complexion, but I saw every one of them now as clearly as I did when we were nine.

"Oh, Johnny, you're right," I said as I blew my nose. "I'm sorry."

"Nothing to be sorry about, Amant, I'm just happy you understand I'm always going to be here for you." He gave me another hug. "I don't care if people look, stare, or point. I never have."

John then leaned in and gave me a kiss. I put my hands around his neck and kissed him back. I kissed him and kissed him again. John eventually stood up. He raised me up, gave me another hug, and then walked me to the door.

"You look so very tired. Get some sleep and then call me for breakfast."

I leaned in and gave him another kiss. He opened the door and gave me a wink.

"Thank you for being patient with me, Johnny."

Johnny waved it off with a nod and a smile. I returned his smile and then walked back to my room. I was feeling tired. I yawned twice before reaching my room. When I walked in, I noticed a message waiting on my monitor. It was another administrative inquiry, asking for my identification. This didn't make sense to me, but I was too tired to give it any thought. I walked into my bedroom and collapsed into bed.

When I woke up, I felt invigorated. That cry yesterday had been so overdue, and it truly felt as if a huge weight had lifted from my chest. I had been carrying that pain for so long, and it was finally liberated. I stretched and then jumped out of bed.

"Computer, location of John Crowley?" A tone sounded, and the monitor listed him as in his room and sleeping. I checked the Earth-relative clock. It showed the time as being 2:17 a.m. EST. I decided to do some more blogging until John was awake. I grabbed my headset and placed it on my head. There was a white light and some hissing noise.

Chapter 14

July 19, 2021

"Okay, let's get this meeting started," Taylor said as the attendees settled into their seats. the president walked into the room. He nodded at Jennifer, and Taylor stood up as the president sat down in his chair.

"Okay, Taylor, give me the good news," the president said as he leaned back in his chair.

Taylor gave him a nod. "Today's report shows a total of one hundred twenty-four thousand people have been healed in the United States from cancer, leukemia, heart disease, and other ailments. Worldwide, we're looking at over two million. We have the auto industries in Detroit, Japan, and Korea now refitting their new 2022 cars with Qyron engines. On average, it will increase cost by five thousand dollars per car, but the engines last fifty years and weigh only thirty pounds." The new secretary of transportation perked up. He looked over at the president.

"Sir, overall this should save the average consumer twelve hundred dollars per year, and car engines will now last for decades."

"Excellent. Let's make sure we highlight this to the American public." The president then nodded to Taylor, who continued.

"The homeless issue is nearly eliminated in Philadelphia and Atlanta. We have new housing set up in both cities, with many of those homeless now employed."

The secretary of housing and urban development stood up. "Sir, many of the abandoned and idle buildings and houses have been replaced with new buildings. It's the damnedest thing I've ever seen. These Qyron have this massive machine that's the size of a city block. It's this incredibly huge tubular device that hovers in midair then literally sucks up an entire building. In less than an hour, the old structure—heck, the entire *block*—is gone. Then another machine hovers over the site and lowers down a prefab building. In one day, they can replace a dozen buildings and up to three blocks. Philly and Atlanta now have several new sections of housing not just for the homeless but also for domestic abuse shelters and halfway houses."

The secretary of the interior then stood up. "These same machines are slated to be used on the landfills, garbage dumps, and toxic waste sites all over the world. The Qyron have placed large sorting machines in orbit. When the waste is collected, including these city blocks of building waste, it's then sorted and repurposed."

The president smiled and leaned forward in his chair. "Incredible— all of this progress in just over a week."

Taylor then continued. "We have begun to mine the asteroid belt, and thousands of people have been sent to Saturn to begin siphoning gasses. The Qyron have three large machines on the west coast that suck in air and remove the carbon. It's some type of catalytic converter. But they say they will be able to restore our atmosphere within a few years. Ten of these same machines are now in high-altitude flight on Venus. They tell me that it will have a dramatic change there, cleaning up the Venetian atmosphere and cooling the planet. I'm told that we should be able to begin colonizing Venus within ten years."

Many in attendance were amazed by the news. A few side conversations broke out. The president sported a large grin and then raised his hand for silence.

"They are also going to deposit some of the gasses and water on Mars so it too can be colonized. That will only take about a year before we can begin terraforming."

The secretary of education, Judith Wanner, stood up. "We are trying to make sense of all of the technology the Qyron bring to us. I have a new subcommittee that is composed of scientists and writers. It may take months to develop new textbooks and lesson plans for our children and adults. We are also setting up exploration tours for many of our scientists. The Qyron are more than willing to transport them through our solar system and beyond."

The president gave her a smile and a nod.

"Thank you, Judith, please get me a more concise schedule when you can."

She said something to her staffer and then sat back down. The president urned his gaze back to Taylor.

"And the bad news?"

Taylor frowned and then shuffled some papers. He dropped one paper and quickly bent over to pick it up.

"Well, at present we have several active marches in a few cities. We've lost some police and military through desertion and resignation. We also have a growing number of suicides."

The president gave a look to his aide.

"I want more positive information posted on our new website, as well as more news coverage, and let's see if we can step up the vice president's national tour." The aide nodded, and the president turned back to Taylor.

The secretary of state then leaned in. "Sir, we still have staunch opposition to any Qyron contact from Russia, China, and North Korea. They are mobilizing their militaries and discussing an active military alliance."

The president acknowledged this and then turned to Jennifer.

"Do the Qyron have any weapons we would be able to utilize?"

Jennifer had just taken a bite of a glazed doughnut.

She turned, "Yhe Qywun ..." She swallowed and blushed. "Sorry. The Qyron don't have any offensive weapons. They haven't had any violence in their lives in hundreds of thousands of years," Jennifer stated while wiping her mouth.

The secretary of defense then added, "Sir, even though we have some defection from the military, it amounts to about five percent, and we've adjusted for the loss. We can and will protect the Qyron as you've ordered."

The president acknowledged him and then turned back to Jennifer.

"They don't have any weapons at all?"

Jennifer turned to Xho and nodded. "Well, they have defensive abilities with a type of magnetic force field. It will protect their spacecraft from missiles and bullets, but they have nothing for individual use."

The president leaned back in his seat again. He ran his hand through his peppered hair.

"Is it possible for them to work with some of our scientists to develop offensive weapons and other defensive options?"

Xho shook his head, and then Jennifer turned back to face the president.

"They have a very firm belief against harm to any other creatures. They are willing to assist with defensive armor and tactics, but no weapons."

The president thought for a moment. His expression changed from a look of intense thought to a kind smile.

"Of course, a truly noble belief," the president stated. "I'm sorry if I offended you, Xho."

Xho nodded slowly. The president then turned back to face Taylor.

"I want to be certain on what opposition we're facing. We need intelligence on any single person or groups that present a threat."

"Well, sir, we have plenty of demonstrations, but I think it's best to have that report from Lance."

Taylor sat down, and Lance Meyer, the secretary of homeland security, stood up.

"We are currently monitoring several new groups. Many people came forward on social media, proclaiming their fears and hatred of the Qyron. At present we've had only a few instances of people shooting at the Qyron or our marines on patrol. Worldwide we have—"

"Let's just keep this domestic. Make sure we have our situation at hand," the president added.

"Yes sir," Lance continued. "We've had only a few instances of violence, and no one has been killed. However, there is a huge groundswell of fear and anti-Qyron sentiment. Our department is working with the FBI and other offices to track and define these groups."

"Good. I want daily reports," the president stated. "Anything more to add?" he asked Taylor.

"No sir, not at this time," Taylor replied.

"Good, because now I have to talk with Congress," the president said. "They seem to be quite angry that I didn't share all of our plans up to now with them. Who knew?" The room broke out in laughter.

The meeting then adjourned into small groups discussing strategies and planning. Taylor walked over to Jennifer, who was standing with

Xho and Rachel. Jennifer caught sight of him as he approached. He had a different look about him. Jennifer was used to seeing Taylor high-strung, wound up, and tense. She became accustomed to seeing stress and tension in his face, but as he approached her, she noticed that his face was soft and his appearance calm.

"Do you have a minute?" he asked. Jennifer nodded, and Rachel turned to face him as well. "Alone?"

"Uh, sure," Jennifer responded as she gave Rachel a nod. Taylor led Jennifer to a quiet corner of the room. He extended his hand and clasped Jennifer's.

"I want to thank you," he began. Jennifer glanced down at her hand now tenderly held by his and looked into Taylor's eyes. They were deep and sincere. "I know I haven't been easy to deal with since you met me."

Jennifer raised her head and began to open her mouth.

Taylor shook his head. "No, please, let me finish." He gently squeezed her hand.

"I know I haven't been a nice guy—probably more of a jerk. I'm so sorry for that. I've been under a lot of pressure and stress, but the worst of it wasn't from work." He paused for a moment and swallowed. "My mother was in the final stages of lung cancer. She wasn't expected to live beyond this month, if not even this week. But last Monday, she was visited by one of the Qyron medics. He gave her an injection, and within minutes she was more alert and responsive. It's been three days, but she's off of the ventilator, walking on her own, and even eating like a horse. I owe you and the Qyron everything for this."

His eyes were large and glassy. Jennifer noticed his bottom lip quiver. He leaned in and gave her a hug.

"Thank you. Thank you so much."

He exhaled loudly and sniffled as he hugged her tightly. Jennifer was speechless. They hugged for a few seconds, and then Jennifer pulled back. Taylor wiped his eyes and gave her a big smile.

"Uh, you're welcome," Jennifer slowly stumbled.

Taylor gave a look to Xho, who stood a few steps away.

"I'd like to buy you both lunch; is that okay?"

Xho walked over to Jennifer and Taylor. Jennifer nodded and then turned to Taylor.

"That's really nice of you to offer," Jennifer said, "but we have to be going. Our schedule has us meeting with industry leaders in Los Angles in twenty minutes. Then we're off to Japan and then Europe."

Taylor's smile dropped.

"Oh, okay," he said. He flashed a mixed smile as he turned to walk away.

Jennifer reached out and grabbed his arm. She put a slightly happy inflection in her voice. "But we'll be back by Friday." She gave another look to Xho. "We should be arriving by 5:00 p.m. on Friday evening. How about dinner?"

Taylor perked up. "Yeah, that would be great. Give me a call as soon as you get in town."

Taylor was now grinning again, and he gave her a nod and then walked back toward the president. As Jennifer slowly turned, Rachel approached her.

"That looked awkward," she said sarcastically. "And we need to be leaving now."

Jennifer's gaze was still fixed on Taylor as he walked over to a group chatting with the president.

"Huh? Oh, yeah, right, we should be going," Jennifer mumbled as she turned her gaze to Rachel. As they started toward the doorway, Rachel tapped Jennifer's shoulder.

"So what was that about?" Rachel asked as Jennifer gave her a grin.

"Just thanking us for a job well done," Jennifer said quietly. She briefly turned her gaze back to Taylor as they left the room.

Rachel, Jennifer, and Xho walked out into the hallway and toward the South Lawn exit, where they were joined by several agents. When they reached the door to the South Lawn, Rachel turned to Jennifer.

"So when you say 'a job well done,'" Rachel prodded, "like …?"

Jennifer flashed her a concerned, annoyed look, but before Jennifer could respond, Rachel put up her hand as if to say "never mind." They walked out of the White House and onto the South Lawn, where a Qyron shuttle sat waiting. Huge crowds along the street watched as they entered the craft. Once inside, they sat down and buckled in, and seconds later the craft lifted up and zipped rapidly into the sky.

Within five minutes, their transport arrived in time to meet with business leaders in Los Angeles. From that point, her team was rushed from one business office to another. They spent several hours in silicon valley, discussing new technologies and brokering deals between the Qyron and various companies. Tuesday and Wednesday was a rushed blur through government and corporate meetings in Japan and Australia. By the time Friday afternoon arrived, Jennifer was exhausted. As they stepped back onto the transport in Rome, Rachel turned to Jennifer.

"Wow, this week has been just crazy!" Rachel said.

Jennifer's only response was a tired look.

"I can't believe all the places we visited and the nightlife!" Rachel gushed. She had a devilish little grin on her face. "I don't know why you didn't want to go out and party with me in Sydney or Berlin. You missed out on some wild fun and some really sexy hunks!"

Jennifer sat down in her seat on the transport and let out a large sigh. As she buckled herself in, she looked tiredly back at Rachel.

"I have no idea where you get all your energy," Jennifer mumbled.

"Are you kidding? All we do all day is sit in chairs in plush offices and discuss trade and technologies. It's boring; I get cramped up half the time. I have energy to burn!" Rachel said with a smile.

Jennifer just shook her head.

"Well, at least you came dancing with me in Tokyo," Rachel said as she tapped Jennifer's hand. Jennifer gave her a smile as the transport lifted up.

"You can't tell me"—Rachel took a deep breath as the transport accelerated quickly—"that you didn't have a blast at that nightclub?"

Jennifer finally cracked a smile. "Yeah, that was fun. But I was so tired that next morning."

"Ah, that's what the weekend is for—to catch up on all of the sleep you missed during the week," Rachel teased. "You act like you're fifty. You need to live a little, Jennifer!"

"I did live a little; I went out with you Tuesday night in Tokyo," Jennifer said as she slumped down in her seat.

"But you missed some of the sexiest guys in Sydney. I can't believe all the hot bodies."

"What about your man back home?" Jennifer asked in shock.

"Ugh. All we've been doing the last two weeks is arguing. It's like, it was fine when he was busy with his construction company and he had to be out of town this day and the next. But let me be busy and out of town, and suddenly he's all moody and angry. I just don't get him, and, well, I'm not about to tolerate a double standard."

Rachel shook her head and smiled at one of the Secret Service agents, John. "John knows what I'm talking about." John smiled back at her and then opened his mouth.

"You know," John began as Tank shot him an angry look. John's face went blank, and he sat back in his seat. Rachel turned to Tank.

"Oh, come on; don't bust on our fun, grandpa!" Rachel snipped.

"Did you go out that night?" Tank asked John without acknowledging Rachel.

John gave Tank a stunned look.

"Oh, leave him alone," Rachel quipped sarcastically. "He was busy protecting me."

"With all due respect, his job is to protect Xho on this trip, and he needs to be alert and well rested." Tank turned his look from Rachel to John. "Maybe he needs to be reminded of his duties and responsibilities or be relieved."

"Don't be a dick!" Rachel yelled.

Jennifer immediately perked up. "Rachel, that's enough!" she snapped.

Rachel sighed aloud, crossed her arms, and then turned her head to stare at the wall. The final two minutes of the transport to DC were spent in silence. When the craft finally landed back on the South Lawn of the White House, everyone unbuckled and stood up. Rachel made a dash for the door, and Jennifer yelled out.

"Rachel, wait up!"

Rachel took a few steps outside and then paused for Jennifer to catch up, her hands resting on her hips.

"Look, I need you to be professional when we're on the job. I don't care about your after-hours fun, but I need you ready in the morning." Rachel exhaled loudly and folded her arms. "And I don't need any drama with the Secret Service!"

Jennifer stared hard at Rachel.

Rachel slowly turned to face Jennifer. She caught sight of Tank standing in the transport doorway, waiting.

"Fine, I'll play nice with the boys, and I won't cause trouble," Rachel said.

She flashed a terse smile to Jennifer and then turned around, snapping her head. Her long hair whipped around, and she continued to walk toward the White House. Tank then stepped out of the transport. The other agents walked out behind him, carrying several suitcases.

"I'm sorry for that," Jennifer said to Tank. "Please don't be hard on John."

Tank stared silently for a moment.

"I'll chalk it up as a learning experience for him," he said solemnly.

She slapped his arm and gave him a big smile. "You old softie," she said with a giggle.

Jennifer stopped abruptly and then looked back into the transport at Xho.

"Oh, okay, you have a good weekend too, Xho." She waved at him.

Xho nodded to her from the craft as the rest of the agents walked out onto the lawn carrying the last of the luggage. The door then closed, and the craft lifted up and away. Jennifer walked back toward the White House with Tank.

"Maybe next time you and I can go out dancing; might do us both some good, ya know."

Tank looked at her as they walked. He finally cracked a smile.

"Yeah, we'll see," Tank replied. As they stepped through the doorway into the White House, Taylor walked over to them.

"Welcome back," he said.

His face was cheery, and his eyes bright. Jennifer paused for a moment. Taylor actually appeared to glow. She also noticed that his normally slicked-back hair was now soft and natural. She approached him slowly.

"What?" he asked with a smile.

"Nothing. Uh, you look, different," Jennifer said as she studied his face. He looked younger, invigorated.

"I feel great," he said. "The daily reports are getting better, my mother is doing great, and the weekend is here; what's not to be happy about?"

Jennifer couldn't help but smile. Taylor's happiness and enthusiasm were contagious. She glanced again at his hair.

"So what happened?" Taylor asked in a quieter voice.

"What do you mean?"

"Well, I asked Rachel if she wanted to join us for dinner, and she growled, threw her hand up at me, and stormed by," Taylor stated with a raised eyebrow.

"Ah, well, she has some issues that she needs to work out," Jennifer huffed. "Dinner sounds good right now; I had a really small lunch in Rome."

She pivoted to her right and winced, rubbing her side.

"What's wrong?" Taylor said, moving to Jennifer's right side.

"Oh, it's my back; it's all tense. We were nonstop this whole week, and it's been acting up since Wednesday," Jennifer moaned as she dropped her overnight bag, rubbing her side.

Taylor nodded as he stepped around her.

"Got it. I know what you need." He turned and leaned alongside Tank. He whispered a few things to him while Jennifer moved to grab her suitcase.

"Don't bother," Taylor shouted as he trotted back to Jennifer. He scooped up her overnight bag and her luggage in one quick motion. "Follow me," he chirped with enthusiasm.

He trotted with the two pieces of luggage into the White House. As the three of them walked by a doorway, the president yelled out.

"How was your week?"

Jennifer stopped and turned. She glanced at the president.

"It was grueling, sir—too much work."

Kennedy smiled. "Welcome to my world. Have a good weekend!" he chuckled. She gave him a smile and then continued to follow Taylor and the agents. When they got to the truck, Taylor placed the luggage in the trunk as Jennifer stepped into the backseat. Taylor then joined her on the other side.

"So where are we going?" Jennifer sighed in a tired voice.

"You'll see," Taylor quipped with a grin.

Jennifer continued to stare at him as they drove. He was a completely different person. His attitude was light and fun, no longer stiff and stuck-up. His eyes were bright and less authoritative than usual. She looked again at his hair. She reached up and touched it with her hand.

He quickly turned his head. "What are you doing?"

"Just wondering. Why did you change your hair?"

"I don't know; just felt like I needed a change. No more sticky gel. Why? You don't like it?"

"No, it's really nice. I think it makes you look younger—more …" she trailed off. She noticed Tank looking back in his visor mirror.

"More what?" Taylor asked.

Jennifer looked over at him and smiled.

"Younger," she finished. The truck then pulled alongside the curb.

Chapter 15

"Ah, we're here," Taylor said brightly.

He jumped out of the truck and ran around back. Tank stepped out, and Taylor was already at Jennifer's door as Tank's second foot hit the pavement. He opened her door, and she slid out. Taylor grabbed her hand and walked her up to the shop door. She stepped through and was greeted by soft music, a wonderful earthy fragrance, and the sounds of trickling water.

"Welcome to our spa," said a tall blonde behind the counter with an air of arrogance. She sauntered around the counter and greeted Taylor and Jennifer.

"Hello, my name is Casandra," she uttered with a stuffy British accent. "We are closing in an hour, but is there something I can help you with?"

She peered stiffly down her nose at Jennifer.

Taylor gave her a trite smile.

"Yes, she needs a massage," he stated. Casandra looked over at Tank and the other agent as they stood near the doorway. "Oh, they're with us," Taylor said curtly.

Casandra gave another glance at Taylor and then the two agents.

"I see. Our rates are rather high," she hissed, "and we only have one masseuse available, so I'm afraid I'm unable to help anyone else."

"That's fine," Taylor shot back. "Money is not an issue, and she's the only one who needs the attention."

His words were forceful in response to her prissy attitude. He pulled out a platinum government credit card and slowly extended it with his fingers. As she reached for it, he retracted it an inch and gave her an angry stare. Casandra sighed, and Taylor then extended it again. She grabbed the card.

Tank stepped forward as Casandra walked behind the counter to swipe the card.

"I'll need to see the facilities," he stated as he walked alongside Jennifer.

His suit jacket flapped open, displaying his side arm.

Casandra took a half step back in shock. "Of course you will," she said slowly.

After swiping the card and handing it back to Taylor, Casandra moved to the door. She locked it and flicked on the Closed sign.

"I will do your massage; please, follow me."

Jennifer and Tank followed her into a massage room. Tank inspected the room.

"If you don't mind him being here, then he can stay, but you will be in a state of undress," Casandra said as she looked Tank up and down. Jennifer peered at Tank and smiled.

"I don't mind if he stays," she said coyly as she began to unbutton her blouse.

Tank stared at Jennifer for a moment and then stepped toward the door.

"I'll be just outside," Tank muttered, stone-faced. He closed the door behind him.

The hour passed by with Jennifer receiving a very relaxing full-body massage. Casandra kneaded out the knots, smoothed out her anxiety, and nearly put Jennifer to sleep. When Jennifer finally exited the massage room, she did so with a dreamy smile on her face.

"That was just pure bliss," she whispered to Tank as he stood up from his chair.

"Glad you enjoyed it. I caught up on messages and some paperwork," he replied quietly. Jennifer gave him a smile and strolled out into the main parlor.

"Oh, Taylor, that was just perfect. Thank you so much," she gushed as she slowly walked to the door.

"It's my pleasure," Taylor said as he opened the door for her.

They left the parlor and drove another two blocks to a steak house. After they ordered their food, Taylor spent the next ten minutes detailing how happy he was with the progress that the Qyron were making and how smoothly the transition was moving along.

Jennifer smiled as she listened. "I see you're really settling into your new position, I'm happy it's all working out for you," she said.

Taylor glanced at her for a moment. He took a sip of his drink and then leaned forward. "I can't thank you enough for how much you've impacted my life. I really enjoy this new position; it's so challenging with every day, so busy."

"Yeah, me too. I never thought I'd visit any foreign countries, and in the past week I've been to more than I can count." She paused a moment. "It's too busy, though; I wish we could slow things down a little."

Jennifer looked over at Tank and another agent sitting at the next table.

"You're doing fine, and I'm sure that you will hit your stride soon enough. Besides, no one else can do what you're doing, so take all the time you need." Taylor smiled and noted the waitress approaching with their food.

Jennifer's mouth watered as she cut into her filet. Taylor enjoyed a juicy rib eye steak.

"So how busy are you?" Taylor asked while cutting his steak.

"Well, right now we have the next two weeks booked up solid. We're trying to make sure we handle as many meetings in one area as possible. So this week coming up, we're spending two full days in England, then a day in Egypt and two other African countries. Thursday we'll be in Mexico, and Friday, Brazil."

"Wow, look at you, a globe-trotter!" Taylor said with a smile.

"Thanks," Jennifer giggled. "Yeah, it's nuts." She took a drink of wine. "I guess I'm just not used to it. Me, a small-town girl, zipping all over the globe. This week they wanted us to keep working past fourteen hours; I was just too exhausted."

"That is excessive," Taylor said as he took a drink. "I'd back it down. Tell them you need to set a limit. I understand that there's a whole world clamoring to share in the new Qyron businesses and technologies, but you're only one person. Strongly suggest no more than twelve-hour days."

"At this point, I'll take anything under fourteen," she sighed.

They continued to dine and chat. The conversation meandered from work and their home lives to their old neighborhoods and even high school.

"Oh, no kidding? I never would have pegged you as a wrestler," Jennifer laughed.

"Well, I wasn't very good at it, but I did enjoy it," Taylor said as he leaned forward. He looked into Jennifer's eyes. "Wow, this was *really* a lot of fun."

Jennifer gazed back at him. The flickering candlelight not only gave warmth and a cozy atmosphere; it softly highlighted his features. She stared a moment at his twinkling eyes.

"Yes, it was," she replied softly as she took another slow drink of her wine. "That massage was so what I needed too, and this steak is to die for."

Taylor reached over and grabbed Jennifer's hand. He smiled and began to lean forward.

Tank stood up from his table, knocking over a glass that clanked loudly and splashed water over the edge of the table and onto the floor. "Sorry," he uttered as he quickly righted the glass. "How are we doing on time?" he asked as he ignored the dripping water and approached their table.

Taylor pivoted quickly to his left. "Oh, uh, I guess we can get going, sure."

Jennifer squinted at Tank.

"What's your hurry?" she said with a gravelly huff.

Tank panned Taylor and then Jennifer. He paused a moment.

"It's Friday. It's late. I thought you were tired and ready to go," he said coolly.

Taylor stood up and pushed his chair in.

"Yeah, that's fine; we can go. It is getting late, isn't it?" Taylor said as he slapped Tank's back.

Tank returned a dry look to Taylor. Taylor stepped alongside Jennifer's chair and extended his hand. Jennifer smiled and grabbed ahold. He raised her up from her seat and held her hand as they strolled toward the door.

With the check already paid, they ambled outside and into the truck. Fifteen minutes later, they were pulling into the apartment garage. As the first agent stepped out and started toward the elevator, Tank stood waiting for Jennifer. Jennifer and Taylor were chatting and laughing in the backseat. They slowly, eventually, shimmied out of the truck.

"That was such a wonderful evening, Taylor; you're so sweet."

Taylor took a step forward, close to Jennifer. Tank placed an arm on Jennifer.

"Is there anything else you need tonight?" Tank asked loudly.

Jennifer sucked air through her teeth as her eyes shot darts at Tank for a moment, and she then exhaled loudly.

"Thanks again, Taylor," she said, still staring at Tank. "I guess my chaperone is hinting that it's time for me to finish my evening."

Taylor cracked a smile and chuckled.

"That's fine," he said. "I had a wonderful evening as well, and thank you again for everything, Jennifer. You have yourself a good evening." Taylor nodded politely and then turned and began walking toward the garage exit.

Jennifer spun around. "Wait; you've got several blocks to get back to your car! Tank, why don't you drive—"

"That's okay," Taylor yelled over his shoulder. "It's a beautiful night, and I could use a good stretch of the legs after all of that rich food. Good night, Jennifer." He continued to walk away and raised a hand to wave good-bye.

Jennifer stood staring at Taylor's back as he walked to the exit and turned down the street. She then slowly turned around. Tank was by the truck, standing tall.

"What the hell was *that* about?" she asked slowly, giving every word complete enunciation.

Tank turned and slowly walked toward the waiting elevator.

"Just doing my job," Tank mumbled as he walked.

"Being a jerk to my date is doing *your job*?" Jennifer yelled back at Tank while she trotted to catch up to him.

"That was a date?" he responded with an air of sarcasm.

"Well, *yes!*" Jennifer said as she grabbed Tank's arm and pulled him to a stop. "I guess," she sputtered. "Yes … yes, it was a date. A massage and dinner!"

Tank stared blankly at Jennifer with no emotion on his face.

"Why? What does it matter to you?" Jennifer spat, putting her hands to her hips.

Tank gave a nod to the other agent, who had been standing for the past several minutes, holding the elevator door. He let the doors close, and Tank turned his attention back to Jennifer.

"Look," he said as he grabbed her shoulders and stared calmly into her eyes. "It's my job to protect you against all threats, foreign and domestic."

Jennifer laughed out loud and slapped his grasp from her shoulders.

"What? Taylor, a threat?"

"Yes. I don't trust him."

"Oh come on, *Terrance*; you're not my daddy."

Tank stood up straight, as if he'd been slapped in the face. He then cracked a smile.

"No, I'm not your father," he said, his tone louder. "I'm your body-guard, charged with keeping you safe."

Jennifer continued to stare angrily at him. Tank sighed and then leaned in again.

"Look; you're a very attractive woman. But I see that you're young, vulnerable, and now quite powerful. That combination is a powder keg of what a lot of predators would dream of preying upon."

Jennifer belted out a laugh, shook her head, and then took a final step toward Tank.

"I'm not twelve, Terrance; I know how to handle myself!" she sneered. "*Your* job is to protect me at work. My *personal* life"—she poked her finger into his chest—"is *none* of your damn business!" She took a step away and then spun around quickly. "And besides, *you* had your chance and pissed it away!"

She whipped around again and hurriedly walked toward the elevator doors. Her heels clacked loudly and echoed through the underground parking garage. She finally reached the elevator and pressed the button repeatedly.

"I made my choice, and I stick by it," Tank said in a low tone as he slowly walked toward the elevator. "I honor my job and my values, and besides, this isn't about me." Jennifer smacked the button several more times. "Your job is too important to be derailed by distractions."

His words hung in the air as he finally reached her, a step behind, waiting for the doors to open.

"How could Taylor wreck things?" she replied softly, still staring at the door.

Tank slowly exhaled. "What would happen if you two had an affair and the relationship didn't work? How would your job feel if you had to see him every day, what with the two of you being a now very pivotal piece in how our government and the Qyron are handled. What do you think the president would say about this? Are you ready for all of the possibilities?"

A bell sounded, and the doors opened.

"I can handle myself," she blurted out.

She took a few steps into the elevator and turned around. Tank slowly followed her into the elevator.

"I'm not a child," she snapped as she hit the 2 button and the doors closed.

Tank stood quietly facing the door as the elevator moved up. When the bell dinged for the second floor and the doors opened, Jennifer burst forward, pushing by Tank.

"Please be careful," Tank said quietly.

Jennifer stopped three steps away and slowly turned around.

"Thank you," she said as the doors closed.

She walked to her apartment and opened her door. As she strolled inside, she saw a piece of paper on the counter. It stated that she had new groceries for the week and the apartment had been cleaned.

"Wow, this is just too good," she murmured to herself.

She sat down on the couch and thought about the evening and smiled. She then grabbed her phone and dialed.

"Jen?"

"Hey, Tasha, how was the honeymoon?"

"Oh my gosh, Jamaica is so awesome. We had a great time swimming in the warm waters, playing at Dunn's River Falls, and even exploring the mountains. Craig is such a sweetie; he treated me to everything. I had this incredible massage at the spa, and then we swam for half the day in the warm waters. I never wanted to leave."

"That's great; I'm so glad you two had a good time."

"So how are you doing, Jennifer? How's the job?"

"Oh wow, it's so incredibly busy. I've been all around the world; you wouldn't believe it!"

"Really, I'm so jealous! Tell me!" Tasha fired back.

"That's not even the best of it. Get this: I work with a guy in the White House; his name is Taylor. Think a young George Clooney."

"Really?" Tasha screamed back.

"Yeah. Anyway, when I first met him, he was a real jerk. Mean to me and all. But when I left on Monday, he was like, 'Hey, when you get back, let me take you to dinner.' So when I get back, I'm all tired and sore from working fourteen hour days all week. So get this: he starts off by taking me to a spa!"

"You kidding? No way!"

"No, Tash, he takes me to this incredibly swanky place downtown, and I get the most incredible hour-long massage. It was from this six-foot-tall blonde British model. It was so relaxing! Then he takes me to this really nice steak house just down the street. I had a steak that melted in my mouth."

"Who cares about the steak; what happened with George Clooney?" Tasha laughed.

"I'm getting to it, girl," Jennifer laughed. "So we all drive back to the apartment."

"We?"

"Yeah, Taylor, me, and the Secret Service agents," Jennifer said.

"Oh, yeah, right. I forgot."

"So anyway, Tank gets all protective when we get back to the apartment."

"Wait, who's Tank?"

"You know, the big black guy I came to the wedding with. He's one of my bodyguards."

"Oh yeah, that monster of a guy. Wait, is he the one that turned you down?"

"Yeah, but now he's getting all 'big brother' on me."

"Oh, tell him to mind his business, girl. You need to break you off some of that George!"

The two broke out laughing. After a moment, Jennifer stopped giggling.

"Yeah, but, I am a little confused."

"About what?" Tasha asked.

"Well, Tank has a point. I work with Taylor, and, well, if we don't—"

"Oh, come on. When's the last time you had some fun, girl? You were with Tom for almost what—seven miserable years? Now you're finally away from him, and you have all these rich, powerful hunks around you. Have some damn fun. If it doesn't work, it doesn't work. You can handle it, Jen!"

Jennifer paused for a moment.

"Yeah, I guess you're right."

"Jen, you like this Taylor guy?"

"Well, yeah. He's really cute and so thoughtful. I just ... I don't know."

"Hey, he's not in your apartment is he?"

"No, Tank chased him away."

"Then sleep on it. But if it was me, I'd let loose," Tasha laughed.

Jennifer spent the next hour telling Tasha all about her week's worth of travels—all of the sights and sounds.

"Hey, did you hear the news today?" Tasha asked.

"No, what?"

"Well, they were talking about several groups that have been sending threats to the aliens. I figured you'd have heard about it."

"Nah, nothing so far, but I'll ask on Monday," Jennifer said with a quaver in her voice.

"Yeah, well be careful, girl. I only want to hear good things about you."

"Don't worry, Tash; I'm safe and sound." Jennifer paused a moment. "Okay girl, it's getting late, and I need my beauty sleep."

"Okay, get your sleep, Jen."

"Give Craig a kiss for me," Jennifer replied.

There was a white light and a hissing noise, and then I removed the headgear.

Chapter 16

I took a long, hot shower. The streams of hot water, beating rhythmically down on me, felt so good. With my smooth jazz playing in the background, I could have stayed in that shower for an hour. A tone broke my trance, though. I finished my shower and toweled off. "Computer, messages."

The first message was another administrative request for my identification. I was confused, as my id tag had been scanned on boarding. I skipped the message and played the second.

"Hey, Amant, I just woke up and am starving for some breakfast," said John's voice. I quickly finished drying off and then put on some yoga pants and a tight T-shirt. I pulled my hair into a ponytail and jetted out of the room. On the way to John's room, I texted him that I was on my way. I was hungry too, and I felt like getting out of my room and away from the Psy-logs for a while.

When I reached John's room, I tapped the door sensor, and it opened immediately. The fragrance of the flowers greeted me.

"Oh, Johnny, these flowers are so delightful," I said as I walked into his living room.

"Thank you," he yelled from the bedroom. "You can take them with you after breakfast if you like."

John then walked out into the living room.

"What are *you* wearing?" I asked him. It was a thin white robe extending down to the floor. "Is that a Qyron robe?" I asked as I laughed. John looked so silly in it.

"Yeah, it's a Qyron robe. It's all the rage," he said as he did a mock runway walk with a serious face, and then a pirouette.

"Sure, if you're a kid."

I couldn't stop laughing. John always loved to get a good laugh, and, well, he was tickling me with this robe.

"Aw, come on; you're just … *Damn!* What the hell are *you* wearing?" John yelled as his mouth dropped open. "That outfit you have on leaves nothing to the imagination," John said as he continued to gawk at me.

I suddenly felt keenly aware of my wardrobe. I looked down in shock. He was right. The tight T-shirt with no bra was just reckless and stupid. I could have used my shirt as a sundial. My yoga pants had the appearance that they were spray painted on me. John's stare started to make me feel more than a little uncomfortable.

"Uh, yeah. Sorry. I don't know what I was thinking," I mumbled as I tried to puff my T-shirt a bit. "I should go back to my room and change."

"What? No!" John yelled out. "You're fine just like that," he said with a grin.

"Yeah, thanks, pig. No, I need to go back to my room and change." I took a step back toward the door.

"If you do," John said with a steady, serious tone, "then I'll eat all of the waffles."

I gave him a smile. He knew how much I loved waffles as a kid. I ate them every morning for six years in a row. He would always marvel at me when he would come over and join me for breakfast. I could eat a dozen waffles without stopping.

"Johnny, no, I really—"

"Come on; I love the outfit. Granted, it's a bit much for breakfast, but I'm eager to show off my new girlfriend."

He sauntered over to me and slid an arm around my waist. He pulled me close and gave me a soft, sensual kiss. He recoiled with a wrinkled nose.

"Ugh, you have morning breath."

"Oh my gosh, I'm so sorry, Johnny!"

I covered my mouth in shock and ran to his bathroom, where I found his mouthwash.

"Come on; I'm only playing with you. Besides, we're going to eat, so your breath will be better soon anyway!"

I didn't pay him any attention as I started to gargle. John walked into the bathroom. He grabbed me around my waist as I finished gargling.

I spit into the sink and then stood up. He spun me around and planted another steamy kiss on my lips. It was so sensual and exciting. I gently pushed him back.

"Look, we keep this up," I panted, "and we're going to miss breakfast. And you know how cranky I get when I'm hungry," I said with a smile.

John gave me a grin, nodded, and then turned and extended his arm. I locked my arm in his, and we walked together. He stopped at his room terminal and put a cleaning order in.

"There. I have to make sure that my room doesn't begin to smell like *your* place," he said with a chuckle.

We started talking as we walked down the hallway toward the dining hall. John was telling me about his dream from the previous night about two Venetian women when I heard a loud voice.

"What the hell is *that?*"

I looked ahead of us, at the entrance to the dining hall. Four men stood defiantly in a group. I slowed my pace, and John, who was busy relaying his dream to me, stopped talking and shot me a nervous look.

"Hey, you cross-breed bitch, you ain't welcome here!" said one man. He was tall and skinny with blonde hair and had tattoos up his arms. He took a defiant stance while he shot me a mean glare. I felt the hairs on my neck stand up, and my body tensed. John took a step forward and focused on the group of four men.

"That's right; leave, sugar glider!" another man yelled out. This one was wearing a brown T-shirt that had "sex machine" emblazoned on it. He was short, stocky, and hairy. I hated that slur. It always cut me to bone when I heard it. The eyes of the Qyron, large and angled, reminded people of the eerily large eyes of the sugar glider possum. It had become the slur of choice among racists, bigots, and, of course, the freedom groups. I felt myself begin to tremble from the inside—not from fear, as I knew I could beat every one of these men, but from ambivalence. My mother was Qyron. She always related to me that love and tolerance went hand in hand. To give in to hate was weakness—not the Qyron way. I couldn't dispel my seething feelings of disgust and hate for these bigots. They despised me for just being me, and that was too much for me to fathom—one of my human traits.

John took another step forward. He had a small grin on his face. I knew what this meant.

"Sex machine?" John said calmly. "You obviously stole that shirt from someone else, because it can't possibly be yours."

Two of the four men burst out laughing. Sex Machine swung his head to both sides, giving his compadres evil looks for laughing. This was John's strength. He was quick witted and never backed down from a good word fight. The problem was, he was rarely able to back up his words with his actions.

"Look," I said, "we just want to eat in peace, so if—"

"So go eat somewheres else, ya ugly sugar glider!" Sex Machine belted out.

"Wait," John interjected. "You're calling my woman ugly?" The tall, lanky blond man now started to step around us. "The only thing more disgusting than the thicket of hair sticking out of your nose are the tufts of hair shooting out of your ears."

The man to Sex Machine's left laughed out loud. He had a huge goofy smile and bright red hair.

"Hey, shut up!" Sex Machine said to him in disgust.

The tall man, Blondie, now lurched forward at John. At the same time, the red-haired man took a step toward me. In that instant, I saw my mother's face; I heard her thoughts. She never wanted me to fight, but she came to grasp the reality of growing up different on Earth. After I came into the house at age eight with yet another bloody lip, a torn dress, and a tear-streaked dirty face, my mother reached her limit. She finally allowed my father to enroll me in mixed martial arts classes. She always taught me that violence was never the answer, but when given no choice …

I threw a fast left jab that landed on Red's face. It stunned him and stopped his advance. He probably has no memory of the right uppercut I delivered in the next instant. It snapped his head back, and he crumpled unconscious to the floor. I knew Sex Machine had to be moving in on me, so I spun around hard, leading with my elbow. I was lucky in that he was, and my spinning elbow connected with his jaw. He sprawled to his right and stumbled at me again. I was already poised and gave him a front kick that shattered his jaw and sent him flailing backward onto his back. I turned to the fourth man, who stood frozen against the wall with his hands raised. The terror in his eyes told me he wasn't a threat.

I spun around in time to see John take a hard right from Blondie. I took a step in and closed his left eye with an overhand right. He fell back and slammed into the wall. A sickening yelp came out of his mouth as he lost all of his wind. I stepped into him and clutched his throat. I used every bit of strength I had and lifted him off his feet with my one arm.

"Amant, don't!" John yelled. I heard his words, but the fire and anger were coursing through my veins. I wanted vengeance at that moment. I was tired of being the victim through life, and he had just punched *my* man. I clutched his throat even tighter. He kicked his legs and clawed at my arm. I pulled him away from the wall and then slammed him hard into it. He fell unconscious, and I dropped his limp body to the ground. I turned quickly and surveyed the scene: Red was lying unconscious to my left. Sex Machine writhed in pain in front of me, weeping and spitting blood and broken teeth. The fourth man was now running away down the passageway, and Blondie was crumpled in a heap behind me.

John stepped over to me, eyes fixed on the scene.

"Are you okay?" he asked. I nodded as I continued to look over the bodies in front of me. Red lights broke my attention. Someone had set off the security alarm. I quickly turned to John.

"Give me your robe!" John gave me a stunned look. "Give it to me!" I quickly pulled it off of John and wrapped myself up in it. "Follow my lead; I'm a Qyron ambassador, and you're my translator."

John gave me a stunned nod as three men dressed in red defense suits ran down the hallway toward us. I pulled the robe on and the hood up over my head, covering my hair.

"You do all the talking, John!" I said as the three security men quickly ran up to us.

"What happened?" the lead guard said. His suit had a gold name tag with "Travis" on it. John gave me a smile and then turned to him.

"These three men attacked us, and Ambassador Shanea defended herself," John said as he rubbed the side of his face. A large red welt showed where John had taken the punch moments before. Travis, whose face was gruff and serious, then looked over at me. I turned my head slowly, eyes wide, and stared at him.

"Oh, uh, I'm sorry, ambassador. Please accept our apology for not responding sooner."

The other two guards were busy grabbing Sex Machine and handcuffing him. Red was now returning to consciousness.

"Rest assured that we will take care of this," Travis finished.

John flashed me a grin. A sudden sinking feeling hit my stomach. Now was certainly not the time for his wit.

"See that you do—Travis, is it? I'm very troubled by the fact that this could happen here," John said with his mock serious voice. I grabbed his arm and gave a squeeze while tugging him. I just wanted to leave. Besides, my stomach was twisting into knots from being empty and I didn't want further attention drawn to us. We should have been detained for fighting on board.

Travis turned back around to face John. "Again I apologize, sir. We had no communication that any diplomats were on board. I can attach a detail to the ambassador if you like."

John stiffened up. I could see the gears turning in his head. I tightened my grip on his arm.

"That sounds like a wonderful idea," John said with his chest out. I pinched the inside of his arm with my thumb and finger. "Ow! On second thought"—John gave me a pained look—"I think we will just limit our travels while on board."

I loosened my grip but continued to tug on John's arm.

"It's no trouble, sir; we'd be more than happy to provide proper security for you and the ambassador," Travis said.

I pulled John's arm. He stumbled and then gave me a panicked look.

"That's not necessary," John responded quickly as we began to walk away. "We appreciate the offer though," he said as we finally started down the passageway. Travis gave us a nod and then bent over to pick up Red. We hurried down the hallway and to the nearest lift.

"Oh my gosh, John," I said as we turned a corner, "I could have smacked you!"

John let out a laugh. "Are you kidding? That was a blast!"

I couldn't help but smile back. John always enjoyed getting us into trouble with his mouth. And I had to admit to myself that it felt good. I did enjoy fighting—especially when it was against someone who deserved it. It felt the same as it did when we were kids, except this time we were grown and I was much stronger and faster. But I recalled how it was usually John's lack of diplomacy that forced us into a fight. He missed his calling as a comedian.

As soon as we got on the lift, we both broke out laughing.

"I can't believe how fast you knocked them out," John said. "You're a lot stronger and faster now."

He pressed the button for Bravo Deck.

"Yes Johnny, I'm all grown up," I laughed. "I'm just glad you weren't hurt," I said through giggles. "That one guy was pretty scary looking."

"One? They were all uglier than sin!" John said. We both laughed harder. When the door opened, a few people were standing in wait. Their eyes grew large when I stepped out of the lift, and they took a few steps back. I continued with my acting, giving wide-eyed stares to the people. They averted their eyes as I did so.

As we walked down the passageway toward the dining hall, John finally said, "Okay, give me my robe back; you've had enough fun!"

I gave him a smile and then took the robe off. As I pivoted out of the robe, my breasts bounced in the skin-tight T-shirt. John gawked, and I felt self-conscious and embarrassed again.

"Eww, it's all warm and smells like girl," John said as he put the robe back on.

I gave him a smile. We spent the next half hour in the dining hall. I had a huge stack of waffles and an omelet. John did some oatmeal and a bowl of fruit. We chatted and laughed over the early morning's events. It really felt good to laugh and let loose. I felt better at this moment than I had in years. As I looked at John while he spoke, his eyes beamed and he had such a beautiful, boyish smile.

"What? What are you looking at?" John asked, spoon in hand as a dollop of oatmeal plopped back into the bowl.

"Oh, nothing," I whispered. "I was just enjoying listening to you," I said as I stood up.

John grabbed his tray. We dropped off our plates and glasses and then slowly walked, hand in hand, down the passageway. I listened to a story John related about a prank at work. It was delightful listening to how much effort he and his coworkers had put into this joke on another friend. He was so animated in his descriptions and quite emotional in his detailed explanations. As we reached the lift, I turned to John.

"Wait, where did you come up with the name Shanea?"

John smiled. "That was my grandmother's name. I just blanked out and pulled the first name I could think of." We both laughed as the door to the lift opened. We stepped in, and Brad was standing in the lift.

"Well hello, Amant, nice to see you again," Brad said.

I was speechless and in shock, feeling as if I had done something wrong. I guess it was because Brad had touched something primal inside me, and here he was, standing in a cramped elevator between me and my Johnny. I stood frozen for a moment. John turned as he entered the elevator and then looked at me.

"Oh, uh, hi, Brad. This is … um …"

John shot me a wide-eyed look. "*John!*"

I motioned my hand toward John. Brad was frozen, looking at my outfit. The tight T-shirt proudly displayed my breasts. I moved my hand quickly and shadowed my heaving cleavage.

"Uh, this is John, my boyfriend." I finally stated nervously.

Brad gave me a little smile and then slowly turned his gaze upon John. He extended his hand, and John shook it. Brad gave a cursory look at John's outfit, and his slight grin turned into a full smile.

"Are you two coming from a costume party?"

We all broke out in laughter—mine being more nervous than jovial.

"Oh no, sorry," I laughed. "We actually just threw some things on to have some breakfast."

"It looks like you did it in a hurry, because it seems he's wearing your clothes," Brad said, still laughing.

"Yeah, it was a rush," John said. "I'm wearing her panties too."

I quickly swatted John's arm. Brad stopped laughing. He looked again at John and then over to me.

"Did you do that to him?" He pointed to the now large red welt on the side of John's face.

"Oh, no. That was, uh, we actually just got into a fight," I said sheepishly.

"Oh really? How badly did you hurt them?" Brad asked, staring at me with an air of confidence.

"One of them won't be eating solid food for a while," John chimed in from the side. The elevator doors opened up on H Deck. The tone sounded, and the letter *H* glowed red.

"Is this your floor?" I asked softly. Brad smiled at me and then looked at John. He extended his hand and shook John's hand again.

"It was nice meeting you, John. Make sure you keep your arms up next time," Brad said as he took a step forward. He walked out into the passageway and then turned. "Nice seeing you again too, Amant." As the doors closed, he added, "Hey, John, you're a lucky man."

I hit the button for John's deck.

John stood silently behind me, arms folded with a small grin. I suddenly felt as if I were in the principal's office. I turned and gave him a pained smile. The lift moved quickly through the letters until we reached John's deck. The doors opened, and I took a few steps out. As we cleared the elevator, John grabbed my hand.

"And?" he said, breaking the uncomfortable silence. "And don't you dare come back with, 'And what?'"

I gave him a little smile as he pulled me to a stop in the corridor. I took both his hands in mine. Two people walked by us, and I waited a moment until they were out of earshot. I took a deep breath.

"It's nothing, really, John. I met Brad in the gym twice. He was posturing for his buddies and approached me. The second time, I was in the gym and thought I was alone. He came up and gave me some help. That's it, John—honest."

John looked down for a moment, nodding. He then peered back up at me.

"I'll be nice with you," John said as he started to walk again.

I skipped to catch up to him. He still had a smile. I grabbed his hand as we walked. We soon reached his door. As he opened it, I asked him, "You'll be, John? You'll be nice, what?" I was intrigued.

He turned in the open doorway.

"I know something happened," John began. "I can see it on your face. But you don't want to share, and, well, I'm okay with that. I know that Brad was just trying to start something, in hopes that he'd have a chance with you. I won't give him that satisfaction; nor will I torture you any further," he said solemnly as he walked into his room.

"John, wait!" I yelled out.

I joined him in his living room, standing alongside the couch.

"Okay, yes, he did kiss me," I admitted to him, peering down at my feet.

"Did you kiss him back?" John rebounded quickly, softly.

I drew my eyes back up to meet his.

"No, I didn't. I pulled away; I protested. I left, John. Honest."

John just stared back at me for what felt like hours.

"John?" I implored.

John leaned in and kissed me. He grabbed me tightly. I kissed him back, passionately, over and over.

"I'm sorry, John," I whispered.

"Shh!" John replied loudly. I shuddered in surprise.

John gently tapped my nose with his index finger, which he then held up, indicating for me to wait a minute.

He gave me the faintest of smiles and then leaned over and grabbed something from his table.

"Turn around," he commanded softly.

I turned around. He stepped in close behind me. His hands came around me.

"Close your eyes," he stated in a whisper.

I closed them. I felt a soft, silky cloth drape over my eyes; then it was pulled around my head and gently tightened. I heard him walk around me, and then he grabbed my hand.

"Follow me," he said softly.

I took a deep breath in. I felt electric—tingly all over. I took a few steps forward and felt his hand pull me hard to the left. I knew from memory we were entering his bedroom. He walked me to the edge of his bed and gently laid me down on my stomach. I heard him walk around the side of the bed. Smooth soundscape music then filled the room. I heard birds chirping and the gentle wash of a babbling brook. Soft violins then joined in. While I was listening to the music, John moved around the other side of the bed.

I felt his hand slide under my shirt at my waist. A soft *ssskkkkk* accompanied his hand as he moved it up my back. My shirt tugged slightly and was then opened up, exposing my whole back.

"John, did you—"

"*Shh!*" he scolded.

My cut shirt now splayed open, exposing my back. The cooler temperature in the room now sent a shiver up my spine. No sooner had the goose bumps arrived than John's hands, hot with wetness, began to stroke my back. The sensation of heat stunned me for a moment but felt delicious. His hands slid slowly over my back. The fragrance of aloe and cucumber washed over me. The hot oil felt so good. I moaned as John rubbed deeper into the muscles of my back. He kneaded and stroked my back, putting me deeper and deeper at rest and into bliss. It must have been a solid half hour of his smooth hands working my back.

He then moved his hands to my waist and grabbed the top of my yoga pants.

"Arch your butt up, please," he said calmly. I raised up as he rolled my pants down. In seconds, they were off of me. Again I felt a chill over my now naked buttocks and legs. Only seconds passed, though, before more hot oil was gently splashed over my legs and thighs.

"Ooh," I cooed. John followed the oil with his hands. I luxuriated as he massaged my legs, thighs, and feet. John was so meticulous but gentle. The only sounds in the room were of nature, violins, and my occasional moans.

When he finally finished, I felt calm, relaxed, and completely in his power. John fumbled with something at the bedside. I then heard the unmistakable *poink* of a cork being removed from a bottle. The gentle *glug glug* soon followed. John's hands were then upon me. He pushed on one side and pulled on the other, rolling me over. His right arm then pulled me into a sitting position. As I was about to speak, his lips met mine.

We kissed several times, slowly and lovingly. John pulled away for only a moment. His lips touched mine again briefly; then there was the cool feel of the rim of a glass.

"Drink," he whispered. I opened my mouth, and a cool bubbly sensation tickled my tongue. I paused, swished it, and then swallowed.

"Mmm, champagne," I said. "I love it."

John gave me another swig. He then took a moment. I heard a few sounds; the most distinguished was the sound of a liquid splashing. A minute later, John returned to the bed. He grabbed me tightly and kissed me. I suddenly felt his naked body lower atop mine. The waft of hot oil on him was strong as his body slid over mine.

"I am going to take you now," he whispered in my ear as his hands removed my blindfold.

He couldn't have been more wrong; you cannot take that which is given freely. I welcomed him in every way: his nibbling, kissing, and caressing. We made love for two solid hours. It was more fulfilling than I could have ever imagined. I had been with three other men in my life, but each of those times was either hurried, awkward, or wholly unfulfilling. This was nothing short of a fairy tale—an adult fairy tale, of course.

"Oh my God, John," I panted heavily. Beads of sweat ran down my forehead. "I have never ... how?"

John rolled over to me and gave me another soft kiss.

"I've been waiting a decade to make love to you, Amant. To say that I've planned this day in my head a thousand times would be a painful understatement."

He laid his hot, sweaty chest alongside mine. I felt him breathing heavily as his chest heaved.

"That was amazing ... incredible. I can't believe ..." I said, panting as I wiped my face.

John bombarded me with soft kisses on my lips.

"I just wanted to convey what you've been missing all of these years—how much I love you, Amant."

I clutched John close. I didn't want this moment to end, ever. As my breathing slowed, I slowly ran the past few hours over in my head. I think I got to about ten minutes into it before I drifted off.

I awoke to the sound of running water. I opened my eyes and looked around. The bedroom was empty, and the lights were off; there was only a streak of light coming from the crack in the doorway. I sat up and swung my legs to the ground. I felt so relaxed that I actually had to make an effort to stand. I was twenty-six, and yet I grunted to get up. I looked at the nightstand, the bottle of champagne stood guard. I grabbed it and walked out of the bedroom. The shower was running, so I slinked into the bathroom. I stepped into the shower behind John, bottle in hand.

"Ah, welcome back," John said with a smile. He turned around and gave me a kiss. He then grabbed the bottle and chugged while I stepped into the stream of hot water. The water beaded up, fighting the massage oils.

"You have the cutest little snore," he said. "I just listened to you sleep for a good twenty minutes."

I lathered up my chest. "How long was I out?"

John placed the bottle down outside the shower.

"It had to be an hour. I left the bedroom over a half hour ago and sent some messages and did a few things for work and decided to shower."

I peered at John's body. He had a very nice physique. He wasn't overly muscular, but he had a nicely defined body with abs and a chest. He also had the cutest little butt; it jiggled when he laughed.

"I don't mind your sweaty body, Johnny," I said as I gave him a kiss. He spun me around and lathered up my back. As his hands slid down my sides, he tickled me. I jumped up and laughed.

"Ah, such an intoxicating giggle," he said.

We finished the shower, and then John gave me a new T-shirt and some shorts. We sat down at the couch and talked for a while. I told him some of what I had witnessed about Jennifer. He gave me some details about his new job.

"So, John"—I looked deeply into his eyes—"where do we go from here?"

John gave me a pensive look. He took my hand in his.

"I'm not sure. We have plenty of options, though. But the only one that will make me happy is the one that has us together as much as possible."

I gave John a puzzeled look.

"Then there's really only one option, John. You just come with me as I do my job. I make plenty of money, so that will never be an issue. The question is, can you be happy not working?"

John shook his head. "As I said, as long as we're together. But why with me not working? I would actually like to finish my work on my psychology degree; then I could do therapy. Granted, we'd be moving from place to place, but I'm sure I could do something."

I gave John a hug. "You've done wonders with me, so why not?"

We spent the next few hours curled up on the couch together. After watching a few movies, we decided to have some dinner. This time the meal was uneventful—no fights with bigots, no bumping into Brad. It was peaceful, calm, and quite delicious.

On the walk back to John's room from dinner, John yawned twice.

"Did I tire you out?" I said with a smile.

"Yes, yes, you did. But *one* of us had a nap afterward, I might add."

"Oh, sure, put that in my face. What kind of worthless therapist does that?"

I laughed, slapped his arm, and ran down the passageway. John gave chase. He caught me as I reached his door. He grabbed me tightly and kissed me. A couple walked down the passageway and smiled as they passed. John opened his door and scooped me up into his arms. He stepped heavily as we entered his room. He huffed as we approached the living room, and halfway to the bedroom he finally had to drop me. I landed softly on my feet, but John was breathing heavily and looked exhausted.

"Sorry, Johnny, you know us Qyron."

"Yeah," John panted. "A lot heavier. Yeah, I get it."

"I'm two forty-five, Johnny, but I carry it well," I giggled. John flashed me a smile. "I guess someone needs to get to the gym more often, eh? No worries; I would love to have a workout buddy."

I wiggled my butt and gave him a devilish little smile. I then sauntered into his bedroom.

John wasted no time in catching up. In fact, he didn't seem to miss a step for the next hour. We made passionate love again. This time it was without massage oils, but it was no less of an incredible experience.

"Oh, Johnny, where have you been hiding?" I whispered. I realized the irony of my statement and waited for John's response.

"In your dreams, of course," he replied softly.

I rolled over and kissed him, happy that he didn't mention that it was I who had been hiding for the past ten years.

"Johnny, I love you," I whispered, and I kissed him again.

"I have always loved you Amant. And I will continue loving you, till the day I die."

He kissed me and then yawned. I giggled.

"You are *so* romantic," I laughed. "So I really have tired you out, eh?"

John blushed. "Computer, Earth-relative Eastern Standard Time."

A tone sounded. "11:42 p.m." was the response.

"Oh, sorry, Johnny; it's way past your bedtime. Does that mean you need a spanking?" I laughed. Johnny laughed along with me.

"Yes, mama, please," John said, and then he yawned again.

I gave Johnny one more kiss and then sat up.

"How about I let you sleep, Johnny? I'll head back to my place and do a little more Psy-logging. It seems Jennifer is nearing a meaningful relationship."

John rolled over. He had a smile on his face.

"So in these logs,"—John rolled up on one elbow and gave me a curious look—"if the person has sex ..."

"Yes, Johnny, you're right there along with them, experiencing it all: every kiss, every smell, and, of course, the orgasm," I replied. "Normally these are edited out by the person, but I guess Jennifer didn't know, being the first person to have the implant."

"Sucks that you're blogging a woman, eh?" John burst out laughing. I dived at him and tickled his sides. He writhed and kicked under the sheets.

"Ah! Stop!" he yelled through the laughter. "Oh please!" he giggled. I finally stopped.

"Careful there, funny man; I'm stronger than you!" I said, laughing.

I grabbed John's robe and cinched it on. John rolled over and crawled over to me, still laughing. He got up on his knees and gave me a final kiss.

"Okay, love, I'll give you a shout when I wake up."

"Good night, Johnny." I kissed him again, and he lay down in bed. When I got to his front door, I said, "lights off" and walked out.

When I got back to my room, I walked in and looked at the monitor. It now displayed two administrative messages. The last one demanded my information. I punched my name and government ID into the panel. It honked at me and came back with "denied." If this wasn't the strangest of things.

"Who the hell are you to deny me?" I yelled. A tone sounded, followed by "please restate" from the computer. I tried my name and ID number again, and twice it came back with "denied" on the monitor.

I walked over to the couch and sat down. I must have taken at least a few hundred transport trips in my lifetime. At no point had my ID ever been questioned. Heck, at no point had I ever traveled in anything but the very best of accommodations. This now begged the question, why was this transport so different from all of the rest? Why had that hairy troll at the ticket counter been unable to enter me on this transport, and why had it kicked back my entry when I came aboard? My mind raced as I tried to think of a logical reason. I got back up and walked over to the monitor.

"Computer, link to administration on the bridge please," I said.

A tone sounded, and a voice stated, "Unable to comply."

"What? *How the hell...* How are you unable to comply?"

Another tone sounded, and then I heard "No administrators are logged in."

Now I was thoroughly confused. *How is it possible that there are no administrators logged in? Who's flying this thing?*

"Computer, who is the captain on this transport?"

A tone sounded. "No captain is logged in." I sat stupefied for a moment. Every transport I'd taken had a full complement on board. There was a staff of at least five flight crew, several engineers, doctors, and security. I know that we had security on this ship, and I'd seen workers in my room cleaning, but we didn't have any flight staff?

I remembered watching classic cartoons as a child. One of my favorites was *Scooby-Doo, Where Are You!*. I could use that Mystery Machine and those meddling kids at this point. I was tempted to walk to the bridge and see what the reasons were, but I figured I'd wait until John was awake. It's always better to have help when you're trying to solve a mystery. For now, though, I needed to take my mind off of this; otherwise I would go nuts rolling it over in my head.

I went to the kitchen and grabbed a flavored water. I drank it down quickly. I guess all the lovemaking had dehydrated me more than I thought. I snatched my headset and sat down on the couch. *Okay, only eight hours*, I told myself. I put the headset on. There was a bright light and some hissing.

Chapter 17

July 26, 2021

Jennifer strolled into the White House. Rachel was on her heels.

"I want a report showing our progress globally. I would like to present this every Monday from now on," Jennifer stated. "I'm also curious to see a list of the demands for our time. We need to schedule more clustered time lines. Xho is pushing harder to have longer days, but we're holding firm at twelve hours."

They approached the central meeting room. Rachel nodded and then ran off to get to a copier. Jennifer spotted Taylor at the table, chatting with the secretary of defense. She gave him a look and a nod. Taylor broke away and came over to her.

"How was your weekend?" she asked

"It was good," Taylor said, "but I would have liked to have seen you again."

Jennifer smiled. "Yeah, me too. Sorry, I got a little wrapped up in a few things. Um, how would you like to come over for dinner, say, Friday night?"

Taylor smiled and nodded. "That sounds good. Oh, will your chaperone be in attendance?" he said with a grin.

Jennifer smiled back. "No, Tank won't be around; he's off this Friday."

Taylor nodded and then pointed to the table. "We need to get started," he said.

They walked into the room and mingled with the rest of the crowd.

A minute later, the president joined the room and the loud conversations quickly died away. As Kennedy took his seat, Taylor stood up.

"This week's good news starts with a total of over two hundred thousand lives saved in the US and over three million globally. We could officially announce that starvation and undernourishment of the human race have been eradicated."

Stunned looks came from everyone around the room. Taylor panned the room with a growing look of amazement.

"Hello, is this thing on?" Taylor tapped the microphone. "We've eliminated hunger worldwide, people!" Taylor said loudly.

The president stood up and began to clap, and the room then erupted in applause. After a minute, the applause died down, the president sat back down, and Taylor continued.

"I know it's Monday, but come on; let's look lively out there." Many laughs followed. Taylor looked over and gave Jennifer a smile. His face glowed, and his eyes sparkled.

He has such a warmth about him now, Jennifer thought.

"To continue, we now have the beginning of production in commercial and residential heating and cooling systems run by Qyron technology. They run at 1 percent of the energy of current systems and have an estimated two-hundred-year lifespan of operation."

Taylor turned to the secretary of energy. "This will decrease electricity demand about 55 percent across the board."

More smiles and applause filled the room. Taylor beamed as he took a brief break. He looked far more calm and composed, lacking the nervousness he had shown last week.

"We're also noting more urban building replacements. Philadelphia and Atlanta are now completed. sixty-five city blocks have been replaced in both cities. The homeless population is still present, but it seems that homeless from surrounding areas have migrated to these cities, looking for the newly available housing. The Qyron have now focused on New York City, Los Angeles, Detroit, Chicago, Dallas, and Oakland. About thirty other cities globally are also undergoing similar changes." Taylor flipped a page. "Besides mining the asteroid belt, ten percent of the Earth-crossing asteroids have been eliminated. We have 6 percent unemployment; that's down 1.5 percent in one week."

The room erupted in mixed banter. The president stood up, and the room came to a hush.

"How is that possible?" Kennedy asked.

The secretary of commerce spoke up. "With the Qyron technology, they've been able to fill about a half million jobs a day. They've linked in with our databases and are able to screen and employ people within seconds. They have small notebook-style computers that contain all job procedures, policies, and frequently asked questions. Even their small work craft are fully automated. Many workers have four-day work weeks and sleep in space stations around their work areas. You have to see it to believe it." The president smiled and nodded. "They still have tens of millions of jobs to be filled," the commerce secretary finished.

Taylor then continued. "Progress on Mars and Venus as colonies continues. The atmospheric conversion on Venus is working; overall global temperature has dropped forty degrees, and more gasses are being added to the planet daily. The Qyron are setting up for a, uh …" He gave a look to Jennifer, who stood up and walked over to the lectern. Xho joined her.

"The Qyron have a method of infusing dark energy to the planet's core. This will cause an increase in density, gravity, and heat. The added heat will liquefy the core of Mars and establish a solid magnetic field. This will allow plants and animals to live on the planet, which will now be protected from the sun's harmful radiation. The same will be performed on Venus, but not until the surface temperature is lowered." Jennifer smiled and returned to her seat.

"Our own planet's atmosphere is now 3 percent cleaner, with a noted reduction in carbon," Taylor continued. "The Qyron are also ready to implement 'well care' to everyone who wants it." Taylor turned to Jennifer again, who stepped back up to the microphone.

"The project Well Care is actually an injection of Meibots. They are a sentient race of microscopic robots that the Qyron initially designed five hundred thousand years ago. Their purpose is to perform medical and restorative procedures. They became a sentient race about fifty thousand years after their initial design. They have since coexisted peacefully with the Qyron. The injection itself comprises about 1 billion to 500 billion Meibots who are given specific duties inside the target body. They can be programmed to adjust DNA, remove toxins, and repair any muscle, bone, or tissue damage."

A slight murmur of conversations now erupted.

Tom Franklin, the secretary of state, then stood up. "With all due respect, how do we know this is safe?"

Jennifer looked over to Xho and nodded.

"It's been over four hundred thousand years," Jennifer stated, "that these micro robots have been working with the Qyron and all plants and animals with no deaths and no side effects."

Tom nodded. "Okay, so what do these Meibots get in return?"

Jennifer turned to Xho and then back. "The Qyron provided them with a habitable moon, which they colonized. The Qyron furnished them with all of the metals and resources that they would need. It's been a peaceful coexistence, like I said, for over four hundred thousand years. The Meibots, like the Qyron, enjoy doing work and are duty bound."

Tom sat back down, slowly nodding in acceptance.

"I was given an injection when I was abducted. They removed lead and mercury from my body, as well as fixing previous injuries I had. They even brought my appendix back." The crowd laughed. "Yeah, they didn't know any better."

When the room went silent, Jennifer continued.

"Anyone who would like the injection, it's basically like getting a shot. The only difference is that the injection tube, which initially glows red, is left on the body for as long as it takes the Meibots to complete their work. When they're done, the tube glows green and is removed. The Meibots are then returned home."

Taylor nodded to Jennifer, and she sat back down in her seat.

"I have the latest poll on Qyron acceptance. At present, 2 percent of the population approves of the Qyron, 28 percent are undecided, and 68 percent are in doubt." Taylor flipped over another paper. He then looked to the secretary of the treasury, Mary Wilson.

Mary stood up. "I'm proud to announce that we've negotiated a currency rate with the Qyron. One US dollar will equal one Qyron bill. Since the Qyron haven't used currency in over three hundred thousand years, they had to set a standard for their goods and services. I will give the facts and figures to Taylor to add to the website. As a side note, for those people who have the mining jobs in the asteroid belt, they're being paid one hundred twenty thousand dollars a year."

The room erupted in chatter.

Mary smiled. "Yes, the Qyron pay very well."

The president smiled and nodded.

Taylor then stepped forward. "That certainly can't hurt come reelection time, eh?" The room erupted in laughter.

Taylor then raised his hand, and the room died back down to silence.

"On the needs improvement list"—he gave a look to Kennedy Myers—"we still have an active suicide rate that's being attributed to the Qyron alliance. The vice president is meeting with some resistance in a few Midwestern states. The marches in cities have begun to lessen, however," Taylor looked at Lance Meyer, secretary of homeland security.

Lance walked up to the lectern. "With our current assistance from the FBI, we have now identified no fewer than thirty solid anti-Qyron groups. Many of them seem to be armed and disorganized, but that's changing by the day. They've been able to secure more weapons and recruit more terrorists than we can keep up with. There have been several skirmishes with our marine detachments that are providing security to the Qyron. Last week, seven marines were injured and one was killed."

The president stood up.

"One is one too many," he said loudly. "How are we progressing with developing defensive devices?"

Taylor piped up. "We have several ideas, but we're a few weeks away from testing anything yet."

"I want maximum attention and effort put into this. We need to ensure that the Qyron and my marines are kept safe, so whatever it takes, are we clear on that?"

Lance nodded and then sat back down.

"We're also getting pushback from the oil industry, namely OPEC. They see the writing on the wall, and in a few years, if not sooner, oil will be worthless. We have also heard reports, as the secretary of state briefed earlier, that some Middle Eastern countries are now starting to open a dialogue with the Freedom Alliance of North Korea, Russia, and China."

The president stood up. "Anything else?"

"Isn't that enough?" Taylor responded with a smile. A few chuckles rang out.

After several seconds, the president nodded to Taylor. "Yes, that's plenty."

The meeting adjourned, and everyone immediately began chatting among one another.

Jennifer walked by Taylor. "See you at 6:00 p.m. Friday," she said as she continued walking. She spent another half hour discussing topics with several secretaries and then finally boarded a transport at 10:00 a.m.

Jennifer spent the rest of Monday in Detroit and Los Angeles brokering business deals. Tuesday was a full day in Japan, and Wednesday found the team in Chile and Brazil.

Thursday morning, Rachel didn't join the group for breakfast. Jennifer called her phone. No answer. As they finished their breakfast in the hotel restaurant, Rachel stepped off of the elevator. She walked slowly and somewhat unsteadily toward Jennifer.

"Ugh, I so don't feel good this morning," she slurred groggily.

Jennifer could smell liquor on her breath and spied the ink stamp on the back of her wrist. She also noticed Rachel was wearing the same outfit she had worn the previous day.

"What's the problem?" Jennifer asked.

Rachel peered at Jennifer, her eyes bloodshot. "I just feel a little sick; I'm going to try to keep up though." She walked into the dining area, being passed by Xho and the agents. "I'm going to grab some food; I'll meet you all in just a minute." She tried giving a smile, but it fooled no one.

On the way back to the transport, one of the agents leaned in to Jennifer.

"Is it me, or does it seem like she got no sleep last night?"

Jennifer just nodded and maintained a stoic look. After they were seated on the transport for several minutes, Rachel finally joined them. She had a cup of coffee in one hand and a cherry danish in the other. They lifted off from Sao Paulo, Brazil, and landed in Mexico City within minutes. As they stepped out of the transport, Rachel made it ten steps before getting sick in the parking lot. Jennifer pulled Rachel aside before their first meeting.

"Rachel, I can't have you hungover like this!" Jennifer whispered angrily to her.

"I'm not; I just—"

"Don't bullshit me. You reek of booze, you're wearing yesterday's clothing, and you still have the nightclub stamp on your hand. I need you right and ready, Rachel!"

"Jennifer, I'm sorry," Rachel pleaded. Her hair was unkempt and smelled of smoke. "I promise this is the last time that you'll ever have this problem with me again. I know I messed up." She paused a moment. "I drank too much. Please, give me another chance."

Rachel grabbed Jennifer's hand, her bloodshot eyes pleading.

"Get yourself together, and let's just finish out the week. We'll talk about this later," Jennifer fumed in disgust.

The rest of the day went without issue. They spent Friday in Canada and Newfoundland. Their transport arrived back in Washington, DC, a half hour early. When the doors opened, Rachel stepped out of the transport with Jennifer close behind.

At that moment, Xho thought out to Jennifer, *This is for you.* Xho extended an envelope for Jennifer.

Jennifer grabbed the envelope and looked inside. It was a check from the Qyron to Jennifer Winston for $675,000. Jennifer stared at it for a moment.

"What's this?" she said in shock.

We apologize for taking three weeks to finalize a currency. This is for all past transactions you have assisted with. We will pay you $125,000 US per Earth week.

Jennifer stood speechless. An agent finally stepped alongside her and nudged her.

"Are you okay, ma'am?"

Jennifer turned to him, mouth open, and nodded.

"Xho, this is too much; I don't know if I can—"

Your services are invaluable to us and your people. This is final.

Xho gave her a smile and a nod, and he then closed the door to the transport and lifted off. Jennifer turned around and slowly walked back to the White House with the two agents. Rachel was already inside. Jennifer slowly placed the envelope in her purse. As she walked into the White House, an aide flagged her down.

"The president wishes to speak with you, Jennifer," the aide said. Jennifer slowly followed him to the oval office, still awestruck.

The president was busy with some discussions. He caught Jennifer's entrance and gave her a cursory wave.

"Okay, let's get that done, Jerry," the president said. "Jennifer, how was your week?"

Jennifer walked over to the president. "It was busy, sir, and I uh ..." Jennifer lost her focus.

"Are you okay?" The president leaned over and touched her shoulder.

"Oh, sorry. Yes, I'm fine, sir. I was just processing something."

"Please have a seat, Jennifer." The president sat down after Jennifer took her seat. "We've had some increasing threats this week—some here in the US, and others abroad. I know that the local governments you visit provide some police and military protection, but I'm going to add a small detachment of marines to your group. I've already cleared this with the Qyron and many of the governments that are in alliance with the Qyron."

Jennifer flashed him a stunned look. "I thought that we were doing okay?" she mumbled.

"Well"—the president leaned back in his chair—"we are making progress every day. However, there is a growing number of scared people who are too ignorant, too defeated, to understand the progress. It will take time. But until then, I will feel more secure with your party's full protection."

He leaned forward in his chair.

Jennifer sat bewildered. She nodded blindly and then stood up.

"Are you sure that you're okay, Jennifer?"

Jennifer was staring blankly at a statue of an eagle on the president's desk. She snapped her attention back to the president and gave him a half-hearted smile.

"Yes, I'm sorry, sir. It's just been a busy week; I'm drained ..." Her voice trailed off.

"I see that, and it's understandable. I'm glad to see that you're adjusting well. Do you need anything else: more staff, an office, or a pay raise?" the president asked with a smile.

"Uh, I may be able to use another staff member. I also have a few issues to resolve, so I'll talk with Taylor about it," Jennifer responded as she stared at a painting on the wall.

"I see you're not paying attention," the president mused. "You didn't even respond to my comment about raising your pay."

Jennifer turned her attention back to the president as he opened a drawer in his desk and pulled out a large file. He handed it over to Jennifer.

"Here, this packet is for you. We have an account set up for you at that bank."

Jennifer thumbed through the banking package.

"Your pay will be one hundred twenty-five thousand dollars a year. This is just a start, as we have no reference for this job. We also have a complete HR package. I was going to have Ross, our HR person, discuss this with you, but I wanted to make sure you were happy with the pay."

Jennifer gave him an uncomfortably blank stare.

"Uh, yeah, that's fine, sir. But the Qyron are also paying me; is that legal?"

Kennedy laughed. "You are precious," he said through more laughter. "So the Qyron are paying you too? Yes, that does actually cross a line." He stood up, still laughing. "I think you're the only person in Washington to actually step forward and admit that."

Kennedy slowly walked around his desk to face Jennifer.

"Jennifer, you're doing some of the most important work for humanity and, well, for the Qyron too. So why not get paid by both? The law was actually meant for other reasons. I'll draft up a new law and have it pushed through." He peered down at Jennifer. She still looked bewildered and tired. "My guess is that you're dealing with more than you're willing to share." He placed a finger under her chin and gently raised it up so her eyes met his. "Take some time for yourself this weekend. Relax and enjoy the area. Recharge your batteries and be back on Monday, okay?"

The president gently patted her on the back and walked her to the door. As she walked down the hallway, Taylor stepped out in front of her as he was leaving another room.

"Oh!" Taylor said with surprise. "There you are."

"Yeah, here I am," Jennifer mumbled. "Tired and so glad it's Friday."

Taylor smiled and then walked with Jennifer.

"I have a few things to finish up here, but I can be by your apartment in an hour if you're still up for dinner," he whispered.

Jennifer sighed. "Yeah, dinner will be good. Maybe I'll take some of the time you're going to be here to grab a nap."

She peered over at Taylor. He gave her a reassuring smile.

"It's a date then," Taylor said as he stopped.

Jennifer smiled and continued walking. Taylor walked back to the room, opened the door, and gave her a wave as he walked back inside.

Jennifer joined her agents and rode back to the apartment. When she stepped into her room, she walked right into the bedroom and plopped down on the bed. She was asleep in minutes.

A half hour later, she stirred awake. Jennifer stretched and stepped off the bed, feeling rejuvenated. She slowly walked out into the kitchen, opened the freezer, and checked on the meats. There were a few steaks, but she really felt like Italian. She grabbed some hamburger and tossed it into the microwave to defrost. The refrigerator was nicely stocked with vegetables, so she started cleaning them in the sink. The phone rang as she dropped the carrots and celery into a large bowl.

"Hello?"

"Miss Winston, this is Tony. I have Taylor to see you."

"Yes, that's fine, thank you." Jennifer's heart raced. She ended the call and quickly rinsed the rest of the vegetables. A knock on the door came a few moments later. Jennifer ran and opened it.

Taylor stood in the doorway. He was wearing a tan dress shirt with a bright red tie. She could smell his cologne. She gave him a large smile.

"Am I too early?" he asked as he took a step inside.

"No, I was just—"

Taylor stepped in close and gave Jennifer a kiss. He closed the door and slowly backed her against the wall, kissing her deeply. His hands grabbed her waist, and she threw her arms around his neck. They kissed for another minute, and then Taylor pulled back.

"You're all I've been thinking about this week," he said in a deep voice.

Jennifer was panting. She pulled him close and kissed him again. "Yeah, me too," she said between kisses.

Taylor finally stepped back. He loosened his tie and pulled it over his head.

"Even with the day as busy as it was, I could only smile knowing that I'd see you tonight," Taylor said as he placed his tie over Jennifer's head. She could smell his cologne on the tie as he draped it loosely around her neck. "It looks good on you. I love the bright ruby red; it matches your lips." He brought his hand up under her chin and then kissed her softly. "So what can I help with in the kitchen?" Taylor took a few steps toward the sink.

"I was washing the veggies for a salad. I have meat thawing in the microwave for meatballs. Spaghetti sound good?"

"It sounds delicious," Taylor said as he stepped to the refrigerator. He opened the door and checked the shelves. As Jennifer returned to the veggies in the sink, Taylor pulled out a bottle of red wine.

"This is a very fine wine; you have such good taste," he said smoothly.

Jennifer blushed and gave him a smile. She then turned and started to brush the carrots and broccoli in the sink. Taylor quietly walked up behind her. He spooned her body as she was leaning over the sink. She felt his body press tightly against hers; then his hand slipped around her waist. She gave out a moan, and he gently pulled her hair back. She felt his hot breath against the nape of her neck; his scruff tickled her. She giggled, and he kissed her neck passionately.

Taylor released his hold on Jennifer. "I know what I'm having for dessert," he said as he walked over to the refrigerator again.

Jennifer gave him a cozy little smile. As she began to cut up the veggies, Taylor pulled out a few more items from the fridge. He began cutting up zucchini, onions, and green peppers, and he then added them to a sauce pan on the stove. When Jennifer finished preparing the salad, Taylor added his sautéed veggies to the sauce.

"There, that ought to spice up that bland sauce," Taylor said as he rinsed his hands. The food was now simmering on the stove. With a few minutes to kill, they sat down on the couch in the living room.

"This is a nice, cozy little place you have here," Taylor said as he gazed around the room.

Jennifer cuddled up close to him. "Yes, it's more than I could have hoped for," she said as she laid her head in his lap. He gently stroked her hair and traced his finger around her face.

"So how was your week?" he whispered.

Jennifer purred as he continued to caress her face. "Ooh, it was stressful, I'm just glad it's over," she mumbled.

"Why so stressful?" Taylor asked. Jennifer just grumbled and rolled over. "Was it the diplomats? The politicians?" Taylor shifted and now massaged her shoulders. "Was it Rachel?"

Jennifer tensed up.

"I see," Taylor said as he pressed harder on her shoulders. "What's the problem?"

The sound of loud hissing now emanated from the kitchen. Jennifer sat up.

"I don't want to talk about it," she said as she stood up. More splattering and hissing noises sounded as Jennifer trotted to the kitchen.

"Maybe I can help," Taylor said as he pursued her into the kitchen. "Sometimes talking about an issue—"

"I think I'm going to have to fire Rachel," Jennifer said as she turned off the burner for the sauce. It was bubbling and splattering on the burner.

Taylor reached for the dinner plates.

"Whoa, fire Rachel?" Taylor turned and faced Jennifer. "What's wrong?"

"She's partying too much. She spent half a day last week hungover."

"Mmm. Yes, that is a problem." He stood for a moment, contemplating. "We all indulge a little too much from time to time though," he replied as he handed the plates to Jennifer. "She's young; she's learning."

Jennifer strained out the spaghetti.

"It's more than that," she replied, "She's also becoming insubordinate."

"Wow, insubordinate. McDonald's teach you that?" Taylor said with a grin. Jennifer flashed him an angry look. "Sorry, I was just trying to—"

"It's just that the days are stressful enough, what with the traveling and all of the meetings and—"

"It's a learning experience," Taylor interrupted. "She's young, and this is all new to her."

Jennifer was plating out the spaghetti when she stopped.

"We're the same damn age!"

Taylor paused a moment and then took a step toward Jennifer. He leaned in close.

"Yes, but you're more mature. You've handled this transition better than anyone."

He placed his hands on her shoulders and began to massage them. She moaned as he rubbed the muscle knots in her shoulders. Jennifer's tense, angry expression melted away as he kneaded out the pain. Taylor grabbed the bowls and the salad and walked to the coffee table.

"Yeah, well," Jennifer shouted out, "I don't think we should show any unprofessional behavior to the world." She finished plating out the spaghetti and sauce. As she walked back to the living room with the plates, Taylor grabbed the bottle of wine.

"Agreed, but I think you should give Rachel more time. She'll come around. Besides, we can't afford the time to train another person right now."

They sat down at the couch and enjoyed a delicious meal while watching a movie. The long, stressful week; the large meal; the comfy couch; and the heat from Taylor's chest all combined to put Jennifer to sleep. As the movie ended, Taylor gently lifted her head from of his chest. He slowly slid around her and lifted her up into his arms. Grunting and panting, he carried her into the bedroom and softly laid her down upon the bed.

Jennifer stirred awake.

"I fell asleep," she said groggily.

He smiled and leaned in, placing a kiss on her lips. He continued to kiss her as he removed his shirt.

"Mmm, no, wait," Jennifer whispered.

Taylor continued to kiss her; his hands tenderly massaged her chest. He then slowly unbuttoned her blouse. Jennifer's heart was pounding. Taylor's kisses were so smooth, so loving. She really wanted him, but she felt this was moving too quickly. He lay down alongside her. Her hand brushed along his side; he was completely naked.

"No, I don't think ..." she said as he continued to kiss her.

He turned his head and breathed into her ear. Goose bumps sprang up. He licked and nibbled on her neck. She moaned and arched her back slightly. She felt his hand on the zipper to her skirt.

"Taylor, no."

She moved her hand down, but he grabbed it and pulled it up. He kissed her faster and more passionately. His other hand now massaged her chest. Her whole body tingled, and she writhed under him. With one hand, he held both her wrists up over her head. His mouth was on her neck again. She was on fire as he licked and sucked. A loud moan escaped her lips, and she felt her zipper pull down. Her head was spinning; he was so hot, so sexy—so passionate. She let herself go for a moment, enjoying the sensations. As she looked up at Taylor, he was now kneeling over the top of her. Her skirt was off and her panties removed.

"Taylor, no, wait, I …" she said as he lowered himself down.

A half hour later, Taylor sat up. His chest heaved as he breathed heavily, and droplets of sweat ran down his chest. He wiped his face and then looked down and smiled at Jennifer. As he stepped off the bed, Jennifer grabbed his arm. She pulled him down close.

"Taylor, I … I think we're moving too fast."

Taylor shook his head. He leaned in and kissed her.

"No," he whispered. "I find you so attractive, and I want to be with you. Don't you want to be with me?"

His eyes were pleading. He brought a finger up and traced her lips. She smiled and kissed his finger.

"Yes, yes I do," she cooed. "I just didn't want you to think that I'm …"

Taylor stood up. "I think you're beautiful. I think you're an intelligent, hot, sexy woman. I think I want us to be together," he said as he slowly walked toward the bathroom.

Jennifer lay back in bed. Her mind was spinning. So much had happened this week, today, tonight. It was all a blur. She heard the shower. Taylor was so sexy, and he had changed so much in the past few weeks. This night was so perfect—the dinner, the movie. She felt a little anxious though. As she rolled in bed, she saw his shirt on the edge of the bed. She grabbed it and pulled it to her face. As she breathed in, she could smell his musk and cologne. It excited and intoxicated her. She closed her eyes and continued to breathe in.

Chapter 18

WHEN JENNIFER OPENED HER EYES, it was light outside. She slowly rolled over, still shaking off the sleep. The previous night's events then flashed in her mind. She snapped awake. Jennifer lifted up and peered at the clock. 8:39 a.m. She looked around the room. There was no sign of Taylor.

"Taylor?" She yelled out.

She stepped out of bed, her panties slung around one ankle. She kicked them off and walked into the bathroom. There was a wrinkled towel hanging on the towel rack. She walked back to the bed. On the nightstand was a note.

> Jennifer,
> This night was so magical. I am so captivated by you. My only regret is that my Saturday is filled with work, so I needed to leave and a get an early start. I will call you. Look forward to seeing you again Saturday night.
>
> Taylor

Jennifer smiled. As she inhaled, the scent of his cologne filled her nose. She felt energized and motivated. After grabbing her phone, she gave a call to Taylor. His voicemail picked up.

"Hey Taylor, yes, last night was a really special night. I will be doing a few things today, but I'm free for most of it. Let me know when you can come by. Um, smooches!"

She hung up and then ran to the shower. After getting dressed and having a quick breakfast, she called to security.

"This is Frank."

"Hi Frank—Jennifer. I want to head out. I need to go to the bank and a few other places."

There was a pause on the phone and a shuffling noise.

"Hi, this is Marcus. Jennifer, there have been some heightened security alerts today. It's best if we stay put."

Jennifer stood shocked for the moment.

"So we can't go out?"

"No ma'am, just that it's wiser if—"

"Where's Tank?" Jennifer inquired.

"He's not on until later this evening. I'm in charge at the moment, so—"

"Well, I need to go out. So can you be ready in five minutes?"

"Yes ma'am," he sighed.

Jennifer ended the call. She walked into the bedroom and grabbed her purse. She looked at the check from the Qyron and the bank package in the folder. She grabbed them both and headed out the door.

When Jennifer reached the first floor, she was greeted by a large group of men: four Secret Service agents in suits and six plain-clothed marines. The marines all wore large dress shirts with only one button fastened. Jennifer gave them a look. Clothing aside, they didn't have the same professional, polished look that the Secret Service agents had.

One man stepped forward. "I'm Marcus; I'm in charge today."

Marcus was a tall Hispanic man with thick black hair and a pencil-thin beard. He wore shaded glasses. He pointed to the elevator. They stepped in as the door opened and then went down to the garage. Two large black SUVs waited. Jennifer sat in the back of the first truck, between two agents. Marcus rode up front.

"So where to, ma'am?"

"Well, I want to go to the bank first, then some shopping."

Marcus nodded, and the trucks pulled out.

When they reached the bank, the second truck unloaded and two of the men walked into the bank. The others stood outside and waited. Marcus jumped out and ran around to the driver's side. He opened the door, and the other agents surrounded Jennifer and escorted her into the bank. As she walked in, several people stared.

Jennifer approached the teller. "I need to speak with someone about my account."

She passed over the information on her account to the teller. The teller looked at it and then pointed to a desk on the far side.

A slender man in a tan suit stood up. "I can help you, miss."

Jennifer grabbed her paperwork and walked over to him. Two agents and two marines accompanied her.

As she approached him, he held out his hand.

"Hi, I'm Patrick Johnson. How can I help you, miss?" He peered at the other men.

Jennifer shook his hand. "I need to set up my account," she said as she sat down at his desk. Patrick continued to peer at the other men. "Yeah, they're with me."

He turned his view to her and politely smiled. "Wait," he said as he gave Jennifer another look. "You're the woman who works with the aliens. They healed my cancer. Thank you!"

He stood up and took a step toward Jennifer. Both agents quickly stepped in, and the two marines thrust their hands into their shirts.

"Oh, no, I was just …!" Patrick yelled as he stopped in midstep. "I … I just wanted to hug her; I'm sorry."

Jennifer stood up. "Marcus, it's okay."

She walked around to Patrick and gave him a hug.

"I'm happy that you're cured," she said with a smile.

Patrick's look of fear melted back to a smile. She sat back down and then slid her bank package over to Patrick. He peered at it and then typed in her account number.

"Oh, yes, I see it here. You have a special account that was set up by the government." He gave her a smile. "You have certain safeguards with this account that you wouldn't have with a normal account. If you read the packet, it will explain it all. You already have direct deposit, and it already has a healthy balance."

Jennifer gave him a smile. "Well, it's about to get a lot healthier." She slid the check over to him.

"Oh my!" he said aloud.

One of the marines peered down. "Whoa!" he said with wide eyes.

Marcus darted his gaze at the marine.

"Hey!" he shouted. "Mind your post, Marine!"

The marine snapped back and stood up smartly.

Jennifer then leaned in. "Can I forward money to someone?"

"Yes, that's also in the packet. You can also access it remotely through the Internet, but we need to set up several passwords for your protection."

He slid a form to her.

"If you can fill this out, I can start this today for you. But your money from this check won't clear for another few days."

"Oh, that's fine. If I have any questions on the information in the packet, I'll give you a call."

Jennifer stood up. She shook Patrick's hand again and turned to leave. A few other people recognized Jennifer. She heard three different people call out to her. She smiled, but Marcus prodded her to continue walking. She waved and continued to leave the bank.

The group then went to the mall, where Jennifer shopped for clothing, some kitchen items, and a few gifts for Taylor. She was recognized several times and stopped to chat with her new "fans," much to Marcus's displeasure.

She then treated her entourage to lunch. Jennifer's last stop was at a grocery store, where she picked up several items for that night's dinner. When they finally returned to the apartment, Tank was waiting for them as they pulled in. As soon as the truck stopped, Jennifer began to grab the bags. The marines came over and grabbed the rest of her shopping bags. As she walked to the elevator, she spotted Marcus chatting with Tank.

Tank stopped her as she approached the elevator.

"Can I have a word with you?"

"Sure," Jennifer said. "Walk with me to my apartment."

They all rode up to the second floor, and Jennifer opened the apartment door.

"Leave the bags here," Tank stated to the marines.

They set the bags down in front of the apartment. Jennifer walked inside. She placed some of the grocery bags down on the counter. Tank continued to bring the items into the apartment.

"Why didn't you just have them bring them in here?" Jennifer said with a touch of anger in her voice. Tank grabbed the last few bags and then closed the door behind him.

She stood in the kitchen with her arms crossed and a defiant look on her face. Tank walked over to her.

"Listen; the current intel is not very positive. I want to—"

"Oh, that's crap. I just went from the bank to the mall and then the grocery store. Several people waved; many wanted to chat. No one wanted to harm me!"

"You can't be fooled by that," Tank responded in a louder tone. "Yes, you may have several people in the crowd who recognize and adore you. But I can assure you there will be some who don't. There also may be those who are tracking you, who mean you harm. We have to be—"

"Oh, you worry too much!" Jennifer said with a huff.

"We have to be vigilant and keenly aware of your surroundings. You can't be reckless!"

Jennifer turned to open a bag on the counter. Tank stepped over and gently grabbed her arm.

"Jennifer, please."

Jennifer turned and looked into Tank's eyes. He was serious and unwavering.

"Terrance, I'm fine. I appreciate you looking out for me." She flashed him a smile.

Tank stood staring at her for a moment. "It's my job to look out for you *and* everyone on my team. I don't want your actions jeopardizing anyone's life."

Jennifer continued to unload the food from the bags, not making eye contact with him. Tank turned and walked out of the kitchen.

"Have a good day, Terrance," Jennifer said in a dismissive tone.

She heard the door open and close.

Jennifer spent the next hour preparing dinner. She had some steaks, potatoes, and broccoli on the menu, with a chocolate cake for dessert. After she put the steaks in the oven, she called Taylor. Again, she reached his voicemail.

"Hey, Taylor, I have a nice dinner cooking. I'll plan to see you by 8:00 p.m. Don't be late," she giggled and then ended the call.

She spent the rest of her evening straightening up the apartment and preparing for Taylor. She wore a sexy little black dress that was very low cut.

When 8:00 p.m. came, Jennifer checked her cell phone. She called Taylor again. No answer. She left a quick voicemail asking him to call her back. She turned off the oven, as the steaks were done. She then turned on the TV and waited. At 9:00 p.m., her phone rang.

"Hello?"

"Hey, Jennifer it's me, Taylor. I'm sorry; I was held up. It's been such a busy day," he said.

"Why didn't you call me back? I had dinner ready over an hour ago!"

"I'm sorry; I'll be there in half an hour."

"I called you like three times!" She sighed. "Okay," Jennifer said, defeat in her voice, "I'm waiting."

She ended the call and turned her attention back to the television. She changed it to a news channel. Jennifer watched as several groups were protesting the Qyron in New York and California. The news shifted to the growing tension with the Freedom Alliance. When the broadcast ended at nine thirty, her security phone rang.

"Miss Winston, I have Taylor for you."

"Okay, send him up," Jennifer mumbled.

She went to the door and opened it. When the elevator opened, Taylor strolled out and strutted down the hall.

"Sorry I'm late," he said as he approached.

Jennifer gave him a half-hearted smile.

"I had a really nice dinner prepared, but—"

Taylor stepped up close to her. He grabbed her, lifted her up, and gave her a hug and kiss.

"Let me make it up to you."

He carried her into the apartment and closed the door with his foot. He continued kissing her and walked her into the bedroom.

"No, wait, I thought we'd have dinner," she said as he laid her down on the bed. He smiled at her as he unbuttoned his shirt.

"First things first," he said.

Taylor wasted no time in undressing. He then kneeled at the bedside and removed Jennifer's underwear.

"Taylor, I wanted—"

Taylor slid up and kissed her. He nibbled on her lips and exhaled into her ear. She could smell a faint scent of a fragrance—not a manly cologne, but a flowery scent. She heard him unzipping his pants. Within seconds he was making love to her. When ten o'clock arrived, Taylor rolled over.

"You're incredible," he said.

"Yeah," Jennifer mumbled as she stared at the wall.

He kissed her lips and then stepped off of the bed. As he pulled on his pants, he peered at the nightstand. There were a few boxes waiting on top, with a card addressed to "Taylor."

"What's this?" he inquired

Jennifer looked over.

"I picked up some things for you," she said softly. "I thought we were going to have a romantic dinner, maybe a movie …" Her voice trailed off.

He grabbed one of the boxes and opened it.

"Ah, a dress shirt, thanks." He continued to dress himself as he opened the next box. Jennifer slowly crawled off of the bed. "Oh, and some dress pants, nice," he said as he tossed the box top aside.

Jennifer stood up and then pulled her dress back down over her hips. Taylor now opened the last box.

"Cologne. Wow, this is expensive." He turned and looked at Jennifer. "You're so thoughtful," he said as he bent over and gave her a kiss.

Jennifer gave him a smile. She perked up and grabbed his hand.

"Come on," she said as she led him out of the bedroom and into the kitchen. "I made us a nice dinner." She opened up the oven, pulled the steaks out, and set them on the stovetop. They looked dry.

"Oh, I'm sorry, I already ate," Taylor said softly as he slipped a shoe on.

Jennifer turned to him, her mouth open in disappointment. He stepped close and gave her a hug.

"Let me make it up to you," he whispered. "I'll take you out next Saturday night for an evening to remember." He gave her another kiss. "You are so sweet," he said, "and you mean so much to me." He kissed her again and then turned to walk away.

"Wait, where are you going?" she cried.

Taylor stopped at the edge of the kitchen. "I'm sorry; I have to be in Philly tomorrow, so I need to get an early start."

"But I thought you would stay the night?" Jennifer pleaded.

Taylor smiled. "I'm sorry, sweetie. I'll call you tomorrow."

He turned and walked back into the bedroom. Jennifer looked at the stove, which was holding the dry steaks, soggy broccoli, and hardened mashed potatoes. She sighed and walked toward the bedroom. As she reached the hallway, Taylor stepped out of the bedroom, boxes under his arm. He pulled Jennifer close and grabbed her chin with his hand.

"You had a wonderful evening planned; I'm sorry that I wrecked it. I can't wait until my job slows down a bit so we can enjoy ourselves more."

He gave her another kiss and then turned.

"Taylor, when am I going to see you again?" She followed him as he darted for the door and opened it. He pivoted around.

"Well, I won't be back from Philly until late, so most likely next weekend. Again, we'll go out Saturday night. I'm sorry."

Taylor blew her a kiss and then closed the door behind him.

Jennifer grabbed a light dinner from what was edible and then trashed the rest.

There was a white light and some hissing, and I pulled the headset from my temple.

"What a jerk," I mumbled.

Chapter 19

As I WALKED INTO THE kitchenette, I grabbed a water and then looked at my monitor. I had another administrative message: "Please input your personal information at once. Failure to comply will cause an immediate lockout of your room. This is the final notice."

That did it. None of this made any sense.

"Computer, John Crowley's room!"

A tone sounded. "John Crowley is asleep."

I checked the time. It had been seven hours.

He's slept long enough.

"Computer, wake John Crowley and dialogue." I heard the alarm tone in John's room.

"Wha? Lights on!" said John's voice. "What the hell is that? Who is this?"

"Johnny, it's Amant. I need you to come to my room right now!"

"What?" John's voice was groggy and raspy. "Amant, are you okay?"

"Yes, Johnny, but I need you to come here right away."

I heard the sound of covers ruffling, a cough, and then the noise of his feet hitting the floor.

"This had better be good! Computer end message," he grumbled.

I went back into my bedroom. I grabbed my large luggage cases and began filling them up. After a few minutes, I heard the tone at my door.

"Open!" I responded. I heard the door open.

"Amant?"

"In the bedroom, Johnny!" I was partially done packing. With the extreme amount of travel that my job demanded, I was a whiz at quickly shuffling and packing clothing—a champion, if you asked me. John walked into my bedroom.

"What's so all-hellfire important that you needed to wake me up?"

I turned around. He was busy rubbing the crust from his eyes, and his hair was sticking up in the perfect bed-head hairdo. I couldn't help but giggle.

"You look …" I laughed harder and pointed. "Oh, Johnny, you just kill me."

"Yeah, I might if you keep waking me up," he said with a scowl as he walked over to me.

He gave me a quick hug and then waited for me to stop laughing.

"I can't figure this thing out, Johnny. I couldn't get a proper ticket to board this transport, and then when I came aboard with a general ticket, it wouldn't accept my ID. Now the administration wants to lock out my room because it doesn't know who I am. I can't give it my ID; it won't take it!"

John stood silent for a moment. He rubbed the last bit of crust out from the corners of his eyes. He took a deep breath and then reached out his hand.

"Give me your ID," he said with a lack of enthusiasm and an exhalation.

I pulled my ID off my nightstand. He grabbed it and walked over to my terminal, opened the current admin message, and then tapped my ID on the panel. It gave out a honk and displayed a red "denied" banner. He turned around and gave me a puzzled look.

"Gee, wish I would have tried that!" Sarcasm dripped off my words.

"Can't we just ask someone?"

"*I tried, John*; the computer said there are no administrators on board!"

"Well, I don't know much about transports," John sighed.

"Yeah, well *I do*, and not a one of these damn things makes any sense. I've taken hundreds of transports John, and every one of them is identical. All of them have first class and are luxurious throughout. This transport, on the other hand—it's like a refitted garbage transport. And now it seems like the transport is on autopilot."

John gave me a nervous look as the word "autopilot" died in my mouth.

"What?" he asked.

"There are no flight staff on board; this transport *is* on autopilot!"

"Autopilot—is that an issue?" John's voice now sounded worried. "We're still going to …?"

"Yes, Gamma Five, but that's another thing." I paced alongside the bed. "John, I know everything about every single human colony. We have ten of them: Venus, Mars, Earth, Beta Lyrae, Tyberon, Marvyn Four, Zon, Theta Nine, Calver, and Dramus. I have intimate knowledge of the people, their governing bodies, and their imports and exports; it's all a part of my job requirements. All of my star charts show them prominently. But Gamma Five was not in any of my training or daily updates, and I had to dig to find it in the general star charts before I boarded. None of this makes any sense, John!"

John now looked a little rattled, and honestly, I probably wasn't looking much better. I was actually a little scared. John sat down on my bed.

"What do we do? Maybe this is all just a misunderstanding?"

"Yeah?" I gave John a serious look. "Have you tried reaching F Deck yet? It won't let you."

"Look, cut it out; you're really starting to bug me out," John said sternly.

"I'm scaring myself, John! An entire deck of a transport *off limits!* Oh, and to top it all off, now my room is going to be locked down because they don't know who I am. So that's why you're here. We need to move my stuff out of here and into your room."

John twitched his head and locked onto my gaze. He stood up from the bed.

"Yeah, well who says I want *you* living with me?" John said flatly.

I know he meant it to be funny, but the joy and humor were out of his voice as well as the mood in the room. He still looked nervous and a bit shaken. I gave him a quick smile and pointed to the last empty case.

"Grab the case and fill it up with what's in the closet. I'm going to pack my toiletries."

We were done within an hour. We dragged the cases out into the passageway. Together we pushed them down to the lift and then up to Alpha Deck and into John's room—well, our room now.

For the next half hour, we sat on the couch, thinking about what to do. I finally stood up.

"Well, time to do some unpacking. You wanted to live together; well, now you're stuck with me," I said with a smile.

John gave a smile back—the first genuine one I had gotten from him since he woke up. After a few hours of unpacking, all of the drawers and closets were now packed, and we decided to shower and have some food.

On our way to the dining hall, we stopped a service member and asked him about the flight staff. He gave the standard "I dunno" response that I expected. It seemed not only that this ship was flying itself but also that the crew on board were the lowest in customer service and knowledge. When we reached the dining hall, I walked with my tray along the buffet.

"Mmm, ooyrd," John said as he pointed to the Qyron meat.

"Ugh, I hate that stuff, John."

"You're half Qyron, and it's a Qyron delicacy," John said with a smile.

"I don't care if it's platinum-encrusted diamond waffles; it tastes horrible, John. You like it, you eat it!"

I filled my tray up with some Earth food and a few Qyron items. There were plenty of delicious vegetables and fruit from the Qyron home world. But as with any food, there were a few things I didn't like. I hated sauerkraut, baked beans, beets, talfeud, and ooyrd. My mother loved the last two and would try forcing them on me. Maybe that was another reason why I hated them so much.

When we sat down to eat, we discussed the mystery. John then gave me a serious stare.

"You don't think they're drafting us into the military to fight in the war, do you?"

I gave pause.

We had been in an intergalactic war with the Pihrae for over a hundred years. We had encountered them when we first settled the Zon system. Our first contact was brief. We tried to communicate with them, but they opened fire on our newly formed colony and killed thousands of people. Since we had no offensive weapons, it amounted to a slaughter. Luckily, the Qyron had stockpiled all of our old nuclear weapons from the twentieth century. We had used several of them on the attacking ships. All totaled, we lost nearly two hundred fifty thousand people in that colony before finally repelling their armada.

"Amant?"

"Huh? Oh, sorry, Johnny. No, there's no reason for them to draft us. We already have over a million Galactic Marines anyway."

"Why don't we visit the bridge?" John stated matter-of-factly.

I felt stupid. *Of course, let's visit the bridge and resolve this whole thing.* I gave John a smile.

"That's exactly what we'll do," I said, feeling silly. We finished our meal and then walked to the front of Alpha Deck. When we reached the door leading to level one, where the bridge was located, the door was locked. I just stood there, miffed.

"Okay, now what?" John asked aloud. I walked back down the passageway until I reached a general terminal.

"Computer, I need bridge access," I stated.

A message responded, "Access denied."

"Computer, I need staff assistance."

A prompt showed my location and an indicator of the nearest available staff member.

John finally walked up to me. "So what's the verdict?"

"I called for a human; they're on the way."

The words were no sooner out of my mouth than a man wearing a white maintenance uniform rounded the corner. He was an attractive man with brown hair spiked up neatly and a cute smile. His uniform had a stitched name tag that read "Casey." When he reached the monitor, he tapped his badge on it and the call for assistance reset.

"How can I help you?" he asked.

"Yes, Casey, I would like to speak with someone on the bridge please."

He gave me a blank stare. I was about to restate my words when he finally opened his mouth.

"Uh, the what?"

John laughed aloud. I spun my look to John and gave him an angry scowl. He immediately stopped laughing.

"The bridge, where people are steering this transport," I said in disbelief. "We would like to speak with those people, please."

The man's face was still a blank sheet. He smiled, but I could see his eyes ping-pong and his face strain as he tried to think of an answer.

"I don't know where the bridge is," he said apologetically.

I gave him a smile and then shot John a stern look. I was expecting him to laugh aloud again. I walked over to the door to the bridge.

"Can you tell me what's behind this door?"

"Yeah, it's a storage locker," he said with an air of sarcasm as he walked up to the door.

He swiped his card, a tone sounded, and the door opened. The lights illuminated as I entered the room. I was accustomed to seeing control panels and seating, and hearing the chatter of the flight staff. On long transport trips, you tend to get bored, so you travel the whole ship and talk with the staff. I had spent many hours chatting with the ship's captain and crew. But here, on this transport, the bridge was filled with crates, boxes, and dust—a lot of dust. I sneezed.

As I continued to wade through the stacks of boxes, I looked forward. I saw where the normal transparent panel would have been to allow forward viewing of space. It was sealed with a large section of metal plating. I stared at it in disbelief.

"Yeah, the only other thing in here is the heater," Casey said.

I looked over at him with a questioning gaze. He was pointing to a forward position. I walked around a stack of boxes and noticed a riser capped by a metal shroud. This was the location of the navigation station. I pressed my hand against the metal riser; it felt very warm to the touch. I looked over at Casey.

"Ah yes, the heater," I said with a smile.

I turned and walked back toward the doorway. John followed, and Casey then closed the door behind us.

"Thank you, Casey; sorry for wasting your time," I said.

"That's no problem," he replied as he walked down the passageway.

"So?" John said as Casey ambled around the corner.

"Well, that is the bridge, John. Did you see the forward viewing windows that were sealed up?"

"Yes. Well, I saw you staring at a blank wall," John mumbled.

"And that heater isn't a heater. It's the navigation port. It was capped with an automatic autopilot. I've seen it on other transports, but they never use it."

John exhaled and then leaned against the wall.

"You know," John said with a grimace, "maybe we're making a lot of something out of nothing. What if this is, like, a first-generation transport that's being used on this newly discovered colony? We saw all of those dirty and smelly people at the space port. They're all workers heading here. So maybe they shuttle us in the low-class transport to a brand-new colony?"

I thought for a moment.

"No, that's not it, John. I was there at the inception of the Dramus colony—both the planet and its moon. We still had complete accommodations in the transport, Johnny, and all of the workers looked middle class. The Qyron don't even have a coach-class transport that I'm aware of. Ugh, my head hurts."

I was starting to get a headache—more from stress than anything else.

John walked over and gave me a hug. "Come on; let's go back to the room."

He grabbed my hand and escorted me back to our room. I took some aspirin and lay down on the bed. Johnny lay down next to me and rubbed my head. It felt so good. I eventually drifted off to sleep.

When I woke, I heard laughing. I slowly slid off of the bed. I felt groggy, but my head no longer ached. As I walked out into the living room, I saw John watching a program.

"What's with all the laughing?" I said as I slid in close to Johnny. He leaned over and gave me a kiss.

"Glad that you're feeling better. I'm just watching a comedy show. Sorry, did I wake you?"

I gave him a smile. "No, I was lying in bed for a bit, and I heard you giggling. Thanks for rubbing my head; I feel so much better now."

"Well, you've had a rich, full day, what with moving your room and then snooping around the ship."

I smiled at him. When we were kids, we used to venture out past the houses where we lived. There was a field and a huge grove of trees.

To us as kids, it was a forest. We spent many a Saturday or summer day adventuring. I loved it. But what I loved most of all was a mystery.

"Yes, it's been quite the day, and all we have is more questions, John. But at this point, maybe it is time to just give it a rest," I said with a sigh. John leaned over and gave me a kiss. His eyes looked tired.

"Is it naptime, Johnny?"

He smiled back at me and nodded slowly. "Yes, I believe so. I feel beat."

We retired to the bedroom. This time I lay in bed while Johnny drifted off to slumber city. He must have been very tired, as it took him only a few minutes before he was gently snoring. I felt nervous and agitated. Part of me wanted to work out in the gym to get rid of the excess energy. But I thought about the possibility of bumping into Brad again.

After lying next to John for twenty minutes, I gently slid out of bed. John didn't miss a beat and continued snoring away. I left the bedroom and sat down on the couch. I didn't want to watch a movie. Jennifer came to mind. I looked over to the coffee table. I grabbed the case and pulled out my headset. I slid it on.

There was a white light and some hissing.

Chapter 20

August 2, 2021

JENNIFER WALKED INTO THE MEETING room. Taylor stood in discussion with Tom Franklin and a staffer. Rachel ambled over with a large stack of report updates. She began passing them out. Taylor then peered over and gave Jennifer a smile.

The president entered the room. He nodded over at Jennifer and made his way to his seat. Taylor broke away from his chat as Jennifer sauntered by.

"How was your trip?"

Taylor gave her a confused look.

"Trip?"

After a moment, his confused expression broke.

"Oh yeah, my trip to Philly. It was good. Sorry, been so busy."

He turned quickly to face the room.

"Okay, let's get started," he shouted over the din.

The room fell silent as Jennifer got to her seat.

"We have nearly three hundred thousand terminal cases cured nationwide. The Wellness Program is also progressing rather well, with fifty thousand already served. It's been a real boost on the news, with so many people praising the Qyron now that their nagging aches and pains have been eliminated."

Rachel finished distributing the reports and sat next to Jennifer. Jennifer noticed a waft of the same fragrance she had smelled on Taylor Saturday night. She stared at Rachel for a moment. Rachel smiled politely.

The president raised his hand up and then added, "What are the weekly poll numbers?"

Taylor smiled. "This weekend's polls have Qyron acceptance at about 4 percent, nearly doubled from last week. Approximately 32 percent are undecided, with 61percent against."

The president nodded and smiled as Taylor continued.

"Urban renewal is progressing well in NYC, LA, Dallas, and Oakland. There were some minor setbacks in Detroit and Chicago. By the end of this week, we should have completed many of the noted areas in all of those cities."

Taylor panned the room and then locked eyes with the president.

"The unemployment rate has continued to drop. The Qyron now have over three million Americans employed throughout the solar system. Mary, you wanted to add some things?"

Mary Wilson, the treasury secretary, then stood up and walked to the lectern.

"I ran some numbers with the Qyron financial projections. Within a year, we'll have all people employed—not just here in the United States, but globally. It seems that with the added jobs and revenue this will bring, our country will be debt free in about fifteen years."

"This is starting to sound damn near too good to be true," the defense secretary chimed in.

"My numbers don't lie," Mary responded tersely. "I worked on them all through the weekend!"

The defense secretary lowered his head.

"The only catch I can find," Mary said, turning another page, "is loss of manpower as we colonize other planets."

"How can these jobs turn our economy around so fast?" Tom Franklin asked.

Mary pivoted to face him. "Do you realize that the starting pay for an asteroid miner or resource collector is one hundred twenty-five thousand dollars a year? The work week is four ten-hour days; the Qyron provide food and housing in space for the workers. If anything, we're starting to see other jobs become vacant because the Qyron jobs offer so much more pay and better benefits. So factor in that we have 10 percent of the previously unemployed now working, the fact that their pay is far above the norm, that tens of millions of other jobs will also be opened up with similar high pay, and that tax money fills in the otherwise increasing national debt."

She raised her eyebrows and smiled back at him, silently saying, "There!".

"I'm going to collect some more data and perform a few additional calculations, but right now, the economy is looking at some very explosive growth." She nodded at Taylor and walked back to her seat.

Taylor adjusted the microphone. "We have a few hundred cars on the road now with the new Qyron engines, and several commercial and industrial facilities have been retrofitted with Qyron heating and air-conditioning units. The Capitol building, Pentagon, and White House are all scheduled to have refits this week. As we mentioned last week, this new technology, on average, is 95 percent more energy efficient." Taylor caught the president's gaze. "Of course, we're providing news agencies and our website with all of these facts and figures."

Kennedy smiled and nodded.

"Now for the bad news," Taylor said solemnly. "As I'm sure you've all seen on the news, there have been a few fatalities over the weekend. We've had three separate attacks on the Qyron—two here in the US. Seven marines were injured, and three died. I have a report, though, that may help." He flipped a page. "With the Qyron research team, we finally have a prototype defensive fiber in testing. It's made of carbon microtubes, and it's ten times more effective than Kevlar in stopping bullets."

The president stood up. "Taylor, I want this in production as soon as possible!"

"Already ahead of you, sir. We have vigorous testing scheduled, and it will be ready for field use by next week."

Taylor looked down at his papers. "We have some ongoing conflicts with the Freedom Alliance."

The secretary of defense cleared his throat as he stood up. "I'm on top of this. We've had a few of our planes shot at, but no one has been hurt. One Russian cruiser fired a missile, but it was shot down. As per your orders, sir"—he looked over at the president—"our ships and planes are keeping a safe distance from the Russians and Chinese as they play their war games."

Franklin, the secretary of state, then walked up to the lectern.

"Kennedy, I'm in talks with all three, and it's looking good that China is starting to waver. They've been monitoring our economy and seeing the news on all of the advancements. I think they'll leave this alliance by the end of the week. They already had a few other minor countries defect, and I believe they will be talking with Jennifer this week."

He turned and nodded at Jennifer.

"Uh, yes sir. We've had to change our schedule, as leaders from Syria, Kazakhstan, Vietnam, and Afghanistan are now willing to talk with the Qyron."

"Well, that needs to be put on the good list, Taylor," the president quipped.

The room broke out in laughter. Taylor smiled, nodded, and then continued.

"The vice president is also receiving more resistance on his goodwill tour. It seems that more people are turning out to loudly voice their fears." Lance Meyer, the secretary of homeland security, then stood up.

"With my increased staff, we've been able to distinguish ten major resistance groups. Several of them have just stepped forward from existing radical resistance groups, and some of the smaller groups have banded together. We are trying to monitor their communications and stay on top of their activities. Regarding the major conflict last week, in which two marines were killed in Los Angeles, it seems that a group, Freedom for All is responsible. This group appears to be disorganized and not very well funded, but they aren't afraid to take chances. I will keep everyone informed as I receive more intel."

Taylor then looked over to the president. "That's all I have, sir."

The meeting dissolved into various group meetings. The president walked over to Jennifer.

"How are you holding up?" he asked. Jennifer peered up at him.

"We're doing fine, sir, but we're going to have to do something very soon, because our schedule is completely insane. Several world leaders have already complained that they're not getting enough time with us."

The president nodded. "Yes, I can understand that. It seems that our preplanning has worked quite well in establishing us in the forefront with everyone clawing to catch up."

Taylor walked over to listen in.

"From what I understand, all of the people who work for the Qyron receive digital notebooks. These have an English-to-Qyron translator that allows them to do their jobs. Why can't we use them all over the world?"

"Well," Jennifer sighed, "those do work for simple tasks and procedures, but the government and industry leaders demand face-to-face communication and negotiations. Even here in the US, we have a schedule pushed out for ten months already, and globally, we're looking at nearly two years."

Taylor then chimed in. "Wait, Jennifer; you have that thing in your brain. Can't we just put that in another hundred people?"

Jennifer looked at Xho for a moment and then turned toward Taylor.

"No. The Qyron have tested over a hundred thousand humans in the past several hundred years; I'm the only one that it's worked on. It has to have a very specific brain pattern in order to work. However, if we get volunteers to screen for it ..." Jennifer looked at the president. "Is that something we can put on the government and job websites?"

Taylor chimed in. "Yeah, sure. I need a job description and salary range."

Jennifer peered over to Rachel.

"Rachel, can you get that to Taylor by the end of the day?"

Rachel nodded. "Yes, but what's the salary?"

All eyes now focused on Jennifer. She smiled and then stated, "Two million a year."

As if choreographed, the president, Taylor, and Rachel all exclaimed, "Two million!"

Jennifer then heard in her mind, *That is not what we pay; we are providing a salary of six million dollars a year.*

I know, Xho; I'll explain it to you later, Jennifer thought.

"Yes, it's a lot of money," Jennifer said while blushing, "so we should have no shortage of people willing to get tested, right?"

"I'm first," the president said. Everyone laughed.

"Yes, I will get that listed and even give it to the news agencies. At that salary, we're sure to have no end of people who want to be tested," Taylor said.

"We need to be going," Rachel whispered to Jennifer.

The group said their good-byes and then walked out to the transport.

"Rachel, we're not going to have a repeat of last week, are we?" Jennifer asked.

"No, I promise," Rachel said as they stepped outside.

"Oh, and that fragrance you're wearing—is that new?" Jennifer asked.

Rachel gave Jennifer a curious look and then added, "No, I've had it for a while. Why?"

"It smells nice; I was just curious," Jennifer said as she opened her laptop.

When they were seated in the transport and the doors closed, Jennifer heard *Please explain* from Xho.

Xho, I would be too embarrassed to tell them that I'm making six million dollars a year through you. Two million is more than enough to get hordes of people to be tested.

I do not want to be deceitful, Xho replied.

You're not; I am. Trust me, Xho. Besides, how many other half-breed Qyron are available to be interpreters?

There are ten more Qyron-human interpreters.

Will that be enough?

It's all we have for now. We were hoping that more humans would be willing to mate.

Jennifer burst out laughing. Rachel gave her a shocked look.

"What's so funny?"

"Oh, nothing. I'm discussing things with Xho; sorry," Jennifer said while laughing.

Xho, humans need an emotional bond, and I'm not sure how a human and Qyron would communicate in a relationship. We'll have to discuss this later.

Yes.

A minute later, the transport touched down in Detroit. They were scheduled to speak with the automakers and then be in California for lunch. As they walked off the transport, Jennifer heard *Please do not be deceitful on behalf of me or the Qyron.*

Okay, Xho, I'm sorry. Jennifer thought back to Xho.

As the group walked across the parking lot, a sudden explosive burst of gunshots rang out. Two marines and Secret Service agents were hit instantly by the gunfire, which came from a group of terrorists on their left. Loud thuds were followed by screams of pain as the bullets impacted their Kevlar vests, arms, and legs. Jennifer watched it unfold in shocked disbelief. Everything seemed to move in slow motion. One of the agents in front of Jennifer was hit in the face and fell backward, spraying Jennifer with blood.

A marine on her right was struck repeatedly in the arm, which shredded as blood sprayed. It dangled helplessly from his shoulder as he fell to the ground. Another agent, Thomas, grabbed Jennifer from behind and thrust her to the ground. She slammed hard onto the blacktop, scraping her face. Her laptop bounced and sprawled across the pavement. Return fire then deafened Jennifer as a few marines crouched down and began shooting back at the terrorists.

A second group of extremists then opened fire from their right side. Thomas fell down on top of Jennifer, shielding her. His back and legs were quickly hit with several rounds. He screamed out in agony as blood gushed out of several open leg wounds. Two marines on Jennifer's left were also yelling in pain, writhing in a pool of blood on the ground.

Jennifer looked over at Rachel, who was screaming and holding her hip. Blood pulsed through her fingers as she tried to stop it.

Jennifer heard a scream from Charles, the lead marine. "We're taking fire!" he yelled into his headset.

A moment later, she heard a loud hum and felt pulsing across the ground. The transport quickly moved into position six feet above their heads. The incoming hail of bullets now glowed red; the projectiles made sizzling sounds as they streamed in a circular arc around the group. The transport's energy field deflected the bullets, which dinged off of adjacent buildings and struck cars.

When the terrorists realized that their bullets were no longer able to reach their targets, they dashed to their vehicles. Charles and the rest of the marines turned and quickly surveyed the scene.

Two marines lay screaming in a pool of blood. Three Secret Service agents were also horribly wounded and yelling for help. The transport lurched at an angle, the side door now wide open four feet in the air.

Charles and another marine grabbed one badly injured soldier and slid him up into the transport. Rachel stood up, screaming and crying, and Xho quickly shoved her into the transport. Jennifer stood up and noticed a gash in her thigh and a large bullet hole in her wrist. It burned with ferocity, but her focus was on the transport. She staggered toward the open doorway as another wounded marine was hurried inside.

Xho turned and quickly scooped up Jennifer. He jumped up and into the open doorway and set her in a chair. Jennifer just stared, mouth open, and watched in shock as the horror continued to unfold.

A few seconds later, the last wounded marine was slid inside, and Charles then jumped into the transport.

"We're all in!" he screamed. The transport lurched back to level and then quickly rose upward. Those who were standing wobbled but quickly regained their balance. The door to the transport started to close, and Charles slapped the Open button again. He reloaded his machine gun.

"Follow those vehicles, damn it!" he yelled.

The transport dipped back down to within thirty feet of the ground, racing to catch the first vehicle.

Xho ran to one side of the transport, snatching a large red case. He opened it and pulled out several Meibot syringes. He began plunging one into each person who was injured. Jennifer didn't even flinch when he pierced her leg with one. Xho then plunged a second one into the more severely injured, then a third.

Jennifer slowly turned, still in shock. Rachel was crying hysterically. She had two syringes stuck in her side. Jennifer noticed that the bleeding quickly stopped. She then focused on a large hole in Rachel's hip. The torn and shredded skin seemed to vibrate. It then moved, as if invisible ants were slowly placing the pieces back together. She saw the hole quickly close up and continued to stare in stunned disbelief.

She turned her gaze to Thomas, who lay on the floor of the transport, also drenched in blood. One large hole in his leg was already closed up, and a second one was quickly sealing itself. A large gasp sounded as one marine began breathing again. She then peered down at her wrist. One of the bones protruded, but as she stared at it, a shiny metallic form quickly engulfed the bone. The red blood and white bone were replaced with a silvery, almost liquid metal substance. The bone then moved and slid back into and under the skin. Jennifer felt no pain. Her mouth opened wide as she watched the bone then click into place and the skin slide back into position.

A barrage of gunfire then deafened the room. The lead marine, Charles, began firing on the van. Another marine clicked into a harness and also began firing. The transport continued following a straight path, parallel with the fleeing van, but tilted slightly, allowing the marines to get a clear shot. After a few more bursts of gunfire, the van swerved hard into a concrete barrier and flipped over. Two blocks away, police cars were closing in.

"Okay, now let's get the other truck!" Charles yelled out. The transport swerved quickly, everyone braced themselves as it pulled hard right. In ten seconds, the transport leveled itself and then tilted again.

"There he is!" screamed Charles. He gritted his teeth as they began firing on the SUV. Jennifer held her hands to her ears, trying to block out the loud reports. As she looked down at Thomas, she noticed the two bullet holes were now closed. No more blood flowed from them. She looked over at one of the downed marines. The large exit wound in his back was now closing up. Xho grabbed him and rolled him over. His eyes were open, and he was staring blindly ahead. Xho then gave him another injection.

The marines stopped firing as the SUV blew a tire and rolled over. Three blocks away, several police cars were in pursuit and approaching fast.

"Okay, let's get to a hospital!" Charles shouted into his headset. The transport veered slightly and lowered in altitude quickly. When it finally touched down in the parking lot of a hospital, Thomas let out a large gasp.

Another agent kneeled by his side. Thomas grabbed his hand, and he was lifted up to a standing position.

"If that's not the damndest thing I've ever seen," the agent said.

Thomas stood and then convulsed for a moment. He coughed, holding his hand to his mouth. As he slowly pulled his hand away, a bullet was resting in his palm.

He has one more bullet; it will be expelled through his belly button, Xho thought.

Thomas then grabbed at his belt. He pulled his shirt out of his pants and then ripped it off. He pulled open his damaged Kevlar vest. He now stood with his stomach out. A small stream of blood then issued from his belly button as he clasped his hands around his stomach.

"Oh!" he said as he gave a look of shock. Another bullet then slid out of his belly button and into his hand. The blood then stopped. A moment later, the two syringes that were shining red in Thomas's side glowed green. Xho pulled them out.

Jennifer looked up in time to see a group of medics with several stretchers approaching the transport doorway. The marines grabbed their fallen men and lifted them out and onto the stretchers. One agent was also set on a stretcher.

Jennifer stood up. The bullet wound in her thigh was closed up. Her two syringes glowed green, and Xho pulled them out. She walked slowly over to the lead marine, Charles.

"You did a hell of a job, Charles, thank you," she said.

"That's my job, ma'am. But you please thank your alien fella for saving our men; we appreciate it!"

Jennifer looked back at Xho, who nodded. Rachel then stepped out of the transport; she was crying and still shaken. Jennifer gave her a hug.

"We're okay; it's over now," Jennifer said.

Rachel continued to hug Jennifer tightly and cry.

Jennifer turned to Thomas and Charles. "The Meibots have repaired all of the major damage, but you're going to be sore for a while."

Xho stepped alongside Charles and pulled out his syringe. Jennifer nodded and then turned to him.

"The Meibots are now out of your system and back in the syringe. We will need to collect the ones on your other men too."

Charles nodded. His satellite phone rang.

"Yes?"

He looked at Jennifer.

"Here, miss, this is for you."

"Jennifer, are you okay?" said the unmistakable voice of the president.

"Yes sir, I'm fine. We took gunfire. All of us were hit, but Xho was able to save us."

"Understood. Get your team back here!"

Jennifer ended the call and handed the phone back to Charles.

"Your boss says it's time to go home."

A half hour later, they were all on the White House lawn.

Chapter 21

JENNIFER, RACHEL, THE SECRET SERVICE agents, and the marines all stood in the Oval Office. The president stepped from behind his desk. He stopped in front of Gunnery Sergeant Charles Gill. He gave him a salute and a smile.

"Gunny, you and your team did a damn fine job out there today. Thank you. I want your debrief by this evening."

"Yes sir!" Charles said. He and his team then marched out of the office.

The president walked over to Xho.

"Thank you, Xho, for your quick thinking in saving the lives of my marines and agents."

Xho nodded.

"He will also pass along your thanks to the Meibots, sir," Jennifer added.

The president then gave pause and looked at Jennifer. "How do you feel?"

Jennifer thought for a moment. She peered at Xho and then to Rachel.

"I don't know, sir; my wrist and thigh are sore, but I guess I'm still in shock."

"That's understandable," the president said. "Take the rest of the day off, and we'll see you tomorrow."

Jennifer still stared straight ahead, not focused on any one thing. She felt her head nod. She then snapped out of her trance.

"Um, sir. Is that what we should do?"

The president smiled and then stepped to stand face-to-face with Jennifer.

"There is no right or wrong here. If I asked Charles and his team, they'd beg to go back to work and would be angry if denied them the chance. Ask any of my agents and you'll get the same answer. But you're not a soldier. Your job is to bridge the gap between the Qyron and us." A soft smile crossed his lips. "Go home, get some rest, and be back tomorrow ready to hit the day fresh. Your meetings can wait a day."

Jennifer gave him a nod and then turned around.

The secretary of defense and Lance Meyer stood in the back of the room. As Jennifer and Rachel walked by them and out into the hallway, she could hear the president.

"Okay, gentlemen, can someone tell me just *how in the hell this happened today? I want to know!*" The door was slammed shut behind them.

As they walked down the hallway, Jennifer looked over at Rachel.

"If you can move all of the meetings back a day, let's see if we can just push Friday into next week and absorb it."

Rachel continued walking alongside Jennifer. After a moment, she nodded, but she maintained her forward stare. Jennifer stopped.

It took Rachel five more steps to notice. She paused and then looked back at Jennifer.

Jennifer walked over to Rachel and looked her in the eyes. Rachel's gaze seemed vacant. Jennifer reached her hands out and grabbed Rachel's.

"Listen; I understand the shock and horror of everything we went through today. Take the next day to sort through your thoughts and feelings. I'll see you in two days," Jennifer said, smiling to Rachel. Rachel gave a look of acknowledgment and smiled back.

"I'll be okay," Rachel replied as she turned and walked down the hallway.

Jennifer was then joined by two new agents as she was escorted to the truck. When she sat down in the back, her phone rang. It was Taylor.

"Yes?"

"Hey, Jennifer, I just heard that your team was in a bit of a melee," Taylor said.

Jennifer paused a moment. A wave of shock and then anger surged through her. A traffic jam of thoughts crowded her mind: Taylor's initial stubborn insensitivity; then the past week, during which he had been so loving and thoughtful; and now this. She stifled the urge to laugh.

"Jennifer?"

"Yes, Taylor, I'm here," Jennifer said tersely, "Melee? It was far more than a melee, Taylor! I had my left wrist blown apart and my thigh shredded with bullets. We all could have died! Thank you *so* much for asking, Taylor!"

The two agents peered back at her and then focused straight ahead. The truck pulled out of the parking space.

"What? Oh. Yes, of course. I'm sorry."

"Yeah, Taylor, you are, Taylor. I'll talk with you later." Jennifer ended the call. A second call came in on her cell phone, and she declined it.

When they pulled into the parking garage at the apartment, Jennifer noticed someone standing at the elevator. The truck rolled into a parking space, and Jennifer opened the door and hopped out. The lead agent closed her door and began walking with her to the elevator.

She saw the unmistakable figure of Tank, standing anxiously at the elevator. As she approached, she noted his genuine worried look. She also looked at his tight faded blue jeans and bulging T-shirt. In a suit, it wasn't easy to see the thick muscles and broad shoulders. The elevator door was open, and as Jennifer approached Tank, he stepped forward.

"Are you okay? I heard everything," he said with an unevenness in his voice.

He reached out and grabbed her hands. Jennifer suddenly felt overwhelmed. Her chest tightened as the images of the firefight flashed in her head: the agent's blood oozing on the blacktop, her wrist being blown apart, the screams of agony, and the deafening loud bangs of the bullets. She felt as if she were a dam, and the shocking horrors of the day, the surging water behind it.

"I was so scared that you may have been killed," Tank said softly. His wide eyes showed sincere grief.

That was it. The dam broke, and the water burst forth. Jennifer tried to say something, but instead she burst out in tears. Tank caught her as she swooned.

He scooped her up in one quick motion and carried her in his arms as he stepped into the elevator.

"Get out!" he yelled to the two agents.

They gave him a shocked look for just a moment and then quickly exited. The doors closed, and Tank held her tighter. In moments they were on the second floor. Tank carried her quickly to her door and then fumbled for his key. Jennifer continued sobbing into Tank's chest. He opened the door and walked her into the bedroom. As he approached the bed, Jennifer yelled out.

"No, I'm a mess."

Tank looked down at the dried blood on her arms and shirt. Her slacks were torn and covered in blood. He turned and carried her into the bathroom. He gently set her down and then turned on the shower.

"Help me," Jennifer wept.

Her hands were shaking too much for her to unbutton her blouse. Tank slowly undid each button while she leaned against him, sobbing. After kneeling down, he unzipped her slacks. Blacktop stains, dried blood, and scratches painted her legs. He slipped her shoes off and then stood up, opening the shower door for her.

"No," she whimpered, "I want you with me." She pulled at his T-shirt. Tank quickly stripped out of his shirt. He then helped her into the shower, stepping in behind her with his jeans and boots still on. She clung to his chest as the hot water beat down.

After several minutes, the stall filled with steam and Jennifer's weeping gave way to sniffles.

Tank grabbed a bar of soap and gently lathered up her back. He massaged her shoulders and then pulled her into the stream to wash off. She slowly spun back around to face him.

"You still have your jeans on," she said softly. She unbuttoned his jeans and slowly peeled them down. He then leaned over and gave her a long, sensual kiss.

There was a white light and a hissing noise, and I removed my headset.

"Wow, that's just too much," I said to myself. "Whew, I need a cold shower now," I mumbled aloud. I stepped into the kitchenette and grabbed a glass of water.

"Okay, so maybe that *is* where my African blood came from," I mumbled as I returned to the couch. I placed the headset back on my head. There was again a white light and some hissing noise.

After an hour of passionate love, Jennifer looked Terrance deep in his eyes.

"Terrance, I don't think I can do this anymore." Her eyes were large and welled with tears.

"Do what? Make love?" Tank replied.

Jennifer shook her head. "No, I mean this job, as a translator. I don't want to die."

Her bottom lip trembled.

Terrance kneeled over the top of her, staring down at her eyes for a moment. He lowered down and gave her a soft kiss.

"I know you're scared; you have every right to be. Just take some time to think it over. Let your emotions clear. We'll get some sleep, and I'm sure you'll feel better." He leaned down again and kissed her.

The phone rang. Jennifer startled while Terrance rolled over and grabbed the receiver.

"Yes?" he said.

Jennifer looked over his shoulder. It was 2:36 p.m.

"Tell him she's not here," Tank said with authority. "What? Fine, then send him up!" His voice was loud, with a touch of anger.

Jennifer stared intently at him. Terrance gave her a look.

"We're about to have company," he said as he stepped out of the bed.

"I don't want to talk to him," Jennifer mumbled. She pulled the covers up to her neck and gave Tank a woeful look.

He smiled at her. "Yeah, I'll do it," he said as he looked around the room for something to put on. He reached down and grabbed one of the wet towels off the floor. He cinched it around his waist as the doorbell rang.

As Tank walked to the bedroom doorway, he paused in the opening. "If you hear him get hit and scream, dial 91. When you hear him hit the floor, dial the other one," he said with a smile.

Jennifer giggled as Tank walked to the door. She soon heard the door opening.

"What the hell is this?" Taylor exclaimed.

"It's precisely what you think it is, Taylor," Terrance said in a deep but calm voice. "You so callously disrespected the woman who had feelings for you, and now, in her greatest time of need, you're late. So I stepped in."

There was a momentary pause.

"Looks like you did far more than step in. Is that what we pay the Secret Service for?" Taylor yelled.

"You'd best check yourself," Tank cautioned, his voice now louder. "Your lady was nearly killed today, but you were too busy to care?"

"I'm here now! And I don't need advice from you!" Taylor replied, his voice now loud and angry.

Jennifer jumped out of bed. She grabbed a robe and began to walk toward the door.

"I want to see her!" Taylor yelled.

"I'm not about to let you talk with—"

Jennifer turned down the hallway, coming into Taylor's line of sight.

"What do you *want*, Taylor?" Jennifer huffed.

"What the hell, Jennifer? The first chance you get, you sleep with your bodyguard?"

Taylor was now trembling with rage and starting to pace in the hallway.

"Really?" Jennifer said calmly as she tied her robe. "Is that what I did? Can I please see your phone, Taylor?"

"What?" Taylor stopped pacing and gave Jennifer a shocked expression.

"Your phone—may I see it please?" Jennifer said softly, smiling at Taylor.

She had a pleading look and extended her hand. Taylor slowly reached into his suit jacket and pulled out his phone. Jennifer quickly snatched it from his hand and then stepped back into the apartment, behind Tank.

"What's your lock code?"

Taylor stood staring at her.

"Your lock code, Taylor—what is it?" Jennifer asked again.

"6969" Taylor said with a huff.

Jennifer shook her head as she typed it in. She tapped a few buttons. Taylor became more agitated.

"What are you doing?" His voice's pitch was slightly higher than before. "Can I have my phone back!" His voice grew shaky.

Jennifer took another step back into the apartment, and Tank pivoted, blocking the doorway.

"Oh, here we are," Jennifer said with a happy tone to her voice. "Let's see, from Rachel. 'Hey baby, can't wait to feel your strong thrusts inside me.' Oh, and now she calls me a bitch; isn't that sweet?"

"My phone, give it back!" Taylor screamed.

The ding of the elevator reaching the floor echoed down the hall, and two agents stepped out. Tank gave them a hand gesture to stop.

"Oh, and here's another one, this time from a Tammy. Isn't that the young blonde—one of the president's aides? Whoa! This one is too graphic to miss. She wants to put her tongue—"

"*Goddamn it, give me my phone!*" Taylor screamed. His face was dark red and noticeably trembling. Jennifer took a step toward the doorway.

"So I'm sorry, Taylor. Can you remind me what you said to me a moment ago? Oh, wait, that's right. You said the first chance *I* get to bed down with my bodyguard. You think I'm an idiot, Taylor?" Jennifer's voice now seethed with anger. "You think I couldn't smell Rachel's perfume on *your* neck as you kissed me the other night? You think you're going to play *me* for a fool?" she screamed. "*How dare you!*" Her voice echoed down the hallway. "I get you your job, save your mother's life, and give you my love, and *this is how you repay me?*"

She hurled the phone at Taylor, just missing Tank's head by two inches. He ducked as it whizzed by his ear and smashed against the wall, breaking into several pieces.

"How many other women are you screwing at work, Taylor?" Jennifer yelled out.

Tank motioned to the agents hovering behind Taylor.

"Time for you to leave, Taylor," Terrance stated calmly. He put his hand on Jennifer's chest, gently pushing her back and away from the door. Taylor stood trembling in the hallway, his eyes afire with anger. He looked first at his phone in pieces on the floor and then over to Jennifer.

"You bitch!" he screamed as he dived toward her.

Tank spun around and threw a punch. It connected hard with Taylor's chest. His feet flew forward as he was thrust back from the punch. He slammed hard to the ground, the thud being joined by a huge gasp. Taylor lost his wind and twitched on the carpet.

The two agents rushed up and grabbed Taylor. They quickly lifted him back to his feet while he was gasping and clutching at his chest.

"Let's go!" the one agent exclaimed with an icy tone.

Tank slowly shook his head, took two steps backward, and then closed the door.

"I've been such a fool," Jennifer said, breathing heavily and trembling as she turned to walk back to the bedroom. Terrance put a hand around her and pulled her close, her back tight against his chest.

"You're young; you make mistakes," Tank said with a whisper as he clutched her tightly.

Jennifer shuddered, and a tear streamed down her cheek.

"You tried to warn me," she sniffed.

"We all learn," he said softly. "Some of us learn better the hard way."

Jennifer spun slowly around. Terrance wiped the tear from her cheek, and she gave him a smile. He picked her up and carried her into the bedroom. He set her down softly, dropped his towel, and then slid into bed.

She crawled up over his large chest and laid her head down. Her arm extended up, caressing his face.

"I should have listened to you," she mumbled.

He gently stroked her hair.

"So what's going to happen now?" she said as she looked up into his eyes.

"Well, knowing Taylor, he's going to blab to my boss about this."

"No he won't," Jennifer responded.

Terrance gave her a big grin. "What? How do you know?" He cleared his throat. "As a Secret Service agent, most of my day is spent standing around, listening. We observe, we plan, we think ahead, but, most of all, we listen. And from what I've heard and what other agents have heard, Taylor is not a person to be trusted or taken lightly. He'll burn you in a hot second, as you just found out."

Jennifer sat up. "He can't get me fired, can he?"

Tank laughed. "Oh heck no," he chuckled. "If there's one person in the White House with a secure job, it's you, Jennifer. No, you're fine. But be sure that he will tell my boss I've crossed a line. Did you see how angry he was?"

Jennifer nodded slowly.

"Yeah, well, men like that don't take to being shamed too well—especially in public. If he could, he'd burn this whole building down. But since he's a coward, he'll do the next best thing. He'll snivel and moan about this incident to my boss."

"Well, don't you worry; I'll talk to the president and—"

"*No!*" Terrance exclaimed.

Jennifer recoiled in shock.

He gave her a sorrowful nod. "No, please don't," he said in a softer tone. "I'm a man of principle; you know that. I can handle my own business and take whatever comes."

"Oh no, Terrance, I won't have that jerk put you out," Jennifer said as she leaned in.

Tank smiled and gave her a kiss.

"That's all right. I'll be fine. If they dismiss me, I can easily get a job training agents. I've already been offered that position a few times."

Jennifer laid her head back down on his chest.

"I'm sorry if I messed things up for you," she said softly.

Terrance rubbed her back and stroked her hair. For the rest of the evening, Jennifer and Tank had dinner, watched a movie, and then drifted off to sleep.

When 5:00 a.m. rolled around, Tank got out of bed and went back down to the first-floor room before his shift started. He already had several changes of clothing in the first-floor apartment.

By seven forty-five, Jennifer was in the truck, ready for work.

"Good morning, gentlemen," Jennifer said to Tank and the other agent.

They smiled back to her as the truck started up.

"I'm glad you decided to come back to work," Tank said as he peered back at her through the rearview mirror. Jennifer smiled back at him. As they started to drive, Jennifer placed a call to Rachel.

"Hello?"

"Hi, Rachel, it's Jennifer. Are you coming to work today?"

"Yes. I got a late start, so I'll be at the White House by 8:00 a.m. I had a rough night."

"Did Taylor call you last night?"

"Taylor? Why? No. What's up?"

"Nothing. I'll see you in a few minutes."

In five minutes, they were at the White House. Jennifer walked into the conference room. Taylor was notably absent. She grabbed a hot tea and then spotted Rachel walking in. Jennifer motioned her into the hallway and pulled her aside.

"Rachel, listen, we need to talk."

Rachel gave Jennifer a surprised look.

"I want to discuss what happened yesterday. It's obvious now that we're a target, but having it actually happen, well, I just wanted to know if you felt comfortable with continuing with this job."

Rachel paused a moment, choosing her words.

"Well, I never really thought too hard about it. I always felt safe with the agents and then the marines. But yesterday was so, so real. I won't lie. I thought about it all last night. I mean, it's just a job, and I don't know if I want to be dying for it, or watch anyone else die around me. I guess I'll stay, but I'll take it day by day."

Jennifer nodded and turned around. She took a deep breath and then pivoted back to face Rachel.

"One more thing," Jennifer said as she gave Rachel a serious look. "I'm not sure if you knew that Taylor and I were getting close socially or not; my guess is that you did."

Rachel feigned a shocked expression. "What?"

"Let me finish, Rachel. With this job, I really need to know I can trust you."

"No, Jennifer, I don't know what you're—"

"Rachel, I read your text messages on Taylor's phone, so cut the bullshit."

Rachel's mouth hung open, and her eyes darted back and forth.

"Jennifer, I'm sorry," she said, her voice shaking.

"No, no, you're not. You're sorry you got caught. The question now is, can I trust you?" Jennifer yelled. "Rachel, we nearly died yesterday," she said in a lower tone as she looked over her shoulder into the conference room. "I need everyone who's on my team to be working as a team. So no more lying, no more all-night partying."

"And Taylor?" Rachel asked.

Jennifer laughed. "Wow, I thought you were better than that." She brushed her brow with her hand. "No, if you want to date or screw Taylor, be my guest. I want nothing to do with him. Just know that he's also sleeping with other women around here too."

Rachel stood shocked.

"Oh, I'm sorry, did that come off as me sounding like *a bitch?*" Jennifer said with a touch of sarcasm.

A staffer ran down the hall, "Miss Winston, the president is waiting for you in the Oval Office."

Jennifer shook her head at Rachel and walked away.

As Jennifer walked into the Oval Office, she noticed Taylor, Lance, and several other men that she had yet to meet. The president perked up.

"Nice to see you this morning, Jennifer; how was your evening?" the president asked.

"It was quite restful, sir, thank you," Jennifer said. She gave Taylor a sneer.

"Please, have a seat," he said as he motioned her to a chair. Jennifer sat down.

Lance then began. "We've been working all night on this attack. We found that the men who attacked your team in Detroit are part of a group called Freedom for All. This group has been very vocal on social media, they've been growing faster than any other groups, and, well, we were woefully underinformed."

Lance stood up and began to pace the room.

"This group is apparently very well funded and quite informed. They seem to have intimate knowledge of the schedules you keep. We have intercepted some communications, and they were planning another ambush on your group."

Jennifer gave the president a concerned look.

"So we are going to change things up a little bit. We'd like to replace your assistant Rachel with a highly skilled agent. Taylor has agreed to reassign Rachel to his group."

Jennifer peered over at Taylor and rolled her eyes. Lance caught the look and paused a moment.

"We will assign someone new, and as a precaution, we will replace your cell phone with a secure phone. In addition, we have a prototype Qyron bulletproof vest for you and Xho to wear."

Lance walked to the side of the room and grabbed a black cloth item. Jennifer stood up.

"You can wear a shirt over this and you should keep cool enough."

Jennifer grabbed the garment. She draped it down and then tried to put her arms through it. Taylor reached over.

"Here let me help," Taylor said as he grabbed her arm.

Jennifer jumped back and quickly swatted his arm away.

"Don't *you* touch me!" she yelled.

The proverbial pin could have dropped and everyone would have heard it clearly. Jennifer nervously looked at Lance and then the president. They had identical looks—that of a person holding his breath in surprise.

"Sorry," she said softly.

One of the men standing in the corner stepped forward. He glanced at the president and then walked over to Jennifer.

"I would like everyone except Jennifer and the president to leave, please."

The rest of the people in the room slowly ambled out of the room. Taylor stood up, looked at Jennifer, and then left the room. He closed the door behind him.

"Jennifer, this is Ernest Baker; he's in charge of the CIA," said the president.

Ernest extended his hand, and Jennifer shook it.

"Please, call me Ernie. Jennifer, I need to speak with you about your communications. The terrorist attack on your group yesterday had far too much precise information about your schedule." Jennifer felt nervous. She gave the president a glance; his face was serious. "Did you discuss your plans with anyone during the week?"

Jennifer looked up at Ernie. He was an older man, in his sixties. His brown hair was thinning and heavily speckled with gray. If he were sitting on a porch with a glass of lemonade, he'd make a really good grandfatherly figure. But here he was, standing over Jennifer while she sat in a chair, making her feel nervous and guilty.

"No. Uh, I don't really talk to anyone about where I'm going—only afterward."

Jennifer shifted awkwardly in her chair. Her hands were cold, and her chest felt tight. Ernie smiled and knelt down alongside her.

"There's no reason to be nervous, Jennifer; I'm just trying to find out how so much information is being breached," he said softly.

Jennifer gave him a smile, but she still felt uneasy. The president stood up. He walked around his desk.

"Stand up," he said calmly.

Jennifer stood up. The president grabbed her hands and looked into her eyes.

"Jennifer, this is all for the good of your team and for your own safety. We obviously have someone among us who is sharing your schedule with a terrorist group. You're lucky to be alive, so we need you to tell us anything and everything you can think of that may be out of the ordinary."

Jennifer nodded. "Well, there's not much that's different than when we started." She looked over at Ernie. "I discuss our plans through Taylor and with Rachel, and she makes up the schedule. I don't tell anyone else. I know she shares the schedule with the Secret Service so they can plan our agents," Jennifer said nervously.

Ernie then gave the president a glance. He stepped in front of Jennifer. "Okay, now I have a few uncomfortable questions to ask you."

The president released his grasp on her hands and walked around his desk and sat down. Jennifer nodded to Ernie.

"I'm aware of some social issues that have been occurring within your group. There have been some statements made, so I would like to hear your side of the story."

Jennifer gave Ernie a confused look. "About what and who?"

Ernie pivoted the chair next to Jennifer to face her. "Why not just tell me everything you feel that's notable?"

Jennifer thought for a moment, "Well, I've had some problems with Rachel. She has an issue with partying all night and not being ready for work the next morning."

"Was anyone with her when she was out after hours?"

"I went out with her one evening, and I believe one of the agents joined her on another night."

"Three nights, actually," Ernie added.

Jennifer shook her head. "Wow, I guess there was more going on than I was aware of."

Ernie nodded and then prompted her to continue.

"She's done a fair job in keeping the schedule, but I don't know if she's talked to anyone; I'm sorry."

"And what about Taylor? It's obvious something is going on between you two."

Jennifer took a deep breath. "Well, we were together socially. But I found out that he's been, uh, having relations with other women here, so I ended it last night."

Ernie grimaced and shook his head. "Do you discuss your schedule with Taylor?"

"I don't; Rachel does the coordinating with him, and, well, since those two have been more than friendly, I guess you'd have to ask them what was shared after hours."

Ernie gave the president a look and then turned his gaze back to Jennifer.

"Anything else?" Ernie asked. "Do you discuss your work with anyone outside of the job?"

"Well, I call my mother and my best friend, Tasha, but I don't tell them any upcoming details. I've mentioned where we've been. I'm sorry; is that okay?"

Ernie nodded. "Past information isn't the issue," he said. "How about yesterday?"

"Well, we started here with—"

"No, after work," Ernie added.

"I went right home after speaking with the president. I stayed in my apartment all day and discussed nothing with anyone."

"You were alone?"

"No, I said that I discussed nothing with anyone," Jennifer said with a touch of sarcasm. "What is it you want to know, Ernie? Because what I did with whom on my own time is my business, right?"

"Agreed, Miss Winston."

The president stood up. "Okay, Jennifer, we will be replacing Rachel with Don. Is that acceptable to you?" the president asked.

"Yes, that's fine. I would like to meet and speak with Don though," Jennifer said as there came a knock on the door.

Ernie walked over and opened it. A man walked in. He was

short—about five foot seven—with brown hair. He had a boyish face with a goatee. He walked over to Jennifer.

"Hi, I'm Don Winters, and I'll be working with you now," he held out his hand. Jennifer shook it and gave a raised eyebrow to Ernie.

"Perfect timing, Ernie," she said with a smile, placing her fingers to her temples. "I'm feeling like a ham and sausage breakfast muffin."

Ernie smiled and shook his head.

"I've already been briefed on the scheduling. I've moved Wednesday to today, and we're ready to go. Xho is in the transport, waiting," Don said.

Jennifer looked at Ernie and the president.

"Is there anything else?" she asked, looking squarely at Ernie.

"No, that's all I need for now," Ernie said.

Jennifer and Don then left the Oval Office. As they walked through the White House, they quickly discussed the planning for today. On the transport to Mexico, they discussed workflow and procedure. When the transport landed, Jennifer waited for everyone to walk out of the transport. She grabbed Tank by the arm. As they began to walk across grounds at the National Palace, Jennifer whispered to Terrance, "So, did anyone say anything to you?"

Tank continued walking in stride with Jennifer.

"My boss asked me if I had discussed anything with you about your job."

"I'm glad he didn't fire you," Jennifer whispered back.

"It's not over yet," Tank said. "I'm expecting some sort of reprimand though."

The rest of the day went smoothly. Don was very efficient with keeping the schedule, and at dinner they chatted and got to know one another. When they reached the hotel in Panama City, Jennifer waited an hour and then sneaked over to Tank's room.

The rest of the week went fairly smoothly. There were a few protests in Japan, Chile, and Spain, but no violence. They were able to work fourteen-hour days to make up for the day lost on Monday. By the time Friday arrived, though, Jennifer was exhausted.

When they landed back in Washington, DC, Jennifer pulled Don aside.

"Don, you've done an incredible job this week, thank you. I wish I would have had you with me from the start. Have a great weekend."

"No problem," Don responded. "I'm glad I was a smooth transition for you." He gave her a smile and then walked away.

Jennifer turned and entered the White House with Tank and the other agent. They were met in the hallway by Mr. Atkins.

"Terry, I need to see you," Mr. Atkins said. His face resembled an angry raisin—shrunken and full of wrinkles.

Jennifer shot Tank a look. He gave her a wink and shook his head.

"I'll be right back," Tank told Jennifer. Jennifer smiled and then turned to see Rachel walking her way.

"Jennifer, wait!" Rachel called out.

Ugh, I wish I could run away.

Jennifer stood in the hallway and waited.

"Jennifer, we have the new safety clothes for you."

Rachel stopped and motioned for Jennifer to follow her. She waited until Jennifer caught up with her, and then she walked with her down the hall.

"How was your week?" Rachel asked.

"Smooth and safe," Jennifer snapped.

"Oh, yeah, mine too. Not as much adventure here; more boring stuff, but ..." Rachel said with a smile, but Jennifer was stone-faced and staring directly ahead. "Jennifer, look; I ..." Rachel grabbed Jennifer's hand, and Jennifer stopped abruptly and pulled her arm away.

"Jennifer, I'm not seeing Taylor anymore. I just wanted to—"

"I don't care what you're doing or who you're seeing, and I certainly don't wanna hear anything about Taylor. I'm done with him and look forward to only having to see him on Mondays in the briefing. Now where is the safety clothing?"

Rachel maintained a smile for a moment longer but then dropped her head and continued walking.

When they reached the end of the hallway, Rachel stepped into a room. It held numerous black garments draped on hangers.

Rachel pointed to one rack. "Your size should be there."

Jennifer walked over to the rack. Several shirts, skirts, and pants, all black and shiny, hung on plastic hangers. Jennifer grabbed a shirt. It felt soft and somewhat slinky in her hand, but it was no heavier than a normal cotton shirt.

"It's very light; I tried one on to verify the size," Rachel said quietly. "The only downside is that it's a little warm."

Jennifer grabbed several outfits.

"Oh, I have a bag for you." Rachel walked over to a table. She grabbed the bag and walked over to Jennifer, who snatched it out of her hands and then placed several garments into it.

"I don't blame you for hating me," Rachel said. "I acted so poorly, and I betrayed your trust."

"Yes, *you did*," Jennifer snorted. "You had a golden opportunity to be traveling the world with us—heck, the solar system and beyond. I just don't understand you, Rachel," Jennifer hissed as she shook her head.

"Jennifer, please, I'm—"

"No, Rachel, *don't!*" Jennifer said sternly.

She turned and walked out of the room. As she marched down the hallway, she saw Robert, her other agent this week, and another man.

"Jennifer!" Robert called out. "Jennifer, this is Demetri. He'll be with us this evening."

Demetri smiled and extended his hand.

"What? Wait a minute; where's Tank?"

"Well …"

"*Where's Tank, Robert?*"

Robert stepped close to Jennifer and leaned over.

"I think he just quit," Robert whispered. "I was told to grab Demetri and—"

"*Where is he now?*" Jennifer demanded as she tried to push by him. Her eyes welled up and her rate of breathing increased.

"Settle down," Robert whispered as he pulled her arm. "I believe he's heading back to the apartment to grab his things. If you want—"

"*Let's go!*" Jennifer shouted, and she stormed down the hallway.

"Amant? Hello, Amant?"

There was a white light and some hissing, and I pulled the headset from my head.

Chapter 22

"JOHN!" I YELLED AS MY reality came back into focus. My head hurt, and the room had a slight spin to it.

"What? I was tired of waiting. I'm starving," John said.

"Damn it, John, don't do that! It's very unnerving!"

"What?" John said with a stunned look.

"You yelling while I'm in a Psy-log. It's like ripping someone out of a dream. It's painful, Johnny!"

John sat down alongside me. He leaned over and gave me a kiss.

"I'm sorry, Amant. I was hungry, and I just wanted you with me."

I felt my anger wash away. John was smiling at me, and his look was truly sincere. It wasn't as much the abrupt tear from the Psy-log that agitated me as it was his pulling me right out of such a dramatic moment. I felt as if someone had snapped on the lights in the middle of a really good scene in a movie. I took a deep breath, closed my eyes, and slowly exhaled. The room stopped spinning, and my headache abated. I opened my eyes to see Johnny and his puppy dog sad face.

"Oh stop it," I said with a grin. "I know you better than that. Okay, let's go eat."

We walked to the dining hall, and I began to tell him about the logs. After grabbing our food, we sat down, and I continued. Johnny was hanging on every word.

While we were eating, Johnny leaned across the table.

"This is awesome," he said softly. I gave him a confused look.

"What do you mean, Jennifer's life?"

"No. Well, yes, her story is really interesting, but this whole thing," he said as he swirled his finger in the air. "I love that we're just talking, enjoying our meal together."

261

He reached his hand across the table and held mine.

"This is really nice," he said with a warm smile. "Why don't we just do this for a few days?"

I gave him a confused look.

"What I mean is, how about we just take a few days to just do us? Let's hang out, watch some movies, play some games, make a little love—just enjoy each other's company. No lengthy Psy-logging, no creeping around the ship, no fights—just you and me."

He was massaging my hand and looking into my eyes.

"Well, sure, Johnny, that sounds great."

I leaned across the table and gave him a kiss. He was right; this did feel great—just us.

When we were done eating, we took a stroll around the transport. We walked all throughout Alpha Deck and then decided to check out Bravo. We noticed that some things were different from one deck to another. The gym on Bravo Deck was a little nicer, but the dining hall was worse. We then made a point to visit every deck to check on the accommodations. After all, we still had about twenty-five more Earth days of travel, so we wanted to experience the best that the transport had to offer, which wasn't saying much.

After a solid three hours of walking, we finally made up our list. The best dining hall was on Charlie Deck, the nicest gym was on Delta, and the cleanest entertainment area was on Golf Deck. Of course, when we tried to access Fox Deck, we were denied. The elevators went past that deck without stopping. I was starting to get tired, so we made our way back to the room.

"So how about we watch a movie in the bedroom?" John asked.

That was fine with me. I was about ready for bed, and snuggling next to John and drifting off sounded perfect. I don't even remember the movie. I was so tired I only made it through the opening credits.

When I woke up, John wasn't in the bed. I saw a message flashing on the monitor.

"Read message," I said.

There was a tone. "Hey Amant, in case you wake up, I'm at the gym. I wanted to work out before bed. See you soon. John."

I stretched and then thought about the time. I would take a shower and then grab a quick bite to eat. By that time, John should be done with his workout and ready for bed. I could Psy-log while he slept for the following eight hours.

So I took a hot shower and then got into some sweats and a T-shirt. As I was about to walk out the door to the dining hall, it opened.

"Oh, hey Johnny," I said as I leaned in. I was about to hug him when his body odor hit me. "Whew, you reek, lover," I gasped while I held my nose.

"Yeah, well, hazard of being fit," he quipped. "Nice to see you're finally up." He smiled as he walked by me. "Are you heading to get breakfast?" he asked. I nodded. "Well, do me a favor and hold up; let me grab a quick shower, and I'll have a small bite to eat before bed."

"Okay, Johnny, hurry up. Tummy is a-rumbling."

I sat down on the couch and grabbed my laptop. I went into the Qyron ship listing. I stepped through every transport in the list; I had been on every one of them. I could not find the one we were on. Then it dawned on me—I had no idea of the name of this transport. I looked over at the desk and spotted John's boarding pass. I grabbed it. We were on the *Dultz*. My mother had tried to teach me the Qyron language. I could speak it well enough to stumble by, but I had never truly grasped the entire language. I was always more interested in going outside and playing, or learning science. The Qyron language was like Latin, in that there were root names. *Dultz* escaped me.

I quickly performed a search of the Qyron Compendium. "Dultz" came up as "cleaning" or "to process." I thought maybe John was right and this transport's purpose was setting up a brand-new colony.

My next inquiry was about Gamma Five. It didn't show up in my directory at all. This was truly odd. Even when we discovered a new habitable planet, it would instantly show in the colony directory. There would be news about it, and the Qyron would immediately initiate terraforming plans. I could find no trace at all on Gamma Five.

At this point, I would normally have linked into the central Qyron database, but this was not possible when on board a moving transport.

John walked out of the bathroom; a cloud of steam billowed forth.

"Uh, with all that heat and steam, I'll bet you're still sweaty," I said wryly.

John walked over to me on the couch. "Sweaty or not, you can't say no to this body," he said smoothly.

He dropped his towel. I quickly leaned forward, staring hard at his groin.

"Johnny, oh my gosh, you've steamed it away!" I pretended to be looking in vain.

"Knock it off!" John laughed. He pushed me back into the couch and then sauntered into the bedroom. "Be ready in thirty seconds," he said.

As we walked to the dining hall on Charlie Deck, I gave John a smile.

"Um, Johnny?" I batted my eyelashes while presenting my best girlishly cute smile.

"Uh oh, I know this look. This can't be good," John said cautiously.

"I know you said you didn't want to do anything but enjoy each other for the next few days."

"Here it comes," he added.

"But, well, I found another mystery. This transport doesn't show up in the Qyron ship registry. I had to dig really hard just to find that it exists!" John gave me a worried look. He sighed and shook his head.

"Then I looked up Gamma Five, and it too wasn't listed in the colony directory." John gave me a blank stare. "John, I've seen two balls of dirt colonized, and in both cases, the instant the habitable planet or moon was discovered, it made it into the colony directory. The Qyron are sticklers for procedure, Johnny. This planet doesn't exist!"

John stopped walking. His expression now changed to one of anger.

"Really!" John yelled. "You had to do this, didn't you?"

"What?" I said in shock, taking a step back.

"All I wanted was a few days to relax and enjoy things. It started out great; we had a wonderful day. Then you had to go and, well, be *you!*"

"What does *that* mean?" I threw my hands on my hips and cocked my head.

"Oh, you *know* what it means; you know *damn well*, Missy!" John yelled.

I hated that name—Missy. I thought it made me sound old and wrong.

"You do this, Amant. You remember your birthday present when you turned eight?"

I was a deer in the headlights. John was now breathing heavily and notably shaken. His nostrils flared as he breathed, and I suddenly felt under pressure. My mind raced, but I couldn't remember.

"The science kit!" John yelled.

Oh, yes, now I remembered.

"Do you recall how you hounded me, how you pestered and hassled me and then finally tricked my dad into letting you into my room when I was at school?"

I giggled.

"It's not funny! You're like a damn, well, like a ... *ugh!* I don't know!" John flailed his arms in the air. "You're tenacious; you don't give up. You're impossible!"

A few people slid by us awkwardly in the passageway, trying not to make eye contact. I stepped close to John. He tried to back away, still angry and miserable in his current fiery state. I lunged forward and gave him a hug.

"Oh Johnny, I'm sorry," I said.

He tried to pull away. I craned my head up and gave him a big, wet kiss. His struggling eventually died away. He finally hugged and kissed me back.

"All I wanted, you badger, was to have a few days of fun and relaxation. But now we're not going to stop until you've uncovered this little mystery of yours. I'm sure it's something stupid," he said, still trying to be gruff.

I reached up on my tiptoes and gave him another big kiss.

"I'm too pretty for you to be mad at me," I said in a very sultry voice.

I playfully licked his nose and then turned around and slinked down the hallway, wiggling my butt as much as I could muster.

"Damn you!" John yelled as he trotted to catch up. He reached me as I got to the lift. I pressed the button, and the doors opened. We got on the elevator and went to C Deck to eat.

We chatted while we ate. I had ten pancakes, an omelet, two bowls of oatmeal, some fruit, and three glasses of juice. I was tired of feeling hungry and knew that I'd need enough food to get through the next eight hours of Psy-logging.

"Okay, Johnny, I want to know why this shuttle doesn't show up in the normal registry or why the Gamma Five colony can't be found. Then there's the lockout of Fox Deck."

My mind was spinning. I was trying to think of any reasons to explain it.

"I'm telling you, it's all new," John mumbled. I gave him my stinky-face look and then continued to think as I ate.

"I'll prove it to you," John said as he stood up.

He walked around me, and I spun around to follow him. At another table was a maintenance worker. John tapped him on the shoulder.

"Excuse me, mind if I ask you a few questions?"

The man turned and nodded, mouth open.

"Are you new to this ship?" John asked.

"Uh, no, I've been assigned here for three years now," the man replied.

"But this is your first trip to Gamma Five?" John asked, flashing me a smug look.

"No, this is my"—the man paused a moment—"seventeenth time now ... maybe eighteenth."

John's smile went flat. "So what's the planet like?" John inquired.

"I have no idea; we're not allowed off the transport when we offload," he said.

"Uh, yeah, thanks," John said without emotion. He ambled back to his seat like a zombie and plopped down in his chair.

"See!" I whispered to him loudly as I clenched his arm. "Now this makes even less sense, Johnny. This transport has been in use for three years, and it still doesn't show up—or the planet! And what sense does it make to disallow shore leave or off-boarding?"

We finished eating quietly. John then stood up from the table, grabbed his tray, and walked over to the entrance. As we put our trays away, he grabbed my hand and walked silently back toward the room.

When we approached the lift, John turned to me.

"So, if your purpose for all of this was to scare me, mission accomplished," he said quietly.

The door to the lift opened. A few people were in the elevator. We stepped inside and pushed the *A* button. I squeezed his hand.

"That is certainly not what I wanted to do, John."

A woman in the elevator peered over at me; her eyes scanned me.

"Excuse me," I said to her. "Is this your first trip to Gamma Five?"

She looked shocked for a moment and then looked at both John and me.

"Um, yes it is, why?" she responded slowly.

"Oh, we're just surveying passengers; it's for a study," I said with a smile. I turned to the other four people in the elevator. Collectively, they all nodded.

"And why are you going to Gamma Five?" I followed up.

One man smiled at me. "I'm starting a new job at Renkers Industries."

The others replied in kind that they were all starting new jobs, just like John.

"Thank you so much for your input; I appreciate it," I said as the door opened to Alpha Deck. We walked out and then stopped in the passageway. The other people quietly walked by.

"So what does that do for us?" John asked.

"Well, it seems that all the passengers are starting new jobs. Maybe if we know why everyone is going to Gamma Five, it will help us understand what's going on, John."

"So why don't we survey Alpha Deck's dining and entertainment halls?" John asked.

I gave him a smile. "Great idea, Johnny. I knew you'd come around!"

I grabbed his hand, and we walked to the dining hall. I asked about a hundred people, and many were starting new jobs. About twenty were going for some form of training. I wrote down the company names on my pad. As we walked to the entertainment hall, John yawned.

"Oh, sorry, Johnny; we'll make this quick," I said.

John flashed me a smile, but I could see that he was exhausted. We surveyed another fifty people and then returned to our room.

"So please tell me you're not going to go creeping around the ship while I'm asleep?" John asked as he stripped out of his clothes.

Damn him. I had actually been planning on doing just that. My curiosity was itching me all over, and I really wanted to dig into this.

John was right; I am tenacious when it comes to something I want. I'm double that when it's a mystery. The problem was, John could always tell when I was lying. That's how he knew I had peeked at my gift when we were eight. I was bad at hiding lies.

"So promise me," John said as he pulled the covers back, "that you're not going to go sleuthing around while I'm sleeping."

"Aw, well, Johnny—"

"Promise!" he said with authority.

I sighed heavily and gave him a pouting look. He didn't budge.

"Fine!" I snorted, and I turned to leave the bedroom.

"Amant!"

I stopped at the opening to the bedroom.

"Where's my good night kiss?" he asked softly.

I stomped over to him and gave him a dry peck on the cheek. He grabbed my arm.

"Oh no you don't!" He pulled me close and locked his lips on mine. We kissed for a full minute.

"Damn, baby! You keep kissing me like that, and I'll keep you up for another hour," I giggled. John smiled and climbed into bed.

I walked back out to the living room, feeling as if I were grounded. There was no way I could sit and watch a movie or even work out in the gym. I had to get my mind off of this. I walked out to the kitchenette and grabbed a water. I looked over at my headset and then sat down on the couch. As I contemplated, I heard the low drone of snoring coming from the bedroom. No way could I sit and listen to that. I grabbed the headset and put it on my head. There was a white light and some hissing noises.

Chapter 23

As THE TRUCK PULLED INTO the apartment garage, Jennifer grabbed her bag and luggage. She jumped out of the truck as Robert ran to the elevator alongside her. When the elevator door opened, Robert turned to Jennifer.

"I'll have Demetri take your bags up to your place, and I'll take you to our room," Robert said.

"Thanks," Jennifer replied as she gave her bag and luggage to Demetri.

When they arrived at the first-floor apartment, Robert opened the door. Jennifer burst through.

"Terrance!" she yelled.

Two other agents were sitting in front of a large set of monitors. They jumped up to see Jennifer as she walked down the hallway toward the bedroom. Tank stepped out of the bedroom, eyes wide.

"Jennifer, what are you—"

"Oh, Terrance, what happened?" Jennifer said as she gave him a hug.

Robert walked into the kitchen, avoiding Tank's look, and the other agents quickly turned their gazes back to their bank of monitors.

"Come here," Tank said as he escorted Jennifer into the bedroom. He closed the door behind them.

"Look," he stated in a hushed tone as he sat her down on the bed. "It was more my choice than his." Jennifer started to say something, but Tank gave her a wave of his hand. "I wasn't about to be reassigned, and I didn't want to continue working with you, having to hide our relationship. I can't and won't work like that."

Jennifer stood up and gave Terrance a hug.

"Oh Terrance, what do we do now?"

He placed his arms around her and hugged her back. "I don't know," he said. "I was thinking of maybe taking a few weeks off to clear my head."

Jennifer pulled back. "What? No! I mean, if you leave, then—"

"I'm not going to leave the area. It's not like I'll be walking the Earth. I just think that maybe relaxing for a few weeks to clear my head might do me some good." Tank smiled.

Jennifer could tell that his expression wasn't sincere.

"What will you do, and when will I see you? I'm gone all week, and I want us to be together!" Jennifer said. Tears began to well up in her eyes, and her throat tightened. "I really enjoyed us being together every night this week," she slurred while holding back. It was pointless, though, and she began to cry.

Tank stepped forward and grabbed her. She tried to pull away, but he held her close and then sat them back down on the bed.

"Jennifer, relax," he said as he held her close.

He gave her a kiss as another tear streamed down her cheek. She placed her head on his chest, sniffling.

She perked her head up. "Wait! How about I make you part of my staff?" She pulled out of his hug and stood up. "Yeah, I can bring you on as an assistant. No, wait, as my own personal bodyguard!" Jennifer's eyes were wide, and she was now smiling while wiping a tear away.

"No, Jennifer, that wouldn't—"

"Yeah, then we can be together, and … and you can do the job that you enjoy while we travel the world!"

She lunged back at Tank, this time giving him an excited hug.

"Oh my gosh, this will be great! We can be together every day, traveling the world, rubbing elbows with world leaders and seeing the sights! Yeah, we can be—"

"Jennifer," Tank interrupted. He pushed her back to arm's length. "I don't know if that would work."

Jennifer took a step back. She gave Terrance a shocked, hurtful look.

"What do you mean you don't know if that would work?" Her voice was now an octave higher.

"Well, uh, how would I, um," Tank took a breath. "You would be *my boss?*"

"Yeah, so what? What's the big—oh, wait a minute." Jennifer's mouth dropped open as she took a slow half step back. "*You* have an issue having to answer to *me*—to a woman?" Jennifer's tone now carried a touch of anger.

"Well, no. I just think, well, that it would be weird." Tank's words stumbled as he dropped his eyes.

"Are you kidding me? You're worried about being emasculated by being under a woman!" Jennifer yelled.

Tank gave her a focused stare and raised his hands to quiet her tone.

"How about we grab my things and discuss this in your apartment?" Tank stated as he walked over to his luggage by the closet.

"Are you serious?" Jennifer shook her head and threw her hands in the air. He grabbed two large suitcases, and Jennifer picked up his overnight bag.

They walked out of the bedroom with not a word spoken by anyone. When they walked into Jennifer's apartment, she dropped his bag and walked into her living room. She turned to face him.

"Okay, wait. Let's get something straight right now," Jennifer said with a calm tone from across the room. "Do you want me, Terrance? Do you want to be with me?"

He set his suitcases down and closed the door.

"Yes, I care for you a lot, Jennifer. I just—"

"Would you like us to be together, as a couple, every day?" she continued. Tank nodded, waiting for her to continue. "Then how do you see that happening when I'm away from Monday morning till Friday evening?"

She gave Tank a stare, her lips pursed and head tilted slightly, with her hands on her hips.

"Um, well. I ... I'm not sure," Tank responded quietly as he took a single step.

"Can you see any other way that we could have any sort of relationship—any way of growing closer and falling in love by only seeing each other on the weekends?"

Jennifer's posture didn't waver. She had the perfect angry woman pose.

Tank stopped in his tracks. His six-foot-six frame now seemed to shrink. He was a little boy, shy and withdrawn, having to explain himself to an adult. His eyes darted about, and he fumbled with his fingers.

"Terrance!" she snapped. His eyes locked on to hers. "Do you want me? Do you want us?"

He nodded, his mouth open slightly.

"Are you concerned about my safety?" She straightened her head, now staring directly at him.

He nodded slowly.

"Who has more training on my security staff than you?"

"No one," he said softly.

"Who has more field experience than you?" Jennifer asked.

She dropped her hands from her hips.

"Well, I have the most experi—"

"Who cares about my well-being on a more personal level when we're out there?" Jennifer said as she took a slow step toward Tank.

Tank smiled and nodded.

"Are you going to cower in the face of adversity and run away from a challenge?" She barked as she slowly continued her approach. "I didn't know the SEALs made cowards! I thought you were a strong, principled, *loving* man! Not like *Taylor!*"

She was now within two steps of him.

"I need a big, strong, loving *man* to be with *me*," Jennifer hissed.

She lunged up quickly and slapped his face hard. Tank took a staggering step back and gave her a wide-eyed look. He stiffened up.

"I need a *real* man to protect me!" she yelled, and she swung again, slapping his face harder.

Tank pursed his lips and stood his ground. He gave her an angry look. His arms stiffened, his fists clenched, and his rate of breathing increased.

"Damn it. I need a *real* man to make me feel like a *woman!*" she screamed as she swung again.

She slapped his face, and he lunged at her. In one quick motion, he grabbed her blouse and ripped it open. The buttons popped off, bouncing around the hallway. He grabbed her tightly around the waist and lifted her up, pushing her against the wall with a loud thud. He kissed her hard while she clawed at his back. Her legs wrapped around him while they continued passionately kissing. She pulled at his shirt, ripping it open. He raised his hands up, clasping her head as they continued to kiss. One of his large hands slid down, clasped around her throat, and squeezed. She panted and dug her nails into his chest.

He then pulled her off the wall and carried her into the bedroom.

A half hour later, Jennifer collapsed onto Tank's chest.

"Oh my God," she panted, "I think ... you broke me."

She stared at the dark red raised welts on his chest.

"Terrance?" she gasped between breaths.

"Yes," he said softly.

"I think I'm falling in love with you," she cooed.

"Good," he said quietly as he stroked her hair. "I'm not alone then."

They both dozed for about an hour, lying in each other's arms. Jennifer finally stirred when Tank slid off of the bed. He walked into the bathroom.

"So how do you see this happening?" He said loudly from the bathroom.

"What do you mean?" Jennifer replied groggily. She cleared her throat. "What do you mean?" she repeated, her words louder.

Tank flushed the toilet and then opened the bathroom door.

"How do I become your bodyguard?"

Jennifer sat up. She rubbed her eyes and slid off the bed. As she tried to walk, she let out a yelp. "Ow, damn!"

Tank turned around while washing his hands.

"Are you okay?" he asked as he peered out of the bathroom.

Jennifer gingerly hobbled toward Tank.

"You need to go a little more softly next time, Tiger. I'm really sore."

Tank watched her as she waddled slowly into the bathroom.

"Hey, you wanted the animal beast, you got it," he said in a low tone. "I'm sorry," he added.

"No, you're right," Jennifer said with a pained smile. "I asked for it."

"Wait, asked? Try slapped—or better yet, demanded," Tank laughed. "So how do you see this playing out?"

"Well, I can ask for additional staff, and I know that no one will question it. The president already asked me if I needed more people. And, well, after this week, who would think twice about questioning me if I wanted more security?" Jennifer flushed the toilet.

Tank nodded. "You're right," he said as he dried his hands. "But who pays my salary? I can't see the government shelling out more money when—"

"I will if they won't," Jennifer blurted out.

She now stood face-to-face with Tank. He smiled down at her.

"You're going to pay *my* salary?" His smile grew. "You know that I make—well, I made—one hundred sixty-five thousand dollars this year?"

Jennifer giggled. It began as a single laugh and built into a full-on giggle. Tank stood, his arms crossed on his chest, as she finally regained her composure.

"What's so damn funny?" he said with a snort.

"Terrance," she giggled, "we don't have to worry about money." She grabbed his hands and pulled them off of his hips. "The government is paying me one hundred twenty-five thousand dollars a year." She paused a moment.

"So how are we—" Tank began.

"But the Qyron are paying me one hundred twenty-five thousand dollars a week!"

Tank's eyes went wide. "Are you serious?"

Jennifer nodded. She stepped in and gave Terrance a hug.

"So do you want to work with me every day?" she asked as she smiled up at him.

"It would be my honor," he said as he kissed her.

August 9, 2021

The following Monday, Jennifer and Terrance made their way down the elevator to the waiting truck. Robert and Demetri met them in the garage. Robert gave pause as he saw them.

"What?" Jennifer asked.

"Well, I'm sorry, Miss Winston, but Tank doesn't have White House access now that he no longer works for the Secret Service. I will have to drop you off at the gate, and you will need to get him a visitor pass."

Tank nodded. They got into the truck and were driven to the White House. When they arrived, Tank, Jennifer, and Demetri walked into the visitor center. As they entered the guardhouse, Marvin spotted Tank and Jennifer.

"Good morning, Tank. Why are you coming this way this morning?" Marvin asked.

"I need a visitor pass," Tank replied. "Long story, Marvin."

Jennifer provided her security badge, and Tank was issued a pass.

"Wow, you've come a long way, Miss Winston," Marvin said as he peered up from his desk. He shook her hand.

"Thank you, Marvin," Jennifer said.

When they reached the White House, they walked into the main conference room. Taylor caught sight of Tank and walked over to them.

"Good morning, Jennifer," Taylor said dryly. He looked at Tank's visitor pass.

"Good morning, Taylor. I'm having Terrance added to my staff as a personal bodyguard."

Taylor smiled at Jennifer and then peered at Terrance again.

"Terrance, eh?" Taylor shook his head. "I'm sorry, but we already provide security with the marines and Secret Service."

"I'm bringing him on to my personal staff," Jennifer stated with a huff.

"You don't have a personal staff," Taylor rebuffed. "Your staff is directly through the White House."

"Fine," Jennifer stated coolly. "I'll speak directly with the president and get it okayed." She spun around and stormed out of the meeting room.

"You know you shouldn't test her; she's smarter than you," Tank quipped.

"Please, I won't be outdone by a blonde brat!" Taylor boasted. He stared at Tank for a moment and then began to walk after Jennifer. As Taylor walked down the hallway, he saw Jennifer stopped alongside the president.

"So I would like Terry Brown to be my personal bodyguard, sir," Jennifer stated.

"Hello, Taylor, getting your morning exercise?" the president quipped as Taylor trotted up to them.

"No sir," Taylor said with a smile, "I just wanted to discuss the suggestion of having Mr. Brown as Jennifer's personal bodyguard. I told her that—"

"Yes, I think it's an *excellent idea*, Taylor. Great suggestion!" the president stated. "Get him on staff at once. I'm really sorry to lose him from the Secret Service, but I'm relieved he'll be protecting one of our most important assets." The president turned and smiled at Jennifer. "So let's get this meeting started, Taylor; it's already past 8:00 a.m.!"

The president started toward the conference room with Jennifer walking along. Taylor stood speechless on the spot. Jennifer peered back as they walked, checking that Taylor was several steps beyond earshot, and then leaned over to the president.

"Sir, that wasn't his suggestion."

"Shh, I know," he whispered back. "I'm just giving him payback for you."

He smiled, and Jennifer stifled a giggle.

Everyone was seated when Taylor finally walked into the conference room. He shuffled his papers and looked noticeably shaken.

"Okay, um, good morning," Taylor began, as he stalled for time to organize his thoughts and paperwork.

"All right, we have more progress on lives saved. We just surpassed four hundred thousand lives, and the Qyron are now in most emergency departments as well, so this number should increase dramatically over time. The Wellness Program is also showing high marks, with over two hundred thousand people served. It seems that word of mouth is causing an explosion of people seeking out the program." Taylor took a sip of his coffee. "Our weekly poll has 8 percent acceptance, 35 percent undecided, and 52 percent against."

"That's an excellent trend," the president added.

Taylor glanced at the president and then continued.

"The urban renewal program has now completed in Dallas, Oakland, Chicago, and Detroit. New York and LA will continue, and we will be adding fifteen more cities, as the Qyron have increased the number of renovation machines. Several third-world countries have also been completed. At present, we estimate that thirty million people now have housing where none existed before."

The president began to applaud, and the room erupted. When the applause finally died down, Taylor smiled and continued.

"The better part of the urban renewal program is that the Qyron are providing it free of charge for the third-world countries. As for the United States, the added taxes from all of the newly filled Qyron jobs will more than pay back the cities for the new housing. On that note, unemployment numbers continue to drop. We are now down to under 4 percent unemployment rate with over five million Americans employed through Qyron businesses."

Taylor took another sip of his coffee.

"All major government buildings are now using the new heating and air conditioning systems, and the Qyron are continuing to refit their engines in existing cars."

The secretary of the interior stood up.

"I just had my Honda outfitted. The power is incredible, and it's whisper quiet. It only cost me three grand."

He smiled and then sat back down. Taylor shook his head and then continued.

"Our new carbon defense apparel is now in service. We will be producing it in massive quantities and should have all police and military outfitted within a month. All of our marines and Secret Service are now wearing them."

Taylor looked over at Jennifer.

"Oh, yeah, I have it on as well. It tends to keep you warmer, which is nice in the winter, I guess, but not so much now," Jennifer said as she ran her hands over her outfit.

"We tested the material and it easily stops .45-caliber bullets and is even effective with armor-piercing rounds. Layered sections can be placed on vehicles, giving them extreme protection." Taylor flipped a page. "China has now left the Freedom Alliance, and it seems that it's losing member countries in a hurry. At present, there are only five countries left in the alliance, Russia and North Korea being the biggest players.

"There have been a massive number of people tested for Qyron interpreter positions. It seems that nearly a quarter of a million people have been scanned"—Taylor paused as he stole a peek at Jennifer—"with no one yet having the precise brain pattern required." He cleared his throat. "Myself included."

Several laughs sounded.

Jennifer stood up. "This is already becoming a serious issue," she stated as the laughter died out. "Our schedule is now past two years, with countless countries and industry leaders screaming for earlier times."

The president then chimed in. "Is it possible to hire more staff and answer questions through social media or maybe have face time on a teleconference?"

Jennifer shook her head. "We've already suggested that, sir; most political and industry leaders are still leery of the Qyron and demand face-to-face negotiations. I just hope we can locate some more translators soon."

Taylor cleared his throat and took another sip of his coffee.

"Now for the bad news. We've lost a total of five marines and seven police officers in terrorist attacks on the Qyron to date. Thankfully, once the new carbon suits and wellness packs are distributed, fatalities should greatly diminish. The attack on Jennifer's group last week was traced back to the Freedom for All group. There are fewer marches and protests, but as the polls show, there is still far more opposition to overcome."

Taylor surveyed the room.

"This opposition is now calling in with more bomb and death threats," Taylor said.

Ernie stood up and waved his hand. Taylor turned toward Ernie. "You would like to add something?"

Ernie had an annoyed look on his face. "Yes, I'd like to discuss this issue *offline*, Taylor!"

Taylor nodded. "So that wraps up this week's update."

The meeting dissolved quickly as everyone tended to other business.

Jennifer walked over to Taylor. "When will we have XXXL-sized carbon defense wear?"

Taylor glanced at Jennifer. "I'm not sure; I'll have to get back to you."

"Since one of my team members is not protected, I expect a response from you no later than the end of today," Jennifer snapped.

She turned, and Ernie was there to greet her.

"If I could get a minute of your time?" Ernie asked.

The president and Ernie escorted Jennifer and Tank out of the room. Don joined them in the hallway. As they entered the Oval Office, Don closed the door.

Chapter 24

"PLEASE, HAVE A SEAT," ERNIE offered. Jennifer sat down as Tank stood alongside.

"Terry, glad to see you stepped up to help with Jennifer." He smiled and shook Tank's hand. "Okay, the reason I asked you all here is that we've received a large number of threats on your group. We don't give credibility to some, but others we do. We've also debriefed the terrorists that we captured in your raid. We've been able to link them to some of the groups in France, London, and even Brazil."

Jennifer thought for a moment. "Wait a minute," she said with a start. "We stayed overnight in London, Paris, and Sao Paolo."

Ernie nodded. "Yes, that's what we've been piecing together," he said as he pulled a chair close to Jennifer. "Can you think of any way that someone would get the information on your scheduling?"

Jennifer thought a moment. She glanced over at Tank and then the president.

"Well, I only carry our weekly schedule. Rachel was the one who has our entire hourly plan." Ernie looked over at the president. "I never went out—I mean, except for that one night. But I know that Rachel normally went out to clubs after work, so that would be my guess," Jennifer said softly.

"Yes," Ernie said as he stood up. "So what I'd like to do is put Rachel back in your group. I want her to be in charge of scheduling again. You will treat her no differently than before. We already have your daily schedule ready, but past today it's all a ruse. We will keep Don with us for now, because we don't want to raise suspicion. Do you have any questions?"

He handed the scheduling laptop to Tank.

Jennifer peered down at her feet and grimaced. "No, but how long will we need to have Rachel with us?"

"Until we can identify how the terrorists are gaining access to your schedule," Ernie stated.

The meeting ended, and Jennifer and Tank walked back to the conference room. They located Rachel.

"Rachel, I got you reinstated in our group," Jennifer said with a fake smile.

"Oh my gosh, that's great!" Rachel exclaimed. She jumped up and down with excitement and then leaned over and gave Jennifer a hug. "Oh, does Taylor know yet?"

Jennifer turned and looked across the room. Taylor was busy chatting with some staffers. Jennifer walked over to him.

"This needs to get done now," Taylor said. He turned to face Jennifer. "I thought you'd be gone by now; it's almost 9:00 a.m.," he stated in a smug tone.

"Well, we needed to make some changes. I have Rachel reassigned to our group," Jennifer responded.

"What? No, that's not how this works! We need to discuss this, and you need *my* approval before you can—"

"It's been approved by Kennedy. If you have issue with that, you can talk to him!" Jennifer smiled politely and turned around. She walked out of the room with Tank and Rachel.

Jennifer spent the rest of the day in meetings in Mexico, Panama, Costa Rica, and then Sao Paolo, Brazil. When the last meeting was over, she let out a huge sigh.

"I'm so tired," Jennifer said, "but I could use some fun tonight."

Tank nodded. Rachel looked back at Jennifer.

"Where are you going tonight?" Jennifer asked Rachel.

Rachel perked up. "Oh, I didn't have any plans. I was just going to relax in my room."

"What? Relax in your room? Wasn't it you that told me about all of the awesome nightlife here in Sao Paolo?" Jennifer replied.

Rachel's face lit up. "Yeah, you should see these two clubs!" Rachel began. She then spent the next few minutes detailing the atmosphere and people. When Jennifer reached her room, she turned to Rachel.

"Okay, well I'm going to grab a quick nap, and then I'll shower and meet up with you there," Jennifer said as she slid her key into the lock. Jennifer and Tank walked into their room.

"You're pretty smooth there, lady," Tank said as he set their luggage down.

"I learned it all from you," Jennifer quipped as she walked over to Tank. "So now that the easy stuff is done for the day, how about we play?" she said as she planted a soft, wet kiss on his lips.

They spent the next hour making love and then lay in bed.

"If you keep treating me like this, I'm never going to let you go," Jennifer said. They continued to lounge in the bed and were deciding on what to do for dinner when her cell phone rang.

"Hello?"

"Jennifer, it's Rachel," she yelled into the phone, as the background music was loud. "Are you coming? It's already jumping down here!"

"Actually, I'm pretty tired," Jennifer replied. "I'm going to stay in and sleep."

"Okay, don't know what you're missing!" Rachel laughed as she ended the call.

Jennifer and Tank decided to eat dinner at a local restaurant with the rest of the crew. Xho drew a lot of attention, but they all enjoyed a really good meal. When Jennifer and Tank returned to their room, Jennifer asked Tank, "So, how do you think the CIA is going to find out?"

Tank smiled. "If I know them, they already have every room bugged and her room wired with video." Tank took off his shirt. "They will have other plain-clothed people following her and watching to make sure they don't lose sight of her or her computer." He took off his pants and slid into bed. "I'm sure they will have an answer by the end of the week," he whispered as he pulled Jennifer close.

They fell asleep in each other's arms.

The next day went smoothly, with Jennifer's team in China for most of the day and then two hours in Thailand. When they got to their hotel room, Jennifer checked the news on her computer.

"Hey, Terrance, check this out!"

The video on the screen showed the president pinning Bronze Stars on Charles Gill's group of marines. The follow-up story had the president officially naming Taylor as his newest cabinet member, secretary of Qyron affairs.

"So now Taylor is *officially* an ass," Jennifer said as she shook her head.

Tank stepped over to her. "Don't let his pettiness pull you down," he said softly. "Rise above it." He placed his hands on her shoulder. "And be the bigger person." He gave her a hug.

She smiled up at him. "You're so good to me, baby."

They had dinner in their room and retired early.

Wednesday and Thursday were fourteen-hour days, as the pressure to meet the demand for their time had increased. As they were on the transport to Malaysia Friday morning, Jennifer was talking with Rachel.

"Yeah, well, let's be sure to not cave to Taylor and his 'Oh, just stop here for a quick visit' requests. We're not going to be working fourteen-hours days!" Jennifer yelled.

The transport landed in Kuala Lumpur.

"He keeps telling me I have to take these add-on appointments since they're—"

"Rachel, you work for me! You don't work for Taylor!" Jennifer shouted back as they walked off of the transport.

A line of soldiers stood in front of the Malaysian Houses of Parliament.

"I'm not arguing with you," Rachel responded, "but it's hard to say no to him when he says it must be done."

Jennifer fired back with "Well I'll talk with …"

They are not real.

"… Taylor when …" Jennifer paused. She looked at Xho, who stopped walking.

They are not real. We must go now!

Jennifer received the thoughts from Xho as the soldiers turned and pulled their machine guns from their shoulders. The marines started to react, but not in time. Twenty soldiers turned and opened fire. Four of the five marines fanned out, shielding Xho, Jennifer, and Rachel. Dozens of rounds impacted the marines, knocking them to the ground. As they fell, the continued spray of bullets hit Jennifer, Rachel, and Xho. Tank instinctively grabbed Jennifer and pulled her backward. As Tank was pulling Jennifer down to the ground to shield her, several bullets pierced his arms and legs.

The transport slid quickly six feet over the top of the group with a loud humming and then rapidly lowered to within two feet of the ground toward the soldiers. The next few seconds were a surreal, macabre event.

The transport accelerated, and as it reached the first solder, the force field of the transport pushed him backward off his feet and to the ground. It was like watching dominos fall one by one as the soldiers were shoved to the pavement. The first soldier then slid underneath the transport, but the force field pushed downward on his body, smashing, rolling, and grinding his torso and limbs as the transport continued its forward movement. At no point did the metal of the ship touch a person or the ground, making the scene look like a horrific slaughter choreographed by invisible magic. As the blood spurted, it too was pushed away and downward from the transport in a ghastly bright red splashing fan shape.

When the transport finally stopped fifty yards away, it left a gruesome, bloody path of mangled bodies, arms, and legs in a massive pool of blood.

The marines quickly rose to their feet and surveyed the situation. All of the enemy soldiers were either mashed and deceased or horribly disfigured and howling in agony. Rachel was screaming and crying, her arm had been hit in two places that her carbon defensive armor hadn't protected. Jennifer rolled over, trying to catch her breath. At least twenty rounds had impacted her body, but all had been stopped by her carbon armor. The force of the impacts had left bruises, and the throbbing pain stunned her.

As Jennifer rolled over, she saw Tank lying semiconscious in a pool of his own blood and screamed.

"Terrance, no!"

His left arm had nearly been sheared off by the hail of bullets. Several wounds in his legs oozed blood. Xho stood up and turned to the returning transport. The marines took a defensive posture around the transport as Xho quickly rushed into and then out of the transport with a red medic kit. He quickly plunged four syringes into Tank, and two in Rachel. He motioned with his arms to go quickly.

Jennifer jumped up and pulled Rachel into the transport while three marines grabbed Tank and pulled him inside. Within seconds, everyone was in the transport, and it lifted quickly. The entire group was pinned to the floor as it accelerated rapidly.

He will need blood now! Xho thought to Jennifer. Xho then peered at Rachel, who was screaming and crying in terror as her bleeding stopped.

Within thirty seconds, the transport was descending quickly in Washington, DC, outside of George Washington University Hospital. It hovered just above the Emergency Department. The marines quickly carried Tank into the building. Jennifer then turned to Rachel, who had stopped bleeding and was only sobbing. She looked at Jennifer.

"I quit; I can't take this!" Rachel yelled.

Jennifer nodded and then lifted her up and walked her out of the transport and into the waiting arms of two medics.

Are you hurt?

Jennifer turned to Xho. "My chest really hurts," she cried.

Xho quickly lifted her shirt. Jennifer's chest and stomach were dark purple with heavy bruising. Xho grabbed the last syringe and inserted it into Jennifer's stomach.

"Ow," Jennifer cried out.

Xho gave her a nod. Jennifer's belly and chest now felt hot. She opened her shirt, exposing her entire chest. The bruising receded quickly, as if someone had poured dark purple ink on her chest and stomach, and then played video of the event backward. A minute later, the tip of the syringe glowed green. Xho pulled the syringe out. Jennifer then put her shirt back down and walked out of the transport. She was met by four of the six marines walking back to the transport.

"These carbon defense suits are incredible," one marine marveled. "I must have gotten hit with over fifty rounds at close range, and I all got was some bad bruising."

"And those were armor-piercing rounds," another marine chimed in.

Four black SUVs roared into the parking lot. Several Secret Service agents jumped out of the trucks as they slid to a stop.

"Jennifer, come with us!" shouted Demetri.

"No, I have to see about Terrance!" she yelled back as she ran into the Emergency Department.

She quickly found Tank's procedure room. He was lying on a gurney with an IV of blood and the four red glowing Meibot syringes in his side. A doctor stood by him, staring.

"Oh my God, Terrance!" Jennifer shrieked.

Both the doctor and Tank startled from her scream. She ran over and gently hugged him.

"I was so scared that I lost you. Your arm … it was …" she blubbered.

"It's the most incredible thing I've ever seen," the doctor chimed in. "His arm was nearly sheared off. When he came to us, it was encased in some liquid metallic sheath. I've been here for a few minutes, just watching his arm reassemble."

Tank's arm was now fully reattached. It was purple and silver at the point of the wound, the colors swirling and the skin vibrating and pulsing. The skin was a window to the rapid repair; a tendon was moving, sliding past a muscle as it was being rebuilt.

"Yeah," Tank said softly. "I have feeling in it again."

He wiggled his fingers.

The doctor shook his head and then slowly walked out of the room.

"Terrance," Jennifer said softly.

"No," Tank replied quickly. "I know what you're going to say; I can see it in your eyes." He reached over with his good arm and gently stroked her face. "It's all a part of the job; relax."

She just stood quietly with a pleading look.

"This is what I do," he whispered as she leaned in to kiss him.

A half hour later, Jennifer was escorted into an awaiting SUV. Within minutes, she was back at the White House with the rest of her group, minus Tank.

Her team was debriefed on the incident. Rachel gave her resignation and left later that day.

When Jennifer finished discussing the attack with CIA and FBI agents, she was escorted to the Oval Office. As they entered the room, the president stood up and walked around his desk.

"I'm so relieved that you're okay," the president said as he shook her hand. "I heard that Tank is doing fine and will be joining us shortly."

Ernie, Taylor, and two other men then entered the room.

"Sorry we're late," Ernie said as he took a seat.

The president gave a nod and then began speaking.

"I'm extremely disgusted that our group can't be protected on their daily travels. This is twice that we've been attacked, and personally, I feel that's twice too many. Ernie, what intel do we have so far?"

Ernie cleared his throat and sat up. "Well, sir, after tracking Rachel for the week, we found that twice she lost control of the computer she used for scheduling. Both times, men she brought back to her room were able to breach the PC and gain access while she was asleep. However, this does not explain how they were able to know where the group was going to be on Friday. The schedule that she had was only correct for the next day, and there was no breach on Thursday. Basically, sir, we have more security issues than we can pinpoint at the moment, and some may not even be on our side."

The president flashed him a look of question.

"Sir, some of the information may be leaked from other nations; we can't be certain."

Jennifer raised her hand. The president gave her a nod. "Yes?" he asked.

"Sir, maybe we could flip this whole thing?" Jennifer said softly.

Taylor exhaled a grunt of disapproval. The president nodded for her to continue while shooting Taylor a look of disapproval. Jennifer gazed over at Taylor while she spoke.

"Well, in my many travels on the transport, I thought about our safety and security. We can't always be sure that foreign governments, people, or even places are safe. So every time we travel, we're taking a huge chance with our lives. Then I thought, with the Qyron being able to drop a building down on a piece of land in minutes, why not have them make us a central building for meetings? We can have a secure structure placed anywhere here in the US. The Qyron can make it solid enough to be a bunker on a mountaintop, in the desert, or here in DC. Then we can make the other business leaders and diplomats come on a transport to *our* meeting site."

"Pssh," Taylor said, shaking his head.

"I mean, it was just a thought," Jennifer said quietly as she looked downward, dejected.

The president sat quiet for a moment. An eyebrow rose, and then he nodded with approval.

"That's perfect; let's go with it. I would guess that the Qyron have enough transports to allow for this?"

Jennifer nodded. "They have hundreds of thousands of transports in a few sizes, ranging from the two-seat models workers use here in our solar system to the ones we use for our travels that hold up to thirty people, and giant transports that can house thousands."

The president looked to Ernie. "Ernie, let's find the most secure location."

Ernie peered back at Jennifer. "I like your idea of putting it in the desert; Area 51 would be an excellent location." He stood up and began to pace. "It would be far enough away from the public, prying eyes, and terrorists."

The president flipped back toward Ernie. "I want your best location by Saturday."

He finally turned to Jennifer.

"Can the Qyron drop a building down on the location of our choice by Sunday?"

Jennifer reached into her leather briefcase and pulled out her transmitter. She placed it on her forehead and a moment later said, "Yes, they can do that. We just need to specify any specific details that we want in the building."

Ernie nodded. "I'll have a list of our requirements for you by tonight."

"Sooner if you can," Kennedy added.

"Oh great!" Jennifer said with a smile as she pulled the transmitter from her head. "Xho just told me that a woman in India has been identified as a suitable translator!"

The president smiled and nodded.

"How many people have been tested so far?" Taylor asked.

Jennifer placed the transmitter to her head again.

"Wow, over one million!" she replied.

"This should help us speed things up transitioning the world," the president said. "Ernie, let's make this building able to house ten separate large conference rooms. I'm hoping more translators will be discovered as the days and weeks go by. Does anyone have anything more to add?"

Taylor stood up. "Well, sir, are we sure we want to have transports from all over the world zipping into our air space? I've heard that the

FAA is already starting to have concerns with transports coming near normal flight paths."

"Give it a rest, Taylor," Jennifer bantered. "I've already had talks with several airlines. They're discussing scrapping their fleets and using Qyron transports. Besides, while the transports are flown by humans and Qyron, they're outfitted with safety features that won't allow for any aircraft or other transports within a mile of them while in flight." Jennifer rolled her eyes as she stood up alongside the president.

"Taylor?" Kennedy said as he gently placed a hand across Jennifer, shielding her from Taylor. "What solution would you propose to keep our team out of harm's way?"

Taylor stood with his mouth open for a moment. He looked around the room.

"Well, uh. I haven't given it much thought, but offhand I'd say send a second transport with more marines."

"That's an idea," the president said, tilting his head toward Taylor, "but instead of incurring more costs with more marines, putting more lives into a potential shooting gallery, it seems like a slam dunk to just have everyone travel to one central location we can control, with little or no public to hide terrorists, and a full security compliment to ensure no weapons are brought onsite. And before you rebut, the decision has been made."

Taylor exhaled loudly. He gave a glance at Jennifer with his lips pursed, and squinted.

"Okay, we'll firm all plans up, have the building put in place over the weekend, and look to begin a new process for Monday morning," the president announced.

The door opened, and Don walked in.

"Excellent timing, Don," the president added. "You're back with Jennifer now, and we have some catching up to do. Jennifer will fill you in. Everyone have a restful weekend; I have more work to do."

Ernie and the other men walked toward the president. Jennifer and Don turned to leave. Taylor started to follow.

"Taylor, I'd like to speak with you," the president called out.

As Don left the room, Jennifer grabbed the doorknob and slowly closed the door. She stopped and leaned on the door to listen.

"Taylor, I don't know what issues you have with Jennifer, and frankly, I don't care. But you had best resolve them *right now!*" the president commanded.

"Sir, I just have issue with someone trying to usurp my authority that—"

"Taylor, let me be crystal clear here: Jennifer is irreplaceable. *You* are not. Is that clear enough for you?"

Jennifer giggled and then pranced over to Don as Tank turned a corner toward them.

"Do I want to know?" Don asked.

Jennifer stopped laughing. "The president told Taylor to quit being a jerk to me or else he's fired."

Tank smiled as Jennifer raced over to hug him.

"Glad to have you back," Don said, shaking his hand.

They continued walking down the hallway. Jennifer quickly filled Don in on the new arrangements slated for Monday morning. When they reached the parking area, Don was fully informed and ready to assist over the weekend.

"Have a good weekend, Don, and welcome back!" Jennifer said as she gave him a hug.

"Thanks, Jennifer, I missed the team," he said as he gave Tank a nod.

There was a white light and some hissing noise, and I removed my headset.

Chapter 25

As I READJUSTED, I LOOKED at the monitor. It had been eight hours since I began my Psy-log. I walked into the bathroom. After finishing and washing my hands, I opened the door and heard a stirring from the bedroom. I slowly walked in.

"Hey baby," John's voice quietly greeted me from the darkness. I slipped out of my clothes and snuggled in close with John. I felt that he was fully ready for me.

"So are you happy to see me, or is this just your morning salute?" I giggled.

"A little from column A, a little from column B," John replied as he kissed me.

We took our time making love for the next half hour. John was so caring and loving. I felt so secure and happy with him—something I had never felt with anyone.

When we finished and I rolled over, my mind wandered back to the lingering mystery.

"Johnny, let's shower and then do some more investigating."

"Ugh, really? I was hoping you'd want to relax and have fun," John moaned.

"But investigating *is* fun, Johnny," I said with a sweet voice.

I gave John a few kisses. He grumbled and stepped out of bed.

"I know it's pointless to argue with you," he mumbled as he walked toward the bathroom.

After a hot shower, we went to G Deck to have breakfast. We thought a change of scenery would also do us some good. As we ate our meal, I related some of my Psy-logs to John. He hung on every word and then gave me a look.

"Is there any way that these logs can be made to show to someone?"

"Well, Qyron law states that they're 'for your eyes only,' so to speak, so unfortunately no. There are historical aspects that are taken for general knowledge, but no one except Qyron and translators have the ability to view them. Sorry, Johnny."

I looked around the dining hall; it was fairly busy.

"With all of these people here, Johnny ..." I said with a smile.

"Let me guess—you want to do some more interviews?" John said with a sigh.

We put our trays away, and then I walked over to a table where a couple was eating. As I approached the woman, she stopped eating and gave me a stare.

"Do you mind if I ask you a few questions?"

"Am I in trouble?" she shot back.

"Oh no! I'm just conducting a survey."

"Well, okay then," she said with a look of relief. Her male companion stared inquisitively at me.

"What's the reason for your visit to Gamma Five?"

"I'm going to get trained. And, well, you mean Gamma Five Alpha, don'tcha, darlin'?"

"What?"

The woman gave me a smile and straightened up. "I'm going to Gamma Five Alpha," she stated confidently.

"Oh, sorry, of course," I replied. "And you, sir?" I asked her male companion.

"Yeah, me too, sweet thing," he said as he looked me up and down.

The woman then gave him a look and slapped him. They began to argue and hurl insults at each other, so I gingerly stepped away and walked over to John. He was just finishing talking with a table of men.

"John, did you know there are two stops for this transport?"

"What?"

"I was just told that this couple is heading to Gamma Five Alpha. I didn't know there was an Alpha."

John stared blankly at me. "And for those of us who have no idea what you're talking about?" John replied sarcastically.

I gave him a smile. "You're so cute when you're confused," I told him.

291

"Gamma is the star name. Five means it's the fifth planet. If it has one moon, then the moon is Gamma Five Alpha; a second moon would be Gamma Five Beta."

John stood still, giving me a 'so what' look. I walked over to the entrance of the dining hall, where it was quieter and no one would overhear us talking.

"John, any time you book a transport, it will tell you specifically all stops along the way. If this transport was heading to Venus first, it would list it. So if your destination is Gamma Five, it should state Gamma Five Alpha, and then Gamma Five."

John still didn't respond. I began to feel irritated.

"John, the Qyron are creatures of habit and procedure; they don't do things by accident, and they don't make mistakes!"

"Calm down; I didn't know. So what does it mean?" he asked impatiently.

I took a deep breath. I didn't mean to snap at John, it was just that every time we tried to get an answer, it ended up giving us a few more questions.

"I don't know, Johnny; it's just one more thing that doesn't make any sense. But the couple I asked did say that their reason was for training."

"Yeah, I've had that response quite a bit too," John added. "That table I just talked to had six guys all going for training."

I walked back over to the table John had just been at.

"Excuse me; do you gentlemen mind if I ask you something?"

The men all gave me smiles and lewd looks. I felt suddenly felt dirty and cheap.

"Are you all going to Gamma Five or Gamma Five Alpha?"

"Why don't you come back to my room and look at my ticket?" one man replied.

The table of men laughed.

"No thank you," I said tersely.

"Yeah, we're all heading to Gamma Five Alpha," another man stated. I smiled at him and walked back to John.

"They are all going for training on Alpha too," I said to John. "Let's make sure we distinguish this when we ask."

We spent the next half hour questioning dozens of passengers. As we walked out of the dining hall, we exchanged notes

"So it looks like G Deck has 90 percent of the passengers heading to Alpha Moon for training, while nearly everyone we polled on Alpha Deck is going to Gamma Five for new jobs."

"Is it strange that a deck on the transport would be segregated?" John asked.

"No, that's normal, actually; it makes off-boarding that much quicker and easier."

"Isn't there someone we can ask on this thing that would know the answers?"

"No, we tried that, Johnny. The bridge is where we would have gone for answers on the destination, and we can't communicate to anyone off of the ship while at this speed."

John was about to say something when it hit me.

"*That's it, Johnny!*"

"What?"

"The bridge—it has several stations. We went there to talk with someone but saw that it was all automated. The bridge is where all data is sent for easy viewing, but there's also a technical station; it would have all of the technical data, the destinations, and the purposes."

"So we need to get back into the dusty box room?" John asked.

"Well, no. That won't do us any good, as there aren't any stations there. I would need to access the intel room. It's a room aft on the transport that stores all of the ship's operating data, all passenger information—everything, Johnny! My computer has a port to access it, since it's all Qyron technology."

I felt energized, invigorated. Finally I had thought of something that should put an end to all of the questions.

"You've done this before?"

"Well, not exactly. I've linked in with it to get general information on other shuttles and such. The problem is, I'm not sure where to look for the answers we need; and, well, we won't exactly be invited."

"Oh, come on! What does that mean?" John asked with a touch of shock.

"Well, there should be at least two people taking care of things in that room," I said as we began to walk back to the lift.

"So," John began with his funny mock-authoritative voice, "it's time for the ambassador to gain access to some data." He flashed me a smile as we walked into the elevator.

"That's actually a brilliant idea, Johnny." I leaned over and gave him a kiss. Two other people in the lift looked at us and smiled.

After we got back to our room, I pulled my hair back into a ponytail and put on the Qyron robe. I took off my pants and slid on some sandals. John came up behind me.

"You look so sexy in that robe," he whispered in my ear as his hands groped around the front of me. I giggled as he tickled my sensitive spots.

"Not now, Johnny; we need to get this done first."

I spun around and gave him a long, sensual kiss.

"Yeah, let's hurry this up!" John said with a grin. "More important things await."

He slapped my butt.

"Seriously, Johnny, let's be quick about this; no hamming it up, understand?"

John gave me a nod, but I didn't really trust him. He would get carried away when he played like this. He never seemed to know when to quit. We walked out of the room and toward the rear of the ship. As we approached the intel room, I peered at John.

"Remember: quick! Let's make this quick," I reiterated as I pulled my hood tight and removed the emotion from my face.

John pressed the door call button. The door opened, and we were greeted with a shower of loud music. Three security guards were busy playing around. One of them was dancing while another was playing a game on a hand console.

"Yeah, what can we—" shouted one guard who wasn't wearing his uniform top. As his view went from John to me, he stopped cold. He turned around and yelled to shut off the music. The other guards suddenly straightened up and shuffled about, trying to hide snack bags and the game console.

John took a step into the room.

"The ambassador needs to link her system in with the ship's intel computer," John stated loudly. "What is going on in here?" He looked around the room with a stern face.

The bare-chested man was now visibly shaken.

"Uh, we, uh … we were just …" he stumbled.

I gave a wide-eyed stare at him, which shook him even more. I saw the terminal at the rear of the room. I nodded and took a step toward the terminal. The guard quickly jumped out of my way.

"I'm sorry!" he said as he moved.

"This is not how this station should be manned!" John continued.

He walked over to the other two guards. The bare-chested one slowly walked over behind John. I grabbed my laptop and cable and plugged it into the system.

"Uh, sir, I've called for my supervisor," another guard exclaimed. The other two guards began to straighten up the mess, and John nodded in approval.

I linked in with the mainframe. It looked different and demanded a level-ten access code. As a translator, I have level twelve, so I punched in my name and code. It then opened to show a very limited menu. I quickly fumbled through the screens until I heard a door tone. The door quickly opened, and Travis, the guard we had met after the fight, walked in.

"Where's the music?" Travis said. He then caught my eye and shuddered. "I mean, what's going, uh, how can I help you?"

John turned around and extended his hand. "Good to see you again, Travis. The ambassador required some further information, so we needed to link in with the system." John exclaimed. His voice was so authoritatively overdone. It was humorous to me, and I would have laughed aloud if I hadn't been more than a little scared that this charade would fail.

Travis gave me a nod as I continued to click through the screens.

"You could have had me paged; I would have given you access," Travis blurted out.

"Not a problem, Travis." John slapped him on the back. "The ambassador has all of the access she needs, and your team was more than helpful."

The security guards all smiled.

"So let's hear more of that music," John said as he peered back at me.

I was busy trying to navigate the screens. I finally came to a location in EDIT mode. Then the music kicked on. It was a loud fusion of techno, dubstep, and speed metal. It was horrible. My love of music tended toward jazz, blues, and some fused rock. This noisy garbage, though, was stabbing at my soul. I had to fight the urge to yell out.

My concentration was completely blown, and I looked back over at John. I couldn't tell if he was seizing or trying his best at dancing. Travis and his crew were enjoying it, so at least it was taking their attention away from me. After three long minutes, I was finally done downloading, although I wasn't sure exactly what it was that I had. I exited the link and then unhooked my laptop. As I walked toward John, one of the guards flailed an arm, and I grabbed it in midair.

"Oh, sorry!" he said as he stopped dancing. The music stopped, and John turned to face me.

"Ah, you're done, Ambassador. Excellent." John walked back toward the door. "The ambassador thanks you for your assistance, Travis."

I looked back and then nodded at them. They all smiled and nodded back. When the door closed, we quickly walked down the passageway.

"So did you get what you needed?" John asked.

I turned and punched him hard on the shoulder.

"Ow, damn! What was that for?" John cried out.

"That music, Johnny! Horrid! It was killing me inside."

I pulled my hood back and gave him a scowl. John massaged his shoulder and gave me a pained look.

"Don't be a baby; I didn't hit you that hard," I said as we approached our room.

John opened the door, and we walked inside. I sat down on the couch and opened up my laptop. As I sat down, John walked across the living room, still massaging his shoulder, and then into the bedroom. I started to scroll through the menus. I found a section that listed all of the names of everyone on board. It associated other statistics to each person. I slowly skimmed through. I then noted that there were two distinct sections. One list of people held reams of data linked with each person; the other list, very little. I continued to sort through the personal data. After a while, my eyes started to hurt. I looked at the clock and realized that a half hour had passed.

"John?" I asked as I stood up.

I couldn't believe that I had just spent thirty minutes slogging through countless pages of data. I walked into the bedroom to find John sleeping. I rubbed my temples. I guess I had been straining too hard at the screen. I turned and walked into the bathroom. I pulled open the shower door and turned on the water. I took a long, hot shower. I let it beat down on my head. It was so soothing and took the tension headache away.

When I finally finished and stepped out of the bathroom, I walked back into the bedroom. John stirred awake. He slowly lifted up his arm and grabbed the sash on my robe. He pulled it, the robe opened up. I pulled the covers back and slipped out of the robe. As I sat down on top of him, I grabbed his shoulder and he yelled out.

"Ow! Damn!"

"Lights on!" I responded.

I looked down at his shoulder to find a large purple bruise.

"Oh my gosh, Johnny! Your shoulder! I'm so sorry."

I gently lay down on top of him and kissed him softly. The soft kisses turned into sensual kisses, then nibbles, then sucking. It didn't take long before we were two sweaty bodies moving as one.

"Oh, Amant," John sighed, "I love you so much."

He held me tight. I caressed his chest and then looked up at him.

"I love you too, Johnny, and I'm sorry for hitting you."

He kissed me. Our sweet quiet time was shattered, though, by a large growl from John's stomach.

"Well, that was rude," I snickered.

John laughed. "Yeah, I guess it's time to get something to eat," he said as he stretched. "And now that I think of it, we should be hitting the gym too; all we've been doing lately is eating, sleeping, and having sex."

I stood up and grabbed a pair of sweatpants.

"Well, let's just cut out the sex then," I said with a grin.

John smiled from across the room. "Please, you're twice as hungry for it than I am; you'd crack first!"

We both laughed, and, well, he was right. Qyron females were voracious for sex.

We went to our favorite dining hall on C Deck. I told John about the huge amount of information and how I'd spent a solid half hour just paging through it, hoping to find something that would shed some light on the many questions.

"Come on," John said while biting into his grilled ham and cheese, "how much data can there be?"

I gave John a blank stare.

"I downloaded eighty-seven terabytes, John."

John returned a wide-eyed stare, "What! That much?"

We finished the meal and started walking back to the room.

"I think I'll take a break, John—maybe do some more Psy-logging."

John squeezed my hand and smiled at me. "That sounds like a good idea; you take the time for yourself. You seem to enjoy that much more anyway. Maybe I'll take a crack at the data while you're living it up with Jennifer."

When we got back to the room, I sat down on the couch and placed a blanket over my legs. I grabbed my headset and looked over at John.

"See you in a few hours," I said with a smile. I put the headset on.

There was a white light and some hissing.

Chapter 26

August 16, 2021

WHEN MONDAY MORNING ARRIVED, JENNIFER and Tank were already exhausted. They had been involved in the aspects of the new building and its site, while their entire month's calendar appointments had been contacted by Don. The newest translator, Navya Malik, had had her procedure on Friday evening and had spent much of the weekend working with Jennifer to adjust to the rigors of translating. Tank's arm was a little sore but fully functional and returning to its normal color. Navya spent Sunday evening at the apartment in her own room.

The team arrived at the White House by 7:30 a.m. and met up with Don. The White House was buzzing with activities as scores of agents and staffers ran about trying to coordinate the coming week.

"Wow, what a difference a few days makes, eh Don?" Jennifer asked.

Don smiled. "It has been nothing short of crazy around here. Oh, and welcome, Navya." He shook her hand and then laughed. "You two look like opposites," he quipped.

Navya laughed as she looked to Jennifer. While both Jennifer and Navya stood five feet tall, Jennifer's blonde hair and fair complexion against Navya's jet-black hair and darker skin did pose a stark contrast. The attitudes of the two women were also disparate. Jennifer was forward and bold at times, whereas Navya was soft-spoken and timid.

While Jennifer walked Navya through parts of the White House, she touched on this personal aspect as a possible hindrance.

"Navya, you need to assert yourself in the talks and negotiations. The Qyron are very blunt with their terms and expect you to convey this. Diplomats and business leaders will try to push past you. I know that because I'm short and blonde; many men don't take me seriously, so I've had to adjust my attitude. I would think that with your quiet shyness, you'll get similar treatment."

Navya smiled. "I understand your concerns," she said softly, "but I am prepared for the male-dominated world; trust me."

"Good," Jennifer said. She then explained the format of Mondays. By the time 8:00 a.m. arrived, the entire White House was jumping with activity. The normally half-full conference room was packed to capacity. When the president walked in, the room came to a hush.

"I want to thank many of you for your very long and detailed efforts over this weekend. We have accomplished so much in such a short time."

Applause broke out, and the president smiled and waited.

"To begin, I would like to introduce our second translator, Navya Malik. She is ready to join the global team, and we welcome her."

Another minute passed as Navya shook hands and greeted the assembled group.

"Our next big announcement is the restructuring of the process. A new office building was erected in Area 51. This large building will now host all Qyron transactions, allowing our team the greatest safety and security from terrorist attacks. We have also relocated additional military to ensure maximum security for everyone."

Jennifer stood up and walked to the lectern. "After our voting over the weekend on the name for the new building—and after much campaigning on my part—I would like to formally introduce the name of the building as the Kennedy Myers Building."

The room erupted in applause, and the president laughed while blushing.

"Honest—I had nothing to do with this," he said meekly.

When the room finally quieted down, Jennifer sat back down and the president continued.

"Seriously, I can't thank everyone enough for their hard work and diligence this past weekend. I'll assign bonuses to everyone as my personal thanks." The president then nodded to Taylor.

Taylor took to the lectern, and the president sat down behind him.

"Since this is going to be an extremely busy day," Taylor began, "I'll move quickly through our progress report. We now have over a half million lives saved and a half million Americans happily served by the Wellness Program. Twelve new cities are now in the Urban Renewal Program, and by the end of the month we should have completion of all the major and minor cities in the US."

Taylor flipped a page. "Unemployment is now at 2 percent, as over nine million Americans are now employed through the Qyron. All military and half of the police departments are now outfitted with the new carbon defense apparel. The Freedom Alliance is now only North Korea, as all other countries have opened up dialogue with the Qyron. Oh, and the current Qyron polling numbers are increasing. We have 13 percent approval, 40 percent undecided, and 43 percent against."

Again the room erupted in applause.

"We are doubling our efforts to uncover the terrorist groups against the Qyron. Through our intelligence sources, we found that the attack last week was a collaboration of a few groups but was masterminded by Freedom for All. The actual military detail was rounded up and executed. The terrorists replaced them and staged the attack." Taylor turned and nodded to the president. "That's all that I have, sir."

Jennifer stood up with Navya. "Ready to start your day?" she asked. Navya nodded. They walked out of the conference room and were joined by their agents. Tank trailed behind Jennifer. After a short walk across the lawn, they stepped into the transport.

Xho greeted Jennifer and then introduced Navya's translator, Kylee. Kylee was also half human and half Qyron. She was crossbred on Qyron, with the assistance of Meibots. At five feet tall, Kylee was the tallest Qyron and also had a fairly full head of brown hair. The normally large, angled Qyron eyes were smaller and softer. Her nose was small, and pointed like a Qyron nose. Kylee was also unmistakably female, with a more-than-ample chest.

Jennifer extended her hand. Kylee looked to Xho for a moment and then shook Jennifer's hand.

"It's nice to meet you, Kylee. Welcome to the team," Jennifer said.

Hello. Nice to meet you, Jennifer.

After everyone was seated, the transport lifted off slowly and then quickly reached altitude. There wasn't much time after the introductions before the transport lowered down in the Nevada desert. As they stepped out of the transport, the cool morning desert air greeted them.

The new Kennedy Myers Building stood before them. It was ten stories tall with a basic square shape covering an entire city block. The corners of the building, however, were angled and covered in a silver metal. While a stone facade adorned some of the main structure of the building, the bright metal connected many of the windows and main structure. As the sun shone, the building actually appeared to glow. The famed airstrip and hangars of Area 51 were a mile off in the distance.

The group slowly walked into the main entrance. They were greeted with marble floors, landscape paintings on the walls, and soft music that played overhead. A large front desk area was manned with two security personnel and a well-dressed man in a gray suit.

"Hello, everyone, my name is Jason Barnes. Welcome to the Kennedy Myers Building. I'm the site manager, responsible for all operations here."

Jason was a shorter man, about five foot seven. He had brown hair that he slicked back and a small, round face. He almost looked like a boy in a man's suit. He took a step toward Jennifer and Xho.

"Miss Jennifer and Xho, your working area is on the second floor," Jason said. He smiled and nodded at both of them. "And you must be our newest addition, Mrs. Navya Malik?"

Navya smiled and shook his hand.

"If everyone will follow me, I will give you all a tour of the second floor. Navya, and—oh I'm so sorry—Kylee," Jason extended a hand for Kylee. Kylee shook his hand and nodded. "You two will have the same setup on the third floor, so please just pay attention to the tour on the second," he said gleefully.

They walked through a very large waiting area where at least fifty seats were set around a dozen small tables. Several television screens were on, showing newscasts. On one side was a large kitchenette with several coffee makers and refreshments. They finally reached the elevator.

When they exited onto the second floor, plush carpeting and soft music filled another waiting room. This room was smaller, with several potted plants around the perimeter. Five thick couches were positioned equally around the room. Two more televisions hung on the walls on opposing sides.

"Okay, so as we come out of the elevator, we have the staging area here. There will be more refreshments placed here daily," Jason pointed to a small table, sink, and refrigerator in the far corner. "Bathrooms are over there." He pointed to the right side wall. A woman sat at a desk in front of a door at the back center wall. "This is Margot; she'll direct all appointments." He smiled at Margot as the group walked by.

He opened the center door. A hallway stretched down to the left and right. They walked to the left.

"Here is Jennifer's office," he said as he reached the end of the hall-way. He opened the door to a very nice corner office. A large oak desk was nestled in the corner. Additional potted plants sat on the windowsill, and a few pictures covered the wall. A small private bathroom door was on the far side. They walked down to the next door. "This is Xho's office." He opened the door.

The office was similar; it was just not a corner office. The following three doors led to large conference rooms. A spacious oval table with twelve plush office chairs sat in the center of each room, and each had full teleconferencing capabilities. At the opposite end of the hallway were more bathrooms and one large collective office for the administrative assistants.

"Wow," Jennifer said, "all of this in just two days."

Everyone nodded and mumbled in agreement.

"Yes, I'm very impressed and so proud to be in charge of this," Jason said, beaming. "If anyone needs anything, I'm on the first floor and my extension is programmed on the phones. Your first appointments will be here by 9:00 a.m." He turned and walked to the elevator.

Jennifer turned to Navya. "Since you're a little new to this, would you feel more comfortable taking one of these conference rooms on this floor today?"

Navya smiled and nodded. "Oh yes, thank you so much, Jennifer; that would be wonderful."

Jennifer then turned to the two agents giving her coverage. "If you gentlemen care to, make yourselves comfortable; get the lay of the land, so to speak."

They nodded at her and walked into the first conference room. Xho also nodded and walked down to his office.

Don then turned to her. "In this new building, you'll have your schedule prepared through this site. I'll be leaving this role today, and you'll have a new admin assistant. It's been an interesting time with you and your team. I'll miss you." He reached out his hand.

"Oh, I'll miss you too, Don, and I'm sorry to lose you," Jennifer said. She pushed by his hand and gave him a hug. "I'm sure this stuff was boring to you anyway," she whispered as she pulled back from the hug.

Don smiled. "Not exactly what I trained for." He looked over her shoulder. "Tank, it was a pleasure working with you; hope to again someday." He shook Tank's hand.

"Take care of yourself," Tank replied. Don retreated to the elevator.

Jennifer and Tank stepped into her office. Jennifer stopped and took in the sight of the room. She then turned to Tank.

"Can you believe this?" she said with eyes wide and a huge grin. She jumped into his arms. "I love this. Wow!" She kissed Tank and giggled.

"I'm glad you're happy," Tank replied, "This is a really nice setup, and so much safer." He put Jennifer back down and surveyed the room as he walked over to the window. "Here comes a transport," he said. Jennifer walked over and gazed down. She watched as the French and German leaders stepped out and walked toward the building.

"I guess our new day begins!" Jennifer exclaimed.

The day cruised by smoothly. They were able to see more diplomats and industry executives with this new system. Navya did a fine job of translating on her first day, and everyone enjoyed the flair and services of the new building.

"I'm glad to see that you did so well today," Jennifer commented to Navya.

"Yes, I was very nervous, but I have more confidence now," Navya replied softly. "Thank you, Jennifer." They walked out of the office together. As they left the building, three transports awaited.

"Aren't you coming back to D.C. with us?" Jennifer asked.

"No, thank you," Navya replied. "I am going back to my home in India, to be with my husband and children. Worry not; my country's military will protect me."

Navya walked into a transport as Jennifer and Tank entered their transport. Xho and Kylee boarded the last transport. Two minutes later,

Jennifer and Tank were back at the White House. As they stepped off the transport, they noted a larger number of marines guarding the White House. They asked an aide as they walked to the parking area and were told that increased threats had been made. Additional marines and agents joined them as they walked into the garage.

"Jeez, now we have four trucks with two dozen armed guards," Jennifer stated nervously. "Why doesn't everyone realize that the Qyron are with us for peace and prosperity?"

Tank gave her a glance as they sat down in the back of the SUV.

"Not everyone thinks like you, Jennifer, and ignorance breeds fear," Tank said solemnly. "We still have people out there that hate me for the color of my skin, so what chance do you think we have of them accepting the Qyron?"

Jennifer sat silently for a moment. She then reached over and grabbed his hand.

"I love you, Terrance," she said softly.

They spent the evening having a quiet dinner and watching a movie. They also caught a news broadcast as they were getting ready for bed. Several anti-Qyron groups had been extremely vocal, threatening violence and demanding that all interaction with the Qyron cease. Tank shook his head.

"What?" Jennifer asked.

"It's going to be a long road," he said. "I don't care what the poll numbers say; I can just feel it."

"Well, I hope the …"

Tank gave Jennifer a stunned look. "What's wrong?"

"I just feel dizzy," she said as she sat down on the bed. "I'm fine. Just felt weird for a moment."

Tank walked around the bed and grabbed Jennifer.

"Are you sure you're okay?"

Jennifer looked up at him and smiled. "I'm fine. Let's get some sleep."

The next morning, they were shuttled to the White House. Taylor intercepted them before they had a chance to board the transport.

"Ernie needs to speak with you," Taylor said. Tank, Jennifer, and Xho walked into the White House and into the conference room.

"Good morning, everyone," Ernie greeted them. "I wanted to let you know we're going to be increasing security for everyone. We have been monitoring communications, and we're concerned."

Ernie turned to Jennifer. "Jennifer, we're going to have some security around your mother. You don't have any siblings, correct?"

"No, just me and my mom," Jennifer said softly. "You really think …" Jennifer stopped speaking in midsentence. She glanced up at Tank, and he nodded to her.

"I'm sorry, but it's just a precaution," Ernie stated. "Hopefully we can relax things in a few weeks or so." They said their good-byes, and the group boarded the transport.

That Tuesday rolled by smoothly. Jennifer and Navya chaired dozens of meetings covering as much in one day as Jennifer would normally have handled in a week. The best part was that they were finished by 6:00 p.m. As they were exiting the building together, Navya turned to Jennifer.

"This is pretty easy work," Navya said with a smile. "I almost feel bad about taking so much money for this."

When Jennifer got home Tuesday evening, she called her mother. They talked about the additional security, and Jennifer reassured her mom that she would be safe. She then called and spoke with Tasha. Jennifer brought Tasha up to speed on her current situation.

After she got off the phone, Jennifer walked over to Tank, who was watching a program on TV.

"Terrance, we've never talked about family," Jennifer said as she slid down on the couch next to him. "I'd like to go visit my mother. You were never really introduced."

Tank looked at her and smiled. "That sounds great; I'd love to meet your mother and see the sights where you grew up." Jennifer's eyes lit up.

"Really?" she exclaimed. Tank nodded. She lunged at him and gave him a big, warm hug.

"Oh, that would be great. I can take you all over. Oh, we'll have a blast!" She continued to hug and kiss him. "Oh, I can't wait," she gushed. Her face then froze. "Wait; what about your family? I don't know anything about them."

Tank gave her a calm look. "Well, there's not much to tell," he began.

"I lost my mother to cancer about nine years ago, and I never knew my father."

"Oh, baby, I'm sorry," Jennifer said as she hugged Tank again.

"It's okay," he said softly. "You're my family now." Jennifer teared up as Terrance pulled back from the hug and kissed her. He then lifted her up and carried her into the bedroom.

They made love for the rest of the evening and then drifted off to sleep.

The next morning, as they were getting ready for work, they overheard a newscast on which it was announced that the US Marines were now using single- and medium-sized transports in an effort to respond quickly to terrorist activities. The president spoke about having rapid deployment and protecting not just the Qyron but all Americans everywhere.

Wednesday's workday was interesting in that the Groom Lake area was utilized as one of many testing areas for training the marine pilots with the new transports. While Jennifer and Navya held meetings, the diplomats and business leaders were drawn to the windows as the flight maneuvers continued. Jennifer eventually realized that there were automatic shutters to dim or completely shield the windows. The rest of the workday sailed by without issue.

When Jennifer arrived home that evening, she called her mother to confirm their arrival for the weekend. Her mother's house wasn't large enough to accommodate them, as it was an old farmhouse. The ceilings in the house were only six and a half feet high, so Tank wouldn't be able to stand up straight. Jennifer made reservations at a local hotel and then informed her Secret Service agents of her plans.

Thursday morning, Jennifer spoke with Xho while they were traveling to work to see if they could use a small transport for their trip to Montana. Xho not only agreed but also stated that they could use a medium transport for their weekend plans and have a small transport for their own personal use. He related to her how to fly it. The images and procedures flooded her mind. She quickly sorted them and gave Xho a nod.

"Thank you so much, Xho. Can we practice in one after work today?"

Xho smiled and nodded in agreement.

When they arrived at Area 51, Jennifer was shocked to hear that an appointment had been confirmed with the leadership of North Korea, the final holdout of the Freedom Alliance. The president met with them at the Kennedy Myers building, and several news agencies were allowed access to film the meeting and conduct interviews.

When the event was concluded, the president spoke with Jennifer in her office.

"I think we've finally turned a corner," he said. "We no longer have any rogue countries."

Jennifer smiled. "Yes sir, I'm so glad that we can now push forward," she said.

"Agreed. Now we have to get a handle on these terror groups." He shook her hand and finished a quick tour of the building that bore his name.

When the workday was over, Jennifer and Tank walked outside to an awaiting small transport. It was shaped like a flattened egg. Silver in color and about the size of a large cargo van, it had several metallic ports on it. The ports were attachment points where other appendages could be added. For asteroid miners, there would be large spiderlike arms for grabbing onto an asteroid and guiding it to a processing station. If they were syphoning gasses from a gas giant planet like Saturn, a large cylindrical container with an enormous suction tube in front would be attached. But a personal small transport was just egg shaped and glowed silver. Xho again transferred how to operate the transport to Jennifer. Since this was the third time she received the complete instructions, she felt like an expert. She sat in the pilot seat with Tank alongside her in the passenger seat.

"Let me give this a try," Jennifer said to Xho. She then turned her view to Tank.

"You ready for this, big boy?" Jennifer asked him with wide eyes and a devilish smile.

Tank actually had a nervous look on his face, like that of a father with a young daughter about to drive for the very first time. He slowly nodded. She closed the doors and then grabbed the controls and pulled up. The transport lifted quickly, but smoothly, upward. Within seconds, they were at ten thousand feet. Jennifer pulled to one side, and the craft moved instantly in that direction. She peered at the video map.

"We're now crossing over Utah," she said. "And there goes Colorado."

Tank peered at her with a shocked look, his hands clutching the seat. "Isn't Xho waiting for us?" he asked nervously.

"Oh shit, that's right." Jennifer pulled on the stick, and the craft quickly arced 180 degrees. Tank let out a loud grunt. In a few seconds they were crossing back into Nevada. Jennifer eased the controls, and the craft slowly lowered to the ground alongside Xho. She touched the Idle button and then opened the door.

"Xho, this thing is the *bomb!*" Jennifer yelled to Xho. Xho gave her a startled look and made several inquiries.

"Sorry; I mean I love this. Thank you!" She laughed and then jumped out of the seat and gave Xho a hug. "Can we take this now?"

We give it to you freely. Xho nodded and then smiled at Jennifer.

Jennifer looked at the two waiting agents and twelve marines.

"Oh, um, is there roof access to our building?" she asked. The one agent looked at the other.

"Uh, yes, ma'am, there is. Why?"

"Well, can you call them and tell them to unlock it, because I'm going to land directly on the roof. This will be much quicker and easier," Jennifer said as she sat back down in the transport.

"Ma'am, I'm not sure if—"

Jennifer closed the door and lifted up. In seconds they were on their way again. She looked over to Tank.

"On that panel there, zoom in and locate our building. I can just use the autopilot, and it will land us right on the roof."

Tank tapped the touch screen in front of him, and in seconds he located the building.

"Wow, this is incredible," Tank mumbled.

When he punched 'access' on the screen, a tone sounded and the craft then homed in on their destination. Within thirty seconds, they were on the roof of the building. As Jennifer opened the door, an agent opened the rooftop security access.

After Tank and Jennifer exited the craft, she concentrated for a moment. The transport then hummed and hovered.

"There," Jennifer said with a smile. "It's locked." She turned to the waiting agent. "Thanks for unlocking the access; I appreciate it." She shook the agent's hand as he stood stunned, staring at the humming shiny metallic egg hovering before him.

"This is how we're going to travel from now on," Jennifer said as she sauntered by him. Tank gave the agent a smile. The agent handed him an access card while still staring at the craft.

When they got to their room, Tank looked at Jennifer.

"You know, you're probably going to catch some grief over this."

"Pssh, please," Jennifer responded with a flippant attitude. "The transport is secure; once we're inside of it, we're completely bullet- and missile proof, and we've eliminated the waste of time of having to drive from this building to the White House. Can you tell me that we're secure in that SUV from here to the White House?"

Tank shrugged, shook his head, and then walked into the kitchen.

That evening, after Jennifer and Tank had dinner, Jennifer outlined their upcoming weekend. She told Tank about her elementary school. She talked about her favorite park and hiking trails. She was ready to burst with excitement as she relived her favorite childhood places. Tank just smiled lovingly at her as she gushed about it.

"I can't wait," he said to her softly. "This time we'll be able to enjoy us."

"Yeah, and no sardine can of a ride, eh?" She broke out into laughter.

Jennifer fell asleep in Tank's arms as they watched TV in bed. He turned it off and fell asleep shortly after.

Chapter 27

ALARMS SCREECHED LOUDLY, SHATTERING THE early morning calm.
Jennifer and Tank shocked awake. Lights flashed, and the alarm wailed.
The clock showed 3:38 a.m.

"Shit, we're under attack!" Tank screamed. He grabbed his carbon
suit and ripped open the nightstand drawer. He pulled out his Baretta
PX4 Storm and three clips. Jennifer was jumping into her carbon suit
when they heard two explosions. One was outside, and the second shook
the building. Gunshots rang out as Tank quickly donned his carbon suit.
Jennifer hurriedly donned her suit, tears in her eyes.

Tank ran to the door and listened for a moment as Jennifer ran up
behind him. He opened the door, did a jump, and rolled out into the
hallway. He quickly looked left and then right.

"Let's go!" he screamed.

Jennifer ran, tears streaming down her cheeks as they approached the
stairwell. Tank quickly opened the door and looked in every direction.
Several gunshots and automatic weapons fire rang out. Screams and
yelling followed. Jennifer and Tank darted up the steps toward the roof.
When they reached the door, Jennifer tried the doorknob.

"It's locked!" she screamed.

"Damn it, forgot the access card!" Tank yelled back.

He pushed Jennifer aside and took a running start and kicked the
door. The door heaved and the frame bent, but the door held firm. Tank
got another running start and jumped with both feet. With a crashing
thud, the door flew open and Tank fell to the ground. Jennifer quickly
ran by and stopped at the transport. She stared at it for a moment, con-
centrating. The transport lowered, and the doors opened. Tank hobbled

over to the passenger side. More explosions and gunfire echoed from the street below.

As Jennifer jumped into the craft, she screamed over to Tank, "*Come on!* Hurry up!"

He quickly hobbled over and jumped in. When he closed the door, Jennifer jerked the controls back. They were instantly thrust down in their seats as it propelled upward.

"What took you so long?" she screamed.

"I think I broke my ankle!" Tank yelled.

Jennifer put her hand between the seats and popped open a red plastic container. It held six syringes. She quickly plunged one into Tank's leg.

"Ow!" Tank shouted. "Go back!" he screamed. "Let's see if we can help!"

Jennifer glanced at him for a moment. Sweat ran down his face, his eyes wide.

"You can't shoot a gun from inside here; it won't work!" Jennifer screamed.

"We can run them over!" Tank yelled back.

Jennifer quickly turned the controls, and the transport dived down toward the street. There were four large vans at the front of the building. Six cars and two government SUVs were in flames along the building. Several agents and a few men dressed in black garb lay bleeding in the street. Flashes of light came from inside the building; then more streaks of gunfire.

Tank quickly swung his head around, trying to get a view of the entire street. Jennifer swiveled the controls, and the transport moved in a 360-degree circle.

"There!" Tank yelled. He pointed to the end of the block. Two vans sat waiting. "Get 'em!"

Jennifer moved the controls toward the vans. A red light illuminated, and Jennifer pressed an override button. The transport pushed hard, directly into the two vans. It never made physical contact, but the vans were pushed and flipped over and over.

"Stop over there!" Tank yelled.

Jennifer brought the transport to a stop twenty feet away. Tank opened the door and took a step. His syringe now glowed green. He ripped it out and tossed it into the transport. As he turned back around, two men in black hoods were crawling out of the first van. Tank squeezed off four shots—two into each man. They both screamed and then fell lifeless.

One man was pulling himself out of the side window of the other van. He caught Tank's view and screamed.

"No, wait!"

Tank shot him twice. Two men then opened fire from around the back of the van. Tank was knocked off his feet by the hail of bullets. Jennifer quickly pivoted the transport and guided it straight at the two men. They continued to fire at her with their machine guns as she approached. The bullets lit up orange and streaked wildly to the left and right, around the transport. Within a second, she was on top of them, crushing them beneath the transport. She then swung it around and stopped just shy of Tank. He sprang up, breathing heavily, and climbed into the transport.

Tank closed the door, and Jennifer turned the transport back toward the apartment. As she approached the building, two medium-sized transports lowered down rapidly to the street. Two dozen marines jumped out. Jennifer quickly raised their transport up to thirty feet. They watched from above as three terrorists tried to exit the building. Several marines opened fire from both angles, killing them instantly.

As daylight broke, the entire city of Washington, DC, was locked down. Jennifer and Tank were safely in the White House, in the conference room. Ernie walked in and stepped up to the lectern.

"We've just been through a massive coordinated attack," Ernie stated as he swallowed hard. "Reports are still coming in, but there have been dozens of attacks all around the world."

He took a moment to compose himself; his hands trembled as he read his notes.

"We've lost at least twelve Secret Service agents, twenty-seven marines, over one hundred fifty civilians, and one Qyron." He cleared his throat. "Several government and industrial sites have been attacked worldwide." He paused a moment, still trembling. "And the vice president has been killed."

The room erupted in gasps and sobs. Jennifer squeezed Tank's hand; she was still trembling.

"There were similar attacks in England, France, Germany, Australia, Canada, Mexico, China, and India."

A staffer handed Ernie another paper. Ernie shook his head and sighed.

"We have also lost Navya Malik and her family."

"Noo!" Jennifer cried out. She clutched Tank's chest and began sobbing. Ernie looked directly at Jennifer.

"We also have a report, Jennifer, that your mother's house was attacked."

Jennifer froze, mouth open, as tears streamed down her cheeks.

"Our agents were able to repel the attack, and we lost one agent during the fight. Your mother was initially injured but was given treatment, and she's now recuperating." Ernie maintained a somber look toward Tank and Jennifer.

"I'm also sorry, Jennifer, but we have a report that Natasha Mills was killed."

"Oh my God, *Tasha!*" Jennifer cried out. She sobbed heavily as the room fell uncomfortably quiet. "I'm not safe!" she screamed out. "They killed my best friend, Navya, and almost killed my momma!"

Tank tried to grab her, but she pushed him away, screaming and sobbing. Everyone took a few steps back as she flailed her arms wildly and screeched.

"I'm not *safe!*"

She began to hyperventilate. Tank lurched forward and grabbed her as she passed out.

When Jennifer awoke, she looked up to see Terrance sitting next her. His appearance was soft and calm. She smiled at him and touched his face. They were in their bedroom.

Jennifer spoke softly. "I had the worst nightmare."

Tank smiled down at her. "I love you," he said softly. He leaned down and gave her a kiss. As he pulled back, her delicate expression changed to one of worry.

"Wait a minute," she said with alarm.

"Jennifer, listen," Tank began. "We're in our bedroom, and you're safe." He pushed his hands gently down on her shoulders. "You were given some sedation so you could rest."

Jennifer's eyes began to well up.

"So the nightmare is true?" she sniffled. "We were attacked. Tasha, Navya, and her family were killed." Jennifer began to cry. Tank lifted her up and hugged her as she sobbed.

"Why?" she cried. "Why did they have to kill her whole family?"

Tank continued to hug her. He stroked her back and gently rocked her.

"Her oldest daughter survived," Tank replied softly. "But the vice president was killed, along with dozens of Secret Service and marines."

"Wait! Then how are we safe?" Jennifer blurted out through the tears.

She pulled back and stared into Tank's eyes.

"There are two transports and three dozen marines standing guard on this block. Nothing will get us," Tank said softly.

"My mother?" Jennifer shrieked.

"Shh, relax. Your mother is in the next apartment, sleeping soundly. She's fine," Tank said softly.

"No, I can't do this anymore. I wanna go home!"

"Just relax," Tank said as he continued to hug her.

Jennifer pushed out of the hug. "No, no, I don't wanna do this; it's not worth it!" she said as she crawled away from his grasp. "Look what's happened. So many people killed—so much death and destruction," she sobbed. "No, Terrance, this isn't worth it. I have over a half million dollars in the bank." She wiped her eyes. "We can go live peacefully in Montana. We can buy land."

Tank shook his head.

Jennifer sobbed louder.

"Why not? We can be happy," she wept.

Tank reached out to her.

"No, please," she cried. "Please. We can't do this anymore, Terrance." She slapped his hand away.

Tank stood up. He walked over to the end table and reached for a small needle.

Jennifer jumped up and off the bed. "No, you're not going to drug me!" she screamed, looking left and right.

Two agents walked into the room.

"No, please, you guys can't let him do this!" she screamed at the two agents before looking back at Tank.

"Baby, please!" Jennifer fell to her knees.

Tank set the needle back down and walked over to her. He kneeled down alongside her and gave her a hug. She continued sobbing in his arms.

"We gotta go," she cried. "We gotta go!"

Tank held her tight and stroked her hair. She continued to wail.

After twenty minutes, Jennifer gently pushed out of his grasp and stood up. Her eyes were red and puffy, her face wet. She grabbed a few tissues and blew her nose. Tank stood up.

"I want to speak with the president," Jennifer said quietly.

One of the agents, John, stepped forward.

"Miss Winston, he's very busy right now. He's talking with world leaders and the Qyron. I'm not sure if this is a good time."

She stared at John for a moment. She grabbed some more tissues and blew her nose again. After a few deep breaths, she composed herself.

"Terrance, I want to see my mother."

"She's still sleeping," John interjected.

Jennifer gave him a nod.

"John, please take me to see the president. I must talk with him."

After a moment, John spoke into his sleeve and then nodded to Jennifer.

Tank, three agents, and twelve marines accompanied Jennifer to the roof and into an awaiting medium transport. In seconds they were on the grass at the White House. Jennifer walked into the building and up to the Oval Office. Two agents nodded as Jennifer approached and opened the door.

The president was busy discussing issues with several men. Thoona, Xho, and two other Qyron were also in the room.

"Ah, Jennifer, I'm glad to see you're back," the president stated. He walked around his desk and gave her a hug.

Xho immediately flooded her with questions. She spent the next ten minutes discussing the situation between Thoona and the president. The loss of a single Qyron was an extreme tragedy to all Qyron, as there had been no deaths outside of natural causes for over four hundred thousand years. Thoona demanded to have assurances against any further violence.

The president then detailed to Thoona the strides they were making with keeping their communications secure with the isolation and protection of the Kennedy Myers complex, and they were feverishly continuing their search for and identification of the terrorist groups responsible.

"Sir, Thoona would like to offer Qyron computers to assist with information gathering for this cause." Jennifer nodded to Xho. "The top Qyron programmers have studied our Internet and have designed programs they are certain will help."

More information streamed in to Jennifer.

"They would also like to replace my building with a more advanced and secure facility." Jennifer turned to Xho. "But I like my apartment," she protested.

Jennifer realized the breach in her professional demeanor. "Oh, I'm sorry!" she said as she flashed looks to both the president and Thoona.

"That's fine," The president said with the slightest of smiles. "I'm glad you're in better spirits."

We will not let any harm come to you. Thoona decisively projected.

Jennifer pivoted quickly and looked at Thoona. "Oh, thank you, sir," she said softly.

Thoona took a step forward and opened his arms.

Jennifer gave Thoona a hug. "Thank you."

Thoona then expressed his deep regret for this attack and took his leave.

After Thoona and the rest of the Qyron left the Oval Office, Jennifer took a step toward the president.

"Sir, if I could speak with you for a moment?"

The president nodded. "I have fifteen minutes before I address the country. What is it?"

"Well, if you're busy," Jennifer mumbled.

"Jennifer, I don't have time for this; *out with it*!" the president stated with authority.

"Sir, I don't think I want to do this job anymore. I guess"—she paused—"I'm resigning."

The president took a step back, as if he had been slapped in the face. Mumbled conversations from others in the room abruptly ceased with her statement. The president stood frozen for a moment.

"Everyone but Terry and Jennifer, out." the president stated calmly.

Those in attendance still stood shocked.

"*Now!*" he yelled.

All involved immediately snapped to and quickly rushed out of the room.

When the door closed, the president sat Jennifer down in a chair. He took a deep breath and paced to one side of the room. He turned and exhaled as he walked slowly back toward her.

"Jennifer, it's been well over a month now. We have—"

"Sir, I don't feel safe," Jennifer said calmly.

"Jennifer, we have—"

"They killed the vice president!" she said loudly.

The president straightened up. His look of irritation lingered for a moment, and then he composed himself. "You stated once that interrupting someone is rude. Is that not what you're doing now?"

Jennifer bowed her head. "I'm sorry, sir."

The president slowly closed his eyes and nodded. He then began to calmly pace before her.

"Jennifer, in our history, many tragedies have occurred, and mistakes have been made. On December 7, 1941, we lost over twenty-five hundred brave servicemen. Sixty years later, on September 11, 2001, at least twenty-five hundred Americans died from terrorist attacks. In both instances, we were angry and afraid. We had decisions to make, and if one thing stands firm in the history of this country, whether it be from oppression of the English royalty in the late 1700s or terrorist attacks in 2001, it is that we *will not* turn and run."

The president stopped his pacing directly in front of Jennifer.

"Jennifer, you began this monumental change for mankind. You braved through your fears—through the terror of first contact. With your help, millions—hell, hundreds of millions—of people all over the world are now better off than they were before. Millions of Americans have better jobs, and millions of people in other countries have housing and food." He gave her a solemn look. "Jennifer, you will go down as the single most important woman in history."

"But I could be killed tomorrow," Jennifer said softly.

Kennedy nodded and took a deep breath. "Do you remember the conversation we had after you were first attacked?"

Jennifer squinted her eyes and slowly shook her head.

"You weren't sure what to do," the president began. "There are jobs in life that are bigger than the person; this is true of police, firefighters, and the military. We can add your job to that list. These changes to the lives of the hundreds of millions wouldn't have been possible without you. It may have happened a year from now, maybe more. But it happened now because of *you*, Jennifer."

The president leaned over and grabbed her shoulders. He eased her up from her chair, still holding on to her shoulders and staring wide-eyed at her.

"Jennifer, you are in the history books tomorrow. Your story will be told. But will your story read that you ran and hid from extreme adversity or that you came back stronger, more determined, like we did after Pearl Harbor and 9/11? I can't make you stay, but I'm damn sure going to make certain that you fully understand the ramifications of your actions in my eyes and those of history."

Jennifer stood glassy eyed. Her bottom lip quivered. She continued to stare up at the president.

"I believe in you, Jennifer!" the president firmly stated as he looked over at Tank. "Terry believes in you. I'm sure that your best friend Natasha believed in you."

Jennifer peered over at Tank. He nodded slowly.

"Thoona and the Qyron believe in you," Kennedy stated as he stared into her eyes. "We know that we were caught off guard, and many lives were lost. But we've learned, and we're going to make certain that those who were responsible will pay for their actions. We will ensure that we're better protected. But we need you, Jennifer, *now* more than ever!"

He reached out his hands. Jennifer blinked, and a tear ran down her cheek.

She reached out her hands. The president grabbed them and squeezed. He looked down and smiled. Jennifer smiled back and gave him a hug.

"Thank you for making the right choice," he whispered softly in her ear before slowly pulling back. "Okay, I hate to speak and run, but it's time for me to address the country." He took a few steps toward the door and then stopped. "Hey, let's go!"

Jennifer smiled, wiped the tear from her cheek, and quickly trotted over to the president.

Five minutes later, the president gave his address to the American public and the world. He listed the lives lost, from the vice president, congressmen, senators, and business leaders, to the scores of marines and civilians. He restated that we were currently under a countrywide state of emergency but that justice would be swift and peace would be restored.

When his speech was over, he turned to Jennifer.

Jennifer was momentarily shocked, but she nodded and stepped up to the lectern.

"I'm still mourning the loss of both my fellow translator, Navya Malik, and my best friend, Natasha Mills," she said softly into the microphone. She cleared her throat and brushed her hair out of her face. A single tear ran down her cheek. "But if one thing is clear to me," she stated, sniffling, but in a louder tone, "It's that I will *not* bow to the cowardly actions of these terrorists. I will continue to work for the better of all mankind."

The newscasters in attendance applauded.

After the meeting, the president was pulled aside by Ernie and a staffer.

"Sir, we have significant developments to discuss," Ernie said. "We have the Pentagon and other world leaders waiting on teleconference."

The president nodded and walked toward the Situation Room.

He stopped and looked back at Jennifer. "Come on; keep up!" he yelled.

Ernie leaned in. "Sir, it's for your eyes only."

The president gave Ernie an angry stare as Jennifer and Tank approached. Ernie then turned and continued walking.

When they entered the Situation Room, several large monitors were currently on. One screen displayed a general at the Pentagon. Four other monitors hosted the leaders of Germany, France, Great Britain, and China.

Tom Franklin stepped forward. "Sir"—he peered for a moment at Tank and Jennifer—"thanks to the implementation of these Qyron computers, we were able to rapidly sort through all terrorist communications. We have identified dozens of locations of terrorist cells in countries all over the world. As you see on the monitors, we have the leaders and their militaries ready to strike, sir."

The general chimed in. "I've got birds in the air, sir, just awaiting your orders."

"We thought it best to have everyone attack at once," Tom mentioned, "to prevent any retaliation or regrouping of the terrorists. Everything is coordinated and ready for your orders, sir."

The president smiled at the monitors and nodded to the other world leaders. "It's payback time, gentlemen. Attack!"

Within minutes, reports flooded in detailing buildings, homes, and meeting sites that were blown up, and terrorists that had been captured or killed.

As the reports streamed in, a man handed Tom a few sheets of paper. Tom pulled the president aside.

"Sir, we have one very disturbing fact to relay to you," Tom said.

"What is it, Tom?" the president asked impatiently.

"We've been able to piece together a leader of the Freedom for All group."

"Yes?"

"You're probably not going to like it, sir," Tom stated.

"*Tom!*" the president yelled.

"It's Butler Andrews, sir."

The president stood quiet for a moment as he pondered his former secretary of transportation. He pursed his lips and closed his eyes for a moment. As he exhaled, he opened his eyes.

"I see it didn't take that backstabbing little son-of-a … Let's round him up!" the president responded.

"Well, sir, backstabber he is, but stupid he's not," Tom began. "In all of the communications we've intercepted, he does get mentioned, but at no point is he giving any orders or making it clear that he's in charge.

321

He's definitely covered his tracks very well, sir." Tom took a moment. "And it gets better, sir."

The president folded his arms.

"It seems that he's starting his own political party," Tom continued. "The Freedom Party is the name, and this time, he *is* the clear leader. The group is very well funded by numerous sources, not the least of which is OPEC, along with a few pharmaceutical companies and some political action groups."

"It looks like he's finally trying to get the power he's so desperately craved," Kennedy mumbled.

"Yes, sir, and I don't have to tell you how things look in 2023 come election time, with the current polls as they are."

The president took a moment. Staffers were busy running around, and the reports continued to pour in. One staff member walked up to the president and handed him and Tom a report. The president took a moment to read it.

"It looks like our attacks were successful. Over three hundred targets were hit globally by fifteen different militaries," the president said. He then turned to Jennifer. "Okay, it's obvious that I have my work cut out for me. What I need from you, Jennifer, is to see how we can speed the acquisition of more interpreters. Speak to the Qyron; see what else can be done." Jennifer nodded and turned to walk away. "Oh!" the president shouted, "and welcome back to the team."

Jennifer smiled. "I never left sir!" She turned and walked out of the Situation Room. As Tank and Jennifer walked down the hallway, they were approached by Mr. Atkins.

"Jennifer, I'm sorry for your loss," he said solemnly. Jennifer acknowledged him. "After seeing your apartment building and dealing with the Qyron, we will be replacing your building on Saturday. We can put you up in another location over the weekend, but we'll need you out of the building all day."

Jennifer nodded. She turned to Tank. "So how about that weekend away in Montana?"

Tank nodded.

"Granted, it won't be the same as I was planning, but we could use the time away," she said.

"Yes, that sounds great," Tank replied. "And when we get back, I can empty out my old place."

Jennifer and Tank returned to the apartment. As their small transport landed on the roof, an agent greeted them.

"Miss Winston, we have people boxing all of your belongings up so we can transition to the new building," the agent said. "We set aside your laptop and transmitter for you."

They walked down to the second floor. Jennifer grabbed her equipment. She met her mother back on the roof as a medium transport waited to take them all to Montana.

Jennifer ran over to her mother and hugged her. "Oh, Mama! I'm so glad you're all right!"

"I was so worried about you too, dear," her mother responded, "and it was horrible hearing about little Natasha."

Jennifer nodded solemnly.

"Mama, this is my boyfriend, Terrance," Jennifer said as she introduced them.

"You look familiar," her mother said as she shook his hand.

"Yes, Mama, he was an agent that protected me. You may have seen him at Tasha's wedding."

"Oh, that's right," she said as her face lit up. "Nice to meet you, Terrance. Thank you for keepin' my baby safe."

The three of them stepped aboard the medium transport.

There was a white light and a hissing noise, and I removed my headset.

Chapter 28

WHEN I FINALLY GOT MY mind cleared, I stood up and looked at the clock. I had been in my logs for over six hours.

"John!" I called out.

"In here, baby," John mumbled from the bedroom.

"What the heck! Why didn't you bring me out of the Psy-log? It's been six hours!"

John was in bed, and his brow was furrowed as he stared at the laptop.

"Hey, I was busy with all of this data; it's ridiculously scary," he said softly, with not a trace of humor in his voice.

I felt a chill as I walked over to the bed. John's gaze on the screen didn't waver.

"First of all, this lists everyone on board, but it goes way beyond that," John said as he peered over at me. He had a nervous look on his face. "This database has some incredibly intrusive information, Amant. What the hell are the Qyron up to?"

"What do you mean, Johnny?"

I sat down on the bed next to John and looked at the screen.

"Well, here, look at this." John clicked on a few tabs. "Here's me, for instance. It lists my name and all of my personal contact information. But then it goes into extraordinary graphic detail on the rest of my life. They have scores in college courses, performance reports on my past jobs, my complete medical history, and my food choices. Amant, this is way too much information needed for me to ride in a transport."

I nodded my head slowly in disbelief. I just stared at the data on the screen. It was very intimidating. As I panned down the listing, I noticed it even had dating choices and sexual preferences.

"Wow, Johnny, this is pretty much you boiled down into raw data."

I looked at John. He was visibly shaken. I wanted to comfort him, but I was nearly speechless and stunned myself. There were pages upon pages of data about every aspect of John and his life.

"Now it gets even more odd," John said as he clicked a few more keys.

A new listing came up, now showing just names and a few basic facts. I looked at the top of the page. It was the ship manifest for Gamma Five Alpha. It was a stark opposite to the passengers heading to Gamma Five. John then clicked back to the pages showing his data. He stared at me, begging for a reason.

"John, did anyone scan you at some point?"

John's gaze trailed off as he thought for a moment.

"Well, when I applied for the job on Gamma Five, they did a health scan of me, and I had a small dose of Meibots. Other than that, I can't think of any other time that I've been scanned." John grabbed the laptop and clicked on the screen.

"How long did the scan take?"

"I don't know; like a minute or two," he mumbled.

A medical scan would have taken only take five to ten seconds. I bit my tongue to keep my mouth from verbalizing that thought. John looked truly nervous; I could feel his fear.

"Look at this, though," he said. "I have no idea what this is."

John continued to click on the menu. He then made a selection. The screen popped up a series of dots, characters, and icons. I grabbed the laptop and clicked on the data. A red warning block appeared, along with text that read, "Level 15 access required."

"What the heck," I whispered.

I had level 12 access and didn't know of anyone who had higher. Even top officials of the Qyron government that I interfaced with had only level 10 or 11.

"Are you kidding me?" I yelled aloud.

John looked at me.

"Yeah, I was that frustrated over an hour ago; now I'm just numb," he said matter-of-factly.

"Okay, enough of this," I shouted as I tossed the laptop on the bed.

"Let's go exercise and then get something to eat!" John flashed me a tired look. "Yeah, I know. You don't feel like it. Well, *tough*. Let's go," I said as I rummaged through the drawer, looking for workout clothes. When I finally found some yoga pants and a workout shirt, I turned around. John was lying down in bed, but now the covers were pulled up.

"John, if I have to get you out of bed, I will drag you out by your *feet*," I said sternly.

John quickly thrust off the covers and jumped out of bed. "Bully!" he said as he walked by me. I spanked his butt for good measure.

As we walked to the gym on Delta level, we mumbled facts back and forth to each other. We were both in a sort of confused soup of thought. The data we had viewed was incredibly pervasive but didn't seem to have any purpose for a general transport. If we hadn't been in transit between planets, I could have linked with people that I knew would have an answer. I had been to the Qyron home world on several occasions, and I knew quite a few genius Qyron. But here I was, cut off and left with one mystery after another. I could feel the tension building, so this gym visit was absolutely necessary.

When we reached the gym, I noticed it was only lightly busy. I stretched out while John hit the weights. A good, long jog then occupied my time as I did laps around the track. I slowly ran over the information in my head. I thought about the inability to board the transport, the lack of acceptance of my identification. I then drifted to the complete lack of any information on Gamma Five Alpha or the existence of this transport. It took much searching just to locate Gamma Five. I quickened the pace of my jog. I felt the sweat slowly saturate my shirt. After four miles, I decided to change over to some weight training.

I walked over to the weights and did some shoulder workouts with the free weights. Two men watched me as I did front flys with fifty-pound weights. I then shifted to lateral raises until my shoulders felt nice and warm. The men continued to stare, so I put the weights away and walked over to the benches.

I set three hundred pounds on the bar and warmed up with two sets of ten. When I stood back up to add more weights, I caught sight of someone looking at me as he passed by the gym. The hairs on my neck stood up.

"Psi?" I yelled out.

I dropped the forty-five pound weight and ran to the front of the gym. As I turned the corner, I saw a man stopped down the passageway. He had long brown hair and stood with his back turned.

"Psi, is that you?" I asked, now two steps behind him.

"Who wants to know?" he responded in a low, emotionless tone.

"It's your favorite half-breed, you Neanderthal," I said with a laugh.

"Amant?" he replied as he slowly turned around.

"Oh my gosh, Psi!" I exclaimed as I took another step to him.

His eyes locked on mine, and he squinted. It was as if he had just woken up and was unsure of where he was. And, well, as I stared at him and noticed he had very long and unkempt hair; a scraggly, misshapen beard; and was wearing a T-shirt over a long-sleeve thermal shirt, I thought he looked like he *had* just climbed out of bed.

"Psi? How have you been?" I said. "And *where* the hell have you been?" I reached out and touched his shoulders. He actually flinched, and it took me by surprise. "I tried looking you up on Qyron the last two times I was there, and I couldn't locate you."

His look of bewilderment worried me, and the energy drained from his face. I then studied the man standing in front of me—a man I had dated years ago.

He looked much thinner than I remembered, his face with more pronounced cheekbones and a bonier chin. His eyes looked sunken in with dark circles surrounding them. I had loved how he kept his hair so short and neat, but now it was long and stringy, bunched up beneath a crumpled hat.

"Yeah, I was busy I guess," he mumbled as he stared through me.

"Psi, what's wrong? What happened to you?"

"So who's this?" John stated.

I swung around, startled. John stood a few steps behind me, in the entryway to the gym.

"Oh, Johnny, this is Psi."

John slowly walked over and shook Psi's hand.

"We met on Qyron years ago," I said as I stared at this new version of Psi. "Psi was doing some really good programming with the Qyron government."

"Not anymore," Psi interjected with a grunt.

I paused a moment, waiting for him to continue, and then began again before the moment turned uncomfortable.

"We met one day after a meeting in the capital building. Psi made a joke about me that I—"

"I don't joke anymore," Psi said quickly.

John gave me a curious look, eyebrow raised, and then nodded.

"Nice meeting you, Psi; I should get back to my workout," John said as he slowly turned and walked back inside.

I looked harder at Psi. He still had the bushy eyebrows and small, beady eyes. When we first met years ago, he made a joke to me that I was a misplaced half-breed, and I called him a Neanderthal because of his eyes. It was our own running joke. But the light in his eyes and the fire in his personality were gone. Only this shell of Psi stood before me.

"Psi, what's wrong?"

"Nothing is wrong with me," he stated flatly. "I should go now."

He turned to leave.

I reached out and grabbed his arm. "Psi, can we talk?"

"No! Not now," he said as he pulled away from my grasp and continued walking. I stood in the passageway, depressed and confused. Psi had always been a fun, adventurous, quirky person. This was a complete opposite of the man I knew—the man I had dated two years ago.

I walked back into the gym. John stood a few feet inside, sipping a bottled water.

"John, that was really odd," I said softly. "I knew Psi years ago; he was so different. He was fun and comical—a lot like you. I dated him for two months. This was not the person I knew."

John took another drink and wiped his forehead.

"Yes, he looked and sounded like a broken man," he panted. "I just thought that he was feeling weird that you introduced him to your current boyfriend, so I decided to leave."

"No, that would have never fazed him, Johnny." I turned back to see Psi walking around the corner. "I just … I don't know."

"Well, sorry if I made it awkward," John said as he turned to grab a weight.

"Johnny?"

He peered over his shoulder and looked at me.

"You're not upset about this, are you?" I asked him.

"What? No, not at all." He set the weight back down. "I love you and trust you, Amant. I'm just bushed. It's about time to get some sleep, and I'm really tired—emotionally and physically."

"Agreed. Well then, let's get a shower and some rest."

As we walked back to our room, I told John about my past with Psi—how we met on Qyron and the weeks we spent together. It was actually Psi's work that had eventually pulled us apart. I had to leave for Venus and Tyberon, while Psi said he needed to stay on Qyron for his job as a programmer. It was a friendly breakup, but one that I have wondered about over the past.

We got back to our room and showered. After a small snack and some lovemaking, we both drifted off to sleep. I woke up a few hours later though. My mind was a jumble of thoughts. I sorted through the flood of memories of Psi and me—and, of course, the lingering mysteries of the shuttle and Gamma Five.

I decided to get up. I walked around Alpha Deck for twenty minutes, but all that did was further my questions. When I got back to the room, I decided to just sit on the couch and escape. I grabbed my headset. There was a white light and some hissing noise.

August 22, 2021

Jennifer and Tank arrived in Montana in the late evening on Friday. Jennifer visited Craig on Saturday morning to give her sympathy to him over the loss of Tasha. She had been present at Tasha's funeral a few days earlier, but she still felt a huge weight of guilt. Jennifer couldn't escape the fact that it was her involvement that had gotten her best friend killed.

Craig was still distraught, but he gave her a hug and told her it wasn't her fault. She knew it was a lie, and it was very difficult for both of them, but it allowed them to grieve and begin their emotional healing.

Jennifer spent the rest of Saturday showing Tank around the town, reliving Jennifer's past. They enjoyed a walk through the park on Sunday morning and a nice quiet picnic as the agents and marines maintained a discreet distance.

Jennifer received a communication from Xho on Sunday afternoon. She had asked him how they could speed up the process of locating more human translators. He relayed to her that they were scanning over a million people a day. He then conveyed that lineage carried the necessary genetic anomaly. Lastly, he demanded that Jennifer disclose the full amount of the salary for the position—$6 million.

Jennifer then called her mother and Pari, Navya's sole surviving daughter. It happened that during the evening of the attack, Pari was with some friends on a trip. So she was spared the attack that took her family.

Jennifer asked them both if they were interested in becoming translators. She left a voicemail for her mother but reached Pari directly. Pari was steadfast in demanding to follow in her mother's footsteps. Her country rallied behind her in the wake of the deaths of her mother, father, and brother. She became her country's banner of defiance.

Jennifer and Tank returned to their brand-new government apartment complex by 4:00 p.m. The building was much taller, at fifteen stories. The roof had been built with raised walls to allow complete security for entering and exiting a transport. Their room looked very much the same, but it was outfitted with a few additional features: there was a built-in transmitting interface so Jennifer could reach Xho even if he was in his room in orbit, there was a hot tub in the bathroom, and most importantly, there was Qyron security. The apartment door had an additional metallic security door that would slam into place if the alarm was sounded. Similar defensive shields were in place over every window, making the apartment a secure panic room in case of attack; but all this was hidden from view, so the apartment still gave the appearance of any other. One window had been fashioned into a door to allow easy escape into a transport if the need arose.

As they relaxed into their new building, Jennifer's phone rang.

"Hey, Mama!"

"Jeniveve, baby, I'm callin' about ya job offer, baby."

"Mama—Jennifer!"

"Oh hush now, darlin'! I carried you inside me nine whole months; I get to name you. And I gave you Jeniveve! Anyways, I was callin' about your offer for me to take the job like you. Baby, I'm really not right for it. I'm not good with all that government-type stuff, like you."

"Mama, it's not like you need to know things. You just relay the thoughts of your Qyron interpreter to the politicians or business leaders. It's just talking, Mama, and you love doing that."

"Yeah, well, I'm not all comfy with those big muckety-mucks, baby girl. I'd feel like a sardine in a box of candies. I wouldn't even know how to dress."

"But you said you needed more money for retirement, Mama!"

"Jeniveve, I can work 'til I'm sixty-five, and I'll be just fine."

"Mama, it pays six million dollars a year!"

There was a long pause on the line.

"Mama?"

"Baby girl, it ain't nice to lie to me like that!"

"I'm not lying, Mama; I'm serious—on Daddy's grave. That money that I sent you last week—fifty thousand—Mama, that's just a small bit of what I get paid. I make one hundred twenty-five thousand a week."

"But they put something in your head?" she asked, a nervous tone in her voice.

"Yes, Mama, it's surgery. There's no pain; don't worry! And no scars, and it's right quick too. I can have them do it, and you'll be fine in minutes, Mama. Plus the government will give you an apartment like you had here this weekend. You can live here next to me, Mama."

"That was a really swanky place. Hmm."

A long pause ensued.

"And heck all, I could even retire after a year," she said with a lilt in her voice.

"So you'll do it, Mama?"

Another long pause passed.

"Yes, baby, I will. But Jeni, you have to help me pick out clothes. I don't want them thinkin' I'm some stupid ol' country woman!"

"Clothes can't hide that, Mama!" Jennifer laughed.

"You watch your tongue, girl!" she sassed back with a giggle.

"Okay, Mama, that's great. I'll be out there in a few minutes, and I'll be with you the whole time."

Jennifer ended the call. Since Tank was listening, he was already ahead of her and had his shoes on. Jennifer transmitted to Xho, and Xho relayed their readiness and the fact that Pari was already undergoing the procedure.

In ten minutes, Jennifer was at her mother's house, walking her to the transport. As she approached the transport, she realized that it was a two-seater.

"Stay here, honey; we'll be back soon, and we'll be safe at the space station," Jennifer said.

"Yeah, you can guard my house, Terry," Jennifer's mother added.

Tank laughed. "That I will, Miss Margaret. And don't you be nervous." Tank smiled as he sat down on the porch.

Within a minute, they were docked at the station in space.

Jennifer's mother gazed at the Earth from a window. "It's so peaceful," she said, staring down at the big blue marble.

"Yes it is, Mama, and we're making it a better place, too."

She hugged her mother and then walked with her into the procedure room. As Jennifer waited for her mother's procedure to finish, Pari and Kylee walked into the room.

"Oh, hello, Kylee," Jennifer said.

This is Pari, Kylee thought.

Jennifer stared at Pari for a moment, stunned. Pari was a shorter, younger version of her mother; the long black hair, dimples, and pretty smile were the same. Jennifer teared up.

"Oh my God, you're Navya!" Jennifer exclaimed as she burst out crying. She leaned over and hugged Pari. The two cried for several minutes. When they pulled back from the tearful hug, Kylee had already fetched two small towels and some drinks. They wiped their eyes.

"I'm sorry, but you're just as young and beautiful as your mother," Jennifer sniffled.

"And you are as kind and sweet as my mother told me," Pari cried.

They hugged again.

"I'm so sorry for your loss; I really liked your mama," Jennifer said.

"Thank you," Pari replied as she wiped her eyes. "I want to do as well as my mother did."

"I'm know you'll do fine," Jennifer said as she mustered a smile. "And I'll help you get there."

They both sat down and chatted for a few minutes until Xho walked out of the procedure room.

Your mother is finished.

Jennifer, Pari, Kylee, and Xho walked back into the procedure room. Jennifer's mother lay on the table.

"Hi, Mama, how are you feeling?"

"I don't feel any different, Jeniveve."

"You won't, Mama." Jennifer turned. "Mama, this is Pari; she's Navya's daughter. And this is my translator, Xho."

Margaret sat up.

"My, you're so pretty and so young," she said, looking at Pari.

You are feeling well? Xho thought.

"Oh my!" Margaret exclaimed. "Who said that?"

Jennifer and Pari laughed.

"It will take time for you to adjust, Mama. That was Xho." Jennifer turned to Pari. "Pari, this is my mother, Margaret."

"It is nice to meet you, Margaret," Pari said.

The three of them spent the next twenty minutes practicing. Pari caught on quickly, while Jennifer's mother fumbled a bit. They were also joined by Tahr, Margaret's Qyron translator.

"Oh my, we left Terrance at your house," Jennifer said abruptly. The group said their good-byes, and Jennifer, Pari, Margaret, and Tahr went back to Margaret's home. Jennifer took her personal transport while the rest traveled in a medium transport. As they descended to the house, another medium transport hovered near the home.

When Jennifer exited her craft, she noticed the dozen marines and five Secret Service agents were standing outside. The lead agent, John, walked over to her.

"Miss Winston, we cannot allow you to just take off like that. We must be with you at all times!" he scolded. The medium transport dropped off Tahr and Jennifer's mother.

"I'm sorry," Jennifer said solemnly.

"Well, who's this attractive gentleman?" Margaret said.

"Mama, this is John; he's an agent sent to protect us," Jennifer said. "John, this is my mother, Margaret."

"Nice to meet you, ma'am," he replied.

"Mama, we should be going. If you want to pack up your things, you can meet us later for dinner in my apartment."

The first transport, with Pari aboard, lifted off, taking her back to India. Jennifer and Tank got in their transport and flew home while her mother packed her belongings with the help of John and his team.

"I was having a nice time sitting on the porch, sipping lemonade, when the cavalry arrived," Tank said.

"I'm sorry; did I get you in trouble?" Jennifer asked as she piloted the transport.

"Yeah, I caught a little grief, having known better. See what your charm does to me?" he said with a smile.

They arrived back at the apartment and settled back in. After a brief shopping spree with her mother, they enjoyed a wonderful dinner and talked until ten.

"Okay, Mama, time to get some sleep. We all have a big day tomorrow," Jennifer said as she walked her mother to the door.

Chapter 29

THE NEXT MORNING, THE TEAM walked into the White House. Margaret gawked at everything with each step they made.

"Mama, stop it; you're embarrassing us," Jennifer said quietly.

"I can't help it, baby; this the damn White House!"

When they entered the conference room, Taylor caught sight of the group. He walked over and peered at the visitor badges Pari and her mother were wearing.

"Giving tours in your spare time?" Taylor asked dryly.

"Not exactly," Jennifer said. "Taylor, this is Margaret Winston, my mother, and Pari Malik, Navya's daughter."

"Not giving tours, eh?" Taylor said with a snort as he turned.

At the same time, the president strolled into the room.

"Oh my goodness, that's the president!" Margaret exclaimed as she tugged on her daughter's sleeve.

Taylor continued to walk away but turned and shook his head at Jennifer.

"Mama, stop!" Jennifer scolded, pulling her arm free.

The president caught sight of Taylor, and Jennifer and gave a raised eyebrow as he approached.

"Mr. President, it is my pleasure to introduce you to our two newest Qyron interpreters. This is Margaret Winston, my mother."

Jennifer then turned to her other side. "Sir, this is Pari Malik, the—"

The president stepped forward and gently shook her hand.

"Miss Malik, you have my deepest sympathy for the loss of your mother. If there is anything that I can provide for you, you need only ask."

He then turned toward Margaret.

"Ms. Margaret Winston. It is a pleasure to meet the woman who raised such a talented and strong young woman as Jennifer."

He shook her hand as she stared at him with her mouth open.

"Mama, close your mouth!"

"I'm sorry," Margaret said. "It's a real kick in the ass to meet you too, sir. I even voted for you!"

The president chuckled as he winked at Jennifer.

"And it's Jeniveve," she added. "I named her Jeniveve upon her birth, so don't let her fool you with no nonsense about 'Jennifer.'"

"Mama!" Jennifer yelled out as she slapped her mother's arm.

The president continued laughing. "Time to start the meeting," he said. "Are you coming with me, Jeniveve?" he added with a chuckle.

"Mama!" she scolded as she walked to the front of the room.

When the president stepped up to the lectern, the room came to a hush.

"The past several days have been the biggest test to our way of life in decades," the president began. "We saw our vice president killed; Navya Malik and much of her family murdered; and congressmen and senators, along with scores of marines, Secret Service, and civilians alike, massacred. We had several buildings and businesses destroyed globally." The president paused, surveying the room. "But in three days, we have recovered. We located many of those accountable and eliminated them or brought them to justice. We strengthened our defenses and our resolve. With the help of the Qyron, we've established a new communications network. I will announce to the public a lifting of the state of emergency."

The president smiled as many applauded.

"My former secretary, Butler Andrews, gave a speech yesterday outlining his newly formed party, the Freedom For All Party. His three-minute commercial outlined the fears and strategies of his party to take over the White House and end our budding relationship with the Qyron. I will be meeting with everyone shortly to discuss our short- and long-range plans."

He looked to Jennifer.

"Before I continue, and to allow Jennifer and her group to start their day, I'll hand this over to her so she can make an important announcement."

He stepped aside, and Jennifer walked up.

"Thanks for calling me Jennifer," she whispered to him as she passed.

"I'll make this brief," Jennifer said into the microphone. "It's my pleasure to introduce the two newest translators in our team: Margaret Winston, my mother"—Margaret stepped forward to light applause—"and Pari Malik, daughter of Navya Malik."

Pari bowed her head as everyone applauded.

"I would also …" Jennifer swooned forward, bumping her head into the microphone. The president lunged quickly and grabbed Jennifer. Four Secret Service agents bolted toward the lectern, along with Tank.

"I-I'm dizzy," Jennifer said. The room erupted in gasps and chatter.

"Everyone be calm!" the president said loudly. An agent ran over with a red plastic emergency kit. Margaret stepped forward.

"Wait a minute," she said as she pushed by an agent.

Margaret grabbed Jennifer's hand.

"Mama, I feel dizzy and like I'm gonna throw up," she said.

An agent quickly brought her a chair. Another agent grabbed a trash bin. As Jennifer sat down, a third agent walked up with a Meibot syringe.

"No, y'all don't need that!" Margaret exclaimed. "Don't anyone know a woman when she's new with child?"

The room fell silent.

"Mama, what!" Jennifer screamed.

"Baby, this is exactly what happened to me when I was pregnant with you."

The president chuckled. "Never a dull moment," he quipped.

The room erupted in laughter.

An agent stepped forward. "We should still be sure," he said. He inserted the syringe into Jennifer's leg.

Tank opened Jennifer's leather briefcase and removed her transmitter. Within seconds, the syringe glowed green. Jennifer put the transmitter to her head.

"Oh my!" she exclaimed. "I'm gonna be a mama!"

Tanks eyes opened wide, and he gave her a huge smile. He leaned over and grabbed Jennifer in a hug, lifting her up. The assembled crowd cheered.

Jennifer smiled and looked over at her mother. "Gramma!" she said, laughing.

"Oh, honey!" she yelled nervously into Tank's ear. He put her down just in time for her to be sick into the trash bin.

"Never a dull moment," the president said as he stepped away.

The rest of the day went much smoother. Jennifer's team chaired meetings all day on the second floor of the newly renamed Malik/Mills Building. Jennifer assisted both Pari and her mother as they learned the ropes of translating. By the end of the week, Pari had settled into her third-floor office and Margaret Winston was enjoying the fourth floor. By Friday, they welcomed another new translator from China, Li Jing.

There was a white light and some hissing noise, and I removed my headset.

I felt so happy about Jennifer being pregnant, and my thoughts suddenly moved to myself and motherhood. I had never really given it too much thought before, as my focus had always been on my career. I had been translating for ten years now and had amassed more than enough wealth. There really was no reason for me to continue doing my job. With ten colonies, we were still very much in need of translators, though, as we had only a total of twenty-six. I stood up from the couch.

I then reflected on my mother. She had drilled the value of loyalty to the job into me at a very young age, so I guess that was the reason why I was still working. I was also a little shocked that Jennifer was paid so handsomely. My salary was still a luxurious $3 million a year, but the Earth government didn't pay me, and there were no sponsored living quarters. Of course, there was no imminent threat from terrorists, either, so I guess I still had it better than my great-grandmothers had it.

As I walked toward the bedroom, I heard mumbling from John. I walked to the room and peeked my head in.

"Hey, baby, why are you up?" John mumbled.

The soft, dim light from the dining area gave just enough illumination for me to make out the details of my lover. He looked so tender lying in the bed with his hair all tousled to one side and the covers up to his neck. I slowly walked over to the bed and slinked out of my nightgown. I grabbed the covers and gently pulled them down.

"Don't; it's cold," he whined as he tried to pull them back up. I smiled and slid one leg under the covers. It was hot under the sheets, and my body was chilly from sitting still on the couch for so long.

"Shh," I said. "Don't you worry, Johnny; I'll take care of you." My voice was low and sultry as I glided under the blanket. My leg rubbed against his. It was hot.

"Jeez, you're freezing," John yelped as he pulled away.

I giggled and grabbed him, rubbing my colder body over his hot skin.

"Come on, stop it!" he whined.

I just giggled harder.

"Oh no," I said slowly, "you're not getting away from me."

I grabbed ahold of his shoulder and slid over the top of him. "No, I'm tired," he mumbled.

I put my hand over his mouth. "No, baby, not too tired for me."

I exhaled my hot breath into his ear. I felt him instantly respond.

"That's it," I cooed. "Good boy!" I leaned down and licked his neck.

"Mmm," he moaned.

I continued to lick and suck, and I then slid over and mounted him.

"You're in for a ride!" I said to him as he moaned.

I made love to John for a solid hour. I'm not sure if it was because of the broken sleep, the Psy-log, or just my raging Qyron hormones, but I wanted John in the worst way. Our lovemaking was actually so little love and so much carnal lust. I was so forceful—even violent. I moved fast and hard. I clawed, slapped, grunted, and bit. I was on fire, and I wasn't going to be denied. When John would resist, I would overpower him. When I finally brought him to orgasm, I stopped atop him. Sweat dripped off of me, and I panted heavily. John looked up at me, stunned.

"What?" I said as I rolled off of him.

John leaned up on his side, perched on one elbow. "Where did that come from?" he asked as he surveyed my glistening body. "You were an absolute animal."

John's expression finally changed. He gave me a smile and ran his hand over my naked chest.

"What can I say, Johnny? You bring out the animal in me!" I giggled.

I stood up off the bed and leaned in. I grabbed Johnny's hand and pulled him toward me. As he sat up, I could see the dark red marks on his chest and neck. John slunk a leg over the edge of the bed. I pulled him up and hugged him.

"I love you, Johnny," I whispered into his ear.

He hugged me tightly. "I love you too, Amant," he sighed.

I pulled away and tugged Johnny with me. We walked into the bathroom, and I started the shower. John glanced at the mirror. The lights illuminated his body. John's eyes opened wide as he examined his chest and neck.

"Damn, you tore me up!" he said as he ran his fingers along the dark, raised red welts. I grabbed his hand and gave him a hug.

"I'm sorry, Johnny; did I hurt you?"

John peered down, noticing his groin and hips were also a rosy red hue.

"I think you chafed the heck out of me," he mumbled. When he raised his head back up to meet my gaze, his concerned look faded. He gave me a smile.

"I've never been manhandled before," he said meekly. I smiled and opened the shower door. "Oh, so what kind of birth control are you using?" he asked.

I grabbed his hand and pulled him inside the shower. The hot water was a bit of a shock, as my sweaty body had been chilling in the open air.

"Oh wow," I exclaimed. I pulled John into the hot stream.

"Whoa, too hot!" he said as he stepped aside.

I adjusted the handle.

"Oh Johnny," I said as I hugged him, "I feel so good with you."

We stood in the hot water for several minutes, kissing and hugging. I grabbed the soap and began to wash John's back. He turned around, and I lathered his chest.

"Ouch," he exclaimed as he stepped back.

He turned and let the water wash his chest.

"It's really sore," he said with a wince. "You have to treat your toys better, or you won't be able to play with them anymore!" he scolded me.

I giggled. "Okay, daddy," I said playfully.

We finished showering, and as I stepped out of the shower to towel off, John looked at me.

"So, you never answered my question," he said.

I wrapped the towel around me and walked into the bedroom.

"What question?" I yelled back to him.

John paused a moment, continuing to dry off as I searched for clean clothing. He eventually walked into the bedroom as I was putting on a pair of panties.

"What kind of birth control are you using?" he asked calmly.

I grabbed a shirt from the drawer and pulled it over me. I gave him a smile and sauntered over to him.

"I'm not using any," I said softly, and I leaned in to kiss him.

He pulled back, eyes wide and lips apart.

"So you're being cavalier and reckless?" His voice and tone were solid and cutting. It caught me off guard.

"What's the big deal, Johnny? We love each other." I opened a drawer and grabbed some sweatpants.

John reached over and grabbed my arm. He pulled me to face him.

"Yes, I love you very much, Amant, but this is all new. It's fresh, and, well,"—John inhaled deeply—"I would really like to discuss our future in the way of making a family. I'd rather not have the decision—"

"Oh, Johnny, you're so serious," I said as I moved to walk by him.

He grabbed ahold of my arm and spun me around. "This *is* serious Amant, and I won't be dismissed!" His voice echoed off the wall. His eyes pierced into mine.

"Johnny, I …" I paused. I could see that there was no humor in him at this moment. "Fine, I'm sorry," I said with a huff, looking down. "I won't do that again. I just thought that you'd want to have a baby. I thought—"

"That's right!" John said. "You thought. You didn't ask."

He ran his fingers through his wet hair.

"Johnny, please. I didn't mean to cause a problem. I love you, and I'm just riding a high with you right now. I let the moment get away with me."

I gave John a serious look. His eyes were darting back and forth. He breathed in deeply and closed his eyes. After a moment, he exhaled.

"I'm sorry, Amant," he said calmly, "I didn't mean to lose my calm."

He opened his eyes and grabbed my hands. His expression softened as he gazed into my eyes.

"I love you, Amant; I want to be with you the rest of my life. But I want us, *us*, to make the decision on having a family." I nodded. "I want us to figure out our future before it lands on us. I'm tired of making mistakes in my life and then having to correct. I'm past that, so please don't force me backward."

I saw John's expression waver. "Okay, Johnny, I'm sorry."

I gave him a hug. I heard him breathe deeply a few times. He pulled back and gave me a kiss.

"I'm hungry," he said. "Care to join me for breakfast?"

"Dressed like that? Sure." I laughed. John gave me a smile and walked to the dresser to grab some clothes.

A few minutes later, we were on our way to the dining hall on C Deck.

"So why do you like sweatpants and T-shirts so much?" John asked.

"Well, I always have to dress up for work, so when I don't have to, I'd rather be comfy and cozy. Is that a problem?"

"Nope; I was just curious. I like it," John said with a smile.

We continued to talk as we walked. I told him about Jennifer and Tank. John and I both remarked on how neither of us remembered Jennifer's mother being a translator. We looked it up on John's tablet. She had translated for a year and then retired. We both knew about Pari, as her role in history was very prominent. She had translated for fifty years and had four children; two of them went on to become translators too.

John took an interest in me telling him about the birth of the Freedom Party. He liked history and politics, so he hung on every word.

"I didn't know Butler Andrews was a cabinet member of President Myers—wow!" John exclaimed as he ate a cherry danish. "He gave the president a really tight race in 2023," he said as he wiped the icing from his face.

"Well, he and his political party left a real legacy of being a thorn in the side of the Qyron; that's for sure," I mumbled. John finished his meal and then gave me a smile from across the table.

"What?" I asked.

John's smile grew.

"What, John?"

"Well, I was just thinking. This is the first time you haven't talked about the transport or Gamma Five," John said as he stood up.

"Oh yeah!" I exclaimed. "Time to get back to the mystery!" I said as I followed John.

John's shoulders dropped. He exhaled loudly.

"Why, why, why did I have to mention that," he mumbled. I tousled his hair and gave him a big grin. He smiled back at me.

We left the dining hall, and I grabbed John's hand. I was bouncing and skipping down the passageway as John tried to drag me back to a slow walk.

"I still can't believe that I reminded you of that," John mumbled.

I stopped and gave him a kiss. "Aw, you're too sweet!" I said cheerfully. "You know I wouldn't be happy unless I'm figuring this thing out!"

As we continued to walk, John looked over at me. "So what's next?" he asked. "Where do we go from here?"

My mind started to fire. I was thinking about all of the information we had, and then our interviews.

"Well, I think we've gone as far as we can with interviewing passengers. We know there's a moon that isn't listed in any star chart or registry, and it seems that a mere 20 percent of the crew are going there for training."

As we approached the lift, John glanced at me.

"What is your friend going to Gamma Five for?"

It just isn't making any sense, I thought. *Any change in the registry would have caused—*

"Amant!"

"What? Oh, I'm sorry, Johnny."

We stepped onto the lift. I gave John a smile. "What was your question?"

John shook his head at me. "What is your friend's reason for going to Gamma Five? You mentioned he did programming; maybe he knows more about this planet or its moon?"

I jumped and hugged John.

"You are so smart; I knew there was a reason I was so attracted to you!" I laughed.

"You mean besides my stunning good looks and unparalleled lovemaking?"

"No, that certainly isn't it; what else you got?" I quipped. The door opened on Alpha Deck as John reached in and began tickling my sides.

"*Aah!*" I screamed as I ran toward our room. John gave pursuit. We dashed by several passengers, who jumped to the side. When I reached our door, I quickly scanned and opened it. John was lagging behind and grabbed his side.

"What's wrong, Johnny?"

He huffed to the door and finally said, "Ugh, I don't know how you can eat and run; I have cramps."

He moaned as he limped into the room. After a large burp, he sat down on the couch.

"Excuse me," he said as he rubbed his stomach.

"Ah, that's okay," I said. "I still love you even if you don't have any manners."

I gave him a smile and sat beside him. John smiled and grabbed my hand.

"So this guy—Psi, is it?" he asked. I nodded. "If he's as smart as you say, maybe he can look at the data too."

I was suddenly irritated. I wondered how I could have missed that; it was so obvious. I leaned over and kissed John again.

"Brilliant," I whispered, "Good-looking, sexy, brilliant, *and* you have a hot girlfriend!" I giggled.

I stood up. "So let's go!" I shouted. I grabbed my laptop.

John stood up. "No, I think I'm going to get a nap, actually; I'm still kinda tired."

I gave John a stunned look.

"Hey, don't give me that," he stammered. "You broke up my sleep, brutally molested me, and then dragged me to breakfast."

"Yeah, molested," I giggled. "That was one heck of a fight you gave me." I gave John a long, sensual kiss. "Okay, Johnny, I'll see you soon."

I stopped at the terminal. "Location of Psi Worly," I asked. I heard a tone and then "Room D21." I turned and left the room.

Chapter 30

I WALKED ALONG THE PASSAGEWAY, thinking of my past with Psi. We had had so much fun in the several weeks we had spent together. We had gone to movies on Qyron; the Qyron thoroughly enjoyed our movies and had a good three hundred years of cinema to choose from. We had also spent many weekends seeing the sights on Qyron and Belvy, Qyron's sister planet. It was a very intense relationship, akin to a shooting star. After only five and a half weeks, I had to leave, and Psi was unwilling to travel with me. I've had regrets about that, and I thought maybe now was the time to put them to rest.

As I approached his room, I felt more than a shade nervous. I took a few deep breaths, pasted a smile on my face, and pressed the door call button. A few moments passed, and nothing happened. I pressed the button again. I could feel my heartbeat accelerate. Another moment passed, and I peered down the right side of the passageway. A terminal was about ten meters away. As I took a step toward it, the door opened. I stopped abruptly and turned back toward the open door.

"Psi?" I said as I walked into the room. The lights were off.

"Lights on," I said.

"*No!*" a voice shouted from inside the room. Two tones sounded. I shot my hand out toward the open passageway, keeping the door from closing.

"Psi, it's Amant!" I yelled into the darkness. "What's wrong? Why are your lights off?"

"Damn it!," he shouted.

I heard some mumbles.

"Psi, turn on the lights or I'll call for security!" I was now quite alarmed. This was beyond weird, and besides the foreboding darkness, there was a strong odor in the air of something very foul.

"Lights dim," he shouted. The lights came on at one-quarter power. I removed my arm from the doorway and jumped into the room as it closed shut. I took a second step in and saw the living room. It was piled with old food, drink bottles, and clothing. I gagged as I got another whiff of the rotting food and moldy clothing.

Psi took a step out from the bedroom. He looked like a scared child as he peered from around the corner.

"Psi, what in the sweet love of everything holy is all of this?" I shielded my nose with my hand, which did nothing. The smell was becoming overpowering, and I was having trouble keeping my breakfast down.

He took a step toward me. It was slow and deliberate, like that of a condemned prisoner walking toward his death. I couldn't take the foul odor any longer.

"Computer, door open and lock!" The door swung open, and a clean breeze blew in. I walked to his panel.

"Request room change!" The screen lit up, showing four other rooms on this deck that were available. Room D43 was the closest. I selected it.

When I turned to my left, I saw that Psi was finally at my side.

"Psi, what is all of this? This isn't you!" I yelled.

He just stared at me. I looked into his eyes, and they were devoid of life.

"Psi, answer me or I will call for a medic!"

Psi finally blinked. "I just … I'm just going through a thing."

"A thing? Are you kidding me? Psi, this is a major mental breakdown!" I was still feeling ill from the foul air. This couldn't be healthy at all.

"Psi, get your things; we're moving you to a new, cleaner room!"

Psi turned and slowly walked back toward his bedroom.

"How long will this take? I can call for assistance!" I shouted to him.

"No!" he said as he walked. "I'll only be a minute."

Psi was good to his word; a minute later he walked around the corner dragging two suitcases. They were large but completely inadequate for someone moving to a new colony. As he reached me, I swooped down and picked up both suitcases.

"Let's go; I can't stand the stench in here any longer!"

We started to walk down the passageway. As I hefted his luggage, my laptop slipped from my grasp. Psi reached out and grabbed it.

"Thank you Psi," I said.

He gave me a weak smile. It was the most I had gotten from him so far. A few moments later, we were at the doorway to D43. Psi tapped his ID at the door, and it opened. As he entered, the room lights illuminated. The air was fresh, and the room clean.

I set his luggage down in the doorway and waited for him to turn. He stood motionless, gazing at the room. I stared at the back of his head. His hair was long and greasy. The shirt he was wearing had stains on it, and it was wrinkled as if he had been sleeping in it and had just woken up.

"Psi?"

He slowly turned to face me. His eyes were so dark, as if he were staring at me from the pit of hell.

"Psi, what was that whole thing in your room?"

Psi took a deep breath. "Long story," he mumbled.

"Boil it down for me!" I barked.

I took a step closer to Psi. I could now detect a similar foul odor from him. It made sense, as no one who spent more than a minute in a garbage pile could hope to leave without the stench glued to them.

"Ugh, Psi, you really need a shower!"

He gave me a cursory look and then turned and walked into the bathroom. He closed the door, and I heard the shower turn on. I grabbed his suitcases and walked them into the bedroom. I opened the first one and found it was filled with all sorts of material. Dozens of memory sticks fell out like raindrops, hitting the ground. I set the suitcase level on the bed. I noticed several papers in the suitcase as well. I leafed through numerous blueprints and diagrams of buildings. I then noted that many of them were labeled "Toncha," which was the highest of security in Qyron. I saw that he had video logs too.

I turned and opened the other suitcase. This one had no surprises, just clothing. I grabbed a pair of pants and a shirt. I couldn't find underwear. But I then recalled that he never wore underwear. "Commando Psi" I had called him once.

The shower turned off, and I heard the shower door open. I grabbed his clothes and walked to the bathroom door.

I knocked. "Psi, I have some clothes for you."

"Come in," he replied. I opened the door. He was toweling off as I put the clothes on the counter. I peered briefly at his body. His once thick and toned body was now skinny and somewhat gaunt. His ribs poked through his chest, and his hips were quite pronounced. He gave me a questioning look.

"I'm sorry, Psi," I said as I looked down, "I'm just not accustomed to seeing you like this." I stepped back and closed the door.

"Things change," he said softly.

A moment later, he opened the bathroom door. Fully clothed and with his hair slicked back, he looked a world better than when I barged into his room. He came over to me at the couch.

"So what do I owe for this Mary Poppins moment?" he asked.

I took a minute. I didn't immediately get his reference, but then it came to me. We had watched the movie *Mary Poppins* together.

"Oh." I smiled. "Psi, what is all of this? What happened to you?"

Psi stared at me for a long moment. I wanted to ask him more, but I thought it best for him to tell me without badgering him.

"Let's just say I'm going through a thing, and we'll leave it at that," he said.

I was bubbling with questions and getting anxious for answers. But I felt it was pointless to keep bothering him. His current state was definitely beyond my help. I hoped that some amount of old friendship would let me into his world, but he wasn't about to budge. He truly was a completely broken man, devoid of life.

"So what is your question?" he asked calmly.

I patted the couch cushion next to me, offering for him to sit down. He just shook his head politely.

"I'll stand, thank you," he rebuffed.

"Well, I have a few questions. First, what is all of that information in your other suitcase?"

His eyes opened wide, and he jerked his head toward the bedroom. "What! What did you see?"

He maintained a stare on me as he walked toward the bedroom. When he reached the opening, he looked and saw the memory sticks on the floor, the suitcase open, and the documents on the bed. He quickly closed the door to the bedroom and stormed back over to me.

"What did you do? What did you read, Amant!" His voice was loud and seething with anger.

"Psi, please, I was just looking for clothing for you, and all of that stuff spilled out," I said as I rose cautiously to my feet.

"Damn it, Amant!" he screamed.

He trembled with anger, and his lower lip quivered.

"Psi, calm down. What is all of that? Maybe I can help."

"No, you can't help!" he yelled.

I took a few steps back and toward the door. My heart was beating faster, and my mouth hung open. I was terrified of Psi. I didn't know him at all anymore, and this changed man scared me. I continued to backpedal toward the door.

Psi ran his hands up over his face and through his hair. He caught sight of me edging toward the door.

"No, don't go!" he yelled. He stretched out a hand, and it trembled as he did. "Please, I'm sorry. It's just that …" He paused as he caught his breath. "Please don't go."

I stood for a moment, watching him as he began to compose himself.

"Psi, you're scaring me," I said softly.

He shook his head and slowly walked forward.

"Psi, you need help—help that I can't give you," I said as I took another step toward the door.

"No, please, Amant, I am so sorry for losing my temper. Please stay."

He stopped and stared at me. His eyes glassed up, and when he blinked, tears fell down his cheeks. He dropped to the floor on his knees. I slowly walked back over to him.

He hugged me at my waistline and cried for several moments.

"It's so complicated. You don't understand," he babbled.

"Psi, what happened to you? What's complicated?" I said softly as I gently stroked his hair.

He slowly regained his composure and stood back up.

"I'm sorry; I'm under a lot of stress," he said quietly.

He walked a slow circle around the couch. When he returned to face me, he regained his calm.

"What did you want, Amant?"

I reached down and grabbed my laptop, keeping an eye on him while I did. I opened it up and scrolled to the unreadable data.

Psi looked down at it and smiled. "Where did you get this?" He looked into my eyes. I could see a sparkle in him again.

"Well, I got it from the ship's main intel database," I said softly.

He laughed, first gently and then more unrestrained. His loud, boisterous laughter was contagious, and I couldn't help but giggle. This was the Psi I knew.

"Oh my," he said through the laughter. "What are you doing, Amant?"

"Well, Johnny and I were—"

"Johnny?"

"Oh, yes, my boyfriend, Johnny. You met him at the gym."

Psi stood still for a moment; his laughter ceased.

"Oh, yes, I remember now," Psi said.

But I could tell from his expression that he was lying. He didn't remember.

"Well, we noticed a lot of things about this transport—and, well, about Gamma Five—that didn't make sense."

I grabbed my laptop and showed it to him again.

He looked down at the data and then back at me.

"Let's get to the real question, Amant." His gaze became more intent, and he stared deeply into my eyes. "What the hell are *you* doing on this transport?"

He caught me off guard. I suddenly felt on edge—cornered. Why was this any of his business? What difference did that make? I tried to think on my feet, but he took a step closer, and it rattled me.

"You're still translating for the Qyron Alliance, right?" His voice was now clear and devoid of any emotion.

"Uh" was all that I could get out. I was on the edge of terrified, and my heart began to race. His sudden shift of tone put me on edge, and the hairs on the back of my neck stood up.

"Amant, you're still translating, yes?" he hissed. His demanding stare pierced me. I tensed up even more.

"Yes." The word barely escaped my mouth at a volume no greater than a faint whisper.

"Then what the hell are you doing on this transport? How did you get on here in the first place?" he said back to me in a slightly softer but authoritative tone.

I could feel my bottom lip move, but no sound came out. I felt my heart beating faster. Psi looked at me again and then stood straight.

"I'm sorry," he said as he stopped his advance and nodded. "Am I scaring you?" His eyes darted back and forth.

I slowly nodded, my mouth still open. He smiled and took a few steps back. He sat down on a chair.

"Not my intention," he said with a weak smile.

He motioned with his hand for me to sit down on the couch. I slowly made my way to the couch, keeping a firm view on Psi as I did so.

"Amant, I'm sorry for all of this. You know me; I don't live like this, and I'm not crazy—honest!"

He closed his eyes for a moment while I sat down. He exhaled and then opened his eyes.

"Please forgive me if I've upset you. So you and John have found some irregularities about this transport."

"And the colony and its moon," I added in a whisper as I swallowed hard.

Psi smiled.

"You're as clever as you are beautiful," he said, still smiling.

He pointed his boney finger to my laptop.

"Can I see it again?"

I leaned over and handed it to him. He grabbed it and leaned back in his chair.

"Hmm, yeah, this is basic encryption. The Qyron are smart, but they're not good at thinking outside the box."

He looked up at me.

"So you would like me to decrypt this for you?"

"Yes, please."

Psi stood up. He walked around the couch and into the bedroom. I heard the rattling of memory sticks and then an "aha!" He walked out of the bedroom and sat back down at his chair. He stuck the memory card into the laptop. His eyes then elevated to meet mine.

"So you want to know what this information is all about. What are you going to do with it, and why are you going to Gamma Five?" He kept an unwavering stare on me.

"Well, I just want to have an answer to many of these questions I have." I said. "And I'm actually going to Beta Lyrae, but I met John in the transport terminal in New York. I thought I would ride with him here and then take a jump transport to Beta Lyrae."

Psi smiled and shook his head. "So you're going to catch a jump transport, eh?" He smiled and chuckled under his breath.

"Yes, why is that so funny?"

Psi shook his head and pursed his lips. "Nevermind," he said as he paced in a circle. "So how did you get on the transport?"

"I got a ticket like everyone else, Psi; why?"

Psi stopped and stared at me for a moment. His expression did not waver.

"Because as a translator you wouldn't be allowed on this planet!" His voice was harsh and cutting.

"Wait; how would you know? What do you know about Gamma Five, Psi?"

Psi began pacing again. He shook his head and smiled.

"I know you're not supposed to be on this transport."

I exhaled deeply. My mind raced, and my body tensed up. I was not enjoying this little game of his one bit.

"Psi, why are you being so cryptic? Can you decode this for me or not!"

I was passing irritated and approaching mad quickly. I felt as if I were in a verbal chess match with a master. Every question I asked was greeted with another question. It was as though Psi were part of this whole masquerade, where every door opened more mysteries, and he seemed to revel in teasing me.

"Okay, fine. I'll decrypt this for you. But realize that sometimes the answers you *seek* may not be the answers you *want*," Psi said as he picked up the laptop again and then sat down.

He clicked a few keys.

"And what does *that* mean!" I stood up.

This had to stop. I felt my heart beating faster, and my breathing was quickening. Psi just stared at me.

"Damn it, Psi, you haven't answered a single question I've asked of you. You've just danced around it with a pathetic arrogance that—"

"Arrogance?" Psi yelled. *"I'm arrogant, am I?"*

He lowered the laptop and stood up. He took a half step forward so now we stood nearly nose to nose, close enough to smell each other's sweat.

"Psi, stop messing around; what do you know about this transport and Gamma Five?" I demanded in a low tone as I trembled with anger.

"No!" Psi barked, and he turned to walk away.

I lurched forward and grabbed his arm.

"Let me go!" he protested.

"Why don't you *make me*, Psi? You can't weigh any more than one fifty soaking wet. No, I'm tired of this." I pulled hard, and he stumbled close to me. "You tell me what you know, or I'll slap you stupid!"

I tightened my grip on his arm. I was angry, tired, and sick of all of his games. The blood was surging through me and I was ready for a fight. I played back my last mean comment in my head, and part of me recoiled. This really wasn't me, but I was out of patience and I had to get some answers. I knew he was aware of far more than he was telling me, and yet he was holding back for some reason.

"You'd better let go of me," Psi said in a calmer tone as he leaned in closer. "You have *no* idea what the hell you're dealing with."

His eyes stared deeply into mine. I saw *nothing* in his—no anger, no emotion—just a cold blackness. A chill raced up my spine, and my mouth drew open. I don't know if I had ever seen the face of evil, but if I had to put a look to it, *this was it*. My tight grip fell away like a dying man's grasp. Psi jerked his wrist from my feeble hold.

"Wa-wait," I mumbled. "What do you mean 'what the hell I'm dealing with'? Don't you mean 'who'?"

Psi didn't answer. He reached down, grabbed my laptop again and clicked furiously for a moment on the keyboard. Then he stopped dead. His eyes slowly rose up until they met mine; they were still cold, still dark, and still devoid of life. He handed the laptop over to me.

I paused for a moment, chilled with the eerie feeling that whatever he uncovered on that screen would lead to my doom. Psi maintained his steely cold stare and then shook the laptop at me to indicate I should take it. My anger had since morphed into a cold, clammy fear; but deep down inside, I still had to know.

I slowly extended my gently trembling arm. I could feel my heart racing and sweat beginning to form on my face. Our stares stayed locked as I felt the laptop touch my fingertips. I finally gripped it tightly, and Psi let go. He slowly drew his hand back and then folded his arms.

"Don't say … I didn't warn you," he hissed.

I suddenly felt as if I were at a crossroads. Part of me was screaming to just drop the laptop and leave. It was the safe thing to do, and the loving me was pleading for it. It was the I-would-rather-be-curled-up-on-the-couch-watching-a-movie-with-the-man-I-love me asking me to drop the PC and run. But then the opposing side of me chimed in, softly at first. *You have to know what's going on here*, it said. *You can't keep uncovering questions. We have to know, and you don't have a choice.*

I slowly drew my eyes away from his cold, dark stare and looked down at the decrypted information. My mind froze as I read it. My mouth dropped wide open, and I felt paralyzed.

"Oh, you have got to be kidding me!" I screamed. "*This makes no sense at all!*"

I looked back up at Psi; he had a slight grin on his face.

"This is crazy!" I said as anger and confusion swept over me. "This data says that F Deck is full of—"

"Yes, it is," Psi said as his cold, pale appearance filled with color. He shook his head slowly, and a sick little smile crept across his face. "You asked for it, now you have it."

I continued to stare in disbelief at my monitor. "F Deck … is full of prisoners?" I screamed.

Thank You

THANK YOU, KIND READER, FOR taking the time to read my novel, The Amant Chronicles – Jennifer's Legacy. I do hope that you enjoyed this first installment. Amant's story only grows in depth and intensity from here so be sure to get your copy of Volume 2 (Dark Secrets). Fear not, I guarantee that volume two is nearly published and will be out by February 2019. You can of course, keep up with current events on my website: www.mjbrun.com

As a new writer, it's important that I hear your feedback and reviews from the folks who've read and hopefully enjoyed my work. So I graciously ask that you do me the favor of giving your honest review to the novel on Amazon. If you have never given a review on Amazon, no worries. It's easy:

1. Log in to www.amazon.com and then do a search for "The Amant Chronicles."
2. When you're on the page that shows *The Amant Chronicles*, scroll to the bottom until you see the Customer Reviews section.
3. Click on the "Write a Customer Review" box.

Since I realize that waiting for the next installment of The Amant Chronicles can be frustrating, let me see if I can minimize the hassle of dead time. I have the following selection of free short stories available on my website. While these short stories have not been edited, I do hope that you enjoy them and continue to visit my website for the latest updates. The following short stories are available for your reading pleasure!

- <u>Speeding Ticket</u> – Officer Weems finds out that a simple speeding ticket is far more than he bargained for...
- <u>Contracts</u> – A contract is only as good as the man who writes it...
- <u>The Old Church</u> – The cold air isn't the only chill for this young boy...
- <u>Card Shark</u> – One man seeks peace, the other, an audience...
- <u>The Children</u> – Sometimes loyalty to your job can lead to unexpected discoveries...
- ~~Transistor Radio~~ Sorry, but the tale of Transistor Radio is such a great story, that I've decided to turn it into a full length novel. So I've removed it from the short story area.
- <u>The Farmer</u> – The complex joys of retirement...
- <u>Daylight Mission</u> – Instead of tilting at windmills, maybe a day spa retreat is the answer?

Thank you again, and I look forward to entertaining you on my website: www.mjbrun.com

See you in Volume 2 of the Amant Chronicles – Dark Secrets!

M.J. Brunnabend

After Thoughts

I BEGAN WRITING THIS NOVEL several years ago. I was already in the middle of writing my very first novel, *Life's Dream*, when I got the idea for this story. My daily work commute was about forty-five minutes each way, so I was given ample time alone with my thoughts. Yeah, I know—scary, right? Well, as the days and weeks went by, this simple idea started to grow. It then exploded on a long vacation drive back from North Carolina. (I had hours in the car with my thoughts!) I seem to get a lot of inspiration on long drives. All the pieces started to come together, from the fact that each novel in the series would be two interconnected stories in which the reader would learn about some of the past translators, to many of the juicy plot points.

It got to the point where I could no longer keep the massive amount of storylines and dialogue in my head without screaming. So as I reached the climax in writing *Life's Dream*, I knew I had to make a choice. While I thoroughly enjoyed the story of *Life's Dream*, I felt it wouldn't be a great first book to launch my writing career. I felt certain that I would need a strong start. So I made the decision to stop at the second-to-last chapter and begin the long journey of *The Amant Chronicles*.

Yeah, I wasn't thrilled with the story title, but it stayed, and now it's grown on me. This was a quick nod to *The Martian Chronicles*, although this is a novel and not a compilation of short stories. But, well, that idea of a chronicle stuck with me.

Anyway, this novel wrote itself. Well, maybe not as much the image that the keyboard of my computer became a player piano and the words shot onto the screen by themselves, but the fact that I didn't design a thorough story line, complete with all of the characters and their interactions. Nope. Instead I had a solid idea of how it would start, how it would end, and some juicy stuff in between. But as I wrote, the story just exploded in my head. Yeah, it even made that *kaboom* sound, eerie, right? One scene quickly tied into the next. Details and minor characters popped up from nowhere. It was as if my loving deceased grandparents were whispering the story into my ear as I typed. Seriously. At times, I could barely type fast enough to keep the words and ideas from crashing into each other.

And no sooner had I finally finished the first rough draft of volume 1 than I began volume 2.

At the time of me writing this, and of publication, all three volumes are written. The fourth and final volume is safe in my head. Hmm … I already have the scenes and some of the dialogue just itching to get out. But, as luck would have it, my hands were ripped off in a freak popcorn accident and can't write anymore. Nah, just kidding.

I am now in the middle of *Bright Future*, a really compelling sci-fi tale. I hope to have that one published soon after volume 2. We'll see. Speaking of volume 2, get ready for even more action, fights, and mystery. It only gets bigger and badder from here.

Well, stay tuned. Keep in touch, which is easiest on my website. www.mjbrun.com I would enjoy hearing your feedback.

About the Author

ORIGINALLY FROM UPSTATE NEW YORK, M. J. Brunnabend has lived in several states along the East Coast. He is a navy war veteran, a nuke, who has also worked in the medical, dental, and insurance industries. He enjoys such things as working out, bicycling, hiking, gardening, and even home improvement. He likes to travel and try new things. But the nagging lifelong question of "What do you want to do when you grow up?" has finally been answered. He wants to write, and does so with his trusty sidekick, Fresca, a Moluccan cockatoo.